Mystik Legends

Jennifer Oneal Gunn

Mystik Legends
Jennifer Oneal Gunn
Copyright© 2015

This book can be purchased in all countries.

Printed in the United States of America.

Abridged Edition

02/012016

ISBN-13: 978-0692300596
ISBN-10: 0692300597

The publisher would like to thank all contributors of this work.

I dedicate this book to some key people in my life:

The first person, my aunt Edna will always remain the strongest person I have ever known and will always be with me no matter what. I miss you and I love you.

The second is my grammy. I love you and I miss you every day!

For my other favorite aunt, JJ, I love you! Thank you for believing in me and what I do. You have no idea how much your love and support will always mean to me.

Mystik Legends

Jennifer Oneal Gunn

Prologue

No one really knows where the life-force goes. We only ever hear stories because no one is around to tell us the truth about what happens after we're gone from the world. Some souls have yet to pass on into another state of being. Some people believe heaven exists, or a form of it does. Some people don't. Reality spreads before them, thick as a quilt until they are shown otherwise, left questioning their own existence. What lies beyond? We always wonder but will never know.

Vision was enigmatic toward dawn, praising the early light, springing free of trappings so boldly displayed in the blood of the young and old, splayed across the bow of a tree. Hanging low, the entwined carcass of a human no longer living, who's soul has vacated his body.

Tendrils of tendons hang from the derisive corpse like tiny chains of a manacle with no need for a lock or key. Hands, feet, and head detached from the body and strewn above in the leafy May vegetation. The torso of the victim sticking in place, trapped by a metal short-handled ax, the blade of which is sharpened so it might cut the fine hair off a man's face in a single slice.

The silence surrounding the area is imminent. No birds calling, no insects chirping, and no people enjoying a lazy day by the creek with children laughing and playing. They'd been forewarned about the place for centuries. It was a custom to leave their world behind and vacation off in an area deemed safely far enough away from the place some of them raised their children, away from their farms and country homes. The legend was musty with age and gossip, but no one, not even the newest of residents took a chance, knowing in these parts, the tales had a way of showing their ugly truth.

Dawn sunlight lit the morning anew with rising colors. Flashing upon the ground, a site of darkened crimson, causing the mud below the tree to turn the deepest brown. Flies and mosquitoes hovered above the staunched area without making a sound, trying to gauge how best to absorb the moisture that was quickly drying as the sun beat down on it. The night before, in the middle of the darkened twilight, the blood was a puddle of rapid drainage as if the human body was the gutted corpse of a deer hanging upside down to be butchered for its meat and pelt. Most of the pool was soaked into the ground, leaving only a muddy spot.

Cutting center stage, the bodily functions necessary in dying, smells surrounding the corpse were a copious edifice of shock and surprise rendered helpless by nothing so much as the unwillingness to die swiftly. The victim's last breath taken shortly, only hours before dawn, shallowly among the stillness of the forest surrounding him. No one heard his gasp, his scream, or his cries for help as he begged for mercy that wasn't granted. The last sight being an ax blade searing toward him, shining in the dark as his neck became severed from his torso.

When the day passed back into twilight, the corpse materialized into the cavern of a deep cave, cool and refreshing to living beings. The remainder of the blood residing inside the main part of the body being taken to an ancient place, for the hope that one day, a trapped spirit might once and for all be freed from the relentless struggle over the curse it's been beholden to for hundreds of years.

PART ONE
The Beginning of a Nightmare

Chapter One

Light danced its way across the murky water flowing through the creek one final time as the sky faded into the night. It was the marked fiftieth year for the ancient cursed ghost, legend from the mid-country, to return to his killing spree. The vengeful spirit of a Viking haunted a part of the country where no one believed in supernatural occurrences other than the Holy Ghost. As he stalked his next victim, he waited for the cover of night to come, shading him from the fading daytime sun.

A man lay on the ground, his thick chestnut brown hair stuck to his forehead with sweat. He was petrified with fear, his eyes wide, barely able to breathe, *What the hell? Am I really seeing this? He can't be real! I'm not seeing this! My eyes are not right! Ghosts aren't real! My parents said he was, but that can't be! Folk Legends are bullshit! Yet…here we are. I wonder if I'm going crazy right now… Am I going to die? Oh, God!*

The specter came closer, gliding, his feet never touching the ground, rags and his weapon belt dragging in the dust. With wide green eyes, the victim stared at Leif Eriksson, Viking warrior and explorer. Shock spread across his face, his eyes bulged further with fear, his pulse raced, and his breath quickened.

Leif smiled a ghastly smile, *Old Scenic* as he was sometimes known, a figure with blood dripping and matted all over him; it seeped from his pores as he hovered over his next victim. The man couldn't scream. His breath rattled in his chest and he was sweating. It made Leif happy knowing he still put fear into his victims. He had his battle ax poised above his head and laughed about the stench of fright he smelled on his victim. He had no time to waste. The damn people, most of them, heeded the warnings. Plus, he promised himself it would be more interesting that year. *Some new people will show up soon and the fun will begin.* He felt them coming closer with each passing hour, his smile grew wider as he looked down at his victim's body shaking on the ground. It was time to kill.

He said in Ancient Norse, "All people with fear such as yours deserve to die a coward's death!" Leif swung his ax with ease, taking the man's head off his shoulders; as it fell to the ground with a thud, Leif saw his eyes were permanently locked in horror. His body fell on the hard earth and went limp as blood oozed out of his neck, pouring out of the new hole his head was previously attached to. Leif went to work cutting the man's body into several pieces, hacking with almost motionless ease, throwing the pieces into the trees above him. He tossed back his head and sinister laughter erupted from him. Feeling victorious, he picked up the man's head by his thick chestnut brown hair and carried it into the woods surrounding the creek in Tipton Ford, Missouri.

***

Where exactly do roads lead? What path were we meant to take? *As these thoughts played inside her head, Rain saw a woman torn between life and death rise from the shadows to stand beside her best friend.*

It felt like they'd live to continue fighting battles no one in the normal realm knew existed. She stood solid as a soldier staring into the eyes of evil, she was unafraid. Her face stone cold, her hair pulled up behind her, her gaze more terrifying than her scream.

Bits of gravel beneath her feet shifted as she stood looking into the face of some horrible monster. The ghastly bleeding face, the blond matted hair, and white-eyed stare were enough to make even the bravest of men fall to their knees. This beast saw much and killed many over his years of torturing people, two angry women didn't appear to be a match for him. Killing them would be easy enough in his mind.

Insanity stood in the way of proper judgment on the road to hell; for every right move, a wrong one waited in its stead. Being matched blow against blow, Jen and Morgan seething and ready to walk away, looked at one another, giving one last smile before getting low to the ground.

Powdery dust flying through the air was indication something bad happened in the woods. The ground shook and the ghost howled in agony. Whatever was left of his chance at freedom was gone.

The beeping of an alarm clock woke the sleeping Indian woman named Rain, who awoke startled and confused. She never had a dream so real in her whole life. Being of Native American blood, she believed sometimes dreams were windows to the past or the future. That particular journey scared her to the core. She lay in bed shaking, thinking about her friends. She knew deep down, this trip would be her last. Finally, Rain did the only thing she could think of. In order to grasp what she saw and to mentally deal with it, she wrote it down and tucked the pages into the open suitcase sitting on the chair beside her bed. Her next move was to decide whether or not to tell them.

Is it superstition? Is it chance? Why is it, I've never had a dream this real before, like a vision in my sleep? As Rain questioned the vision, she worried over her friends and hoped the trip would go smoothly. She hoped it was nothing but stress, messing with her head.

Chapter Two

As the sun rose, birds began to chirp, waking everyone who was softly sleeping, waking the neighborhood in the quiet part of Sioux Falls, South Dakota. Suburbia at its finest, white picket fences, flower gardens in bloom, and yards always mowed. Sunshine peeked in the windows of a house in the neighborhood; a place where roses grew and laughter sometimes consumed the occupants. Two couples arose from their slumber. The first to move out of her bed was Jen, the one of Native American descent of the two women living in the house. As she turned to roll out of bed, her fiancé Warren grabbed her by the waist, pulling her in close, hugging her. She smiled and told him good morning. He smoothed her long dark hair out of her face and kissed her forehead. In another bedroom in the house, Morgan, the blonde who resided there, was also being awoken by her boyfriend. He slid his hands around her and kissed her. With closed eyes, she returned his kisses. As she kissed him, her eyes slowly opened, looking into Blake's eyes, her heart overflowed with her hidden emotions.

The two female research assistants' home was quaint and cheerful. Jen looked at the place as if it might be the last time she would see it. The two-story yellow house had dark blue wooden shutters and roses growing high on the side picture window. She sighed and looked at the small covered porch on the front of the house with a few chairs and a porch swing swaying in the breeze. This picturesque scene made her regret wanting to leave it. She looked at the roofline, imagining nothing in particular. The lawn was manicured neatly. The grass was short and green. Jen thought the place was beautiful for what it was. She especially liked the flowers lining the outside edge of the house. And she was glad the house sat in a quiet part of town. It was a peaceful place with wonderful memories attached to it.

A little while after breakfast, Jen and her friend Morgan, the fair one of the two, were outside helping get the gear together to make a trek to Tipton Ford, Missouri. Both women gathered and read all the material on the place surrounding the legend of Old Scenic. Their boss gave them a book someone recovered and sent to the Old Courthouse Museum in their hometown of Sioux Falls. As the two of them leafed through it, they began believing it was bullshit. The intended mission was, go to Missouri and see if the legend was true or not. This meant getting away from South Dakota for vacation reasons.

It was time to go. Warren fired up the engine in the Suburban, hollering at everyone to get in so they could hit the road. The windows were rolled down and the girls' hair was blowing in the wind. Warren picked up speed as he drove the small group to meet up with some more of the team. Jen took one last look at the neighborhood she was leaving. The foreboding feeling she got earlier was stronger as she, her best friend, and their boyfriends drove away. She wondered if it was natural to feel apprehensive before something good happened.

***

As soon as the two couples made their way out of town, an extra vehicle followed them with more friends inside it. Rain was an Indian expert who worked with Jen and Morgan at the museum. Pauly was a cameraman and friend they met during some of their travels. The group kept in contact via cell phones as soon as they reached the highway.

Pauly thought about his life while on the long drive, all he'd seen and been through since he could remember anything. He thought about his parents, his dad's job and his mom's habits. He thought about how after he graduated high school, he went into the same business as his father. Killing without remorse took its toll after a few years as the main hit man for a sector of the New York mob. After killing people who were put on a list for about twenty years, Pauly got out the only way a person is able to, he faked his death with the help of a friend on the outside.

He started over in someplace new and tried to stop the nightmares he was having fifteen years into the job. Waking up for years in cold sweats with chattering teeth was almost enough to drive a man insane but, he had to play the game until he got enough cash and formulated a plan. Pauly's whole world had to go dark, everyone he knew believed his was dead, he was free of the job and the worry, free of the migraines and the constant nagging to do as he was told because the boss would kill him otherwise.

Too many times, Pauly dreamed of walking into the office and blowing the boss away. It would have been a matter of time before he got himself killed if he hadn't kept his mouth shut about the mob and the boss. He was tired of keeping his mouth shut, so after the well thought out plan was executed he started over in Sioux Falls, far away from the drama of Brooklyn. The northwest was as good a place as any to start over and learn something that had nothing to do with killing anyone. That didn't mean he wasn't always prepared, this trip was no exception to the rule.

As Pauly drove and Rain messed with the radio, he thought about how much he liked the changes in his life. Being a cameraman might not sound like much to some people but, being considered normal class was fine with him. It wasn't hard work and he enjoyed his job. He got to travel with the kids, filming whatever they told him to. He thought they were nice enough just sort of stuck up, but not like he couldn't handle a couple of spoiled little girls. The guys he actually liked, they were real people. Pauly smiled and thought about his life, *Not too shabby, not too shabby at all.*

***

The intrepid travelers went about the first part of the mission with enthusiasm, not stopping often in order to make it on time. Starting mid-morning Wednesday, they set out to get to Tipton Ford on Thursday about midday. The whole group was in general high spirits.

Staring out at the sun, the visceral heat radiating off the ground coming up, expanding the shining spaces in the road an oasis awaiting them on the other side, they thought. Life wasn't as simple as they wanted it to be or without complications, they decided even if the myth wasn't real, they'd enjoy the time away from daily life. As the road was winding out before them, the group of young souls descended upon the world unknown to them. A lot of their lives was spent being told legends were false, yet they were on their way to find out about logical truth and their path in life, leading them into an unseen world beyond human existence.

The trip started on a happy note, but the closer they got to The Ford the harder the car radio was to tune, they kept getting *Dragula* by Rob Zombie, the tuner would wind but nothing else came on. The group looked at each other with that *What the Fuck?* look on their faces then decided to turn off the radio. Shortly after that, they reached the pick-up point in Iowa where they loaded up the rest of the team, a grizzly mountain man type named Cledus and a Hispanic named Jorge. The mountain man had a tale to tell and knew the area, and the Hispanic was there for cheap labor. Both were hired off the Internet through some work contacts from the museum the ladies worked for.

Cledus Jones was a man of means. To him, the trip was a way of paying his bills only. He wasn't thinking about what might happen even though he knew, he was there because he knew the area, maybe even too well. He grew up there as a boy. He saw things he wouldn't talk about until now because he wasn't doing well financially and telling the truth was finally going to pay off. Money and jobs in his field were getting pretty scarce for men his age. Without much savings, he couldn't retire when he wanted. He did odd jobs such as travel and scout for rich people who didn't know their way around. Mostly, the same type of work he was on now except he never took people home; hell, he never went home himself. He never thought about it much, until about a month ago when the group from South Dakota contacted him about taking them to The Ford. Now, they were going to pay him to take them there and tell them his story. *Wow, life can really be funny sometimes...* he thought. He also thought about how the place taunted him all those years and how he was looking right into the eye of a dragon, waiting for it to spit fire on him.

He ran his hands through his gray hair until he got to the ponytail and stopped, putting his black leather cowboy hat back on his head. He looked down at his work boots and dusty jeans, he hadn't thought much about his mother or the day she died since he was a child. It still scared him and he wanted no part of those memories, this job would make those memories surface whether he wanted them to or not. He hoped he wouldn't get too sentimental in front of the others when the time came. He always wanted his mama to be proud of him even after she was gone. He always got the notion she probably wasn't, so he gave up giving a damn about his family and put them to the back of his mind. He was honest and never tried to screw anyone over, that had to be enough.

He thought the whole thing might warrant a few hundred-thousand drops of whiskey. Good thing he never went anywhere without it. Ever since he was old enough to drink, he has. It was something to take the edge off so he could sleep without the nightmares coming back so often.

Jorge, on the other hand, was a different story. He was a muscular Hispanic fellow and from what Cledus could tell, he was only brought to help lug around stuff the rich people brought with them. His job was simple; he was a laborer, as he had probably been his whole life, this trip would be easier on him too. He looked like the type of guy who often wondered what a real vacation would be like and thought that the trip was probably the closest he'd get to knowing what it was like. Cledus shook his head. He knew what was coming, even if no one else did. *Poor bastard*, he thought.

Jorge Rodriguez was a stocky muscular man, built for heavy lifting. He worked his whole life to build a decent home for his family, his wife and kids never did without what they needed. The jobs he did might not have always been legal, but they paid him money to get by on. This job he signed on for was one of the easiest he'd ever been on. From what he gleaned thus far, there was a ghost story behind their mission. Although his Catholic heritage taught him to never leave home without his bible, he kept the rituals for soul saving in his mind. Memorizing them, he never left home without God by his side.

With a rosary in his pocket like always, Jorge sat silently in the vehicle, listening to the other three people talk about all the things they knew while soaking it in. They were mostly well educated and not from the same part of the United States, he could tell by listening to the way they spoke. The conversations they were having were interesting, seeing as how they'd only known each other for mere hours. While he was trying to listen to a debate about horticulture he drifted to sleep while sitting beside Cledus.

Blackened blank expressions were on the faces of the dead staring at him from amidst the trees. Bloody and hollow, the pale faces with white dead eyes came rushing toward him as he stood still with the woods.

As the dead bodies lurched forward, Jorge stepped backward and toward a ledge, rushing water cascaded off the sharp rocks below him. He looked behind himself, watching the creek race on. The dead-eyed bodies came at him faster, he wanted to scream loudly but knew no one was around to hear him.

A few feet to the left he saw the circular stacks of rocks with dripping blood on some of the stones. The small torches, dimly glowing, were barely visible around the center of the circle and the old wooden burning pyre.

Jorge was stricken with fear and didn't understand what he was seeing, his heart was pounding as the dead were closing in on him. He could smell the creek and the decaying of the bodies as they got within feet of him. He saw the rags they wore, the whiteness of their eyes came into his view, as the noiseless corpses grew closer, coming to take his soul and rip him to shreds.

Jorge suddenly awoke with a start and Cledus was staring at him. "Ay Dios Mio! Bad dream!" The more he thought about it, he knew it was a warning and a nightmare. He got an acutely bad feeling about where they were going and couldn't turn back.

Chapter Three

The group of eight found a small, secluded hotel in the middle of nowhere that Cledus told them about. As they drove up to the establishment, they were reminded of horror movies of the past. It was eerie to look at in the daytime but more ominous at night. An old tattered flag was flying in the wind. The house must have been a fine two-story red brick mansion in its younger days. In the present, moss grew up the side of the building. Weeds protruded from the cracks in the foundation. The courtyard of the past was a lump of dead and dying overgrown bushes, the mixed foliage of days gone by. The once beautiful stone figures stood scattered, now gruesome and dark amongst the brambles.

The travelers walked onto the porch of the hotel and noticed it was seconds away from falling on them as they stood there. The roof above them sagged and insulation was peeking through the hole, pink and fuzzy. Before they rang the bell, Jen turned to look at Cledus, who stood in the back of the group, and gave him a glare. Then she started asking questions about the place.

"Why did you direct us to this rat-hole in the middle of nowhere?" Jen was mad. She thought, *Hillbillies probably doesn't know much about anything.*

"I know this place. I been here travelin' loads of times. It might look creepy, but it's cool, promise. First time I ever stopped on the porch o' this place, I thought the same thing."

"How come this house hasn't fallen down yet?" Jen questioned.

"The people are good and the rooms'll do for a night. And from the sign I read, they're a B and B now. It's all right, 'lil lady, you can spend one night here. They won't pull the *Psycho* treatment on ya. I swear, ma'am," Cledus said, promising her.

"I don't know..." Jen said. She had a suspicious look on her face, she met the man only hours earlier and trust wasn't something she doled out like compliments.

"If I'm lyin' I'm dyin' and I lived a long time so far," he said.

After ringing the bell, they stood on the porch until they heard creaking footsteps and a doorknob turn. They felt a whoosh of air conditioning, then saw Buzz, the owner and manager of the bed and breakfast. Buzz was of middle height and middle weight. He was balding and had a gentle face. He wore wire-rimmed glasses, a sweater, and slacks in the summer. His senior years had, thus far, been kind to him.

"Yes? Can I help you?" said Buzz in a kindly voice.

"Yes. We saw the sign by the side of the road that said you have vacancies. This is a hotel right?" Warren asked.

"Yeah, yer at the right place. Follow me inside and we'll get ya fixed up. How many rooms do ya need, for how many days, folks?" Buzz asked them.

"Okay, let me see. One, two, three, four, um…we need five rooms but only for one night," Warren said to Buzz.

"If you'll follow me to my desk, we'll get y'all processed." Buzz ushered them in and closed the door.

Cledus remembered seeing the shabby but neat furnishings in the hotel, like the last time he was there. He was no longer standing in the entryway on the moth-eaten burnt orange shag carpeting. The walls were dark wood panels with two large windows flanking the hand-carved wooden door behind him.

"If you don't mind me askin', what brings y'all out this far? Oh, never mind, don't answer that. My wife's always tellin' me to stop bein' nosy. If y'all will sign here and follow me, I'll take ya to yer rooms," Buzz said.

"It's okay. We're passing through on our way to a place we were told had great campsites." Morgan sort of lied.

"Oh, really, where might that be?" Buzz inquired.

"Tipton Ford, Missouri," Blake said from the back of the group.

"Really?" Buzz went white. His eyes were bulging with surprise. He heard the stories too but what he heard was quite different. "Well, right, this way then." He wore a nervous smile.

"This place is older than the museum and that was built in the eighteen hundred's," Jen whispers and laughs to Morgan on the stairs on the way up.

"Okay, here we are. At the top of the stairs and to the right's our first double bed and across the hall's another. Down the hall a bit's a single room for our third lady. The fella she rode with, in the single across the hall from her. And Cledus, the last room to the right has two singles and the bathroom is across from ya there. If y'all need anything, we stay up until ten pm. And the wife and I serve breakfast at eight in the mornin'. Just ring the bell if you'uns need us." Buzz wanted to be away from the group as soon as possible. His nerves were on edge. He shuffled away as quickly as a scared old man could.

Cledus felt the bad vibes too, but he felt them because he was the only one that truly knew the truth about the legend. It was real, realer than all the gold in China. On the outside, Cledus appeared to be handling the journey well, but he wasn't. He was so scared his mind was racing with horrid thoughts of the past. If his shaggy long gray hair could've gotten grayer it would have. *Why am I doing this?* He thought, *No amount of money is supposed to make you sell out your past.* It felt wrong to him. He knew he would probably die at the hand of the ghost. Inside he was petrified.

***

Warren grabbed Jen by the hand and led her to the door of their room, opened the door, sitting the luggage inside. "Hey Jen, come here, look in here. I've never seen anything like it." He winked at her. Jen knew from his mischievous smile what he was up to.

"It's just a room...oh okay...I think we need to look at it. Bye everybody," Jen said as she turned and waved at the group, gave Morgan a wink. She walked into the room, shut the door and looked Warren in his beautiful blue eyes. "What? What haven't you seen yet?" The love of her life was only playing a little game they played when they were alone together. The two lovers turned and looked at the room they were in for the night. Holding Jen by the hand, Warren swirled her around like on the dance floor, whirling huge pink and yellow roses set into cream wallpaper passed her vision. The window was dressed in simple white lace that let in the sun and the brass bed was adorned with a lovely yellow coverlet.

"Well, I haven't seen what you look like with no clothes on in this room yet. Come sit by me where it's comfy," Warren said to Jen after she stopped spinning and started smiling at him. His blue eyes had a wanton look in them.

"So dirty, but I love you, so it's okay. And you're a hunk…and…kiss me…" Jen said. She put her hand on his face. Then she ran her thin piano fingers through his black locks. She loved staring into his blue eyes and running her fingers through his hair. She loved playing his little love games, too. *They're so cute*, she thought. Both Jen and Warren took it slow most of the time and enjoyed each other. Jen liked it when he showed his love for her. It was the reason she knew she could love him. With him, everything was different.

They spent their time entwined in each other. Everything revolved around only them. Time always passed slowly when they were with each other, almost standing still. She had her own Poet and he needn't say a word. She was enthralled.

***

"I wonder if anyone else feels as awkward to be here as I do. Oh my God! This is not five stars. This place is lucky to get one. Oh!" Morgan complained. She was freaked out about being there too. All around her, she saw blue. There was blue on the bedspread. There were blue roses with a little lighter blue background for wallpaper. The curtain on the window was pale blue lace. It didn't give the appearance of filth, but Morgan wasn't used to staying in such shabby motels.

"They don't have bugs so stop checking. You're so funny! I wonder what the others are doing..."

"Umm duh! I know what at least two of them are doing. When Jen and Warren give each other a certain kind of look, you just know. That's what I saw in the hall earlier. It's pretty sick knowing that much about people, but what can I say? I've been there from the start of that relationship," Morgan stated.

"Yeah, that's kind of disturbing. Anyway, since we're away from the gang, there was something I wanted to tell you and it's a secret. It's something I have never told you. Sit with me," Blake said.

"Am I in trouble? Are you mad at me?" Morgan wondered as she sat on the bed beside him. She was a little scared. That relationship was the first one she had actually *wanted* to happen. She worked to make it good. And he was the best guy she had ever known.

"Oh, hell no. Look at me and just listen, please. Okay, I'm very nervous, so I'm just going to say it. I love you! I'm in love with you, heart and soul! I've been scared to death you won't love me back. I thought, maybe it was too early but—" Blake exclaimed.

"I LOVE YOU, TOO! Wow, I thought it was just me feeling this," Morgan said as she kissed him, her blonde hair getting in her way, falling down all around her. The surprise was amazing. *He loves me too! Wow*... She ran her hands through his neatly cropped dirty blond hair while looking into his deep brown eyes.

"No, you're amazing. How could I not love you?" Blake said while looking at her.

They embraced for a long moment. Outside the window, the two lovers see the wind kick up and blow leaves off of the dry trees. They smiled at each other and sit on the edge of the bed holding hands. Morgan's thoughts were elsewhere.

Imaginary bells rang in Morgan's head as she saw herself walk down the brightly lit middle aisle of a church. In her daydream, *Blake was standing at the head of the aisle waiting for her.* When she awoke from her daydream, he was still holding her hand and they were lying on the bed holding one another. He smiled watching her. It had been his mission to make her smile often. He loved to know he was the one that made her so happy.

***

Everyone started opening doors to rooms about an hour later. The group gathered in the hall and walked down the stairs to ring the bell. All of them wanted to talk to the owner for a minute. Everyone was laughing when they looked at each other in the hall. Buzz came in and the gang asked him about going outside to look around. He assured them all was well and not to wander to the road, he said the road was highly dangerous. When the gang got out of the house, they laughed and talked about him being crazy. What they didn't know was that Buzz lied because he didn't want to lose his business due to a few scary neighbors who had lived out there too long. They loved to creep out his possible customers and drive them away.

Outside a warm, breeze blew. The group passed the garden on their way to the woods. With the wind blowing, the figures in the garden looked gloomier than they had earlier. Some of them were almost black with age and no maintenance. The group didn't look too long, but could tell the rain wore lines into the faces of the statues as if they were crying for a long time. It also felt like the stone figures were staring at them.

The young women took the men on a little nature walk on a soft trail through the woods. The bugs and bees were buzzing all around. The sun was shining through the thicket. Flowers were blooming by the small stream in the middle of a wooded area. The wildflowers were pretty shades of purple, yellow, pink, and white. And everything was green. The sound of the water flowing through the stream was relaxing to all who heard its gentle voice. No one dared say too much for the fear of ruining the tranquility. *This is a vacation,* the four of them thought, *this is living!*

***

It was a few hours after dark, battle axes were being thrown into a couple of trees with loud ka-thunk sounds. The handles quivered from the bodies caught at the necks by them. The two victims were still kicking and screaming as Leif came into view. His matted hair, bloody and stuck to his face, covered one eye. He laughed that horrid, evil laugh which sent his victims into uncontrollable fits of terror. The sounds were no longer audible with axes sticking in their throats binding them to the trees. Leif got so close to them that if he had breath they would have smelled it. He gathered their blood for his blood ritual. They died with their eyes wide open and their voices gurgling to silence. He got as much of the blood as he could, quickly glided away to place it in the burial ground then back to finish up his work. He knew his other visitors were coming, and he didn't want them to run too soon. Hiding the bodies had become an art form over the years. It never took him long either. Those were his woods and he knew them well. He also knew how hard to throw his ax so he didn't carve up the trees by the road, that way no one knew what they were getting into when they came to see him by accident. He liked the little games he sometimes played with his victims out of pure boredom. It was about time he thought up a new one, all the screaming was annoying. The time was nearing an end and it was time to get down to business. He had waited too long to be mortal again and wanted it bad. Valhalla wasn't even an option. *Maybe Valhalla doesn't even exist,* he thought. *Who cares, either way, I'm tired of this.*

Chapter Four

The group of eight got up in the morning and ate breakfast, paid their bill, and vacated their rooms. They had to keep traveling or they would never make it and Cledus would chicken out. The closer they got, the weirder his personality became. In fact, the closer they were to Tipton Ford, the stranger people acted when the gang inquired about Leif. This commotion made the group think there might be something to the legend after all. Cledus knew, but of course, the others were not thoroughly convinced. He thought it was nuts to go on a trip because of the stories in a book. His story wasn't in there. They needed to find more clues as to what happened to Leif Eriksson, a man who died one of the most horrible deaths of his time. Cledus knew why he died. He was an evil bastard. His time had been 1405 C.E. The Museum the ladies worked for sent them to check everything in that book and hopefully find more evidence. This wasn't sitting well with him. Something he hadn't read in the book, Leif shied away from crosses because for some reason he feared them, or it could have been his barbaric nature. He didn't know why. It was his only fear, the gods gave him no notion of the emotion otherwise. The girls brought many Catholic crosses with them because they *had* read it. Morgan brought her Rosary and Jen brought one her grandma gave her as a child. They were others around their necks every day. Cledus knew better than to chastise a woman for trying her best to protect herself. When they were all together and the men started teasing the women, he didn't say a thing.

***

After being on the road for a couple more hours, everyone thought it might be a good idea to take a pit stop. They needed gas. They found a station off the highway and pulled over. Warren, Blake, and Pauly went to get gas and the rest of them stayed back to chat. After that, the men went along checking the vehicles and supplies. Warren didn't, however, he wanted to be with Jen alone for a bit.

"I need to stretch my legs. Hey Princess, are you coming?" Warren said.

"Yes, of course, I am."

Jen and Warren walked along the highway in some part of central Missouri looking at the blue sky, thinking about nothing in particular, completely oblivious to the fact that a murder was happening on Old Scenic Road. Long grass was brushing their thighs as they walked hand in hand, her long hair blowing in the breeze. It was getting hotter as they got further south and almost to their destination. Sweat beaded on their foreheads as they walked in the sun. Before the two turned back, they stopped and just stared at each other. They both smiled.

"I love you so much," he said to her.

"I love you more," said Jen.

White flowers were blooming alongside the highway. Warren bent down, picked a few, and handed them to Jen, saying something sweet to her as he did. She loved getting flowers from him. He never gave them to her out of guilt for bad deeds. He gave them to her because he thought she deserved pretty things. Jen said thank you and pecked him on the cheek. She held them in one hand and held his hand with the other. Their time together had always been simple and bittersweet. *How can I not love every minute with him?* She thought. After they were married, she dreamed it would only get better. It had been her dream for a long time to have a family with a loving husband and two great kids. It appeared that that dream would finally come true. She was happier than she ever imagined she could be. She was still so scared. She learned not to trust her feelings a long time ago. Warren knew this about her, but he was trying to prove to her, he was the one she could trust. It was a hard job, but he took it on with ease. He loved her too much to let it end over the fact that she needed to learn to trust him. He understood her. That was more than she could say about any other man. The light Warren always had in his eyes when he looked at her, assured Jen he meant what he said when he told her loved her. No one ever had the kind of light he did that resonated from him.

***

Leif found he was doing something similar to the repeating of his achievements with his killings. He made it into a little game, collect as much blood as he could until his visitors finally got there and supplied him with the rest. He kept up killing for a third time until his guests arrived. Twelve was the magic number and it looked like he'd luck into it that time. There was only so much blood a ghost could take anywhere so it never seemed like enough to him. He could feel his visitors coming. It made him salivate more for the blood he needed. He was like a rabid jackal about his blood. He wanted to be mortal again badly. It had been six hundred years since he tasted real water or ate real food, extremely frustrating for a ghost. Killing was the only thing that satisfied his tortured soul. He wondered if his new visitors would be wise enough to try to take him down or would they be scared like all the rest. While he pondered these thoughts, he smiled vehemently.

Hopefully, his final game would start soon. His last bout of fun and then he could finally die, immortality be gone with ye. There were enough of them to finish the job that time. Eight. That was it. His mind ran wild with excitement and joy about being mortal again. It was the first time in a long time he thought about joy. The last time he thought about it was when he was still in Scandinavia with his family before he came to the wretched country known in present times as the United States.

In American slang, Leif thought to himself that life sucked. His did, he was tired of being an old ghost and wanted to be alive again if only for a day. He never yearned for much in all his years as much as he wanted to breathe again.

Killing can only hold its luster for so long, he thought. *I hope it all goes as planned.* He waited and pondered as the remaining eight came slowly to him. He grinned in anticipation of them. He had to make his arsenal ready. Time was calling him to sharpen his axes and fire up his crossbow. It would be fun to see their faces as they tried to run away from him for the last time.

Chapter Five

Jen looked around the Suburban at the others. They were her friends and family. She loved them all. Blake was like a brother, Morgan like a sister, and Warren she already thought of as a husband. Even though she had a feeling of foreboding, she felt happy to be with them. If the possibility of dying came to them, there was no one she'd rather die with. Rain, who rode with Pauly the camera guy, was also someone she loved enough to die with and for. Jen also knew when the world seemed perfect it usually was anything but.

"Well, I don't know about you all, but I hope to get a tan and spend some much needed time with my lady," says Blake. He winked at Warren, who ran his fingers through his hair, smiled, and looked at Jen, who in turn, blushed. She wasn't a kiss-and-tell type of person. Nothing extreme happened on the walk, but she was shy about telling details of any of the time she spent with Warren. He was too special and good to her. She used to tell Morgan everything, but with him it was different. She never told her friend, but Morgan always knew by the look on her face.

"I agree with you about treating this like a vacation but, we also might have to be a little on our guard because we don't know the area," said Warren.

"The natives may be nut jobs. Did you get the feeling the last people we talked to were crazy? They were trying to make us feel like the crazy ones for going out there. They acted like we were going to die or something if we went. I wish you two would've seen their faces. You ladies should've seen them…totally crazy," Blake said, swirling his finger in the air.

"Were we still walking when you ran into these crazy people?" Jen asked.

"No, the guys were paying for gas. It was the guy behind the counter that was the craziest though. Blake told me about it when you guys were walking. He said he was creepy. He told me, the guy started yelling when they told him where we were going. I had to go check for myself. And his eyes, they were freaky as hell!" said Morgan.

"Yep, it was nuts," Warren said, looking at Jen as he said it.

"You're just now telling me?" Jen said, looking inquisitive.

"I didn't want to worry or upset you. I get the feeling here lately, something is going on with you, so I didn't want you to be mad or cry or something. I'm sorry, baby," Warren said to Jen. He was right, she was feeling emotional and indecisive. She thought it was stress about marriage. She knew nothing was perfect even though it could feel like it was in her world. She was getting one of the good ones, this scared the shit out of her; she wasn't used to being the one that got the good guy, the good friends, and the good life.

***

Pauly, being from a New York mob family as he was, he tried to shed the bad image. He still had a bad habit of carrying too many guns when he went on location to film. Sometimes he lost jobs he was freelancing to keep a low profile because of the guns. He wanted out and the only way was to fake his death and run like hell without looking back. He was also the best cameraman Jen and Morgan ever had the pleasure of working with. That's how he got the job he was currently going on. He met them when he applied to go on one of the other jobs the girls had gone on. He was definitely Italian, if the dark skin, hair, and eyes weren't enough, if you threatened his ma he'd shoot you.

As for Rain, she was full-blooded Native American, dark skin and hair to go along with it; the best friend of both of the girls. She also worked at the museum in the Native American Artifacts Department, which was a different branch all together at the Pettigrew House on Duluth in Sioux Falls.

She had long raven hair and deep brown eyes, the type a person could get lost in. Her spirit could haunt a man forever. She was beautiful. She was the one with the tribal knowledge. They always brought her in on the missions involving Indian artifacts or burial grounds. All the things Pauly heard about her sparked some interest.

"Eh, what you wanna listen to? I got no preference, I go with anything," said Pauly. He didn't mind playing whatever she wanted. As they talked more and more he began to really like her.

"I'm like the other two girls on that one. I like Rock and Alternative. Unlike them, I like the upbeat stuff. They don't care as long as it's got a beat," Rain told Pauly.

"Okay. Rock it is. What about this?" Pauly asked to her. He took a CD of Guns 'N' Roses out of the overhead CD holder and put it into the CD player.

"That'll do. Do you have any Ozzy or Trapt?" Rain asked him.

"Well sure. I'll take this thing off the visor and you can look through it and see what ya like. The radio is all yours," said Pauly. They started talking about subjects they may have in common. Who knew a guy from the Lower East Side in Brooklyn would know anything about Quantum Physics or the definition of a Begonia X Argenteogutta, commonly known as the Angelwing Begonia? As it turned out, there were quite a few things those new friends had to talk about. The conversation went on for hours, which made their time in the car fly by.

While the conversation between Pauly and Rain took place, Cledus and Jorge played cards, gambling the money they were going to make on that trip back and forth in the back seat.

***

At last, they arrived, two SUVs parked alongside the road on Old Scenic Road, across from the creek bed, close to a rock formation sticking out on the other side. It was dusk on Thursday, May 29, 2005. All five of the men got the gear out of the vehicles and started making camp. By nightfall, camp was set up and the roaring fire was crackling to life. This was the perfect time for Jen and Morgan to start weaving their tale of how Leif became The Old Scenic Slayer. After dinner was cooked over the campfire, the tale began. Jen reached in her bag and produced the book the boss gave them. Jen leafed through the book and found the place she wanted to start the story. She wanted to start with Matthew Hardaway. He lived in the area in 1805. His was almost the first entry. He started recording things that summer before the ghost got him too. Right before that was the history of Leif the two young researchers got off the Internet.

"How shall we start this tale of torment?" Jen asked.

"Pauly, would you get the camera? We have a ghost story to tell. This should be interesting," Morgan said.

Everyone was positioned around the campfire ready for the story. They were eager to get that part over with so they could enjoy themselves.

"Let's officially kick this off by reading a news article we found, printed just days ago by the local newspaper, shall we?"

Man Slain in Ancient Indian Ritual 1405 C.E.

[Joplin Globe Special Editions, May 2005]

[Joplin, MO] *Leif Eriksson, the son of Eric the Red, Viking warrior, was finally discovered as the man who haunts the Tipton Ford, Missouri area every fifty years. And it is suspected his ghost might have been responsible for the disappearances of many local people over the years. It is speculated that he's killed over a thousand people in the six hundred year killing spree. The locals only have records from 1805 C.E. to present.*

It was finally discovered, through DNA testing on a set of bones believed to belong to Leif Eriksson, the cause of death was a sacrifice. He was burned and bled out, his bones were found charred and holes were found in his ribs.

According to the old records, one hundred years passed before the community started seeing a pattern and began recording it. The journal dates back to the fifteen hundred's, the first pages with dates were as far back as the Sixteenth Century. The book, found in 2004, was said to have the names of all of the people who were murdered throughout the macabre past. The book started with a handwritten account of one of his earliest kills. The man who wrote the account was the friend of the victim. His friend was near the creek fishing at night when Leif caught him by surprise then he disappeared. His body was found weeks later scattered in the trees. According to the account, it took the search party a couple of weeks to fully gather his body and bury him. Supposedly, people got wiser over the years, anyone who truly believed the tale would leave for a month every fiftieth year.

In 1855, on the same day of the year, two people came up missing. It took the families more than three weeks to find their bodies, which had also been dismembered. The families of the two people hardly survived themselves. The only way was to stay away as long as they could think of. The legend goes on for six hundred years.

Also according to these legends, Leif, sometimes referred to as Old Scenic, was one of the first whites to inhabit the continent. He was a Viking warrior and the son of Eric the Red. He only spoke in Old Norse. He was hated by his family, shunned by his father, and disowned by his clan. His Berserker ways were produced by ingesting mushrooms that gave him savage hallucinations. His tortured soul only lived to torture others. The Indians had had enough of his evil ways.

One night, while he was sleeping in the cave he claimed for his home, the Indians used herbs he wasn't used to ingesting to drug him so they could properly restrain him. They tied him up and dragged him out of his home. The Indians then tied him to a sturdy stake in the ground in which they made a fire all the way around him. When he awoke, he smelled smoke and was afraid. When he saw, it was the Indians who captured him, he was furious and tried to get away, but couldn't. He soon discovered that the more he moved, the tighter his bonds became. The Indians wasted no time with him. In those days, the Indians didn't want to anger the spirits, so they sacrificed him immediately then burned his body to release his soul and please the spirits. He was said to be a tortured, now trapped soul who remained on earth to hunt and kill as many as stepped in his path. So the legend of the six hundred-year-old ghost remains, of course, a mystery.

"Wow! Just wow, guys!" Jen said. "There's a bit that might not be in this history."

"This sicko has a trophy collection of sorts. This is the really nasty part guys, so don't go getting all girly on me now. He sometimes cuts off the male victim's balls. The cops can't find them when they clean up the crime scene," Morgan explains.

That little bit of information made all the men cringe. After that, they began discussing Matthew. Jen told them about his life. According to what Jen and Morgan gathered, he lived in the woods alone most of his life. He never married because he was so young. He was a woodsman and a scout for hunters. He told them where to go and how to trap animals if they were the rich type and had no idea how to hunt. He lived a comfy life by himself until the fate-filled day he died.

***

No one paid much attention to the life and times of Matthew Hardaway, the man that was only second in line to start keeping records of the area's killing spree. All of the men were more concerned with the loss of their balls and simultaneously shouted obscenities.

"You're yankin' our chain, right?" asked Pauly.

"No, according to this, I'm not. Look," Morgan said as she showed him the book and the place stating the passage about the trophies.

"What does it say about his weaponry? Supposedly he has been a ghost but he uses weapons to kill," Jen added.

"Absolutely, according to this, he's fond of arrows and hatchets. But the news clippings say he has also used short swords and battle axes," said Morgan.

"I have something to add here if that's okay," Cledus said. It was Cledus's turn to get it over with. He couldn't wait any longer.

"That's fine. It's one of the reasons we picked you," said Jen. She smiled kindly at Cledus.

"All right, here goes. Well, when I was a kid the story had grown. As y'all already know I lived here growing. My parents didn't believe it. They thought it was crap. When I was about ten, I learned it was them who was lyin'. The funny thing is, they didn't know they lied. They just thought it was some crazy rumor, but when he killed them, I found out. I was hidin' so he didn't see or sense me, I guess. Or maybe there was a reason for him only killin' them, I'm not sure. He took my parents away from me, so I'm back here to prove he's real and possibly find a way to get rid of him. He was the scariest thing I had ever seen as a child. Even as a grown up, he's still scary as hell. He was tall. He had blond hair drenched in blood. His beard was even covered in it. His face was hollow and horrible, there were cuts all over him and his expression was deadly. I used to have nightmares about him, in them dreams, he'd sense me and just stare at me. And he always said he would take care of me next time." Cledus stopped talking, stroked his beard, and sat silently for a while, staring at the fire. He was drinking so he was half lit and everyone was talking again about other stuff. Then after a while the gang heard screaming in the woods. They never noticed Cledus got up and walked away. When the screaming started, the group looked around and saw one of the eight was missing.

Chapter Six

"That was Cledus, wasn't it?" asked Warren. "Oh, shit!"

"How come no one saw him leave? I feel selfish. We weren't even paying attention to him," Jen said. Everyone agreed with her. "Could someone just go find him? Maybe that wasn't him." She started to tear up a little. Her emotions began to get the better of her, she was scared.

"Jen, it was *him!* There isn't anyone else here but us," said Blake.

"Yeah," said Pauly.

"Somebody just go find him! Did we tell you that he only starts killing after dark because he thinks it's more fun to sneak up on you?" Jen was starting to panic.

"Jorge, I nominate you to go find him. Take this lantern and this walkie-talkie with you. Hurry back," Morgan told him.

"Okay, Señorita. Be back soon." Jorge left and as he did, he grumbled all the way, cussing about them in Spanish. After he left, everyone sat silently by the fire, huddled closer together. Pauly was the first to speak.

"I hope the Mexican finds him. We need to get rollin' on this. I don't see us stayin' this whole weekend. The thing about stories is, they ain't always fairy tales, and the way you told that one, it seems like a bad time to be here just now. I'm from fuckin' Brooklyn and I seen a lot of bad stuff, but I don't know about this one. I never heard anything like this in my life!" Pauly exclaimed.

"Does this mean you're wussing out on us?" Warren asked.

"Hell no, this ain't no sissy. I shot guys point blank who were as big as freight trains, but this shit is crazy. How the hell you gonna defend yourself against a fuckin' ghost? Guns don't matter to somethin' that's already dead."

***

The gang heard another scream from somewhere in the trees. They tried to contact Jorge on the talkie and got only static. Then they heard an ominous laugh on the other end of the talkie and some Norse phrase they couldn't understand because it wasn't loud enough or audible.

"WHAT THE FUCK WAS THAT?!" Warren shouted. He tossed the talkie in the air.

"Oh my God!" Jen screamed. She was beginning to panic.

"I think it was him!" Morgan said.

"Now what do we do? I should probably tell you guys something. I had a premonition. I've never had one in my life, but my tribe is notorious for having the second sight. My grandma was a descendant of a medicine woman who strongly had the gift and they always came true. I didn't say anything, but I saw them both die in my head. We gotta do something before these visions continue and I see someone else die," Rain said.

"What the hell do you mean you see things? How come you never said anything before?" Warren asked.

"She never even told us and we've known her for a while," said Jen.

"Okay, big deal. Back to the problem at hand. What the hell are we going to do? We just heard what was supposed to be the Slayer, now what?" Blake wondered.

"I don't know. Read the book, I guess. That way we can possibly find something in there about slowing him down," Morgan said.

"This is fuckin' crazy. I say we get the fuck out. I'm not gonna die over no fuckin' documentary about a fuckin' ghost of a dead Viking. Fuck this!" Pauly spat. He got up off the ground and shut off the video camera. He walked over to the SUV, put the camera in the front seat, and closed the door. He put the key in the ignition and cranked it. The SUV wouldn't start. He cussed out loud then got out of the SUV and slammed the door. Pauly lifted the vehicle's hood and started messing with the engine. He cussed louder. The gang came running over.

"Hey man, thought you were leaving? What the fuck is that?" Warren asked.

"Yeah, that's what I'd like to know. So, which one of yous fucked wit' my car?" Pauly asked accusingly.

"What are you talking about? We were with you at the campsite the whole time. And the better question would be, *who are you accusing?* Because you know these girls don't know a carburetor from a camshaft," Warren said.

"Yeah, that only leaves two other people besides you. And let me tell you, I don't do stupid shit like that cause I'm an actual upstanding citizen. I don't just play one on TV," said Blake.

"Pauly, are you really *that* scared? I thought you knew us better than that?" Jen asked him. Jen's eyes welled up and she walked a little way away from the group.

"So we aren't your friends anymore and you think we sabotaged you?" Morgan asked. "Fuck you."

"Whoa! Hold it. We need to stop this. We know we didn't do anything," Warren said.

"I thought I knew you all, too. Look under this hood! It's a mess!" said Pauly.

"I see it but how could we have done anything? You sat beside us all evening. You're our friend. Rationalize this, will you, please? We were with you and you know us. The only ones you don't know are missing right now. They were also sitting there for the majority for the evening and no one was near any of the vehicles. There is only one more explanation here and no one wants to hear it, but I think it was Leif. We were all distracted for about a half hour when Cledus was telling us his part of the story, remember?" Jen explains.

"After we took over again, he came up missing, remember? He could have done it then. We were still distracted for a few more minutes before we noticed him missing," Morgan said.

"If it was Cledus, we would have heard it because the car isn't that far away. The engine latches are noisy when people go messing with them," Warren said. "Maybe it *was* this damn ghost."

"I know. Eliminating the impossible, whatever is left no matter how improbable, in this case, ghosts, it must be the truth. The story is good, but not *that* good. I would have heard someone messin' wit' my car. I got an idea. You guys should try to start yours, too. I wanna know if it's just my ride or everyone's," said Pauly.

"I'll do it, gimme the keys," Blake said, annoyed. He then walked up the short path to the road. The gang watched him get in the Suburban and heard the engine try to crank over with no success. A little while and a few cranks later, Blake returned to the small crowd with a frown on his face. "Well Pauly, don't you have some apologies to make? We're all stuck, not just you."

"Yeah, you're right. I'm sorry, yous guys," Pauly apologized.

"Apology accepted, Pauly," Jen said.

"I have another suggestion. Have you guys got your phones on you?" Warren asks everyone.

"We all brought them. I haven't had reception though since we were on highway seventy-one. I doubt if we have any now," Blake said.

"Let's check anyway," Jen said. No luck though with the cell phones. That scared her. After seeing the mess under Pauly's hood, she didn't need to see under theirs to know it was also a pile of cut wires and grease. They were trapped.

"It was worth a shot. I'm tired. I think we should try to sleep if we can, then get up and try to find the others tomorrow or a house with a phone or something." Morgan yawned loudly.

Everyone agreed, although not much sleep went on that night. Everyone was too scared to close their eyes for long, which would have been hard anyway since Pauly and Rain whispered all night. It wasn't until morning when they finally stopped hearing every blade of grass rustling around them. They woke up at ten am when it started to get warm. When exiting the tents, they saw words written all over the ground. The words were in ancient Norse.

"Hey girls, what's all this?" Pauly asked pointing at the writing on the ground.

"It's a message in Norse. He was right outside our tents last night and didn't kill us. He wants something from us. I read last night, there was a burial ground around here somewhere. I wonder if it has to do with that," Jen said. She could read and speak many old languages, but she needed her special book for that one. She hadn't seen it since the days she studied abroad.

"You're the Ancient Language expert. What does it say?" Morgan asked.

"It's not that simple. I didn't have a chance to get re-familiarized with Norse before we left. All I have to go by is this book and a stupid book about writing languages that no one uses anymore. It's going to take some time, but in the meantime, be careful not to smudge those symbols or we're screwed, guys," Jen said.

"Oh my, the princess said a semi-swear word!" Morgan said, laughing hard.

"Shut up and help me!" Jen said scowling at Morgan.

"So, what are we supposed to do while you're decoding that shit?" said Warren.

"Well, cuss mouth, you three guys could go find the burial ground. That would be helpful. We're going to have to go there too, you know."

"Yeah, you guys go find it and come back. We women folk will stay here and do our jobs. This is serious, no time for foul-ups. Go across the bank over there. It seems like it will be near water because the Indians needed a water source. If you find the other guys tell them, their little prank from last night wasn't funny. If I wasn't a lady, I would smooth kick their asses," said Morgan.

"Do I take a gun just in case we see somethin'?" Pauly asked the other guys as they walked away from the girls.

"What the hell are we gonna need a gun for in the daytime? Also, are you gonna try to put a bullet in a ghost? How stupid is that?! Start walkin', fool," Warren said. "You're the one who told us you can't shoot a ghost, dumb ass."

The guys said goodbye to their women and kissed them, Pauly waved and smiled at Rain. As they went in search of the burial grounds, they found their missing companions, blood was more than scary in the vivid light of day.

The ground was dark crimson and brown from the night, the blood soaked into the dirt and grass around the trees where the bodies hung. Horror was permanently frozen onto the faces of Jorge and Cledus. In the center of a thick tree line, there was a blank spot with trees planted in a circle, the corpses were facing the inside of the circle and couldn't be seen from the outside. In the center, there were jagged edges of rocks from the bottom of the deepest part of the creek, symbols were drawn and the rocks used to help tell a graphic picture tale of torture and murder. Dried blood ran down the arms of both Jorge and Cledus having dripped on the ground all night. The victims had missing teeth and the groin areas of their jeans were soaked red. Cledus's long gray hair was disheveled and hanging over the huge scratches etched into his skin. Before much contemplative thought could take place the three men ran out of the circle of trees and found what they were looking for.

Chapter Seven

"FUCK! I'm glad they left. Now we can work. Are you figuring out any of the symbols yet?" Morgan asked Jen.

"Not yet, like you said, now it's quiet. If you could read the book some more that would be great. I need to get Rain to look at the tribes of Indians that were living here when Leif was. I also need to grab my books from the car. I'm just glad I brought books instead of trying to rely on the Internet. I had a feeling it would be no good here," Jen said as she walked to the car and got her book about Norse language and symbols then returned to the other girls.

The three of them spent the next half hour reading. The drawing of the symbols on the ground appeared to be: ᛑᛏᛘᛖ

"I think I have it! The first symbol means 'death' and then we have 'to all' after that it says 'who enter here.' So roughly that means 'death to all who enter here.' After that, it says something like 'once you enter you will never leave alive.' I think it's a warning to us that we're going to die here. He all but spelled it out for us and I think the reason why he didn't kill us last night is because he wants to play a game with us," Jen said.

"It's my turn now. The tribe that lived here in 1405 was Cherokee. I brought books too. I always carry copies of the historical documents and maps as well. Back then, they were very savage and used to use human sacrifice as a means to please their gods. If the guys find the burial grounds, I can show you what all of the stones and the positions mean," Rain explained.

"I also found out some more about Leif in this book. We need to bone up on Viking rituals, too. That might be how we get to him if need be," Morgan added.

"I have a book about that too."

The three girls kept reading until the sun started to shift a little in the sky and turned light orange. The day was already beginning to end and it was only around eleven am. They heard the babbling of the creek water and the sound of wind blowing slightly in the trees. One thing no one mentioned was the sound of the wildlife. There were no sounds coming from the indigenous creatures supposed to inhabit the area. Everyone was focused on and rattled by the possible loss of people in the group they hadn't stopped to observe the silence in an otherwise naturally noisy spot.

***

At noon, the women started hearing voices and looked up from their books at the same time. The men returned. They were anxious to hear news.

"Ladies, we have good news and bad news. We found what we were looking for, but we want Rain to look it over. I'm no expert, but something is wrong about that place. It's hard to explain," Blake tells them.

Warren swallowed hard. "Bad news, we found the missing guys. They weren't playing a prank. They're dead and all over the place." His eyes glazed over and he started mumbling about blood everywhere and body parts in trees. He saw so much blood he still saw nothing else in his mind but red.

"It was gruesome, ladies. The thing Blake thought was wrong with the burial grounds is there's a lot of fresh blood on this circle in the middle. You three really gotta see this. It's hard to explain," Pauly said.

"We're done here. I was just telling Jen and Morgan about Indian sacrifices. So maybe it has something to do with that," Rain said.

"Yeah, maybe it does. The blood looked human and fresh," Pauly said.

"We better get up there and look so we can get back well before dark," Rain suggested.

The remaining six members of the group took off for the burial grounds with their books in hand. It took them a while to get there because the men took them a little bit different way than the original path. Dead bodies were not something they wanted the ladies to see. It was getting later in the afternoon, the sun was changing positions in the sky again. They didn't have much time before nightfall, which was going to be a total bitch. *Ah, sweet success, we finally reached the burial grounds*, they all thought.

***

Everyone reached the grounds on top of the hill in time to see the sun peeking through the trees. The Ancient Indian burial grounds were what one would imagine. In a clearing, there were piles of rocks everywhere. The circle in the center had a wooden post in the center of it. Around the center circle, there were many smaller circles formed from rocks. Outside the center circle, they saw a crude altar made of stone with a few objects laid across it. The objects belonged to some of the victims of Leif. Once inside the big circle, they noticed the blood the guys talked about at camp. They touched the rocks with their fingers and looked at them. It was fresh!

"The Indians used to put the blood of humans on these rocks and did ceremonial dances to their gods here. Sometimes they would burn the person after they bled them out. That's what the post is for," Rain explained. Her expression almost frightened and sobering, she glanced across at her friends.

"I get it. I also think that may have been what they did to Leif because he was such an angry person they may have thought they needed to release his evil soul, but something went wrong," Jen said.

"Maybe they did that to him as a revenge killing because he was a bastard while he was alive. According to the first recorded recordings in the book, he ate this certain kind of mushroom that had the effects of LSD and it turned him into what history calls a Berserker. And that is a fancy word for a Viking gone madder than a hatter. The most common side effect was horrible rage. If it was a revenge killing, I'm sure they had a good reason," Morgan explained.

"The sun keeps moving and we're losing daylight. We better get back to camp so we can get prepared for tonight. I think Jen's right about him playing a game with us, so we need to get ready for him," Warren said.

"I *do* think he's playing a game and I know that he doesn't have that many days left until he has to wait another fifty years to be free to kill again. So, I go with

Warren on this. We need to get back. It's going to be a long night." Jen sighed.

"Okay. I just want to take some pictures first," Rain said. Then she snapped several pictures with her digital camera. "All right, I'm done now. We can go."

The gang walked off toward camp and they were almost there when Rain had another vision. She started shaking, almost convulsing.

The blood dripped slowly down the side of her brow as Rain stared into the face of death himself. At first, she couldn't speak or yell, his hollow horrifying appearance built terror inside her. Soon she saw the blade of his ax shining in the moonlight. She finally produced a scream before he swung the battle ax over his head sweeping then connecting with hers, slicing it off in one foul swoop. As her body hit the ground, she seemed to be looking down on the entire scene from above it. She gasped, no one heard her make a sound as Leif picked her head up off the ground by her long black hair, carrying it into the woods and disappearing into the trees.

"NOOOOO!" Rain screamed.

"What the hell? Are you all right, girl?" Pauly asked her.

"No! I'm not okay! I just had another one of those visions or premonitions or whatever the hell you call it!" Rain screamed at Pauly.

"Huh?" Pauly said.

"What? What did you see?" Jen asked her friend.

"I don't know what's happening to me. I saw death. I witnessed my own death. Pauly, you die too," Rain said fast and breathlessly.

"This is truly the first time you've ever seen things like that? Are you sure?" Morgan asked.

"Never before this trip, have I seen anything," Rain admitted to everyone.

"We really need to hurry back. This is getting serious," Morgan said.

The group looked at each other with shock and surprise. The six of them ran the whole way back to camp. The sun was fading, getting lower in the sky, turning shades of red and pink then orange and blue. It was getting dark. Back at camp, the gang tried to get into survival mode. The girls read their books and prepared with information while the guys prepared with protection strategies. A lot of black coffee was brewed over the newly lit campfire. They tried to hold out as long as possible then they started drinking the coffee. It wasn't going to be a quiet night for them.

Dusk faded into nightfall, the group was sitting up waiting for the inevitable. It seemed like a long wait. Leif was watching them from the trees on the other side of the creek. They took no notice because it was hard to see a ghost covered in blood in the dark. He was waiting until they were distracted or alone to pick them off one by one. Some of them couldn't get the memories from earlier out of their minds. Part of them were still in a horrible daze, which made Leif think the timing was perfect. Time was growing terribly short, the days were passing too quickly. Leif got more desperate to kill as many people as he could to become mortal again.

Chapter Eight

Through the trees, Leif continued to watch and wait, then the opening came that he was waiting for. They couldn't hold their water for forever, they were human, after all.

"Hey, I gotta pee. Am I supposed to just piss myself or is it okay for me to take a leak? You guys are borin' the hell out of me," Pauly said.

"No one goes into the woods alone, remember? You came up with that rule. Somebody has to go with you. Oh, and just so you know, you're no barrel of laughs right now either," Warren said.

"I need to stretch my legs from so much sitting. I'll go with you," Rain said, winking at him.

"Okay. I really gotta go, so no funny business from me. No worries," Pauly said to Rain putting his hand in the air. After they were away from everyone he asked her, "Do ya really buy into all this?"

"Yes, I do. First off, I've never had a vision in my whole life until this trip. I went on mission trips with the other two ladies before and not one vision. They know I don't lie or make anything up. I have no reason to do that. Second, I know they wouldn't do something to scare us. I'm very scared of what's happening here and no one can make someone else have visions," Rain stated.

"Scared of dyin' you mean?" Pauly said.

"Yes and I'm scared my friends won't be strong enough to handle this mess without the guys. No one knows this, but I saw the girls' boyfriends die in my vision, too. I came out of it before I had a chance to see it come to an end. I didn't tell anyone else. You're the only one who knows. Promise me, you won't tell them. I don't think the girls could handle knowing any more of this," Rain said to Pauly.

"You got it. My lips are—" Pauly didn't get to finish his sentence.

The two of them stopped in their tracks. They walked into a thicket of trees. In the middle there were no trees. It was a barren circle with many symbols carved into the dirt. It was pitch black, but the flashlights they had in their hands pointed at the ground and all the symbols on it. Some of them were wet with blood.

Leif picked his moment well. He came down upon them and paralyzed them with fear. They couldn't make a sound. Pauly pushed the button on his talkie in Morse code. He tapped S.O.S., standing in the middle of the trees. With a smile on his face, Leif cut Pauly's head off with one silent swing of his battle ax and it flew to the side. His body hit the ground with a thud. Rain, standing beside a headless corpse, finally found her voice and screamed loudly one time before he decapitated her. Blood gushed all over the ground in the dark. This pleased Leif a lot.

***

Back at camp, everyone heard Rain scream. Then they realized Pauly was trying to contact them via Morse code. They heard it one time and that was the last time they heard it. The woods were deathly quiet that save for their voices.

"Was that an S.O.S.?" Warren asked.

"Yeah, man. That's exactly what that was," Blake said.

"What about Rain? That was her screaming! She's dead! I know she is! I can feel it!" Jen exclaimed. Chills went down her back and there was no wind. Her heart raced with panic.

"Those screams from last night were the missing people the guys found. We gotta go find them. We have to make sure!" Morgan said.

"Come here, Mo," Blake said to Morgan, looking at her in a serious manner. "Get your pack together, grab only the stuff you absolutely need. We need to try to find the others if we can, but if we can't, we need to get the fuck out of here. To hell with your job. I'll find you two new ones when we get home. Fuck this place," Blake said. He hugged Morgan and told her to hurry.

"I agree with that. Let's get the hell out of here," Warren said.

The two young women gathered the books and the things they would need, it was pure necessities at that point. The four of them took off into the woods to try to find their friends. Leif was staring at them the whole time and they walked right passed the tree he was standing behind, again unnoticed by them.

The woods always looked thicker at night, but the four of them had flashlights. After walking about three-fourths of a mile into the woods, they came to a less wooded area with symbols carved into the trees. They looked them over and Jen explained the Norse writing. The symbols in the trees were in a circle, they stood in the center of it. After standing in the circle long enough to determine they needed to leave it, they looked up and shined the light up as well, to see if there were more carvings. They saw the bodies of their friends strewn among the trees. Everyone screamed at the same time. Then they finally put their hands over their mouths for fear of being heard and found.

"Shhhh! He'll find us! We gotta go now!" Blake whispered.

The gang ran through the woods, dodging old arrows occasionally and hearing ominous laughter in the distance. They never knew it, but Leif was with them the whole time. He tailed them at a distance so when they looked back they never saw him. After they ran for a while, they sat down to rest.

"This is only Friday. We have one more night of this," Jen said.

"You don't have to remind us," Blake said to Jen in an annoyed tone.

"Maybe we do and maybe we don't. I don't know about you, but I'm ready to stop running and start facing the truth here. There's a possibility we may not come out of this one alive y'all. Admit it," Morgan said.

"You may be right, but I don't think we need to give up. Yes, our friends are dead, but do you think they would wan t us to give up? Because I don't think they would," Warren said.

"What about standing up and fighting this thing? Is there any way of fighting back at all?" Blake wondered.

"Baby, it's a ghost. It's gonna be hard to fight a ghost. Isn't that what you told Pauly yesterday? If there's a way, we'll have to try to find it. We brought some of the books, only the ones we thought we needed," Morgan said.

"I think if we can outlast him 'til he goes away in the am then we can read and find out. We need to get going again, he could be watching or listening," Jen said.

"He seems to like picking us off while we're alone, so we're staying together and we're gonna keep moving, then maybe we'll have a better chance of surviving the night," Warren said.

The four of them got to their feet and started walking again. It was too quiet. There were no nature sounds to be heard; no birds, no barking, and no babbling from the creek. The four of them walked all night until it started to get lighter. The sky was a pale blue so the group guessed it might have been around five am. They sat down, too tired to speak, soon the gang of four fell asleep.

***

A few hours later, the cool dew and sun shining in their faces woke Jen and Morgan up from their uneasy dozing period of sleep. The light was beating down on them, it turned warm and sweat was forming on their faces. The ground made a stiff, chilly bed. After they both rubbed the sleep from their eyes enough to look around without wondering where they were, the girls noticed something was wrong.

"Hey, where'd the guys go? They were right here a few hours ago," Jen wondered.

"I don't know. They should be close. They made the rule about us not going anywhere by ourselves," Morgan said.

The girls started screaming the names of their men. They got silence in return. Panic instantly filled Jen and Morgan. The girls jumped to their feet and took off running, hollering names. Again nothing was returned. They stopped. As Jen and Morgan were turning around to go back the other way, they looked up at the trees. They saw the bodies of the men attached to tree trunks with battle axes holding them in place by their necks. Blood cascaded down the trees in sheets and started to dry at the bottoms. The sight sent Jen and Morgan into fits of hysterical screaming so loud the birds got scared and flew overhead trying to get away from the noise. The sound of flapping wings was drowned out by painful shrieking cries.

Soon, the two young female research assistants stood rooted to the ground in silence, staring at the bodies with no heads, motionless. In pain, tears streaked their faces, insanity instantly plagued their minds. A transition between good and evil happened in both of their hearts, something inside them died. As Jen and Morgan mourned, they realized they were going to avenge the men they loved. Madness crept into the recesses. Morgan was the first to vocalize it. She wanted to kill the bastard who took them. She convinced her best friend to do the same. Anger fueled the fire to find their strength, standing before the bloody corpses of their beloved men.

"I'm only gonna say this once, so listen good." Morgan's voice was ragged. "We gotta kill that motherfucker! TONIGHT! No more of this stupid fuckin' game. Got me? No more! It ends this weekend, baby girl! I don't care if ya barely got the guts to go on, cause yer gonna! He's gonna die, damn it! We will survive for *them*!" Morgan said and then she pointed at the bodies stuck to the trees. "We're gonna get him for all of 'em!" She put her arm around Jen, leading her back to camp.

***

Two unnerved young women walked down the trail closest to the where the SUVs were still parked. Morgan began to wonder what exactly the plan was going to be. She thought of some things as they got to the road then saw the SUVs. She suddenly remembered there was extra stuff in them.

"Hey, baby girl, you need to snap out of it. We got work to do. We need ta check them cars an' see if there's anythin' that may be of use. You check our car an' I'll look in the back hatch of Pauly's," Morgan said.

Jen was still pretty out of it, but she slowly started coming back to reality. She walked to the car with a haze hanging over her. After she finally threw up, she looked for food and weapons. She didn't know if she would find anything. She didn't really care about food. Her thoughts consisted more of throwing up and screaming so loud it would hurt her own ears. She needed something to do. It had been at least a half hour since she'd spoken at all. *How am I going to make it if my heart isn't strong enough to ride the pain out until all of the madness is over?* She pondered. The more she got back to reality, the madder she got. She realized it was pure anger that would be her fuel too.

"Hey, your facial expression's lookin' better. Are ya feeling a little better? Hey, guess what I found? Pauly had a whole trunk full of stuff. I think we gotta thank God for a gun totin' bastard," said Morgan.

"Yep," Jen said as she crossed herself. And they both looked down at a trunk filled with C-4. "I wonder what he thought he needed that for."

"When he said liked to blow shit up, he wasn't kiddin'. This could come in handy," Morgan said.

"Do you really think we're gonna need all this? He's a ghost and if you can't shoot 'em, you sure as hell can't blow 'em up."

"No, but every ghost has a home. Those do blow up and that motherfucker don't need no home or cave or whatever the fuck he lives in," Morgan spat.

"I feel yer right, but where d'we begin? We don't know how to blow shit up," said Jen.

"Pauly, that crazy son of a bitch, I love him! Look! It's a book for buildin' bombs with C-4. Think about it, how could he know this might happen?" Morgan asked Jen.

"Well, I guess let's try an' do this then. This's better'n no plan at all. We only have t'day. It'll be too late after that. Look what I still got." Jen showed Morgan the books she had in the pack she had on her back all night long.

"Nice, forgot all about them. Maybe we can mix this with that an' come up with somethin' good." Morgan smiled a maniacal smile.

"I was gonna read up an' on spells an' such, see if there's anything to use in these old books to possibly keep us goin' til mornin'. I'm thinkin' we may need to blow up the burial grounds too. That'll really piss him off," Jen said. She thought about the blood she saw on the stones and knew there was a reason for it, but didn't know what it was.

"Good idea, now yer thinking, that's m' girl. Anything else, just spit it out as it comes. We got no time to spare here," Morgan said.

Jen started reading with lightning speed. A maddening smile stretched across her face. Morgan tied up her hair and looked at the diagrams and built the bombs, she had the more level head of the two as the adrenaline was fueling her. By midday, they had the bombs placed in their designated areas. The spells were memorized and the incantations close at hand. It was time to lie down for a while and try to sleep while there was some daylight left. After about a half hour of trying, the girls decided sleep wasn't an option and continued with their work. They practiced how to shoot guns and how to quickly load them. The darkness was advancing on them, it was almost time to start their crazy plan to stay alive.

"Ya do realize, we could get stuck there, don't ya? We might have ta fight 'im there. What're we gonna do if that happens?" Jen was worried that nothing was going to work.

"We try the spells and Viking stuff first. If that don't work, we blow up the grounds an' run our asses off for camp. The cave's close to that. If nothin' else, we got remotes for the bombs. Don't worry girl, we got this. If we can help it, that bastard ain't gonna get us." Morgan tried like hell to be positive.

The girls ran to the burial ground in record time and checked the charges they set. It could be blown up with a remote. Before they could pry themselves away from it, they looked at the center circle and it was mostly covered with blood. The girls knew it wasn't that way the last time they saw it. They both read enough of the book to know, Leif was vicious and killed ruthlessly for some sort of purpose and had to kill again to finish the job. The two women stayed too long at the burial grounds, they had to run hard and fast to camp before it got completely dark. As they lit up their campfire, they heard a loud, close cackle from Leif coming from somewhere in the nearby foliage. They huddled closer to the fire acting scared. The maniacal laughter sounded closer the next time they heard it. The girls remained silent with small smiles of satisfied hatred on their faces.

Chapter Nine

Leif stepped out of the woods to face them as they sat staring through the campfire waiting for him. He laughed at them. "So you think you are going to defeat me? Many have tried and all have failed, as will you," Leif said in English.

"Push the button! Now!" Morgan whispered.

"Okay. Your precious burial grounds are gone in five! Four! Three!"

"No! Don't! Please don't! I have to be mortal again!" Leif screamed at them.

"At the expense of so many people, I think not! Push the damn button!" Morgan yelled to Jen.

"She pushes that button, I kill her!" Leif said.

"No matter what we do, we'll die. You ain't got enough blood for yer sick ass ritual without us. So, one way or the other, we're gonna die. Well, good thing we don't care for yer way o' thinkin', ain't it? Push that button girl, cause fuck that motherfucker! Remember what he did? He killed your future husband!" Morgan said.

"Here goes nothin', asshole!" Jen pushed the button with an evil grin on her lips.

"No! You shall die a thousand times for that!" Leif screamed.

"How can you die a thousand times? Ghosts're morons!" Morgan said, laughing she grabbed Jen by the hand and started running, then turned around and stared at Leif.

***

Inside, peeking outward, swirling and raging were the insane thoughts of a deranged man. Outside was the seemingly scary reddening visage of a killer. His thoughts trampled his own conventions, the thought of spending even one more day as a ghost drove him to his breaking point. He wanted those two incessant women dead, they wouldn't stop. They wouldn't help him either. They didn't understand it. Six hundred years as a vengeful spirit not only angered him, it pushed him to the point of insanity. It had been too long living in a hell he couldn't be released from because of a curse bound tightly on him. He didn't know how all of it worked, but he'd found out he could take mortal form after he had most of what he needed. He still couldn't properly die. He tried to cut out his own heart and couldn't, there were only so many ways to try to kill yourself, even for a ghost. He tried everything he could think of in solid form, nothing was going to help him. After he learned how the anti-curse ritual worked, he'd been trying to accomplish it and failed for many seasons. His chances were few since he was only allotted time every fifty years. There was a lot of time spent stewing over how he messed up, which made the rage grow.

As he stood stock-still and straight on, the women before him thought they had to fight. In his mind, it would be easier if they gave up, giving in to death. His look of trepidation should have been the clue. He saw that look in their eyes before, it was a look of broken insanity. He wasn't sorry he was the cause of it, he knew the women were now unpredictable and he didn't know what to look for next. Their behavior changed over the course of a few days, he'd observed them from the tree line to glean information about the group when they arrived; he saw the changes. These prim and proper women grew into creatures of instinct. The normal beauty they exuded so well was hidden by the mask of rage, with dirt and blood covering their outer shells, the way they carried themselves changed. Their glittering eyes and wide smiles became dull. He noticed the start of the change in them with the first kills of the eight. They were scared. He also left them for last because he thought they'd be the most fun to kill. He imagined all the screaming Jen and Morgan would do, as he came after them, it made him shiver with excitement a few days ago. What stood before him were not those two scared little girls he noticed in the beginning of his observations. These women were dripping with pain, hurt *he* caused them. He couldn't sense their fear. As he stared at them, he noticed the crazed smiles painted on their faces. He had never seen women like these before.

***

Pieces of trees sailed past their heads as Jen and Morgan ran from the blast, ducking in a large cut out section in the ground. Splintered wood, dust, and fire exploded around them, smoke billowed into the night sky. Greenery from the new May growth was destroyed, chunks of huge rock came flying toward them. Morgan ducked Jen's head further into the homemade foxhole, washing the world of the only 'demon' they knew existed.

Jen was laughing between coughs as the smoke got closer to them, making it harder to breathe. She was thrilled to be a part of the demise of what she thought of as pure evil. Her heart raced and her entire body shook with adrenaline. Her tiny body started to convulse a little and she threw up. It didn't bother her to spit out what she ate, it woke her up, further sobering her soul to what she was witnessing. She bit her tongue on purpose and spit out the blood, still laughing as the raging fires now tried to consume the bomb site about a quarter of a mile down the road.

The scenery on Old Scenic Road changed. The houses closest to the burial grounds were ruined masses of flaming, sagging wood. The siding was melting off and running onto the ground from the intense heat of the fires that came from the blast. The battlefield was cloudy and fire lit in the places in the darkness. Pieces of wood and stones splashed into the water below the burial grounds. The fence standing on the edge of the land across the creek was gone, it fell into the running water. The girls stood up in their foxhole looking in horror at Leif, wondering what to do next.

"It's spell time, Jen," Morgan finally said. "Hurry before he kills us."

"Gods of Valhalla hear me. Send us Odin the God of Wisdom and War, to help us defend ourselves from evil," Jen said in Ancient Norse.

"Was that it?" Morgan asked.

"Yep. I asked the God Odin to help us," Jen said.

When Jen started speaking in Leif's language, he stood staring at her in shock and amazement. Then he laughed his awful, horrible, guttural laugh. He knew it didn't do anything.

"That will not help you. There is probably no longer an Odin or Valhalla. You should have just prayed to your God. Even he can't help you. It's time to die," Leif said sneering at them.

"No, it's time to say the other spell, then, we get the fuck out! Hurry up, Jen!" Morgan shouted.

"Many moons pass and many moons fade. Fade this ghost in front of us. Fade this ghost in front of us. Fade this ghost in front of us," Jen said quickly. Nothing happened but laughter from Leif.

The two young researchers took off running in the other direction from the campfire. They heard Leif behind them the whole way, laughing. Time passed as they kept going. Leif was so angry he would never get to be mortal, he kept chasing them, not daring to get too close because he wanted the chance to savor his last killings for fifty years. It would seem like an eternity until he got to do the only thing he had ever loved, killing. After all, it was all he had left to look forward to.

***

Time lapsed a little more. An hour passed and the girls ran until they could no longer see Leif. He was never far behind, even if they couldn't see him. He was dragging out the inevitable. The girls had to fight with all the will and cunning they possessed. Those females had no desire to die at the hand of a monster. The next crazy thing the girls tried was an old fashioned exorcism from the bible, Catholic and in Latin. They both knew, since the Viking incantation and the magic spell didn't work, the bible thing probably wouldn't either. They didn't have time to slow down long enough to think about it. It was now or never.

"The bible says we need holy water from a Catholic church. We don't got any. It probably ain't gonna work," Jen said.

"Let's just try it anyway," Morgan said. As she said that, she opened the bible to the page they marked before they left home and the two of them started to read.

"*Ave Maria, gratia plena: In nominee Patris et Filii et Spiritus Sancti. Profectus indedaemon. Vade et amplius noceat nemini. Profectus inde daemon. Vade et ampliusnoceat nemini*!" They both said it together and repeated it together, crossing themselves as they did. They both looked up and listened.

"I don't think it worked. I hear 'im laughin' again. And he's growlin' at us now. Time to go," Morgan said. As the girls stood up to run, Leif appeared directly in front of them.

"You think your religion will hurt me? You make me laugh!" Leif said.

"Go the other way," Jen whispered to Morgan.

"I can't. Water's behind me," she whispered back to Jen, standing on the edge of the riverbed.

"Shoot him or something. We can't just stand here!" Jen pleaded with her best friend.

"We can't. And we can't use the other bomb yet," Morgan said.

"What other bomb? Yes, I'm standing right in front of you and I heard you," Leif said.

"Umm, we got two bombs," Jen said sheepishly.

"Yep and we just found out how much we love to blow shit up," Morgan said, the maddening smile returning to her face. It widened a little from the grin she had earlier in the day.

"Not if I kill you first," Leif said calmly. He reached for them and they both dodged him. Again he reached and they dodged. Then they turned to run and he grabbed them. "You bitches have eluded me for the last time! I have you now! And I'm going to kill you both horribly! You stopped my plans for mortality! You ruined everything!" Leif said.

"Okay, *killer*. I have a question for ya. Why the hell would you want to be mortal again? You called us stupid, but that sounds stupid as hell," Jen said.

"If you must know, I wanted to be a mortal again so I could die again on better terms. I'm stuck like this and I HATE IT! Even more than I want vengeance, I want to finally die a better death and stop being a ghost that kills people every fifty years! I had a life once, it wasn't a good life, it was fraught with peril every day, but it was better than being stuck in between. And yes, all the stories are true. I was once an evil person, there's no doubt. I deserved what the Indians did to me. I don't hate them for killing me. I hate them for trapping me this way. I know they were only trying to protect themselves from evil. And I *was* evil. Part of it backfired on them," Leif said.

"You just had to ask for his life story, didn't ya?" Morgan said to Jen and rolled her eyes. "You never got that close to the goal before, did ya?"

"No and for that you must die. The damage is done now, females. You shall see your version of

Valhalla before me, if such a place even exists," Leif told them.

"Where you takin' us?" asked Jen.

"That matters not. You are going to die and that is all you need to know," Leif told them.

Leif carried the girls by the back of their collars to his cave across the road from the creek, then tied them to a stalagmite in the center of the cave. He told them that for ruining his chances to see whatever else was waiting, he was going to torture them a lot before they died.

***

The girls were still tied to the stalagmite in the cave. Leif cut off some of their hair. They were bloody and bruised from trying to fight him off. He still didn't know where the second bomb was or that it was anywhere near his cave. The girls couldn't push the button yet. The women were thinking of a way to get away from him so they could blow the place up. It took what felt like hours trying to come up with a plan, being tied up made them anxious. The color of the sky was changing from pitch black to midnight blue, the darkness was slowly becoming morning. Something miraculous happened while the light change occurred. The other side of the stalagmite glowed for only a flicker of a moment. The girls noticed and stared in amazement. Silently, they saw a new figure who was also a ghost. He was an Indian from ancient times. At first, they thought Leif summoned him to help kill them.

The new ghost only shook his head as if to say he wasn't helping Leif. When he gently grabbed the girl's shoulders they saw him truly. He wore his hair long and straight. He wore leather shoes and pants with feathers tied in pieces of his hair. He was the first victim of Leif's, who died as a sacrifice. The Indian was no friend of his. He was able to come back because Leif got too close to his goal of becoming mortal and was there to stop him. He showed the girls what happened to him and so many others, six hundred years ago. They almost gasped, but he put his hands to their mouths. Tears streamed down Jen's face. Leif couldn't see her cry in the dimly lit cave.

The new ghost wiped away the tears so Leif couldn't see them then decide to possibly torture her more. The new ghost was an Indian warrior and knew how to be quiet. He told the girls to remain silent and he would help them. He said no more people were going to die because of Leif Eriksson, aka *The Old Scenic Slayer*. He slowly and quietly untied the girls. They remained still until he instructed them otherwise. He went over to create a distraction for them so they could run.

"Hello, Viking! How are you?" said the Indian.

Leif looked at him in shock and horror. He had never seen another ghost let alone one he made. Bloody lines showed on his face. His blood-soaked and matted blond hair still dripped fresh blood on the ground as he stood perfectly still.

"How is this possible?" Leif asked.

"It's simple. You haven't seen me because you have never gotten this close to being mortal again in six hundred years. Since those young women put an end to your plan, as a reward, I was sent back to help them kill you."

"You can't kill a ghost, not even with another ghost." Leif laughed at the Indian.

"Yes, it can be done. We just have to destroy your home. You still have it, but not for long. I can get rid of it. And I know where the other bomb is," said the Indian.

As the Indian was chatting with Leif, the girls were running away from the cave slowly and quietly. They ran back across the street to where the camp was and got under cover of the cut out that led from the road down to the camp. The Indian told them to do that when he was using his mind to show them the murdered people.

"In my cave?! How did they know to do that?" Leif asked.

"They didn't. They just got lucky, as the people say these days. Bye now. Rest in Peace, Leif," the Indian said.

"NOOOOO!" Leif shouted.

The second explosion consisted mostly of debris flying out of the cave and across the street. That time, fire shot out of the entrance and across the top of where the women were hidden, trying to dodge it. They remembered everything the Indian had shown them. He made sure to show them his own death. It was the first of many for the Viking. The Indian had been killed with arrows then hacked to pieces. He was the first to be thrown in a tree bit by bit, the first to have his balls removed as a souvenir. That was one reason the gentle Indian ghost wiped away the tears from Jen's face in the cave. The girls no longer had to worry about Leif, but they were still hiding after the blast was over, just in case.

The Indian ghost came to the girls when the sky was turning another shade of blue as dawn was slowly approaching. He spoke to them one last time.

"You are free now. Leif is gone for forever. Thank you for freeing us all. I know you only did it by accident, but sometimes accidents aren't really accidents. I have waited for a long time to be set free. We all have. You are safe now. Leave this place as we too will go," the Indian said as he faded away.

The girls looked up into the sky in time to see vapors floating higher and higher as the sun started to peek over the edge of the horizon line. They smiled at each other, something they thought they might never do again in the eleventh hour of that night.

Broken and bloody, Jen and Morgan sat on the edge of the rocks close to the creek bed. They heard the water rushing passed and birds chirping. Two things they never heard the whole time they visited Tipton Ford, at least not until Sunday morning. There were fires and smoke around them and that's when they heard sirens down the road. They sat and waited for the rescue teams to show up. They weren't as worried about them as they were the police. They were going to have lie out of their teeth about what happened. No one was going to believe the truth anyway.

Chapter Ten

Fire Engines and ambulances pulled up in the middle of Old Scenic Road not too long after Jen and Morgan heard them in the distance. They knew they looked like hell and couldn't explain it the truth to anyone. They smiled because they had a secret, the Indian and the other people that were killed were finally freed.

The police asked a lot of questions. The girls were normally too honest to lie, but they ad-libbed pretty well. They said some crazy hitchhiker came across them, went nuts then left. No one had to know a bloodbath happened or why. The police acted like they bought it. If a forensics team had gotten involved, it might have been a different tale. There were no bodies anymore because when Leif vanished so did his last victim's bodies. The girls rode in the ambulance and got checked out at the hospital because of the beatings they suffered from. When they were released from the hospital, they returned for the last time to get their things and the Suburban, driving back to South Dakota where they belonged. The ladies remembered to retrieve the tapes from the vacation from hell so as to convince the boss it wasn't a hoax, although they didn't need them, the constant nightmares were going to be enough.

***

Two days later, Sioux Falls, SD:

Still bruised and shaking, Jen and Morgan walked up the stone steps of the Old Courthouse Museum. The two women marched straight through the wooden door into the curator's office in the back of the first floor with the footage in their hand. The chubby, balding man was flushed in the face. He looked furious. His palms were sweaty and his glasses looked fogged up.

"I am supposed to believe some wild story, right? How is it that if the stories were true, you're alive? Answer me that, will you?" The boss wasn't happy at all.

"You won't believe us, but another ghost came and saved us. We have no proof except that we're alive. The video might be junk, we don't know," Morgan said as she handed him the tape.

"What am I looking for when I play this?" asked the curator.

"We have no idea. It's supposed to be all of us sitting around a campfire talking about The Old Scenic Slayer. Since our friend left the camera in his tent before he died, we didn't think about it until we were leaving, we thought there might be something else," Jen said.

"All right then. If it's not something real from our supposed slayer then you two are fired," said the curator.

The tape was put into the VCR and the TV was turned on. He was watching the tape of all of them on the last night they were all together. It was painful for the girls to watch. They had almost forgotten what the guys looked like. It had only been three days since they died. The moment the tape went black, their boss gave the girls an angry look then turned back to the TV where he saw something glide passed the camera and say something in Norse, "I'm going to get you! Die!" And then the tape ended.

"What was that?" The curator was curious.

"It was Leif. Oops, it was 'The Slayer,'" Morgan said.

"And he said, he was going to get us and then he told us to die," Jen translated. "The camera must have been on that last night when he was chasing us."

"I'm not convinced. That could have been orchestrated. Where are the people you took with you?"

"They all died, for you! You crazy asshole! We almost died too!" Morgan yelled at him. "What other evidence do you need?"

"More than you can supply. I knew it was a hoax all along. Tell your friends to stop hiding. I don't believe it, good prank, but you're fired."

Jen jumped to her feet and proceeded to grab the boss around his throat. Morgan grabbed her. "Jen, no, don't do it. Fuck all that. We've got life. That's more important than him. You know what happened and so do I. That's all that matters."

They got him to give them the tape back before they left his office. The glares he got after he returned their property were of sheer contempt. He'd never seen them react or talk to him in that manner before. *Maybe they told the truth after all. Why else would two perfectly gentle ladies go insane enough to try and attack me or maybe want to kill me?* It was so unlike them both.

The girls left the building then got into the Suburban, while preparing to drive away, they looked in the back seat. There was a box with many carvings on all four sides and funny looking pictures of something on the front. Jen looked at Morgan and screamed hysterically.

PART TWO
Never Thought It Was Possible

Chapter Eleven

Her golden eyes sparkled in the moonlight as she brushed her black hair from her face. Mr. Anders saw her caramel skin which showed a touch of the paling effects of death. She was still living, feeling cursed, for more than two thousand years while she protected those who had no idea she existed. She wanted it that way after the maddening episode where she destroyed Egypt in the early years.

She stood tall looking at the ground, examining the dirt grains and watching it slowly pulsate from the worms working the earth from below. The greenery shifted slowly as it grew and only someone with her hearing could hear it. She turned her thoughts to the castle she remembered well, she saw the archaic stone in her mind. It had been a long time since the medieval times in England. She was unwittingly being taken back to its new place of residence.

When he found her, she was caught off guard and he took advantage of that. Pandora tried to get away, but she couldn't, he was strong and had henchmen this time. It was wise of her to have already sent what he was looking for to some humans. After her capture, he put her in an iron box that seemed to be made for her; lock, stock, and barrel.

Don't look straight into his eyes, she thought as she started to look up from her feet. She avoided his gaze for so long, she was afraid to look at him and let it overpower her like she had centuries before. He finally captured her, but she didn't want the torture to be excruciating. One look at him and it would be. His powers to confound people had grown, she could feel it.

The rest of the journey, Pandora spent in a guarded metal coffin with no air holes. If she wasn't quiet in the box, he would be alerted and the guards would probably take the lid off so he could make her silent. He put small wooden stakes in the sides of her body. If she gave too much hassle he would shove them in a little deeper to weaken her almost to the point of death, then he would remove them and put them somewhere else.

Mr. Anders had other ways of keeping her quiet, that one was the quickest. So Pandora laid in the box with her eyes shut tight, making no sound and listening to the others around her to try to figure out where she was and what was going on.

Soon she listened long enough to figure out she was finally in the hull of a plane. She must have been disguised as a dead relative that was being shipped back home for a funeral. That would have been cover enough to get her where he needed to take her. He was taking her to his castle he had moved on barges in large shipping crates, then fully rebuilt in America. It was now located in Salem, Massachusetts instead of England.

***

When Pandora opened her eyes the next time, she was chained to the wall in the dungeon of a castle. Mr. Anders walked into view in front of Pandora.

She tried to reach him, but she couldn't. She sneered at him. He laughed at her. His eyes had gone from golden to dark red in an instant as he chuckled at her.

"Do you honestly think those two stupid humans are going to save you? How mad you've become, my dear. You bloody well know you can't get away from me. I have always found you, I always will. I will find a way to open the box. No one has ever been able to open it but you. I will find out your secret. When I do, love, this world will experience chaos as they should have back when I was the king," Mr. Anders explained.

"As soon as I find a way to free myself, I will kill you! Even if that means hunting you the world over just so I can kill you, I will! Yes, you, the so-called King of England! You will die by the very hand that you loved! I will make sure you suffer as you have made others suffer!" Pandora yelled at him.

Mr. Anders laughed in Pandora's face. He guffawed so hard it bent him over making his brown hair fall into his eyes. That made her angrier. She didn't know it, but she was in for a long stay.

***

Ten months later, Jen found it hard to sleep with a crying baby and nightmares from Tipton Ford that wouldn't go away.

The box the two women found in the back of the SUV was hard to pinpoint. No books had any information and the Internet lacked useful references. The girls had no idea why it was put in the back of their car or what it meant. The symbols in the four sides had no visual meaning. Even delving into the most ancient languages turned up nothing about the oldest wooden box they'd ever seen.

She and Morgan had their friends and men commemorated in Missouri. Jen and Morgan knew they weren't missing. It was a hard decision, but one they made together. The police didn't know there was anyone else in Tipton Ford that day but them. They wanted to get it done and put it passed them, which was easier said than done. A few days later, Jen found out she was pregnant. Jen and Morgan decided because of the baby, they had to make sure the men and their friends were laid to rest in order to ease their minds.

Jen used the pregnancy to force herself to do better, despite the nightmares, she ended up having a healthy baby boy. She named him after his father.

Jen and Morgan lived together in the same house as before losing everything they deemed precious to them, on the same quiet street in Sioux Falls, South Dakota. Since the museum incident, they worked less. The curator fired them that day then made it hard for them to get a job anywhere else. That bastard sucks, Jen thought. So Jen and Morgan became freelance researchers.

It was no gold mine, but they got paid. Jen didn't care if she came from wealthy people anymore. People died, it didn't matter if they had money or not. Since they had their run in with the Viking ghost from hell, she couldn't care less about money and was not taken in by the thought of being rich. She didn't care about the inheritance, shopping, the perfect little suburban life; it was all non-consequential to her after battling for her life against the supernatural.

That day, however, became another pivotal moment for the young researchers. Jen went out and got the mail, another letter requesting their services. This letter was particularly odd, it reminded her of the old style parchment letters she used to carefully catalog at her old job. The envelope was the letter. There was a blood red wax seal that had to be popped off to open it. The paper was folded so the text was in the middle of four triangles folded over it. The script was written with a quill. It wasn't old though because it wasn't falling apart or brown, it was still new parchment.

"Hey look! It's a letter from Salem, Massachusetts," Jen said, thinking about the archives.

"So read the damn thing, why don't ya?" Morgan said.

"Okay, give me a minute," Jen said. "Here goes–

Dear Jennifer and Morgan,

Hello. My name is Mr. Anders. I am trying to reach you regarding a mysterious problem our town has been experiencing. Furthermore, I have information about the box you received. I sent it to you. Since I noticed you have not been able to find the right people to contact about it, I am contacting you. The box is called Pandora's Box and it is known as the Box of Chaos. It was actually constructed for an ancient vampire named Pandora. She received it as a gift before she was turned into a vampire in Egyptian times. Yes, she is supposed to be a work of fiction. I assure you, she is very real. She and I actually are the ones who need your help. I am writing on her behalf.

Our town is in great duress. Every day and night is spent in chaos. We need your help and we need to get her box back to her. Please call me for more information. My number is listed below. I hope to hear from you soon.

Cordially, Mr. Anders

"–That's all it says and the phone number is at the bottom," Jen said. "Oh, look at this!" She held a news article in her hands.

100 B.C. to Present Day:

[Cairo, Egypt] *Pandora was a two-thousand-year-old vampire who saw many things. She tried to change with the world, to blend in, to live among humans undiscovered. For most of her immortal life, she succeeded.*

She lived a good life before her change. She was a well-treated servant to Queen Nefertiti in Egypt. She prayed to gods, was fed well, and treated with much respect and friendship by her queen. For one of Pandora's birthdays, her last before she became a vampire, her queen gave her a box now referred to as Pandora's Box, the box of chaos. She was told it had the power to destroy the world if its keeper couldn't learn to control it.

On the day of her eighteen birthday, she mysteriously found herself naked and confused, walking alone in the desert. I wonder if the box did this, she thought. She saw what she thought was an oasis but when she got there, what stood in its place was the scariest place she had seen in her young life.

The trees were sick and dying. The grass was yellow and burnt. In the middle of the trees was a pool of black water that looked like ink. Off to one side of the pool stood a tiny shack, broken, slowly falling down. All around the lake, the sand looked as if it had been shifted and moved even though there was no wind in the place.

She turned to run, but her weakened state made it easy for a hooded figure to come up behind her and tug her back into the shrouded secret world. She was reluctant to be led back in but had no energy to fight it. That was the day life changed for Pandora. She fainted from the weakness.

She awoke sore and unaware of what happened a few days later. She let her eyes clear and become focused. Everything looked different than before. Every grain of sand on the ground she sat on was like the tiniest piece of glass. She then noticed she wasn't naked anymore and the blanket that covered her was stitched with great care. She could see the individual stitches. It was amazing to be able to see a single piece of something amidst thousands of others.

She heard things clearly and much louder than she did before too. It hurt her ears to hear whispers in the abyss, echoing off the ground made of sand. She was afraid to scream, she didn't know if it would make her deaf.

She looked down at her own hand and saw her golden Egyptian skin had a white overcast to it. She found a piece of mirror sitting beside her. When she glanced upon herself in it, she saw she no longer had dark brown eyes, but they turned golden. What happened to me? she wondered.

She gained a heightened sense of smell, the odorous, obnoxious scent of death came from the black pool outside the door of the hovel she was in. Suddenly, she smelled the coppery stench of blood, she began to crave it uncontrollably. It burned her throat. The more she thought about it, the more ravenous the craving became.

She rose shakily from the ground of the dwelling and stood in the doorway. She could tell it was night time in the abyss, she walked out the door and passed the pool of ink to the opening where the desert lay beyond. She looked at the sand and saw every grain. To her, the sand appeared to be many grains of salt in the moonlight. She decided she needed to return to her queen immediately.

She discovered she had the gift of great speed. Her return to the walls of the kingdom she served only took her an hour. The queen was still awake when Pandora returned. She was overtaken with emotion. She worried for days that something happened to Pandora. Something had happened to her, the queen didn't see it yet.

Within days, Nefertiti believed something awful had befallen her dearest friend. Pandora's appearance and mannerisms changed completely. If she came out in the day, she never let the sun's rays touch her. She remained in the shadows even though she used to love sitting in the sun with the queen, chatting the day away. She used to pray to Amun-Re, the sun god, for prosperity. In her new life, she prayed to nothing and no one. She never broke bread or said anything to anyone anymore. She used to have a lively, happy soul and now she acted like she had no soul because she didn't. This worried the queen.

At night, while everyone else slept, Pandora's anger grew, as did her knowledge of the chaos box. She learned the magic behind it and how to control the chaos within it. Also, the time when she was learning about her box, people started coming up missing then dead. They were drained of all their blood. Suspicions were mounting and fingers were pointing. She occasionally was the one the rumors and fingers pointed toward because of how drastically her personality changed. She decided to take the box with her and hid for what seemed like only months to her.

When Pandora came back out of hiding one hundred years had passed. She found out what happened to her queen and she was angry, rage made her open her box and let the chaos out all over Egypt. The ground shook and the rain poured. Structures tumbled and fell. People tried to hide, but they couldn't stop it. The new pharaoh died and the country was left in ruin when she finally called the chaos back into the box.

Vampires aren't generally known for compassion, but after the tirade she let loose, Pandora remembered her human emotions and never opened the box again. She spent the rest of two-thousand years protecting it and keeping it from falling into the wrong hands.

"I see the look on yer face. Girl, yer outta yer damn mind! This guy's nuts! There is no such thing as vampires," Morgan said. The curiously excited expression Jen wore scared the hell out of Morgan.

"Suppose there are. Suppose she's real and she really needs our help?" Jen said. She thought it would have been an excellent opportunity to find out if vampires were real. They used to think ghosts weren't real and that turned out to be false. Jen wondered if they followed through if vampires would turn out to be real too.

"Bullshit. It's just some weirdo trying to get the box they put in our car back," Morgan said.

"Suppose it's not, though. Remember, we didn't truly believe in ghosts, but we now know they exist. Who's to say vampires aren't just as real as ghosts?" Jen asked.

"I know what you're thinking, but don't you remember all that running, the chasing, and the screaming? I do, vividly. What if they are real? Let's say for arguments sake that they are, if we go there, they might just want their box back. Then they'd probably kill us so we won't talk. Think about it, Jen," Morgan said.

"Yeah, I know. And I know my premature curiosity is rather foolish. I still see what happened last time every time I close my eyes, but I have to know if she's real. I want to know why she wanted us to keep her box for her. There has to be a reason. No one just gives you something like that to hold on to without an important reason," Jen explained.

"Curiosity got your future husband killed! It put your unborn son in danger! We could have died! Do you not realize what could have happened if things had been different? If it weren't for sheer will, we would have both fallen apart and then what? Without the help we got from the Indian ghost, the fact we went insane and were willing to take a stand, we would have died. There would be no little Warren to look at and love. You're crazy as hell, you know that!" Morgan said.

"No, I'm not! I want to discover what's hidden. If we have kill them, we know how. It's in all the books, remember? I do. If that doesn't work, then we'll try everything else there is to try. Oh, please, let's go find out if she's real. I want to figure out the mystery. Say yes, please!" Jen begged.

"I can't believe I'm about to say this…you've always known I love a good mystery. Sometimes, I really can't stand you. Okay, let's do this. The first sign of danger, we get the hell out of dodge, got it?" Morgan said.

"I got it. I don't wanna die, I just wanna know. I guess, I'll let him know we're coming," Jen said. Life without a mystery to solve was strange to Jen having worked in a museum setting since finishing college, being without it was not normal. She wanted a little bit of her old life back. With or without the danger, she wanted to feel useful again and more like she used to be.

Chapter Twelve

The airport was a vast and busy place. Many people milled about, trying to find their way. With their suitcases and tickets in their hands, people were scurrying around like ants, trying not to be late for departures as the two young researchers stood watching them at the ticket counter. Normally, the usual semantics of how people acted would have annoyed Jen and Morgan, but now it seemed unimportant to the girls. Morgan tried to remember what normal life was like, it was simpler in the past. She remembered, they stood at the counter before, when life was different, that seemed like so long ago.

Morgan and Jen took their seats in the waiting area along with the other passengers going to Massachusetts. They both sat and observed a young mother of two children. She was telling them to be quiet and behave, they would get on the plane soon enough. The children were too excited. She sat there smoothing their clothes and hair, fussing over them. She had a stern, tired look on her face. The girls assumed she was flying alone with the children.

Morgan also observed many people who looked like they might be flying home from a business trip or a convention. They were wearing business attire and chatting with one another about who knew what. Arguably, it looked like there was a never-ending debate going on that was probably work related. Their tone never got above a whisper so it was hard for her to tell.

Morgan began to get antsy as she sat there waiting. It was worrisome. Her thoughts began to weigh on her heavily about the real reason they were picked to handle a box of unknown origin then to return it months later. She was skeptical of the whole thing. The airport almost didn't let them take all of their stuff through the gate either. Wooden stakes on a plane were outlawed since nine-eleven by the NSA and Homeland Security. The guards laughed about the Holy water. They assumed the girls had the Holy water because they were scared to ride on the plane. If it weren't for the fact they had to tell security the things they brought were movie props, they wouldn't have gotten any of the weapons on the plane.

As Morgan sat waiting impatiently to catch the plane, she started thinking about the few days leading up to that day. She thought about the priest at the St. Joseph's Catholic Church the most.

Morgan remembered the sound of the church bells and birds flew into the sun as they walked up the stairs of the biggest church in Sioux Falls. Big ornate oak doors opened and revealed the many pews and the pulpit at the end of a long room. In front of the opening of the door, off to the right side was a bowl decorated in gold and silver flowers standing on a wooden pillar. It was customary to bless oneself before crossing into the main service room of the church. They did so. After blessing themselves and crossing themselves, they strode up to the first priest they saw.

"Hello, children. I'm Father Michael. How can I help you? Have you come for confession?" the father asked the girls. The priest had a kind face. He was tall

and younger than most of the clergy in the church. He had short dirty blond hair and green eyes.

"I'm sorry, Father, but no we haven't. We need your help with a serious matter. Is there somewhere that we may talk to you where no one can hear? It's of the utmost importance," Morgan said, remembering her South Dakota etiquette.

"Yes, follow me," Father Michael said. He led Morgan and Jen to the ornately carved confessional and said they could talk in there.

"Father, we have nothing that needs confessing. Why do you choose this?" Jen said.

"Well, because no one else in my congregation eavesdrops on me in here. Speak now of your urgent matter," the priest said quickly.

"Please believe me when I say this will be hard to tell you or say out loud to anyone. I never thought vampires were real. Of course, I never thought ghosts were real either until we met one that tried to kill us. So, I don't know what to think here, but I know that they may be real and we don't want to die. We're going on a trip to give an ancient artifact back to the owner and she's said to be a very real vampire. We need your help. We didn't know where else to turn. Unfortunately, we reach out as the stereotypical females in distress, Father. Can you help us or do you think we're nuts too?" Morgan explained.

"You aren't crazy or wrong to come to me. Unfortunately, it has been a while since I've dealt with them. I believe you and that's a start. They do exist and they're powerful, especially the old ones. I moved here to get away from them. They've been trying to kill me for years now. I've been a thorn in their side you see. I

can help you, but I won't go with you. I can give you supplies and advice and hope you understand what to do. How long do you have until you leave to find these vampires?" the father asked.

"We leave tomorrow. We have only two days to prepare for anything. We tried to look everything up online and found nothing. This person doesn't want to be found, it seems. We need as much knowledge as we're able to gather beforehand. We also have this box that belongs to her and we're supposed to return it. All the letter we got says is that it's called Pandora's Box. Other than that, we have no idea what's written all over it," Jen explained.

"Come with me. I think I may have some things in my office you may need," Father Michael said.

The three of them exited the confessional. The girls followed the father to the inner sanctum of the church. The church was big and old; there were many rooms and hallways to get lost in. Lamps that resembled the old gas lights lit the halls dimly. The walls were gray stone like castle walls. Tapestries of Jesus and Mary were hung on the some of the walls. They were actually replicas from Rome. They finally reached the office of the clergymen a few minutes later.

"Sit. I want to show you something before I give you the things you need," the father said.

He turned around behind himself and grabbed a book off of the bookshelf. It was no bible. It was gold embossed with a seal. The seal was a lion's head and golden swords crossing each other. He opened it then turned the pages until he found the passage he was looking for. He quickly turned the book to face his visitors.

"Here, read this. It talks about Nosferatu. That's the ancient name for them. They're the children of the damned. This will tell you all that has befallen them and all that you might do to protect yourselves from them. They are very strong and have the heightened senses of animals, but can be as civilized as you or I. All that can make them very dangerous. They live in shadow because the direct sun gives them headaches and can burn them badly, but unlike the movies, they don't have to hide from it completely. Take this book with you so you can read it before you get to where you're going. And here, take these, wooden stakes through the heart is still one of the only ways to kill them. Also, we must go to the basement and get bottles for Holy water. They still hate that being thrown in their faces, too. Come, let's fetch it," Father Michael explained as he handed the girls a box of wooden stakes.

They all rose and the girls followed the priest to the basement of the large old church. This time, it was a little scarier because the basement reminded them of a smaller dungeon.

"Here in this box is what you need. I hid it here under the stairs in case I needed it again. We must make haste. No one knows about it or my days as a Van Helsing wannabe." Father Michael laughed a happy laugh.

The small group turned to go back up the steps and out of the small dungeon. The group ended up back in the main service room of the church. The girls were standing in silence holding the boxes that contained the weapons as if they contained something more valuable than gold. They were waiting for the father to fill the bottles with water and bless them. He took his time and filled them well. The blessing was short and sweet.

"Tell the people at the security desk that you're taking these things to a movie set of a Catholic Church in Salem for me. If they don't believe you, tell them you're taking them to a fellow priest at the Catholic Church there in Salem and give them this note from me. Go, my children, and return to this church and confess yourselves when you're done. We will meet again and your smiles will tell me of your success," Father Michael said handing them a note written in Latin. At the bottom of the page was the Church's insignia.

"Thank you, Father. Bless you," Morgan said.

"May the Lord bless you and keep you," Jen said to the priest.

They looked at him one last time and nodded goodbye. Father Michael stood in the doorway smiling at them as they walked away. Then they walked out of the church and into the sun once more.

Memories were good to have when you didn't have much else to cling to, but Morgan had to get back to reality.

Morgan was done reliving the past few days. She sat in the same room in the airport still waiting to board the plane. She straightened up in her seat, then tugged at the messy bun on the back of her head. She always wore this hairstyle these days, it was far more convenient to have it already up out of her face.

Finally, the plane started boarding. She and Jen both sat and read the book Father Michael gave them. It took only three hours to reach Salem. That's when Morgan started to get nervous. This is it, she thought, time to face our inevitable fate…one we chose. When Jen and Morgan arrived at the Logan International Airport in Boston, a car waited to pick them up and they rode the rest of the way to Salem. Their destiny awaited them like the plague; at first it can't be seen, then it's too late.

Chapter Thirteen

Slow torture was Mr. Anders' specialty. He had lots of time. Being around for thousands of years longer than one wants to be would do that to a person. Mr. Anders didn't know life or death, in that case, would eek by so slowly. If he'd known that fact back then, he might have told the whore who changed him to just kill him instead.

Before the girls arrived, Mr. Anders had one more conversation with Pandora. It too wasn't at all pleasant. He was mad as hell at her for the last five hundred years that he chased her all over the world. If they had modern technology back then, it wouldn't have taken long to find and capture her again. Everything was so damned primitive in that time frame, when he got close to finding her, she'd flit away again for several more years. He never liked difficult things. It made the spoiled king come to the surface and he was too refined for that.

"Hello again, poppet. I've just come to share the news with you. I'm so excited to tell you. The two humans I contacted are coming. They arrive today. This is so much fun. In a few days' time, you will have playmates or dinner, whichever you fancy. And I shall have your box," Mr. Anders said. He smiled showing his teeth to her.

"No, you will not! Those women won't just hand it over. They trust no one and that's why I sent it to them. I'm still going to kill you. I don't care how long I have to wait. I hope they're smart enough to figure you out and get away from here," Pandora whispered in her weakened state.

"I very well doubt that will be the case. I read up on them and they let all their friends die before they left last year in Missouri. They probably want to know all sorts of things that will be the death of them. It's too funny. They don't sound that smart to me," Mr. Anders said. He chuckled almost spitting on the floor.

If the humans are so smart, then why haven't they figured out that this is a ruse? he thought. How can they not know? I all but told them so. He laughed at himself that time. Everything struck him as funny. On his scoreboard, he was winning, which was the way he liked it. He lured unsuspecting humans into the lion's den.

His humans would arrive in a matter of hours. It was getting closer to time for him to start his 'acting career.' He thought it would be fun to fool them. And acting like a wolf in sheep's clothing was easy. He'd done it loads of times in England in Medieval times. It was, in fact, his favorite game to play with humans before he sucked them dry.

He left Pandora in the dungeon and returned to the main floor of the castle to make sure all of the arrangements had been made and taken care of for the guests. He wanted everything to appear on the up and up. So the rooms had been cleaned and things were set out to accommodate the humans.

***

A black car arrived two hours later in front of the English castle entrance. It still had a drawbridge that remained open so cars could pass through it. There was no moat, although it was dug, it was dry. The castle even had a stone wall up all the way around it, like in the movies, for fortification. There were two flags on the front of the gate to the drawbridge flapping in the light wind. The flags were red with black trim and a black shield with two swords crossing over each other.

After the car took them into the grounds of the castle, it parked by the main entrance. When Jen and Morgan got out of the car, they looked around at the courtyard. There were statues and gardens all over. The road leading to the castle entrance was paved with small gray cobblestones. All the gardens were edged with the cobblestones and the flowers were not yet in bloom, so they were covered to keep out the frost.

"Wow! This guy must be really rich! This place is huge!" Morgan said. "He has a moat and a wall with a drawbridge and everything."

"I bet he is. He paid us way more than the going rate," Jen reminded Morgan.

"Right this way, ladies," the driver said. The driver escorted the girls into the main entrance of the house then brought their bags inside and shut the big oak doors. An old Persian-typed woven rug was at their feet; vibrantly it lay there on the floor for feet to wipe themselves upon.

A maid came into the entryway and beckoned them to come with her, they followed. She took them to a set of adjoining rooms at the top of the stairs.

"This is your suite of rooms while you are with us. There are two bedrooms with a bath in between and a living area. Have a wonderful stay with us. And if you need anything, just pick up the phone and someone will assist you. Good day, ladies," the maid said, faking a smile as she left.

"Thank you so much," Jen said.

"Is she gone yet? Okay, this is like one of those places in the movies. They all have big scary houses in them. I'm just hoping this won't turn into a scary movie like last time," Morgan said.

"I really hope so too. It would suck if the running, chasing, and screaming happened here too. It looks like it might have been a cheery place once upon a time," Jen said. She looked around the room. "What a shame."

"Maybe, but I'm keeping my guard up just in case. I trust no one but you," Morgan said.

"Same here, I trust no one but you. We can't afford to," Jen said. She and Morgan decided they weren't about to get drawn into anything if it was possible.

***

A bell rang and both ladies went into the hallway then down the stairs. Mr. Anders told them to follow him. The three of them assembled for dinner in the great dining room. The large hall was decorated ornately in British finery. Large tapestries hung on the walls of the great crusades and of kings and queens in history. Large wooden sideboards flanked the walls on either side of the massive oak table that was long enough to have banquet parties. Twenty people could have sat there, but alas only three sat at the table that evening. The chairs they sat in had high hand-carved backs and lush pads in the seats. The colors in the room were reds, black, and gold. It was reminiscent of the medieval time period, extravagant. The same design on the flags outside was hung on one of the walls over a buffet table. It had to be the family crest.

At the head of the table sat Mr. Anders enjoying a glass of crimson red wine. At least, that's what he wanted the ladies to think. He was dressed in a conservative business suit. He stood as they came in, ushering to them to sit down. Jen and Morgan obeyed him and sat on each side of the head of the table.

Both ladies looked around as they were led into the room. It was so richly assembled they had to ask the obvious questions, like if Mr. Anders was related to a king or other such royalty in order to acquire all of those lovely things, etc. He told them he was related to a king. He told them he was related to many kings. He said he researched his family line to almost ancient proportions. He said he found out he was related to several of the kings of England. He told them of how he bought the old unused castle. Then he regaled them with stories of how he found all of his possessions from different collectors over the years. When a collector had a piece for sale that belonged to his relation, he was the first one they contacted. What he neglected to tell them was the truth, he had, in fact, been a king himself some one thousand years ago. Many of the things surrounding them, if not all of them, were his to start with. He didn't collect antiques really, he had all the family wares packed up and stored for him for hundreds of years.

"I hope you are having a good evening, ladies. Your trip went well I trust?" Mr. Anders asked them, acting like he gave a damn about stupid human things like flying in a plane.

"Yes, it went very well. Thank you," Jen said. She thought he was being too nice. It was a little eerie to her that he should be so refined and yet wanting to live in the U.S. No one that refined ever stayed unless they had motive or reason, unless they worked for someone in the U.S. maybe, but he didn't appear to be the working type. His hands looked too soft and pale.

"Yes. Thank you," Morgan said.

"I asked you here to discuss the matter I contacted you about in my letter. Did you bring the box with you?" Mr. Anders inquired.

"Yes, we brought it. We have no idea what's up with it, though. We've never seen the writing before. All the books we have tell us nothing about this ancient writing," Morgan said.

"That's because the language pre-dates normal Egyptian Hieroglyphs. Only one person knows what it says, Pandora," Mr. Anders said. Oops! He didn't want to bring her into the conversation yet.

"Is she here? Will we meet her?" Jen was curious. She didn't think he was a vampire and she wanted to meet one that might not try to kill her right off the bat and tell her a story like in the Anne Rice book. She thought it would be pretty exceptional.

"Not currently. However, you will meet her very soon," Mr. Anders lied.

"She's not here now?" Morgan questioned.

"No. She had a pressing matter that she had to attend to, but she will return. Don't worry, she is just as curious about you, as you are about her. She finds mortals from this day and age very fascinating, especially the modern feminist. She is very anxious to make your acquaintance," Mr. Anders said to them. He lied some more so as to not make them suspicious and to get them to stop talking about her. He didn't want to slip up again.

"She's not going to kill us is she? If she wants to eat our flesh, we're leaving like right now!" Morgan said.

"No, no, no! That is absolutely not the point of your coming here. It was to figure out how to get the box open and how to put the chaos back into the box once it's released. It's already destroyed some ancient civilizations. If any more of it gets released into our world in these present times, it could spell certain doom for all of us. Do you understand? There are many people who would pay handsomely for it, just to release the chaos. And many more who would seek to steal it. We cannot let anyone get their hands on this box," Mr. Anders said.

"Yeah, we understand. We just never thought we'd be part of saving the world from total destruction. Saving our own asses is different. Thanks for the pressure," Jen said.

"But you are capable of trying something or you would never have been asked to come. It's pretty late, time for you two to get some rest. Maybe you'll feel better about saving the world tomorrow. Good night, ladies. I bid thee adieu," said Mr. Anders.

***

He left the dining room and entered a secret passage that no one saw. He ran down the narrow stone staircase to the dungeon. Here he laughed in Pandora's face.

"Those stupid human ladies think they will save the world. You should have seen it. You would have loved the performance I gave. They bought it hook, line, and sinker, my dear. I must say, it was rather brilliant," Mr. Anders said.

"You won't get away with your little scheme. They can't be that dumb. Like you told me the other day, they were the only survivors in a massacre that took place in the woods in Missouri about ten months ago. Why do you think that is? They don't strike me as strong so there has to be another reason. When they do catch on, you will have three females who hate you, willing to try to kill you. What will you do with them then?" Pandora asked Mr. Anders.

"I will simply kill them first because I am stronger than they are. It will take more than two female mortals to best me. But this you already knew. They brought me your box, now to open it," Mr. Anders said.

"You have no idea what you're doing with that. It's not the toy you believe it is. It will destroy everything in its path, including you. It has the capabilities to kill anything I command it to kill. I mean, anything," Pandora said.

Mr. Anders snarled at Pandora and left the room swiftly, she hardly saw him whiz past her. Up the stairs and out of the secret passageway, he found himself angry and lingering in the hallway. He muttered ancient curses at the passage. The researchers heard none of it, they were sleeping off their jet lag.

Although it was creepy being in the huge castle after dark, they were too tired to be scared that night.

Chapter Fourteen

The next day was one of many mysteries and challenges for the two women. Jen and Morgan had to try to unravel the mystery that was the 'Chaos Box.' With no keyholes or places to stick anything, it wasn't going to be easy for them. The looks that Mr. Anders gave them were bad. The girls thought they saw daggers coming from his eyes. It was not going well. Finally, Mr. Anders started asking them questions.

"Do you know what you're doing with that?" Mr. Anders asked.

"We've never come across a box without a keyhole or a way to puzzle it open," Jen said.

"You can have a look at it yourself. It has no riddle or shape puzzle. If there's a code, it could be the pictures, but it would be older than anything we've ever seen before. I think it tells some kind of story, but it's not the kind of story that would open the box. If I can read these carvings correctly, it tells a life story. If not, we got nothing. Look here," Morgan said.

"So, with whom does the story tell?" Mr. Anders asked.

"Pandora's, of course. That is, before she was made into a vampire. These symbols and markings are ancient Egyptian, which pre-dated the normal ancient hieroglyphs. My theory is, it's the story of her life until she received this gift. The article didn't say who gave it to her or what it was actually supposed to be used for, we just assumed it might be dangerous. There was no note to go with it, it was left in our car one day when we left our old job. The Internet hasn't been of any help. We can't locate this box in the history books anywhere. Believe me, we've tried. We cannot make out the true origin other than Egyptian and that's only because of the article you sent us. It makes me curious about her more than anything else. I know this doesn't help find the key at all," Jen said.

"This is making me quite angry. I brought you here to figure it out. If you can't, then I'm afraid I have no further use for the both of you," Mr. Anders said with anger.

Morgan and Jen looked at each other with surprise. *Here it comes*, they thought, *the dangerous part*. Would they be sent home in a box? Would they be sent home at all? Would that weird slightly older gentleman just kill them for being in his house? They never did get to see if Pandora was actually real. Was she? Or was she just the bait he used to get them there to kill them? This was a doubtful bunch of thoughts.

"Now, we will take a break from all of this frustration. Follow me, ladies. There's something I wish to show you," Mr. Anders said.

"Hey, it's not our fault we don't know all about that box. It was thrown in our laps. There's nothing about it anywhere, we looked for anything that might lead to answers about it back home," Morgan said.

"That's not the point. I want to show you something. Do you enjoy making people angry with you?" Mr. Anders said. "Is that Holy water I smell?"

"Yes. How can you smell it?" Jen said the bottle of Holy water was in her pocket.

"Only vampires can smell Holy water," Morgan said as she looked at Jen and thought, *Oh shit!*

"Because I'm a vampire," Mr. Anders said calmly. "Get it out of here. It *stinks*."

***

Fear and shock spread through Jen and Morgan, they held fast to their emotions, staying silent. Neither of them knew what was going on, so they followed a man who could tear them to shreds. They made no sudden moves. The girls silently walked behind him into the lower extremities of the castle. Both women were leery of him, taking stock of his every move. Jen and Morgan were caught off guard when he finally spoke to them again. They also knew they were standing in front of the door leading to the dungeon.

"I could tell by the look on your faces yesterday, you don't think Pandora's real. Well, ladies, you're about to get quite the show. Be careful and stay behind me. She's a mean one," Mr. Anders said.

Never showing his teeth, he hissed as he unlocked the door to the cell he kept Pandora in. Jen and Morgan could hear her call out. Pandora was whispering curses under her breath, the words sounded like barely audible guttural sounds of the undead. She sounded mean. So that was his plan, he was going to get Pandora to kill them!

The researchers entered the room. It was small and made of stone, precious little light came in. The stones smelled of death and decay. The stone must have had the blood of thousands of prisoners soaked into every pore of it. Moss and mold grew up the walls. Hay littered the floor. Shackles and chains hung on the walls, most were bare of bodies. One set was made out of iron to hold something stronger than a human. The prisoner those manacles held looked every bit as human as the two young women who entered with the false king. Pandora stood, attached to the shackles with great iron chains, facing the door so she was made to see who entered the room. Her hair was black and her eyes were golden. Her skin was pale olive, the hint of a darker skin from a former life. Under normal circumstances, she would have been exotic and beautiful. Now she was menacing. Her brow was furrowed and she hissed loudly in the direction of the people standing before her.

"Anderson, what are you doing?" Pandora asked.

"I brought you a snack. It's been so long since we dined together. I thought it would be nice," Mr. Anders said grinning so that his fangs showed.

"Are these the girls who brought my box here?" Pandora said.

"Yes. They have no clue what they're doing, love. You should have picked someone smarter," Mr. Anders said.

"They weren't supposed to figure it out. They fulfilled their objective as long as they could, without their knowledge too. And that was to keep it away from you as long as possible. They wouldn't know how to open it. No one knows but me, I told you that. They aren't part of this, just let them go," Pandora said.

I don't think so. They know too much about all this. And they know what I am. You know how I am about getting rid of witnesses and evidence," Mr. Anders said, smiling again.

"No, you don't have to do that. You can just hold them captive like me. You don't have to kill them. They would starve down here in a matter of time," Pandora said.

Mr. Anders smiled widely, showing the girls his teeth again. They knew he was bent on bloodshed. They hoped it didn't include them. All the stuff the priest gave them was three floors above them. Was Pandora on their side or his? It was hard to tell. She mainly acted like she was mad at him and mad to be in the dungeon.

"So just lock them up. Don't kill them yet. You'll have plenty of time for that. Remember, we're vampires, we have all the time in the world. We own it. You can kill them later," Pandora said.

"What you say does make sense, poppet. I don't have a deadline to end the world either, but I want it done just the same. Hmmm…all right then. I will lock up these lovely morsels for a little later then. Since you won't tell me how it works and they don't know, I have a lot of work to do."

Mr. Anders grabbed Jen and Morgan by the wrists with one of his large hands and dragged them to the wall where the old shackles hung. This was the first time they got a taste of how strong he was. He secured them to the wall with rusty manacles beside Pandora in her iron and silver ones. There was nothing left to do but wait to die. Mr. Anders looked at them with the eyes of longing thirst. He swiftly walked away, creating wind as he hurried. The door slammed and locked suddenly.

For the first time since entering the room, the girls saw Pandora's expression soften as she turned to appraise her new young companions. She didn't appear to be trying to figure out how to harm them. The girls assessed her but neither had the will to speak yet. Not five minutes before, they found out vampires were real.

"You don't need to be afraid of me. I'm not going to hurt you. If I can get off of this wall, I will make sure he doesn't either. You don't even know you walked into. There is so much to tell you," Pandora said.

"I told you she was real," Jen said poking Morgan in the ribs.

"Yeah, I'm real. And I will keep you from dying if it's possible. I don't know what Anderson may have told you before bringing you down here, but I'm not going to eat you. I'm not a normal vampire. If I can help it, I don't kill humans. I don't have much time and I have a lot to say to you, so I'm going to tell you with my mind," Pandora said to them as she reached for their hands.

"I was born in Egypt a very long time ago. I was young, eighteen in fact, when I was lost in the desert. I found an oasis. I was so tired that I barely made it inside before passing out. The creatures there bit me, and days later I awoke as one of them.

"It was my birthday, the day I was lost in the desert. That was the day I received the box. Earlier in the day, my queen had given it to me at the party she held in my honor. You must understand, this is important. I was a servant, raised to serve my queen with every loyalty, but just as I was loyal to her, the Queen Nefertiti was my loyal friend. We were more like two friends who just spent all day talking in the

*sun rather than my being her servant. She loved me
very much and knew my heart very well. I still miss my
queen even though it has been centuries. She was to me
what you would call a best friend.*

*"I didn't have a chance to master my gift before I
was changed. I had received it one day and was
damned the next. The magician was supposed to teach
me its function and purpose later on but never really
got the chance. I was too changed and everyone knew
it. Even my magic changed.*

*"The queen told me that my gift had been made
especially for me. She thought I was special and
deserved something to match. Before I was reborn, I
would have said I was just like her, loving and loyal. I
would have asked her if that was a bad thing and she,
in turn, would have answered, "No, it was good."
After I came back, she was the first to notice my
changes. She knew right away I wasn't right. I had no
emotions.*

*"In those days, people vied for power by putting
poisonous snakes in your bed or lacing your food or
drink with poison. Those were common ways for
royalty to die. Even though my queen was fair, she was
also just. If a crime was committed, then it was
punishable.*

*"No one caught on for a while that occasionally a
person came up missing until someone finally found
one of the bodies and examined it. They were all in
fear instantly. I hadn't learned to use my gift without
anger for a while.*

*"When the fear of the people came on, my queen's
days were numbered. She never came up missing so no
one really thought she had been killed, rather they*

thought she died of natural causes in her sleep. She died and I knew it wasn't natural. I later found out she had been peacefully executed by her most hated cousin. He wanted her power. He poisoned her dinner with a slow moving poison that left no traces in humans. My vampire eyes see things human eyes can't see. I saw the poison on her lips.

"In the sheer horror of the event of losing my queen, I set to the task of destroying them all. I opened my box, not caring the outcome. I shrieked and cried aloud, swearing my revenge. After a few moments of chaos attacking people's minds, I saw the crazed and scared faces, horror struck me like a white-hot branding iron. I asked myself, what have I done? I immediately ordered the chaos back into the box. I looked at the scene of destruction with so much shame that I buried myself in the ground with my box. Deep inside the earth, my box and I remained so that I could not hear the screaming for over a hundred years. My pain was enormous. When I awoke, I saw the signs that still remained from the mess I caused. My heart shook. My grief was great.

"It wasn't until I awoke that the coven who made me finally helped me to be able to deal with my guilt. They also told me that with my human emotions returning, I should be able to control my box because it worked off of emotions.

"It took a while to understand that as the keeper of chaos, I could help the world balance itself with good and evil by putting some extra chaos into the box, to keep the world from overflowing with dark deeds."

"Mr. Anders wants me to open the box, so he can use chaos to destroy the world," Pandora said aloud.

"Why would he destroy the world?" Jen asked.

"He's just a bastard like that. Troubled human makes for a troubled vampire, I think," Pandora said.

"He hides it really well," Morgan said.

"Yes, he does. I'm older, but he still feeds off of humans, which makes him stronger than me. If I still did, my age and my knowledge combined with my fighting skills would have been his ruin. He was able to trap me because I don't drink the blood of humans, so I remain in a weakened state compared to him. It's easy to trap a veggie vamp, all you need is an iron box, a silver chain, and a few silver tipped iron spikes. There is still so much I want to tell you, but time is growing short. He's coming back soon and he's mad. He thinks there's another way and there isn't. The key is me. My soul, my heart, and my mind control it. From the sounds above, I can show you a little more, but we must be quick about it," Pandora said.

Chapter Fifteen

Pandora saw her life flash.

"Which of my life stories would be the most important to tell them? she thought. We don't have much time, Egypt first. I awoke one hundred years later and I could still see the traces of the rampage. I was now two hundred and eighteen years old. Life had progressed more slowly than I had thought. Blood tears streaked down my face as I stood there in the dark, surveying the town. I took my handkerchief out of my sleeve and wiped my tears. With my box in hand, I decided to leave Egypt, my only home. There was a taboo about the sun. I stayed in the shadows, only in the daytime, by the way. It's like having the worst migraine ever and it hurt my eyes so much. It doesn't burn us like most humans think. I stood there watching the town sleep, "This is where you walk away, old girl," I said to myself. "Just walk away.

"The next place my mind shifted to was England, poor old England. I sort of feel bad about that whole King Arthur story. It's not true. The English need a better fairy tale.

"I was able to hide in England without running into any of my kind for many years. Then one day when I was in the woods gliding around, learning my abilities and watching deer, I saw him. He smelled me and turned in my direction. He kept sniffing the air. I wondered if that meant I smelled good or bad. Suddenly, he was standing in front of me, looking in interest. I stood silently, thinking that I probably

looked strange to him. I was pale, but not chalk white as he was. Anderson looked at me and his smile widened.

"Then he spoke in a language I found odd. He spoke English and I did not. He said hello and asked me if I was from England. He asked me if I had ever seen any of our kind before. I nodded that I had. I didn't fully understand what he said. I spoke Egyptian, not English. He asked me if I spoke English and I shook my head. I saw some of my own kind before, but none like him. I only had a brief knowledge of what I was. He could see that on my face. Did he know that I could not completely understand him? I don't know. He said he would take me in, teach me to blend in with the English people, and learn the language. I understood, so I nodded in acknowledgment. He walked away and I followed him.

"In the years that passed, I learned a lot about my new world and my existence. I learned his language, too. This helped a great deal. I learned many languages in my two thousand years and languages have been important.

"It was Anderson, who told me what I actually was. I had no idea other than 'Abomination.' We were companions for about thirty years. He grew too possessive of me. He felt things I didn't know how to feel with my vampire heart yet. And his nature began to scare me. I didn't want to be possessed or the object of obsession. I could see jealousy every time he glanced at me in a crowd or gathering. His face would only distort momentarily, but that was long enough for me to notice.

"As he mentioned in the present day, he was a descendant of kings. That's where the castle and the money came from.

"I found out that he killed his whole family and took possession of the place. Hundreds of years later, he had it moved to the United States. I left it long ago. But I still remember every inch of every room of this place.

"Back then he said he wanted my box out of curiosity, now he really wants it for vengeance. He is a dangerous kind of vampire that I would never afford myself to be. I think that at that point in knowing him, I learned to see the true treachery in the face of him. He could lie to anyone, vampires included. No one knew his true nature but me. This made him doubly dangerous. The edges were sweet and they lured people in, but the middle was bitter. By the time this was discovered, it was too late, especially for his prey.

"My box was buried somewhere in the forests of England back then. I left it there a little while longer as I decided how to move on again alone. I came up with a plan and acted on it. Wordlessly, I ran as fast as my speedy feet would take me, back to the spot in the forest that I had been hiding my box and quickly reclaimed it. And thus began the centuries of looking over my shoulder.

"I have lived in every corner of the world and seen all the gifts that the world can provide. I have learned many languages and hobbies. All the while, running when I sensed danger or thought I smelled my old companion.

"This was because he thought he could force me to show him the secrets of the box. No one ever controlled me that way, nor would they.

"He thought that if I showed him, he would have the box to himself to use as he pleased. I had tried to explain that it didn't work like that before I decided to run. He wouldn't listen. So there I was, on the run at a moment's notice. And this only got worse in the twentieth century and into the twenty-first, that's when technology became such an apparent necessity in the normal human places. He was smart but for hundreds of years, I had been smarter. Now I have two humans to try to save and that would prove difficult being chained up like one."

"Did you see?" Pandora asked the two female humans.

"Yes, we saw. I've never seen into anyone's mind before. Wow," Jen said.

"That's an interesting way to tell a story," Morgan admitted.

"We don't have much time. He'll be returning soon I can hear him walking above us," Pandora said.

"Do you think he's going to kill us?" Jen asked Pandora.

"If we can't think of a way out of here, then yes I do," Pandora said.

"Damn it! I did it again! Mo, I'm sorry. You were right. I'm a glutton for punishment."

"Don't worry so much. We'll think of something," Pandora said.

"Tell us more about the box. Any information we can get might be good right now," Morgan said.

"As you wish…my box is called 'Pandora's Box.' The expression 'opening a whole new can of worms' was created after the fact, of course, and you know it means ripping off a scab and letting the 'demons' out. Really, it started out being called that because it belongs to me. There aren't any keyholes on it because there's no traditional key. I am the key and that's why I'm still alive. And the box was made by an Egyptian magician or sorcerer, whatever you want to call him, as a birthday gift when I turned eighteen. It was supposed to take a great deal of my mortal life to learn to use it. I shouldn't be alive now, when every human is born, we normally get the one mortal life. The magician hadn't counted on my being turned into a vampire. Back then, vampires were pretty rare. The three that made me were an oddity," Pandora said.

"How does your heart come into play if it doesn't beat?" Jen asked out of pure curiosity.

"When I say my heart, I mean my emotional heart. It took time to recover my human emotions, but I did. And that's when I learned to use the box for its intended purpose, which is to give balance to the good and evil in the world. At my command, the chaos I trap inside can come out and fill the minds of innocent people in an instant. Or with another command, I can suck more chaos out of the world and into the box for safe keeping, therefore, bringing about a balance of good versus evil," Pandora explained.

"Why not just suck up all the evil?" Morgan said.

"I have never tried that before. I don't know if it can be done, or if it would be safe to upset the balance like that," Pandora said.

"It would be like walking a tightrope, too far either way and you fall. If the balance shifts too far one way, we all fall," Jen said.

"Yes, it's almost like that. Girls, we have to think of a way out of this. If I don't do what he wants, he'll kill me. That would be fine with me because I have had a very long life but, who would protect you from him?" Pandora said.

"How is it that you don't want to kill us?" Jen asked.

"Oh, please! I'm not the same as him. I only chew on criminals or small vermin. You'll notice that we don't have much of a rat problem down here. We should have them bad," Pandora said laughing cheerfully.

"Oh, okay…so that one thing I was right about," Jen said. "I was hoping you ate rats and not people."

"I guess so," Pandora said still laughing.

"She heard about you and wondered if you were real. If you were real, if you would like us or want to kill us?" Morgan said.

"Ouch, that hurts. Curiosity is not a friend to you, young lady. It can get you killed and not just by people like me. You had no way of knowing I wouldn't. You should not have come here, as you now know. My best advice if we survive this is for you both to find a new line of work," Pandora said.

"This isn't our first near death experience," Morgan said.

"And we lost everyone," Jen whispered, her voice cracked.

"If I can help it, you won't lose me. I think you're both good and would like to be your friend," Pandora said smiling at them.

"I think I speak for both of us by saying we would like that. How long have you been down here?" Morgan said.

"I've been down here almost a year. It's okay. I've been underground for a hundred years before. I had vermin to eat. I always have control of my needs. Don't worry about me," Pandora said.

Pandora didn't understand the question was asked out of pity, not fear. She thought it was asked because they thought they would somehow become targets the second they were all free. That wasn't true at all. The girls were only curious as to her nature because they were both trying to understand her better.

"No, no, dear Pandora. I think you misunderstood her. She was merely curious. She doesn't think you will hurt us. I can say that because I know her very well. We both chose the research field because we both have very curious minds. We always want to know why," Jen said.

"I thought only crazy people would want to know the truth about me. Are you crazy too?" Pandora asked.

"No, not the clinically certifiable kind, at any rate. After last summer, I sometimes wonder why not. When Jen said we lost everyone, she meant it, almost literally. We lost our friends, people who could have been friends, and our soul mates. She was supposed to marry hers and my future was a little less certain, but I loved him. The only thing we carried away from our battle, besides our lives and our grief, was the child whom no one knew Jen was carrying. She didn't even know. Sometimes it hurts her to look at her son's face. He looks so much like his father. I always tell her, she's lucky. She has a part of him," Morgan told Pandora.

"But what did your love leave you?" Pandora asked with sadness on her face.

"He left me with the knowledge that love exists, his especially. He told me a few days before he died. I knew, I could feel it, it radiated off of him. It wasn't an illusion or my mind playing tricks. I was loved, even though it was brief. He was the man who showed me how it feels and for the first time in my life, I knew it wasn't a lie," Morgan said as tears welled up in the corners of her eyes.

"Oh, M…" Jen said with tears running down her face.

"I'm sorry. I didn't mean to—" Pandora said.

"It's okay. You didn't know how we still feel about all of that. Sometimes our best defense has been to not think about it at all. We loved those men with every fiber in us. But, now we project it into my son and that helps some, too."

"We really need to get out of this," Pandora said.

Chapter Sixteen

After a while, Pandora stood silent and still as stone but her eyes were moving. She was thinking hard over all of her memories. Especially those about the castle they were in. She knew every inch from her time there. If every stone was in the exact same place it had been in while in England, it would be easy to map out in her head.

Just then, spells flickered into her thoughts, like forgotten memories re-emerging for the first time in centuries. At first, she tried to make her mind flick them away. It made no sense to be getting bombarded that way. But the visions in her head kept coming back to the sorcery she learned. Spells, why the spells? she thought.

"My memories of this place give me a mental map of this castle. I think I might know where he's hiding my box. How to get it from there is going to be a mystery unless either of you knows magic," Pandora said.

"What? Magic? Are you serious?" Jen asked.

"How would that help?" Morgan wondered.

"If my memory serves, then it just might. I don't think I can do magic anymore, but if either of you could that would be really good about now," Pandora said.

"My last attempts at magic and summoning failed miserably," Jen said.

"Did you ever try, Morgan?" Pandora asked.

"No, I never did. I left that up to Jen. She seemed more suited for it," Morgan said.

"You should. It might be our only hope," Pandora said.

Morgan was afraid. She tried to talk herself out of the only reasonable plan they had so far. She tried to reason within her own mind, tell herself it wasn't logical. There was no way she could use magic. She never had any abilities other than smarts. Nothing happened because she willed it to. It wasn't possible. There was no way she would be able to do it. She spent her whole life never exhibiting signs of any special gifts. She knew she had the courage to stand and fight, if necessary. That was already proven. Otherwise, she never knew there was anything extraordinary inside her. At that moment, she needed to use that strength of will to push herself to try something new.

"Okay, Pandora. What do you want me to try?" Morgan said feeling apprehensive.

"Don't be scared if you can't do magic. It will be okay," Pandora said, trying to reassure her.

"Our lives depend on us figuring out a plan. This is part of it, let's just do this," Morgan said.

"Close your eyes and repeat after me. 'As I lay me down to sleep, dreams and messages I will seek, Spirit Guidance, come to me. Show me what I need to see,'" Pandora said. Morgan repeated it.

Morgan saw Blake as vividly as if he were still alive inside her head. He stood there smiling at her. He looked the way he did before he died. He spoke to her, "Baby, you can do this. You have to. You will live…" The vision vanished and she opened her eyes.

"I saw Blake, Jen. He told me, I could do this. Pandora, what was I supposed to see?" She was shaking and her voice cracked, tears ran down her face.

"The sights are always different. I didn't tell you to pinpoint any one thing in particular. You saw what your heart wanted to see most, the man you love. You were just telling me how much you miss him. That means it worked and we can use this to help us. Now concentrate on the box. See if you can picture where it is. Say the spell again and concentrate hard," Pandora said to Morgan.

"Okay. I'll try," Morgan said.

Morgan transfixed on an image of the box in her mind and said the spell. In a few short moments, she was staring straight at it in her head. She described the room to them. Pandora immediately knew where it was. It took them a while to find the key to the shackles that held them in the dungeon, but they succeeded in finding it.

"We found one of the things we were looking for. I'm going to teach you the spell for getting those keys on the hook outside the door to this room. This is going to take a lot of your strength. We don't become witches overnight. I know I didn't at any rate. It took practice, from when I was five until I was eighteen and had to stop," Pandora said. "We need a summoning spell, let me think a few minutes."

"Is there such a thing?" Jen said.

"There is, but I don't remember. It's been two thousand years," Pandora said. "I think I know another way. Have you ever heard of teleportation?"

"Yeah, but it's not real," Morgan said.

"Yes, it is. I have seen it done before with nothing more than your mind. We don't have much with us right now. Our minds are here for the using," Pandora said.

"What do we have to do?" Morgan asked.

"All three of us have to concentrate really hard, that's about it," Pandora said. "I can put the image we need in your minds, but I need you mainly to concentrate."

"Oh hey, we have Holy water and wooden stakes up in our room. We could probably use those too if we can get them here," Jen piped in.

"I think we'd better try to get the box first, then the other things," Pandora said.

"Okay, so let's try this then," Morgan said.

In the minute after they closed their eyes, the three females started to see the image of the room the box was in. The room was made of gray stone like all the rest. It had red curtains and wall hangings. The bed was a four-poster bed with red curtains tied back to the posts. The floor was stone with Persian rugs on it. The vanity table had a golden crown hanging from the corner. A pair of men's trousers and a long sleeved dress shirt were on a hanger slumped over a chair and dress shoes were tucked underneath it. The box the ladies were looking for was sitting on a table in the middle of the room.

All the ladies had to do was concentrate on that object. They tried hard. It flickered in their minds. They continued to see it. All of a sudden, it was gone from view. They all opened their eyes quickly. The box was sitting at Pandora's feet like a long lost pet reconnecting with its owner.

"We did it!"

***

A loud crash three floors above and a loud howl of raging madness was heard in the dungeon. Mr. Anders saw the box disappear. Footsteps were everywhere above and Pandora heard one set getting steadily closer to them. They had to hide the box.

"We have to hide this! He's coming, I hear him! He's coming fast!" Pandora said in a quick whisper.

They tried again to concentrate with the impending threat of a madman. It was harder, but they managed to hide the box in a corner that had a pile of skeletons in it. He was getting closer faster. He must have been far enough away from the servants that he was whizzing around the dungeon.

He arrived at the door in lightning speed and unlocked it with same whirring speed as well. The girls had never seen a door open that fast in all their lives. Even through all of the stuff they saw last summer, nothing moved that fast.

It would be nearly impossible to get the stakes and Holy water so soon. Mr. Anders was mad. He knew that Pandora had had magic powers when she was a mortal. When she told him she lost them when she became a vampire, he didn't believe her. Funny thing was, it wasn't her. Morgan had the power and he didn't know it. Maybe they did have a secret weapon after all.

"Pandora, how did you do it?" Mr. Anders said.

"How did I do what?" Pandora said.

"Where is it? What did you do with the box?" Mr. Anders accused her.

"How am I going to do anything with the box all the way down here?" Pandora asked. "I've been down here for months. I don't have access to the other floors. Maybe you should talk to your employees."

"They don't know about it," Mr. Anders said.

"Are you sure? Maybe one of them took it to get it cleaned up or something. It could have been dusty," Pandora said as she used mental vampire powers on him.

"Maybe, I'll go check. Then I'm coming back and I'm gonna hurt you if you don't bloody tell me what happened," Mr. Anders said, not realizing what she did to him.

"Okay. See you in a bit," Pandora said.

Mr. Anders whizzed out the door and locked it before the girls had time to look at each other. Pandora smiled.

"We have very few minutes then he'll come back. We need to get your weapons from upstairs. Yes, I confounded him. I'm older than he is, even in my weakened state I can still put the occasional idea in his head," Pandora said. "I had to buy us a little more time."

The two young researchers smiled and looked at Pandora. She nodded. It was time to look inside their minds at the rooms they stayed in when they first arrived at the castle. It was the only way to see where the weapons were.

The suite of rooms was stonewalled and floored, but it was drastically different from the other room they saw in their heads. It was done in pastels. There were two beds in the suite and both had coverlets of pale pink, purple, blue, green, and yellow silk on them.

The curtains were also cheery. The four-poster beds had been painted white and the hanging drapes were all five colors attached in the middle of the post with silk flower bouquets. The dressing tables were white with vases of silk flowers on them. The stone floor had white high pile rugs by the beds and the closet had a small chandelier. The crystals were catching the light and throwing it all over the floor. They found the part of the room they were looking for.

The bag with the weapons was on the floor above the girls' clothes, which hung in the closet. It was black and leather, this nondescript suitcase. The lining was padded to help the water be more undetected. Everyone saw the suitcase and concentrated on it heavily. This time, it took a few minutes to flicker and disappear from the upstairs room; they were getting weak. It didn't take long to sap their strength when the girls hadn't been fed since the day before. Morgan got dizzy and sat down on the floor of the cell when they finished teleporting the case.

"We don't have long. I know that took a lot out of you, but you need to get up," Pandora said. "We need you just as much as you need us right now."

"I know. This ain't the time for weakness. Right now, I need to just sit here. I need to think of a place to hide some of this stuff, so we can have access to it," Morgan said.

***

Time passed slower even though there was an impending threat on his way back to them at any time. The three females were thinking of places to stash stakes and Holy water. It was a mad scramble, but they had to hide the weapons quickly. Their time as prisoners was coming to a close. Whether they got out alive or not at all, they were going to fight. Most likely, they would get hurt badly or die. It didn't matter as long as they were free. The light was drawing to a close. Pandora would have the dark on her side but so would Mr. Anders. It would be a tough battle for them all.

Morgan wished she had time to learn more magic in order to have a secret weapon, but they already had a secret weapon and didn't know it yet. Pandora was going to unleash chaos one last time. She didn't tell the others it was a last resort plan. They had to get rid of that guy one way or the other, even if it meant taking a chance on the other two girls trying to kill each other before the chaos was returned. It was a chance they would have to take.

***

Mr. Anders returned before the ladies had a chance to talk about a real plan. It was dark out the tiny window. The night was cloudy in Salem. That only helped the vampires because it was even darker.

Mr. Anders was dressed in traditional kings clothing from the Tudor age instead of a business suit. He wore the crown that hung on the vanity mirror in his room that the ladies saw earlier in the day. It was gold encrusted with diamonds. He was wearing his rings and his gold chains from the age that he was born. He wore stockings instead of socks, a jacket with poofy shoulders lined with ribbon, and a pair of what appeared to be shorts but were old trousers that kings used to wear. His plan was to conquer the United States and reign as king with the box and Pandora by his side, it was more apparent to the three women seeing him in his old fashioned clothes. That had to be the reason she was still alive.

In all his finery, Mr. Anders was a sight to see. When he spoke, he was the same man who wanted to kill them. His teeth were showing, especially bright now that he was so mad at them.

"Hello again, ladies. We meet again for the last time, I'm afraid. The time has come for you give me what I want and Pandora, I mean everything I want. You other two will be dinner for us. How nice," Mr. Anders said.

"No, I don't think so," Pandora said. She then closed her eyes and anger led her thoughts to the box, which then released the chaos upon him, mostly. While he was busy trying to figure out what they had done, Pandora instructed the girls, "Stop fighting and stake that bastard! Now!"

"What are you all doing, love?" Mr. Anders asked because now he was confused.

"Getting rid of you, once and for all," Pandora said.

The girls were fighting, fighting each other and fighting against the chaos in their minds. It was maddening when the chaos entered their heads. They managed to focus the rage the box gave them on the golden monster in front of them.

The three of them simultaneously threw Holy water in his face, melting it like hot candle wax, making him fall to the floor screaming and writhing in pain.

All three of the ladies knew that was their chance. They moved the hay around that was scattered on the floor of the cell, trying to find the stakes. They stabbed Mr. Anders with one stake each. The first one caught him in the chest. The second was planted in his back. The third was in his abdomen.

Pandora was able to put the chaos back in the box a split second after they threw Holy water at Mr. Anders. Pandora didn't want to have to take the chance that Jen and Morgan might have tried to kill each other, but they'd have had no other choice. It wasn't like they didn't have things they hated about each other, they were human.

It was easier to fake being locked up than last time; it was harder for them back then. That was twice the two younger women had to lie it in order to live. They wanted to be free since the moment they were locked up.

Morgan was told to concentrate on conjuring the keys to the cell. Once Pandora had them, she unlocked the door and ran out. When she returned, she came back with an ax and proceeded to chop Mr. Anders' head off. As she did, the blood from his most recent kill came spurting out of his neck rapidly, spraying all the women. Jen ran up behind them with the box and handed it to Pandora. They were leaving. As they were walking up the stairs and out of the dungeon, Mr. Anders' employees stopped and stared at them. No one said a word all the way up and back into the main hall. Pandora put the head of the dead vampire on the shiny marble floor, her bare foot on top.

"Here is your king!" Pandora shouted. Her voice echoed off the walls, scaring half the servants away that hadn't already fled at the sight of the blood covering the white shining marble floors.

It was time to get out of Salem. They made it up to Jen and Morgan's room. Pandora took the liberty of packing the girls' bags because she was extremely quick. The three of them trotted out of the bedroom door and toward the front door.

One maid hadn't run away from the three bruised, broken, and bloody figures. Believing she had the courage to step toe to toe with the ones who killed her employer, she faced them in the large foyer. Her stern glare told Pandora the woman believed she murdered the evil bastard who paid her to clean. Suddenly, the maid produced a butcher knife from her pocket in an attempt to get revenge. That wasn't a good idea. Pandora grabbed her faster than she could blink and sucked her dry, tossing her body on the hard stone floor. She wiped the blood off her mouth, glanced over at the girls and said it would never happen to them. The girls knew it wouldn't, they trusted her.

They walked out the door, three female prisoners of war. The black car that two of the survivors came to the English castle in was sitting by the door, ready for its next departure. The driver was nowhere in sight, but the keys were inside. It took no time for them to decide to take the car. It was the first time Jen and Morgan ever stole a thing, but they hopped in and fired it up. Pandora drove like a maniac. She didn't care because she wanted to be as far away from that castle as possible so her two human friends would be safe. She drove all night because vampires don't sleep. Jen and

Morgan slept the whole way back to Sioux Falls, South Dakota. Pandora had to wake them when they got to town. She didn't know where their house was.

Chapter Seventeen

It didn't take long for Jen and Morgan to show Pandora where they lived. They showed her with their minds because they were exhausted. Before long, they pulled up in front of the roses in the front yard. It seemed like a year since they'd been in their own home.

Nothing looked mysterious or out of place, so they decided to go inside. When they reached the porch, it was a different story. The door was ajar. Pandora entered first, just in case the place was the site of a break-in. As they walked through the door, they noticed the inside was trashed. There was stuff everywhere.

"This is not how we left the place," Morgan said.

"Figured as much, no one goes away and leaves their house like this. Someone came in here looking for something, they didn't find it and still think you have it, or they lost interest and gave up. I can't smell any others but you two," Pandora said.

"We need to get my son. He's at my mom's house," Jen said.

"Yeah, whoever did this might try to use him, to get to us, to make us give up whatever it is they've been looking for. I'm going to get us some more stuff and lock up. You might wanna gather up some of his stuff, Jen. We can't stay here," Morgan said.

"No matter what's going on, I will protect all three of you," Pandora said.

"We don't even know what's going on yet, but thanks," Jen said as she tried to sift through the piles of stuff thrown around the living room.

The girls found clothes and things they needed to stay in a hotel. After that, the three of them went to pick up little Warren at his grandma's house. They flew down the roads that took them there, the drive was less than five minutes.

They pulled up in front of the white English Provincial style home. It had red roses growing up over the two front picture windows. The shutters were black and the door was red. It was like a picture in a magazine. The second-floor windows were dark, but the picture window to the left was dimly lit.

It looked like no one was home. Before the three ladies could exit the vehicle and make it to the porch, Jen's mom came sprinting from the house with the baby in her arms.

She looked panic-stricken and scared. The dark-haired, blue-eyed baby had dirty tear stains on his face.

"Mom, what's going on? Why's he dirty? And why do you look so scared?" Jen said, starting to panic herself.

"These people came by here looking for the two of you. They didn't know we were here. I peeked out the window and I didn't recognize them. Since you didn't come home when you said you would, I got scared. The baby's dirty because the basement is dirty. That's where we were until just now when I saw the headlights of the car you were in and then through the basement window, I saw you all. I ran up here as fast as I could," Jen's mom said. "I was hoping it was you. I'm so glad you're alive. I was so worried about you."

"Mom, do you have any idea why the people came looking for us?" Jen asked.

"No. I didn't talk to any of them, I was too scared. They tossed my house like they were looking for something."

"Maybe they were, we just don't know what it is. They tossed our house too," Jen told her mom. "Get your stuff together, we're going to a hotel for a while until we get this figured out."

***

"Does she know anything about what you all really do for a living?" Pandora asked.

"No, she doesn't. Either she probably wouldn't believe us or she'd haul our asses off to the loony bin," Jen said to Pandora.

"Okay then, I won't tell her about me. And I won't try to train Morgan to be a witch in front of her," Pandora said.

"Good thinking. We don't need someone else thinking we're crazy as hell," Morgan said.

"Besides you, there's only one person we can trust and he'd probably try to stake you the first chance he gets. You won't be meeting him for a while," Jen said. "He's a priest at our local Catholic church. He gave us all the stakes and Holy water that we used on 'the king.'"

"Good man," Pandora said.

Jen's mom returned with a suitcase of her things ready to go to the hotel. Everyone piled into the stolen car. The group was now five. When they got to the hotel, they asked for two rooms. Jen, baby Warren, and her mom stayed in one room while Morgan and Pandora shared the other. Morgan needed to be trained.

Everyone slept for hours on end except Pandora. It was a good thing they brought the laptop. She was busy trying to hack into a system somewhere and find out why the others were being endangered. And who might have set that ball in motion. It was morning again before the others woke up and Pandora could tell them anything she found.

"I know you just woke up but I want to tell you, it's the CIA that's looking for you. I don't know if it's for hostile reasons, the forms didn't say. But your ordeal in Missouri was brought to their attention somehow and they're looking for you. They probably think you did it," Pandora said to Morgan.

"That's crazy. Do they have us marked as terrorists?" Morgan asked in her sleepy haze.

"No, they think you're both crazy as mad hatters," Pandora said.

"That's because we are. Trauma will do that to ya," Morgan said. "We weren't before then."

"We have to go tell Jen," Pandora said.

"No, let's give her a few minutes, she had a bad dream," Morgan said.

"How did you know that?" Pandora questioned her.

"I always know. I even know what it was about. She projects when she dreams so I always see it. We live in the same house and the whole time she was pregnant I saw all of her weird dreams like I was having them myself. I even saw all the nightmares she always has since we left Missouri," Morgan told

Pandora. "I thought it was because she's my best friend and I felt for her."

"No. Do you ever feel really sad when she does or do you feel happy as hell when she's happy? Have you ever felt happy and walked into a room with her when she was sad and she suddenly feels happier than she was?" Pandora asked.

"Yeah, but I always thought it was a best friend making a best friend feel better," Morgan said.

"Nope, you not only have magical abilities, but you sound like you're an empath, too," Pandora said. "That's how you see her dreams. She's not projecting. You are."

"Son of a bitch!" Morgan screamed.

"What? Why are you angry? You have abilities that if you honed, could come in handy if you all found yourselves in another scrape," Pandora said. "You need to be grateful not mad."

"All I want is peace and quiet, not powers," Morgan said.

"That doesn't look like your lot in life, sorry M," Pandora said.

"Stop feeling bad, it's making me sick to my stomach. I know you didn't do this to me," Morgan said trying to console Pandora so her tummy ache would go away.

"Sorry about that, too," Pandora said.

"Let's get dressed and go over now. We've wasted enough time. The dream is over and she's calming down. I feel it," Morgan told Pandora. It was strange how in-tune she was with her best friend, she never realized it. It became second nature. She didn't think about it.

"Yes, there is so much to tell her," Pandora said.

***

Jen stayed in a hotel room with her son and her mom. She screamed herself awake like always. That startled the baby and he started crying. With tears running down her face, Jen got up, got baby Warren out of his playpen and tried to console him. Her mother was confused. She must have never noticed. When Jen and her little one were together, it was their daily routine.

At least, another night and another nightmare have passed, Jen thought. The daytime was her favorite time of day. Most bad things happened to her at night. The sun was shining and the baby was starting to calm down. That day felt like it might be a good day to her. However, that was still yet to be seen.

There was a soft knock at the door of the hotel room. Morgan and Pandora stood in the doorway. Both of them looked serious. They came in and asked Jen if she could come with them to their room for a minute that they needed to talk about business.

Jen got dressed and went to their room with them. They explained how the CIA must have been looking to question them all. Pandora told her what she found, and that they were probably looking for them to question them about Missouri. When people disappear mysteriously no one believes how or why they disappeared. Jen thought it was farfetched, and if they tried to explain all of it, they would get laughed out of the CIA building. Or they would get locked up in the nut ward somewhere. That wasn't all that Morgan had to tell her about.

She told her the reason she always felt and saw Jen's dreams was probably because she was not only a witch, she was an empath. When Jen was sad, Morgan made her happy by being happy, somehow filtering it to Jen and calming the sadness without knowing it.

"Wow, that does make sense, you having some sort of weird influence on how I'm feeling. I used to ask myself how I would feel so happy all of the sudden sometimes. That's amazing and thank you for that. It helped so much with the baby," Jen said to Morgan, hugging her.

"I didn't even realize I did that until Pandora asked the right questions about it a little earlier this morning," Morgan said.

The three of them talked a little more about all the new information then sent Jen back to her mom and the baby. Back in her room, her mom was wondering what was going on. She couldn't tell her the truth and risk her getting hurt by anyone in the process because she knew too much. Jen told her the CIA was looking for them to question them about some of the missions they went on in the past, about artifacts they found, and some of them were classified. They couldn't talk about them. This satisfied her mom.

Jen sat on her bed in her room thinking about everything when the CIA busted through the door. The door came off the hinges and banged up against the wall. This sudden loudness scared everyone inside the room. The baby cried loudly and the two women screamed.

"What the fuck!?" Jen screamed. "Who are you?"

"The CIA, ma'am. We have to take you all in," a CIA agent said to Jen.

Jen looked surprised they were being taken in, even if she suspected what the other two told her was true. Surprised as she might have been, she calmly gathered her things and her baby then marched out the door with her mother following her.

There were black SUVs in the parking lot of the hotel waiting to take them to the headquarters of the CIA. Several men in black suits sat in them with loaded guns in their laps, in the event they were needed. It was a serious matter, considering the manpower and arsenal involved.

Jen's dark hair flowed in the breeze as she walked to the SUV the captain of the team directed her to. She stood there waiting to see if Morgan would come out without problems. After 2005, no one wanted to rattle that cage. If Jen weren't holding her baby, they wouldn't want to rattle hers either.

***

This same scenario happened in Morgan and Pandora's room. Pandora could have fought, but she didn't because she didn't want to get anyone in trouble if they weren't already. Hiding who she was turned into a pastime for her. She was good at it. Both ladies came out peacefully as well. All five people, mortal and immortal, were taken into custody.

The CIA building was a stark and austere place. It was gray concrete inside and out with institutional white tiles and white walls. The chairs were hard and plastic. There were mirror glass panels in the conference rooms.

The group was separated then told to sit and say nothing until it was their turn for questioning. They were all interviewed and asked about a lot of different things. The CIA had a long list of situations they'd been following involving them or Warren and Blake.

We got captured, again. This is getting old. Three times in approximately a year is bad, Morgan thought.

The line of questioning was strange. They thought they were there to talk about how their boyfriends and their friends died so suddenly and mysteriously; they weren't. The questions the agents were asking had to do with buried treasure. Apparently, the men found some gold or something made of gold, sometime in their younger years when they visited Scotland. Then they buried it somewhere in the U.S. on a camping trip they went on when they were eighteen years old. No one else knew anything about it. The ladies had no idea of its location or what exactly they agents were looking for.

Warren wasn't from South Dakota originally. His father was from Scotland. He lived there as a young child and until he was eighteen, he had to go there and visit his father on summer break. His mother moved back to the U.S. when he was about three years old.

The CIA knew of the divorce and contacted both parents then found out Warren died when he went to Missouri with his fianceé and friends in May of 2005. However, his parents didn't know anything about treasure missing from Scotland. No one questioned the girls about what happened in Missouri, although it was mysterious. No one knew about what happened only days ago in Massachusetts. Somehow all the mysterious and weird happenings were being swept under the rug to an extent, but the group was still under the scope.

**

The CIA had to let everyone go. They couldn't hold anyone because no one knew anything about gold from Scotland. It was something the CIA would have to figure out without the help of the people that loved Warren and Blake the most. The gang walked out of the CIA building when the sun was shifting into the afternoon. They called a cab and went back to their hotel rooms to get their stuff so they could go home. Pandora didn't have a home and hadn't had one in so long she was moderately confused.

"You look like you don't know what to do. You're free now and you can come home with us," Morgan said. "I would really like to learn how to use my magic, so I can defend us in a bad situation."

"Yeah, that makes sense. Okay, I will come with you and Jen," Pandora said.

Jen walked up to the empty doorway of Morgan and Pandora's room and looked in. She smiled because she heard Pandora say she was coming home with them. She felt protected with Pandora around.

"We're ready to go now, ladies. It's going to be so much fun cleaning up when we get home," Jen said still smiling. "Don't forget the laptop." She glanced at Morgan who began shutting it down and packing it, getting her research put away so she could go home.

PART THREE
Never Ending

Chapter Eighteen

The Whereabouts of the Missing Gold

[Sioux Falls, SD] *Be highly aware and on the lookout for a golden statue in the image of King David I of Scotland. It's rumored to have made its way to the United States. It's been missing for a number of years and the hunt is on to find it safe and sound. This artifact is, in fact, one of the oldest original statues still in existence belonging to the Scottish people.*

Its last known Scottish location was the Carlisle Castle, which used to belong on Scottish soil until the English fought and took it over many years ago. Since then, the castle inhabited the descendants of the first king of the realm. Any and all relics and artifacts have been stored or displayed within the castle walls.

Unbeknownst to the current owner and descendant, the golden statue of King David I was stolen by teenagers passing through on a pilgrimage to their homeland in the continent of the United Kingdom.

As part of a secret sector in a well-known secret organization, which shall remain nameless, the current castle owner and ancestor of the king, has been using all of his known resources to track the object. He found, the last known whereabouts lead to the United States. In Sioux Falls, South Dakota, a place his son used to reside, he hopes to find the object.

In his attempt to get the object back, the Scotsman tried to obtain the help from his family members. It was important to get the object out of the hands of civilians as soon as possible. There was a secret he didn't tell the regular media. The golden relic was cursed many centuries ago with a fast-growing version of the plague that only struck people who were not of the royal bloodline.

It's got one other trick up its golden sleeve; it can open a gate to release demons on earth, making it doubly dangerous in the wrong hands. Yet another reason to keep it under lock and key, also the main reason recovery is imminent. Witches around the world, having studied mystical objects their whole lives, knowing how to handle it and not to touch it while opening the door to command the demons they unleashed, would make for Armageddon.

***

For six months, the CIA had been looking for the golden statue and for six months Pandora trained Morgan in the ways of magic. She knew everything there was to know, she just couldn't perform many spells anymore. Teaching someone else to do it was a chore, but she knew Morgan might need it, considering the line of work the girls were in. She needed her magic to help with the survival of herself and her best friend. The road they were on was not an easy one, they seemed to be so unlucky that dangerous people sought them out. They had no choice but to fight, so they needed something to fight with.

Pandora knew she couldn't stick around forever and wanted to be able to leave knowing the girls would be okay. There were so many spells to teach Morgan that she and Pandora started a grimoire to catalog them in. Morgan never thought she would be the owner of such a thing. She thought about it and the more she thought, she realized the legends were coming to light for them; the three of them knew about and saw things no normal person did. It was only natural the next thing they might have to face would be magic. Something or someone would eventually come into their sights that could do magic whether it was demons, more ghosts, or witches.

***

The golden object was eventually found by some treasure hunting idiots because they searched since the story broke in the newspaper. The Scottish relic was a golden statue of one of their founders, King David I. It was ancient. It depicted the ruler in all his glory; his face was an exact picture of the original. The statue wore traditional attire from the time King David I lived. The people who found it died of what looked like the plague, four days before they could hand the statue over to the CIA. It never made it out of the hole it was in. It was speculated by the coroner, they caught the strain of plague in the woods surrounding Sioux Falls. Teams of Health Department testers were testing the site and found nothing telling them the virus came from anything in those woods. The autopsy reports came back showing the virus was detected in all the bodies but, the factor causing them to catch the disease remained unknown.

The girls were perplexed about the mysterious disease they heard about on the news and in the papers. Supposedly, there was no connection between the disease and the statue, but the girls weren't buying it. It was time to start the behind the scenes investigation. They were about to unravel another mystery.

***

The first thing to do was the most obvious. Jen called Warren's father in Scotland and asked about the object. He told her it was a statue of King David I of Scotland. It had a curse on it, anyone who wasn't in the bloodline of King David I could touch it without getting the black plague and dying within a week of coming in contact with it.

He warned them, if they did find it not to lay their hands directly on it but to wrap it up and take it with them, so they could send it back to Scotland. Warren's family were descendants of the king and they were the only ones who could touch the statue without dying. The O'Connell family had two remaining members of the bloodline, Warren's father and his son.

Warren O'Connell Jr. was born and lived in a Scottish castle until he was about three. When he was older, he took the statue when he went to visit his father. No one knew it was gone for a few years or who might have possibly taken it. At the time, Warren had no way of knowing how dangerous the statue was. He just knew it was old and wanted to get back at his father for not being around much when he was growing up. His father was in 'business' and that meant he and his mother were neglected but had money when he was smaller. That was really what he knew of his father, never being around much, when he came to visit, his dad was always in a meeting. His parents got a divorce because his mother was tired of being alone in a strange country all the time. After the divorce, she and Warren moved back to the states. His mother never knew what kind of business her husband did or what he dealt with, he was never home and never explained his business trips to her.

After Warren died, his father connected some dots and came to the conclusion that he may have taken it and he was right in that assumption. Now it was up to Warren's love to find it.

***

"So, we have to go searching for this thing our boyfriends took?" Morgan asked Jen when she got off the phone and told her what Warren's father said.

"Yeah, it looks that way, doesn't it?" Jen said.

"Oh shit. Yet another mystery that we pretty much fell right into!" Morgan said, exasperated. "Damn it."

"Looks like you're going to need a little help with this one too. Neither one of you can touch the statue. The only one who can is the baby," Pandora said. "I'm already dead so the plague won't hurt me."

"This is gonna be great…just fuckin' great!" Morgan said. She had her own fears, she let them out in the form of sarcasm. She didn't want to go into the woods at night, the idea filled her with dread.

"Remember, life hasn't been a picnic for a long time and it won't be again. We just gotta deal with it," Jen said. "You keep telling me that."

"I hate it when you do that. No one likes it when you use their words against them," Morgan said, she sneered at Jen. "Ya wise ass."

"You two are so funny. You sound like married people," Pandora laughed.

"We are married to sisterhood and friendship, loyalty, and all that," Jen said.

"I know you are. I could tell that when I first met you two. I could almost smell those things," Pandora said. "If that's even possible."

"No, that was the fear. We didn't know for sure if you were going to kill us or not," Morgan said, she laughed a little at the thought because she knew better now.

They all laughed at that thought. It was funny because Pandora didn't take in human blood. It had been almost two thousand years since she did when she sucked the maid dry in Salem. At the time, the girls didn't know and had a premature fear. That fear dissolved and brought them together quickly in the short time they were locked up together. It was a good thing Pandora was strong enough to use her mind to tell them her story. It would have taken too long to explain in words.

Most of all, she was glad she knew them, they knew what she was and they weren't afraid of her. She'd proven herself time and again. Life was finally good. It only took two thousand years and two people who were alive to make her feel that.

***

While the girls on U.S. soil were laughing, in the far away country of Ireland, Celtic witches were casting spells trying to find them. They read about the statue in the local newspaper where they lived. They wanted to get away from the hovel they dwelled in and the remote village in Ireland. They wanted the statue for themselves. They knew it could be used to raise evil spirits and demons to kill their enemies. The witches had many more enemies than friends, the statue could help them out of their destitute situation faster than people would.

An old stone cottage house also known as a black house, which had been placed roughly between two small rolling hills, housed three Celtic witches. In the main room of the house, they hovered over the top of a book of spells and a map as they were using, desperately trying to scry for two American women. They thought those women must have some knowledge of the whereabouts of the statue, much like the American CIA surmised at first.

The room was musty and the furnishings were old. The stick furniture was plain, straightforward, and falling apart with everyday wear and tear. The color scheme of the place was 'Village Peasant' browns. There were also no modern conveniences in the cottage. The floors were made of packed earth and covered with rugs made from animal furs. The windows were holes with fabric over them and the place was dimly candle-lit. The thatched roof was starting to leak from lack of upkeep. The only thing that kept them from freezing was the stone fireplace in the center of the kitchen and living area combined with thick stone walls. The bedroom was the only other room the cottage contained. The sisters slept in one big bed to keep warm.

Those witches hadn't thought they needed all the modern conveniences in the past. They got along fine on little for a long time. They had a plan would take them passed that life and into a brand new, exciting existence wherever they wanted to live. They wanted the sunshine. They'd spent most of their lives in gloomy Ireland and it was time to move on. The witches were going to make it happen, even if they had to rip every hair from the heads of both females who were trying to get in their way. If it came down to it, the witches would kill them all.

Chapter Nineteen

Back in South Dakota, the moon was full but the cut-out on the floor of the woods below the thick overgrowth of trees was dark without the moonlight. Summer was once again opening up new nightmares for the young researchers. Jen and Morgan didn't like the woods at night, not since the time they spent in Tipton Ford. If it hadn't been for buried statues, they wouldn't have never imagined venturing into the woods again.

Flashlights weren't much use in the dark with Pandora standing nearby, she had a predatory night vision, seeing any and all moving things when normally it was pitch black. They used her special vision and searched night after night, when finally, two weeks later, they found the statue. It wasn't easy, only going at night so as no one would suspect them of criminal activities. This left the days for mapping routes to take in the dark. After searching so long, they found a statue that was ten inches high made of pure gold. It was an exact replica of King David I of Scotland, crown affixed, beard and all, exactly like Warren's father described to Jen over the phone. It didn't look dangerous, but then again, the evilest things usually didn't.

The statue was wrapped up in a big piece of cloth and hidden in the basement until Jen could send it to Scotland. There was something about the statue that seemed off somehow. There was something besides the curse Warren's father neglected to mention. It felt wrong. Jen couldn't put a finger it, but they all felt that a part of the puzzle was missing.

The statue had powers King David I didn't know it had. He was a war-filled king, but he didn't use his power to control demons and specters. He only used the statue as a decoration of his being the king. It was like a golden self-portrait to him and nothing more.

The witches of the age of King David I didn't like him and they didn't like the peace from war over the territories. They used their ancient magic to put more than one curse on the statue, hoping it would kill him. Instead of killing him, it killed anyone but him or his family bloodline. The part of the curse few people knew about brought about demons and evil souls to do the bidding of whoever had possession of the statue. If evil witches took possession of it than evil could be brought forth. It was as simple as that. The statue had a lot of things written about it over the years, but none of the curses were in any of the literature.

"We've looked everywhere and can't find a thing about that curse dear old dad warned us about," Morgan said to Jen. "Do you think it could be bull?"

"I've learned to take things like this at face value. If he said there's a curse, there probably is. I hadn't even heard about this until he told me. Warren never said a word about any of it."

"Neither did Blake. They knew they could trust us, but still didn't say a thing. Maybe they died before they ever got the chance," Morgan said with a sullen look on her face.

"Stop. Stop feeling that way. When you feel sad, it makes everyone in the room feel like shit. I really wish you weren't an empath. That part really sucks," Jen said.

"Yeah, I know. Sorry. I miss him so much sometimes, especially after seeing him in your nightmares all night. That sucks too," Morgan said, then she sighed.

"Please, think about something else. I love Warren still. You know that. I can't sulk about it right now when we have this to try to figure out," Jen said, feeling sad because of the empathy.

"You're right, Jen. I just miss him is all," Morgan said.

"I know," Jen said, trying to be understanding, which became one of her newfound powers.

"I'm so glad to know the two of you. Life is never boring here and the two of you are so much like my queen and I used to be. It's comforting to think that there's still real friendship out there," Pandora said.

"We are all we have now besides baby Warren, my mom, and now you," Jen said. "We lost everyone else."

"And Morgan is right. I hear you screaming at night too. I always want to run up the stairs and look in on you, but I know I don't have to because she always does. I hear that too," Pandora said.

The three of them talked a little while longer about how things changed and about what life was like before all the scary stuff turned into reality. What would life have been like if they decided to veer off the road a few days and got to Tipton Ford behind schedule? Dreams were only dreams.

Jen explained how she and Morgan had been raised to Pandora and how different they had become after the weekend they spent in Tipton Ford, Missouri what felt like many years ago. She told her, being spoiled wasn't all it was cracked up to be. Warren and Blake used to try to teach them how to be regular people before they died and how they misunderstood what the guys meant. The aftermath of their deaths taught the girls *too* much. They finally understood what it was to be an adult and not a spoiled brat.

Pandora understood that sometimes it was a hard journey to get where you wanted to be. Something she knew all too well. The girls told her their story, which helped her know them better, so she listened intently.

***

On the other side of the world, two small groups of people were preparing an attack against each other and they didn't know it yet. The witches were practicing up on their Black Magic and Druid practices, so they could resurrect an army of demons. Warren's father and his 'company' were gathering information to fight whoever might get in the way of retrieving the relic from America, he decided to go there and get it instead of Jen sending it. Two weeks passed by while arrangements were made and Jen and Morgan found the statue.

No one knew if it would be a bloody battle or not, but everyone was coming prepared. The sect of the Free Masons in Scotland that Warren's father belonged to, they believed in justice and serving it up Wiccan style if necessary. They were not above using magic themselves to defend the cause. The ancient and hidden organization wasn't above anything, they kept it a secret from everyone else in the world. People weren't supposed to know such a thing existed.

Everyone on every side of the battle hoped it wouldn't be a long fight, even though they all knew it could be. The witches wanted to exact a villainous plot. The Free Masons wanted to save people from the violence the witches planned on. Jen and Morgan just wanted to be free of the dangerous thing putting them in the middle of yet another supernatural scene. The battlefront was decided; Jen and Morgan would have to deal with it at home this time.

Wars were raged every day in the most ordinary of places. This time, it would be in front of the roses and the big picture window of a yellow vinyl sided house, on some quiet street in the middle of suburbia. It would appear too strange to be real. There would have to be a way to erase it from the minds of the neighbors somehow and the girls would have to cross that bridge sooner than they wanted to.

"It's 'bout time we paid yer almost daughter-in-law a visit, ye kin it? We need tae secure tha' item 'fore someone finds out they 'ave it an' try an' take it from 'em, aye. I know they was supposed to FedEx it an' I dinna trust it," Sir MacAfee said.

"Aye, I dinna kin if they believe any o' what I told 'er on tha' phone. I dinna kin if I trust 'em either. I never met the lass, an' therefore, dinna kin if she's in good standin' or no," said Mr. O'Connell.

"Well, we ain't got time fer ye tae meet 'er an' have the trust conversation wit' 'er. The lass loved yer boy, that's got tae be enoof," Sir MacAfee said.

"She was 'round him when he was killed, ye kin? Still dinna ken if I believe she wasna directly involved," Mr. O'Connell said.

"I kin it, we ain't got time to get into it, until after it's doon. We're gonna get the statue back, so them witches won't do noothin' awful wit' it. Top priority righ' now. After tha', ye do all tha' family stuff ye wanna, old son," Sir MacAfee said.

"I've a grandson to be protectin' also. Dinna be forgettin' tha'," Mr. O'Connell reminded him.

"Never," Sir MacAfee told him. "That's why we do wha' we do, protectin' the innocent."

After a short conversation, the two gentlemen sat at desks facing each other in what used to be a library, busying themselves, making travel arrangements to the U.S. They knew exactly where they had to go. *Thank you, Google Maps*, they both thought. The lives they led in the Free Mason secret organization allowed them to be like the FBI or the CIA and track anyone anywhere they needed to in order to do their jobs. In the Present, it wasn't too hard to put a trace on someone. The old sect of Free Masons didn't have computers. They used wire tapping, phone tapping, video surveillance, and many other arcane methods to find someone.

It was decided they would leave for the U.S. in the morning. Flights out of Scotland were not hard to get if you knew who to talk to. It was like being well connected in the mob. There were Free Masons fixed into every important place and job in the world. That good old buddy system was for helping others instead of making money and murdering people, they only killed when they absolutely had no other way. And then, that particular person just came up missing to never be found. No one cared because it was usually a criminal or some other evil person like a vampire or the occasional lycanthrope, they killed people.

***

The witches of Ireland saw that the two Free Masons were on their way to the U.S. the next day. It was time for them to depart as well. They were going to wait until morning to teleport themselves where they needed to be, then they would have time to do some recon. Planes weren't their style. Time was short. They were going to have to 'bring it' when they got there. The demons weren't going to wait forever.

They wanted to be released again so they could roam the earth and wreak havoc on society. They were holding in a lot of rage. If the witches didn't release them, then the demons would find a way to kill them horribly. They had no masters, but they valued life.

These sister witches were different and had different powers, but one common goal bound them together even more than their bloodline coven. The goal to set the demons free on earth so they didn't perish for not doing their sworn duty.

One of the witches, Lahar, was tall with long fiery red hair. She was thin, they were all thin, from living off of nothing but scraps for too many years. Her eyes and her face were flushed when she was concentrating on her spells. Her cheeks were hollow and her face sallow from malnutrition.

The second witch had black curly hair and blue eyes, her name was Edon. She was also hollow and sallow-faced; they all were. She was the shortest of her sisters, but she was the smartest of the three. She knew more about magic and runes.

The third witch had blonde hair and green eyes, she was called Isador. She was the prettiest one of them, but she was also suffering from hunger and rags looked no better on her than her sisters. She was the kindest, but considering how they lived, that wasn't saying much. She healed animals behind her sister's backs.

Life was bad for those witches. All they could think about was releasing the demons and having a better life. They were void of modern conveniences and were damn tired of it. They were going to fulfill their mission or kill those 'little girls' if they got in the way. At least, that was the mindset the witches turned over and over in their heads until morning when they would go to the battlegrounds and take what they wanted. They had no idea about the level of difficulty they could be facing to carry out their plan.

Chapter Twenty

Trees swayed in the warm breeze and the sun was shining brightly in the mid-morning. Birds chirped and the occasional dog barked throughout the neighborhood; it was still too quiet, even when the joggers passed the house, no one thought a thing of it. Everything appeared picturesque and normal. All was not as it seemed. In the house, the girls were preparing for the Free Masons to come. They called early in the evening the night before, which with the six-hour time difference, they must have caught a red-eye non-stop flight from Scotland, so they would be in the U.S. in a few hours.

The witches were lurking in the bushes across the street in the neighbor's yard. That was where they would be for the majority of the day, staking the place out and thinking about their plan of attack. They were waiting for the Free Masons to arrive and attempt to protect the women across the street from them.

It was May. It was going to be a warm day. Those witches were going to sweat a lot in the bushes. They only had one set of clothes and they were for winter more than summertime. It was a good thing the neighbors across the street were on vacation. They would have alerted the authorities if they'd seen someone hanging out in their bushes.

It had only been two months since the girls came home from Salem and stillness put them on edge. They didn't know how to respond to it. They didn't trust it. To them, it was the 'quiet before the storm' and that was worth worrying about. Life was unpredictable. Too much silence made the girls want to climb the walls. They didn't exactly want all the creeps of the world to find them, it just so happened, they were starting to get used to it.

The girls sat in the house staring out the windows wondering why they felt like something was wrong. It was supposed to be a good day. They were going to meet baby Warren's grandfather. The day felt wrong. It was like the day Warren Sr. called Jen for the first time about the statue.

Those witches hid well. Every time one of the girls looked out the window, they saw nothing but their normal looking neighborhood outside. Pandora convinced them to stop looking so they would stop driving themselves crazy.

"I smell new people out there, but it isn't getting stronger. They must be staying at a distance from this place for some reason. You two really need to calm down. If anything happens, I'll protect you," Pandora said.

"I don't like having the baby here just in case something *does* happen today," Jen said.

"I can run him to your mom's if you want. I will go so fast no one will know I'm there. Don't worry. It would be like running a football down the field, only faster," Pandora said. "Much faster."

"I know. Just be careful. I don't know what that kind of speed would do to him," Jen said.

"I will. I've grown very fond of him. I don't want him to get hurt and being here might do that to him," Pandora said.

"I'm glad you brought it up because you're right. He doesn't need to be here just in case something bad happens later," Morgan said.

"Okay. I'll be back in a flash," Pandora said. She ran and got the baby. Then she ran back down the stairs with him, he was laughing and waved as she zoomed past the girls and down the road in a blur. Little Warren laughed some more as Pandora hugged him close to her like a football so she could run at top speed and no one would see her.

The witches in the bushes thought the wind had gusted hard when Pandora zipped past them. They never saw Pandora at all. It only took her five minutes to get all the way across town to the edge of Jen's mom's house. That was where she stopped running and started laughing with the baby.

Pandora knocked on the front door and told Jen's mom Jen sent her to ask if she would watch the baby. She said she would, she never questioned anything when Pandora asked her because she was a little afraid of her. Even though she didn't know what Pandora was, she knew something was different about her. She took little Warren inside the house. She loved to have him come and stay with her, she didn't need a reason why. She assumed it was work related. A lot of the stuff that went on with her daughter and her best friend, in her mind, was work related. Jen and Morgan never truly clued her in on what was really happening. She didn't exactly know their new line of work but, after the stint with the CIA coming after them for questioning, she figured they didn't tell her on purpose so she had nothing to hide if it ever happened again.

She wouldn't have believed it if the girls fessed up anyway as to the true nature of the work they did.

Pandora raced back after giving the baby to Jen's mom who took the little one inside the house. It took her another five minutes to return to Jen and Morgan's. The girls were alone for about twelve minutes. Nothing happened except a lot of staring at bushes that moved occasionally and looking at the trees blow in the wind. It was really boring waiting for impending doom to start.

Chapter Twenty-one

Jen was sitting at a small table in the middle of the dining room, staring out the window that faced the street. She concentrated, glaring out the window. Occasionally, she thought she saw a bush move in the neighbor's yard. She wasn't sure if it was her imagination or not, it was windy outside. Once or twice she thought she saw a flicker of a mirror or gold of some kind coming from the bush, she'd look again and the flickering would be gone.

Everything looked normal in the neighborhood, but it wasn't, something was going to happen there. It was unknown as to what it would be, but it felt like when Jen and Morgan were trapped in the dungeon in Salem, waiting to die at the hands of an old pissed off false king. She felt it. She sat there waiting for Pandora to return and Warren Sr. to arrive so he could tell them what the hell was really going on. She thought there had to be more to the whole thing than what he told her over the phone. She thought he acted like he didn't want to talk about it over the phone to begin with, like someone could have been listening in.

She ran her fingers through her long raven hair and sighed. Impatience ran long and thick in her family, creating an impatient Jen. She started playing with her hair, trying to wait it out as long as she could, then she would have to find something else to do. Just as she was pondering her thoughts, Pandora whizzed through the back door. Jen looked up and smiled at her friend. She barely heard Pandora close the door as she entered the kitchen. The smiling face of her friend beckoned Pandora to come to the table and sit.

"What are you staring at? The witches in the bushes?" Pandora asked Jen.

"Witches in the bushes?" Jen asked back. She didn't see any witches.

"Yeah. There are three of them out there watching us. That's why I wanted to hurry back," Pandora said.

"Oh, so it wasn't my imagination every time I saw something shiny flicker over there," Jen said. Her heart started to race. She knew why she felt like there was something going on out there, because there was.

"Don't worry. It'll be a short battle. Morgan is really good. I know you've had your hands full with the little guy so you couldn't watch, but she really took to it. For someone who said there was no way, she's amazing at it," Pandora boasted.

"I'm glad but we only got one witch. There's more than one of them. You said witches, plural. Damn it!" Jen said feeling her anxiety rise within her.

"It'll be fine, Jen. I got this," Morgan tried to reassure her.

"I'm fuckin' glad somebody does. Now, what the hell am I supposed to do? Sit here helpless and thus not helping?" Jen spat. Sarcasm seeped from her pores.

"You can calm down, that's what you can do. It's not going to help with everyone worried about what you're up to," Morgan said.

"Fine. I'm going to my room. Maybe I'll be calmer after a while when Warren's dad gets here," Jen said still seething.

It was hard for her to accept the fact that she really couldn't help with the impending battle. She didn't have to sit on the sidelines before and watch while everyone got the shit kicked out of them. *Why now?* she thought. She hated that she had no powers of any kind. She wasn't a vampire. She didn't have magic to help with. She had nothing to give back. Even her strength of *will* couldn't help her.

She sat on her bed feeling sorry for herself then she laid down and she cried herself to sleep. She didn't know what else to do. Knowing it wasn't one of her stronger moments, she held her eyelids closed tightly, forcing the water that remained behind her eyes to exit and fall down her face as she slowly ebbed into sleep. She didn't care about crying in her room alone, she knew it had to come out whether she liked it or not, it was better before the battle than during.

***

Downstairs, Morgan and Pandora knew Jen was up in her room crying and they left her alone. Both of them felt bad about her not having real powers, so she could help them. Pandora decided it was best to let her sleep a little until Warren Sr. was due in. As the time grew closer, she would wake her up and talk to her. Morgan agreed Jen needed to talk to someone with more experience with who she was than Morgan would be able to. Morgan told Pandora, all her life, Jen had been extra sensitive emotionally and things got to her easier than everyone else. Morgan informed Pandora, Jen didn't get a chance to mourn properly and she had to be strong through everything that happened. She told Pandora how Jen used to cry at sad movies and kittens and all that cute stuff, but now she ignored it and acted like it didn't even exist. She dramatically changed from the loving, sweet person she used to be into an angry person who actually hated things and people. It wasn't part of who she was.

Pandora promised to talk with Jen, in the hope of helping her come back to the person she was before her life-changing experiences. It was something Pandora believed would help her sanity, feeling the line was thin for Jen, who might do something stupid to try to prove her worth to the team.

Everyone was concerned, but no one really had time to address the issues on a bigger scale than talking. Warren Sr. was due in a few hours. It would take more time than they had to do a proper intervention. They'd have to consider it later. That was going to be a long day, maybe two. Thinking and sunshine was giving Pandora a migraine, so she shut the curtains to the dining room and sat down at the table with Morgan.

Chapter Twenty-two

Lahar's fiery hair and her emerald green eyes distracted even the most pious male souls. She thought about how she used so many men over the years. She used them for money to eat in the harsh Ireland winter season. As she smiled, her red hair swirled around her in a cascading shower of sunny fire. Finally, she and her sister witches would be free from the hell of being destitute, living in an old Irish black house. Lahar cast another seeing spell and she watched intently as she saw a grouping of three women, one didn't seem to have any powers, one was a witch...and the other? *Vampire? Surely not...* She saw the golden colored woman smile showing fangs a little as she did. *Blimey, a damn vampire! Well, didn't see that one coming at'tall, mind ya...even after watchin' so long. Have to up the game, we will!*

Lahar ushered her sisters to come over and look in on the Americans too. Edon and Isador came quickly and looked in the glass surface of the bowl filled with water at their nemesis. Neither understood until Lahar pointed out Pandora to them. "Vampire..."

"I see and what in bloody hell we supposed to do about that?" Isador asked.

"Kill her of course. Can't let her catch hold of us, now can we?" Lahar said to her sister.

"Not on yer life and yer life ain't worth nothin'." Isador laughed.

"And yers be worth tons more 'n mine?"

"Nah. Either way, we bloody well better be prepared for that one, yeah."

The sister witches looked on, studying the American women, learning all they could from watching them.

Lahar hoped it would all end the way she and her sisters pictured, with mayhem and macabre being the main events.

If they could set about gaining access to the statue the women recovered, the one that gave them chills when they learned about it from their book of shadows, they would finally be able to bring about the apocalypse as promised in the old texts. With demons roaming the earth, the witches would finally get their comeuppances. Lahar couldn't wait to see what the earth looked like with a new décor and fire everywhere. She, Edon, and Isador would reap the rewards of their task, placing the demons on earth as rulers once more. The time had come to sacrifice human life for a better one. Unleashing hell on earth would be their greatest triumph amongst humankind. There would be no more living like Paupers and fending for themselves.

The wind billowed out of the windows of the drafty cottage. Candles blew out. Smoke rolled from the fire and three witches cackled like a maddening force of nature to be reckoned with. All too soon, the time would come to fight for what they wanted more than anything, to leave their mortal lives behind them.

***

Time was crawling by in South Dakota. For the two Free Masons, they were on the longest plane ride they'd ever gone on. There wasn't a faster way to get to what was left of Mr. O'Connell's family. His son might have been missing or dead, but he had to protect Jen and Little Warren. He never heard much about her but, what he heard were good things. He didn't believe she had anything to do with his son's disappearance. And the Scottish "They take care of their own."

While time was crawling so slowly, everyone that came in contact with the statue had a hard time breathing because of the impending possibilities of doom, their mind's thoughts were fraught with peril. Warren Sr. had nothing to do, but sit in a plane seat and contemplate scenarios. He was too worried to sleep. His age was beginning to show.

He wondered if she knew much about him at all. He wondered if Warren ever talked about him. He thought probably not. Warren Jr. spent a long time being angry with him. His mother was partly to blame. She was still upset at him for not being around much and when he was, he wasn't allowed to talk about work because it was dangerous and top secret. He couldn't tell her that he was out there fighting to save the world. He was always on missions to quell threats, but he could never tell anyone.

Warren Sr. sat on that plane also thinking about how much he still loved his son's mother even though she hated him. He paid his alimony, but he still had the same feelings he had for her all those years ago. He also loved his son, no matter what his son thought of him. That was why he was going to America, to help his family.

The plane would land in a few hours. Warren Sr. was glad. He was tired of sitting on that plane. He was ready to exterminate witches if he had to. Most of all, he was ready to finally meet his son's family, the ones his boy hadn't gotten the chance to bring home for a visit to Scotland.

With Sir MacAfee sitting beside him sleeping and snoring in his ear, Warren Sr. wasn't going to sleep. He opened the spell book he brought with him to memorize. It would have been good for him to brush up on his skills as a warlock, in case he'd needed to use them. He didn't know there was one witch and a vampire there to help them fight as he'd had little time to discuss anything with his would-be daughter-in-law.

Chapter Twenty-three

While Jen was sleeping, Pandora had a serious talk with Morgan about how the fighting was going to go. They formed a plan they would later have to tell the Scotsmen about. While she and Morgan were downstairs, she found and opened a box she sent for from a far off place she stored her things when she was running from King Anderson.

Pandora placed the box on the table. When Morgan saw the box, at first, her eyes widened. She feared wooden boxes as they had the means to kill her or others around her. That particular wooden box was a small six-inch by two-inch box and it had ornate carvings on it that reminded Morgan of some of the ancient Egyptian hieroglyphs found on the Chaos Box. Pandora saw fear and smiled her gentlest smile, beckoning Morgan to sit at the table with her.

"This was given to me by my magic teacher to protect me when I was human. The box simply says, 'To Protect the Ones You Love.' I want you to have it. I think you could use it just in case things go bad in the fight. It will protect you. If someone sends a spell your way while you wear this, it will deflect off of you and hit the caster instead." Pandora opened the box and smiled down at the old talisman she used to wear. It had been hundreds of years since she looked at it.

"How is a necklace going to help me?" Morgan asked her.

"Like I said, this is no ordinary necklace. I will have to have someone else try to hit you with a spell for it to work. You know I can't really do much magic anymore, not enough to show you what it does," Pandora said. She took the necklace out of the box. It was a big red ruby-looking jewel surrounded by gold on a golden chain. It would have gained great heirloom status had it been in circulation. "It could have been worth a lot of money if anyone ever found it and tried to sell it, good thing they never knew it existed. It also has a special power. It can sometimes work its own bit of magic using your courage. It glows and when it does, something really special happens," Pandora added.

"Wow. Is it a real ruby?" Morgan wondered.

"No, it's a red crystal. They're really rare. This is the only one I've ever seen and I've seen a lot of different things in my day," Pandora explained to Morgan. "Go ahead and put it on. You need to get familiar with it. When I leave, you must never take it off. I don't want to be out there in the world, worrying about you two," Pandora said in a kindly voice.

"Don't worry, I won't. We seem to need all the help we can get these days." Morgan stood up and hugged Pandora for the gift.

"Consider it a gift from teacher to student and from friend to friend." Pandora hugged her back.

They both looked at the time and saw it was dwindling. It would soon be time to wake Jen and talk to her about everything, in hopes of trying to help her. Neither of them really wanted to have that kind of talk with her. They both felt she was slowly going insane. However, the risk of her being in the middle of everything without a way to help fight would put them all in danger and they couldn't have that.

Just as they both decided they had to wake her up and talk to her, they heard Jen screaming. It sounded like someone was killing her in her sleep. Pandora raced up the stairs before Morgan could hardly move. When Pandora reached her room and walked in, she saw something unexplainable. It was a good thing Morgan decided to haul it up there as fast as she could, or she might not have seen it.

There was a whirling blue light in the middle of the room and in the center of the illumination stood a figure. Jen was still asleep on her bed, but she was screaming, she was having another nightmare. Morgan wanted to know what was going on so she asked the figure what it thought it was doing. The figure held its silence and smiled an angelic smile at her.

Morgan raised a hand to hurl a spell at the apparition, but it put its finger to its mouth as if to say, "shhh." She lowered her hand and stood there gawking. All the while, Jen went from screaming to talking in her sleep. Whatever the apparition was, it was calming her down while she slept.

Finally, the whirling blue light started to vanish and the apparition began to look familiar to Morgan. When the light completely faded, she couldn't believe her eyes. She saw Warren standing there. She never knew how the screaming stopped all those times before. She had tears in her eyes, looking at him. All he did was stand there, smiling at her. She wanted so much to ask him about Blake and if they were okay after they passed away.

It was as if he read her mind, he whispered "yes" to her. And all the while Pandora stood there frozen, her mind running a hundred miles an hour, trying to contemplate what she saw.

Morgan thought to herself, *Will you come again?* He whispered "yes" again to her. After that, he disappeared.

Both Morgan and Pandora tiptoed back out of Jen's bedroom to talk in the hall.

"What the hell did we just see?" Pandora asked Morgan.

"That was Warren, I guess, in spirit form," Morgan said, still shocked.

"What? How? How is that possible?"

"I don't know, but that was him. I guess he's really the one who's been looking out for her when she's sleeping, not me," Morgan said, smiling.

After seeing the apparition, Pandora wanted to quickly explain what she planned to do to help Jen, so Morgan wouldn't be caught off guard with her methods.

"I'm going to have to confound or compel her. I'm doing it, so I can make her forget about her outburst so she stays sane. She needs the help and we need her, so I don't see a choice. I think your magic will work better if she's beside you so you know she's okay," Pandora explained.

"Just like in the dungeon, she was right there, stronger than ever and pissed. Yeah, I agree, we don't need her to be a mess. She needs to be there. I really don't think I could do it without her. She gives me spirit I don't have without her. And you're right, we need her strong again instead of the mess she turned into," Morgan said. "I don't know her like that and I don't like it."

"I know. She'll eventually be okay, but right now we have to force it. After all of this is over, you need to tell her what we just saw in there. I think it will help her to know that in a way he's still here looking after her," Pandora said.

"Okay, time to wake her up," Morgan said, deciding to deal with her however she awoke.

Pandora and Morgan walked back into Jen's bedroom. They both sat on the ends of her bed and Morgan called to her softly, shaking her lightly. It never took much to rouse her, so she opened her eyes. They were squinty at first. Then she glared at the others. She was mad at them both.

"I heard you. I'm not letting you use mind control on me. No matter how much you think it would help my broken heart," Jen said in between seething glances at the two figures on her bed. "I have the right to grieve like a normal person. And for your information, I would have stood beside you in a fight no matter what. You guys didn't have to think you needed a plan to get me to do what you wanted. It's not like you really need my help anyway."

"That's where you're wrong. I seriously don't think Morgan would be as powerful if you weren't here. She tries to be strong for you. Magic is tied to emotions a lot of times and without you and your son to think about, she wouldn't be very effective. She's better because of the two of you," Pandora said.

"I think she's right. When I know I have my best friend beside me, I feel like I can do anything. Maybe that's your power. You help others be better. It's not real magic but maybe it is. I mean, you're special in your own ways and I need you with me in this. There's no way I can do it without you. Please, don't be mad at us for trying to help you feel better. All we wanted was for you to stop feeling so sad and helpless," Morgan said. "You're not helpless, girl. You're so damn strong. I used to wonder how you could do it. After the guys died and you found out you were pregnant, you didn't fall apart like I figured you would."

"People change, Morgan. We changed. That doesn't mean I'm strong. That means I'm a messed up danger whore. That's about it," Jen said with her resolve starting to break.

"Yes, it does. Damn it. You and I have seen some of the sickest stuff a human has ever seen and we're both still alive. That means something, I know it does," Morgan pleaded with Jen.

"It just means we're some sick ass individuals, sicker than we realized," Jen said.

"Okay, enough of this, both of you. We need to be preparing for our company and the battle ahead. Come on, let's get on with this," Pandora said. The three of them descended the staircase and went to sit in the living room and wait for Warren Sr. to call them for directions to their house.

***

The plane landed when the sun was still up and the moon was beginning to show in the sky. It was stark and blue. The Free Masons called and got directions to their destination then called a cab to get them there.

Warren Sr. was quiet in the cab like he had been on the plane. He was anxious and nervous about the circumstances with which he would meet Jen. He wished they were better ones. For a man of fifty, he didn't appear as weathered on the outside as his heart felt on the inside. His mind took a beating as well over everything that happened in the past two weeks. He also never sat down and thought about his son being dead until then. He had a hard time with that as well. There would never be a good time to ask Jen what *really* happened to him. And he surely didn't have any intention of offending her or hurting her feelings.

He kept telling himself, his emotions were not going to get the better of him. He was in control of himself, he wouldn't make an ass out of himself, nor would he worsen the situation by being around. He also knew too much time had gone by for his son to still be alive.

His thoughts bounced back and forth until finally he and Sir MacAfee arrived on the curb of the house Jen and Morgan lived in. Sir MacAfee shook him out of his daze and they both exited the cab with their things, paying the driver before they walked up the little sidewalk leading onto the porch and to the front door.

Warren Sr. felt something strange as he did this, as if he was being watched. He didn't know that he actually was being watched, although he felt it. He scratched his head, wondered for a moment, then he knocked quickly on the door, hoping they would open it fast and the feeling would go away.

Jen opened the door at the first knock and ushered the two men inside. Warren's father smiled at all of them. He was glad to see their faces. He liked to put names with faces so he would remember people better. Everyone introduced themselves then he hugged Jen and shook hands with the other women. He was genuinely happy to finally meet her.

While the meet and greet was going on, Pandora slipped out the back. No one noticed she was gone because they all started talking to each other right away. There was so much chattering going, everyone was busy quickly getting to know each other. Everyone said they wished they'd met on better terms and a lot sooner.

Chapter Twenty-four

Her eyes sparkled, shining with a brilliant light, slowly fading in the horizon until the darkness fell upon the land.

It was too late to turn back. She knew what she had to do. There was no other choice. She never wanted to kill. In the up and coming battle, she knew she might have to kill again. The thought of it terrified her. She would do what had to be done but not without guilt. When the battle was over, she'd have to leave. She didn't feel worthy of her human friends anyway. They had living, beating hearts. She loved them for their compassion, but she feared for them too.

Has life really come to this? Will leaving always be my pattern? She was so used to leaving to prevent danger from following her. It was such a tiresome way to live but, she felt after all these years, out of habit she almost had no choice.

Her golden eyes shed blood red tears. She didn't want to leave, but she had to. Those two young women had to find their way back down the path to normalcy, with her in the picture it would never happen. "When you love something or someone you have to let them go sometimes in order to do what's right for them."

The tears flowed a little while longer until she saw bright lights that looked like lightning in the direction of Jen and Morgan's neighborhood. It was time. Pandora wiped away the blood tears and ran toward her friends as fast as she could.

Even as she ran, she saw multi-colored lightning. It scared her. She wondered what the neighbors would see and what they would think was going on outside. Most of all, she wondered about her friends. She hoped the Free Masons had their back. She also wondered what they might do to her when she showed up seemingly out of nowhere. *Are they going to understand I'm on their side?* She definitely hoped so.

When Pandora arrived in the neighborhood, things were flying through the air because the wind picked dramatically. There were seven people standing on opposite sides of the street from each other. She saw her chance to go up to her friends. Morgan and Jen stood on their side of the street holding hands with intent looks on their faces. They both looked at her and smiled. The Free Masons, on the other hand, didn't pay too much attention to her just yet.

She put her hand on Morgan's shoulder to tell her silently that she could handle the fight. Morgan looked at that hand and then up to Pandora and smiled a mischievous grin of understanding and looked on more intently than before as if to say "Thank you, friend."

Pandora's black flowing hair blew in the intense wind, but Jen and Morgan remembered to put theirs up so it wouldn't be in their way during the fight. They also wore the appropriate clothing, jeans that weren't too snug and a t-shirt in case they started to sweat. They fought often enough with myths to know when and what to be ready for.

Pandora, on the other hand, hadn't fought anything but her own kind out of pure necessity.

The Free Masons finally noticed she joined them because of her hair blowing in the wind and looked at her in surprise. They didn't know what she was. Jen looked at them as if to say "It's all right." Warren Sr. relaxed a bit. Pandora stood there sheepishly smiling at them with her fangs showing. *Better late than never,* she thought.

Pandora noticed as she stood there, the three witches across the street were staring at her too. She came out of nowhere and surprised them. It was by far not an even playing field, five against three, but the witches were still going to try to change that. They had their hands raised and their eyes focused on the two older gentlemen. Pandora saw this and went to stand beside them. And if she had to, she would stand in front of them. They were human and had to live, she was already dead. She wasn't going to let any of them die if she could help it.

***

It became a day of reckoning. Jen was scared but knew she'd give it her all. She had everyone she cared about, except her mom and son, by her side. It wasn't going to be easy, but she would try with every fiber in her being to help protect the world from demonic takeover.

At that moment, standing in the street, she thought about so many things. She was trying to remain focused but, she was losing her nerve as her thoughts drifted in and out. She thought about Warren and what his take on their fights with supernatural beings might have been. She thought about her son. She thought about other things that seemed silly to her. For some reason, she was losing focus fast and didn't know why; her friends sensed it.

"Jen, pull it together. I need your help. I can sense you ain't with me on this. What're you thinkin' about?" Morgan asked her.

"It's hard to explain, everything, I guess. At first, I was thinking about Warren, then I thought about Little Warren. Then it got all jumbled up and silly," Jen said, baffled.

"I think it's a spell. One to make you lose concentration, so I can't harness your energy," Morgan said. "I've heard about those spells, they're old."

"Damn it! Is there any way to make it stop?" Jen asked her.

"Yeah, stop thinking about anything at all. It's inside your head. It can only take hold if you let it. Stop letting it. Just meditate something over and over," Morgan said.

"Okay, I can do that. I practice a mantra for times like these." Jen winked.

The true fighting had just begun. Jen wasn't going to let them break her spirit. Even if that meant being down on her knees begging God to make any pain they inflicted on her stop. She wasn't giving up or giving in.

***

As Morgan stood beside Jen holding her hand for dear life, she saw curses fly and people stand like it didn't have any effect on them, even though it did. The witches stared at her like she was the main target of their death assault. She didn't want to die. Her confidence was fading and that was no spell. She shouldn't have been thinking about losing the battle. She should have been thinking about winning it instead, but she wasn't.

Morgan wondered what would happen if they lost, then she trembled at the thought. Jen turned her head in Morgan's direction. She felt her friend shudder. Morgan held on tighter and held up her other hand, saying her spells with enthusiasm. She didn't want to die that night or any other night. She had to find the confidence to do what she needed to do. She wasn't only battling for herself but for the world. As heavy as it was, she had to make it good for the sake of all.

No matter what, Morgan had to try her best. Without her, they would surely lose the fight. She was needed and wanted, cared about. She hadn't gotten it through her head yet that she, Sir MacAfee, and Mr. O'Connell were the only ones with enough power to stop them at their fingertips. If she'd thought about that instead of mainly deflecting spells, they could've cast spells together which would have been more effective from the beginning.

The other witches knew that tactic. However, it didn't matter. *We're here to win*, Morgan thought, *whatever it takes.*

***

The curses and spells flew in both directions. It was hard to deflect something when no one knew who was aiming at whom. It took a while of throwing whatever they could at each other before both sides of the fight began to become exhausted.

The sky turned green, giving off the appearance of an impending tornado, something that wasn't indigenous to South Dakota and made neighbors curious about what was going on outside. There were a lot of eyes on the group. The wind stopped blowing and the trees were still. No birds made a sound. The outside climate gave off the definite appearance and aspect of a tornado, but there wasn't one coming.

All the people in the street looked up into the sky. Many of them had never seen such a thing, they were unaware that they were the cause of it. While Morgan and Jen's group were looking up, the witches took the chance to blast them. Suddenly, the Talisman Morgan wore glowed bright red and flashed its own magic at the witches, throwing them to the ground.

Before the Irish witches could stand up again and prepare for another assault, the wind froze and objects carried on the wind stuck in mid-air as if time were frozen. The swirling blue lights came again. This time, they were brighter and there were more of them. Two familiar figures stepped out of the swirling lights. Everyone but Morgan and Pandora gawked at the sight of Warren and Blake reincarnate.

Warren's father shed a tear when he saw his son. "M'boy… What tha' hell's this, now?"

"We came to stop all the fighting, Da. We accidentally caused this and I'm sorry," Warren's ghost told his father. He then looked at Jen and smiled. "Baby, I'm so proud of you. You're so strong."

"Warren…" Jen said with tears in her eyes. "I miss you so much."

"I know you do. I wish I had more time to talk to you, but we have to finish this," Warren said. "Maybe they'll let us come back soon to talk."

The conversation and emotions were the same for Blake and Morgan. Then the two ghosts turned to the three enemies across the road who stood staring in shock the whole time.

The light that surrounded the two ghosts grew bright again. Both extended their hands and fire came from them, shooting across the road like fire from a water hose going full blast. The witches were being burned alive. The flames rose into the sky like a bonfire. The sounds the group heard next were excruciatingly painful cries of agony.

Finally, the witches disappeared into dust floated off in the returning gale force winds. When the ashes were gone, the blue swirling lights grew brighter. It was time for the ghosts of Warren and Blake to go back to wherever they had been.

"I guess this is good bye, again, at least for a while," Warren said to all of them, looking into Jen's teary eyes.

"Yes, we have to go now. We love you, though, very much," Blake said as he stood near Morgan with sadness on his face.

It was harder to leave that time because even though they had no choice, Blake and Warren wanted to stay with Jen and Morgan. They both knew how hard life had been for the two females without them and how much they suffered, they also missed them and were secretly watching the whole time. Morgan knew because she caught Warren in Jen's room earlier in the day comforting her in her sleep.

***

Morgan shed a lot of tears when the bright blue swirling lights and the figures disappeared. Jen hugged her and cried, too. Warren Sr. and Sir MacAfee stood there contemplating the last five minutes. Tears flowed slowly down Warren Sr.'s face. His suspicions were fully confirmed, he son was dead. With the truth came a longing sadness.

Everyone walked up to the porch and sat on the colorful chairs and the porch swing. For a while, no one said a word. They were exhausted and the night wasn't over yet. The neighbors might have seen something. It was up to Sir MacAfee and Pandora to put the neighborhood right again. It had to appear as if a storm hit over the last few hours, at least for the neighbors.

The whole group waited until the fight was over before they ever said a word about what they saw or what they had done. When they started talking, it was loud because everyone started talking at once. No one noticed the tired feeling giving way to adrenaline. They were on a natural high that kept them talking until morning. The house was lit up like a raging kegger was going on, but the noise level wasn't as bad; there was talking, laughing, and a little drinking going on.

They all laughed at how shocked the three witches were when some of the fighting was going on. When the guys showed up, the shock the witches displayed was the funniest thing they'd ever seen.

Chapter Twenty-five

It was early in the morning before anyone got the notion to go to bed. The night was spent enjoying the company of others after the battle was over. Jen thought it was the best night she had in a long time. She really liked Warren's dad and Sir MacAfee was interesting, too.

He made them laugh a lot telling them about his thoughts during the battle. Being brought to laughter after such a traumatic experience was healthy for them, Jen thought. It was normal.

Jen looked at all the faces sitting around the table from her and smiled a warm smile. Family used to mean everything to her, she felt like it would again, which was as it should be. She thought about sunshine, flowers, and her son. She also thought about what the world was going to be like without the imminent dangers they'd faced in it anymore. That made her happier.

Later that day, Jen drove over to get little Warren from her mom's house, so he could meet his grandfather. She explained to her mom that she knew he was going to come in late and didn't want to have to wake the baby to get him from the airport. Her mom bought the story. She also told her mom what the CIA was looking for a couple of weeks ago was something Warren Sr. came to the U.S. to find. Her mom bought that story, too.

After retrieving the baby, she drove back home. He was happy to see her and acted like he slept well.

He cooed at his house when he saw it. Jen laughed out loud and brought him inside. Everyone was happy to see him and played with him until he got tired and had to take a nap. Warren Sr. especially enjoyed his company. Pandora took pictures of the group playing with the baby.

All seemed good in the land of Jen and Morgan, but there were still a few tasks left. Jen could feel something was left undone. She was right. Pandora took the chance to tell them she was leaving after Jen put little Warren down for a nap. It crushed her that Pandora wanted to go. Pandora hugged both Morgan and Jen, explaining how dangerous it would be for her to stay and how it would screw up their chance at a normal life. Just because it made sense for Pandora to go didn't mean any of them wanted her to.

***

Pandora left a few days after the battle. She wanted to make sure her friends were okay and would adjust to everything in the real world again. Pandora knew things took time, but hers was passed. She did what she set out to do.

Again, she watched the town from a hill overlooking it at dusk. She stood beside a big tree on the hill looking down, seeing the people and cars below her moving on with their lives like she never existed. To them, she didn't. That's the way she wanted it.

She looked down beside the tree she was standing near and saw flowers growing around it. She picked one and sniffed it. The mortal world had many things she would miss, she was glad she got to act like a part of it, if only for a little while. She smiled at the sky as dusk changed its beautiful colors again to darker shades closing in toward twilight.

The memories she made with Jen and Morgan would be her favorites, there was no question. Her immortal mind would hold them with fondness forever. She felt a deep sadness inside her heart for them, too. She also knew without a doubt that a fighter with a warrior's heart and spirit could survive. That's what her two human friends were. No matter where the wind blew her, she would think of them and rejoice in knowing they were fine again.

It was time to go. The stars were shining and the moon was full. She put the flower she picked inside her jacket and zipped it up. She ran as fast as she could away from a place she grew to love. The life of the undead was a lonely one, something she got tired of over the years, but she knew she couldn't change it even if she wanted to. She never wanted the humans to get hurt or killed for knowing her. So, it was back to solitude and on the roads she traveled again. This time, it was for leisure instead of hiding. She could finally take in the wonders around her without worrying so much about being hunted like an animal.

There were so many things she'd like to have had time to see, it was time to see them. Although her fondness for her human friends would probably warrant a silent visit or two over the years, to make sure they were okay and to see how big the baby would grow.

***

As neatly as it began, another chapter in the life of Jen and Morgan ended without a sound. A door came open and was now shutting on the old life, once again opening a window to something new. New relationships with relatives formed. Mortal bonds with other humans came to be, new friends surfaced and old wounds healed themselves. For Jen, that was a huge relief, a weight lifted from her shoulders. She and Morgan could carry on with being who they wanted to be, no more nightmares from the past to haunt them, no more sadness and mourning. Pictures of new memories were all they needed to remind the two of them not to turn back the hands of the clock or look in their mental closets anymore. The memories were too lonely to visit anymore. It was time to move on and make the most from their life that was trying so hard to forge its way into the present. The rest of the year would be a good year if it killed them.

PART FOUR
Possession

The Light (Battle March)

Come ye witches…cast your spells
Let demons, take your flank.
Present your queen, but we'll not kneel
For evil has no rank.

Send forth your magic; we will stand
Our banner, proud unfurled.
Our weapons wield, with righteous hand
Will render void, your world.

And if we die, we will not die
Like cowards, cowed in fright.
But with our last breaths, we will sigh
We go now to the light.

You think us weak and hardly foe
That's worth your while to meet
But you'll think differently, I know
When ye lie at our feet.

We ask no quarter and you'll find
We'll give just what we get.
Prepare to be, with darkness twined
Your lives, will pay your debt.

And if we die, we will not die
Like cowards, cowed in fright.
But with our last breaths, we will sigh
We go now to the light.

—Chris Birrane

Chapter Twenty-six

Morgan awoke for many nights as a child with nightmares, the kind she was abruptly awakened from again in her adult life. She felt like she did when she was a child, sweaty and scared. Morgan never told a soul about them and doubted it would do any good as an adult to spill her secrets onto the floor like a fool, but she thought she might have to anyway.

She sat up in bed thinking something was different about that particular dream versus the others. She never knew the true origin of the nightmares or why she had them. The historical figure, Rasputin, was never in them before. In her dream, he kept calling Morgan by a different name. He called her Catherine, which confused her further. He kept saying he was coming for her. He said, *"I'm coming for you, Catherine, my love."* She was baffled and scared, she didn't *want* to understand.

Morgan crept down the hall, across the crème Berber carpet, to the staircase on the top floor of the house she shared with her best friend. She crept down the stairs and into the living room where she sat on the couch in the dark thinking about what her mind had shown her. She needed to find out why she had dreams of the same ornate room in the same palace as she did when she was a child. What did a man fitting the horrible description of Rasputin, the trusted adviser to Alexandra Romanov, have to do with her? Why would he come to her in her dreams and talk to her while she looked at her own face in the mirror? None of it made sense to her. The black beard as long as his waist, the staff with the green glowing orb sitting on top, his green glowing eyes, the same shade as the ball on the stick in his hand. *I don't remember him being in the dream as a kid. What changed so drastically that I'm seeing ghosts again?* she questioned herself. *What upcoming event is making this happen?*

Something must have been getting ready to come to their door again. She knew the tell-tale signs of something unwanted and dangerous seeking them out. She and Jen were pros at spotting them.

She had more questions, such as: *Why does he call me Catherine? Catherine who? What does he want with me?* She pondered her thoughts until the sky got lighter blue, which meant daylight was coming. She and Jen had another full day of chasing a little curly-headed boy all over the house.

Mediocrity had become something the best friends craved, being as they never saw it much in the days of their life as Research Assistants/Mythical Warriors. Playing all day with little Warren was a favorite pastime for them. They both tried to seek adult company and it never worked out, so they simply relied on the child to give them peace and fill their hearts with happiness. It usually worked until last night, when Morgan's head was filled with an old dream and a new fear. It was time to bring up an old secret, open an old wound, and find out why she had those dreams when she was a child. She didn't have a choice.

***

Hundreds of Russian Artifacts Stolen, Still Missing

[Russia, 1917] *The streets were paved with gray cobblestones. Fires were burning here and there. Wild-eyed, starving people stood around the burning fires trying to stay warm. Their ragged clothing and kerchiefs didn't help when it was cold and snowing. The chilly wind attacked them fiercely.*

Some of the wild-eyed people looked into the streets at the many piles of bodies gathered in heaps. Blood ran into the lines of the cobblestone roads. It crept into the cracks in the stones, seeping into the earth below. The bodies were a way of showing the war was not over, there would be more to come.

It didn't matter how much blood was shed, only that it was. Those bodies had not only been shot but gutted as well. Entrails and open carcasses of humans littered the streets. Something wasn't right about that war. It was the bloodiest time Russia had ever known.

No one in the rest of the world had seen a more horrifying battleground as that one. Families were completely destroyed in front of their homes and children dead but still clinging to their mother's hands.

Horrifying wasn't a proper description for what was seen by the barely alive survivors of the massacre. They weren't sure what they were really seeing as they stood there looking on with the dazed eyes of crazed men and hunger forcing them to see what may not have been there. They saw a demon stroll through the wrecked streets like it was on vacation in the happiest place it had ever been. They could not recall for sure though because they thought their eyes may have played tricks on them.

Aremis, a demon of death and war, grinned ear to ear as he walked among the humans. He craved blood, with the dead and dying souls all around him, his heart sang a lovely tune of resounding joy.

[Russia, Present Day] *Aremis in Rasputin form lived in the Underworld and he was tired of it down there. He became a demon to live longer. He thought it would help him gain the power he needed to conquer the world. The only thing he ever accomplished was making the ruler of the Underworld mad at him for not getting enough souls to join him there. His powers were great, but human nature to be good must have been stronger. Oh, he had fun getting some of them to come with him but not all would go. The loophole had always been self-sacrifice.*

In Russia, there were still at least one hundred and seventy-eight missing, lost, and stolen artifacts missing from museums. Many teams of people had been sought out to help Russia find its treasures. The treasures included many famous paintings, jewelry, religious icons, silverware, and richly enameled objects worth millions of dollars.

Amidst the thievery going on, no one had a clue a demon was behind it or had anything to do with it, the country of Russia assumed it had to do with hunger and poverty. The reality was, the demon Aremis, who disguised himself as Rasputin, planted the ideas that made the thieves take the art.

He wanted to destroy the Russians by any means necessary and to get his Catherine to come back to him. He had finally thought he found her after searching all across time for her. It had taken him many decades to find Catherine the Great. She was no longer in Russia. He formulated a plan to get her back to her country. Aremis was working on the soul of her descendant for a long time, preparing it as a vessel for her. She looked exactly like Catherine, but she didn't know who she was. He used to visit the girl in her dreams at night, she grew up still not knowing her true heritage. He was going to get her to Russia and teach her. It was the only way he could think of to get Catherine back. He missed her all those years.

His Catherine was a warring, territorial queen. He loved that passion about her. It could come to that again. He also had an old score to settle with the people of Russia for how the court—including Catherine—died. No one knew he was anything more than a trusted ally, but he was so much more to her and she was more to him than a queen.

Aremis's eyes used to only glow green when they were together and all alone. His magic was something he hid from the entire court except her. She knew exactly who he was and he knew her intimately. He spent too much time without his love. He didn't much care how long or how much of power he used, he would have her.

This was before Aremis used the guise of Rasputin. He looked like another trusted ally back in the days of Catherine. He was known as Serge back in those days. The 1700's were a time of war and passion. She hated her husband, he used that information to get close to her. He came in the form of a lover who gave her a son that hated her and only knew the king as his father. After she died, he remained dormant until the reign of Nicholas and Alexandra in the early 1900's. He befriended

Alexandra and used the friendship to gain influence in the kingdom.

Back then, Aremis used the guise of Rasputin and he stayed in that form until the present, where he saw his chances and took them, in order to resurrect the kingdom of Russia with Catherine and Alexandra by his side.

Chapter Twenty-seven

She sat at the table by the window overlooking the back yard, like she did many times before, looking out at her little piece of the world. She was once again thinking about her life. It was something vastly different than what she'd imagined. She never fathomed for a minute it would have turned out like this. She and her best friend strayed quite far from the path they each set for themselves. *So much for pompous assumptions and idealistic fantasies.* Sunny days used to mean much more to Jen than their current meaning. Now, when winter was finally over, dread filled her. She knew it was time to meet another supernatural creature that would try to kill them. *Spring be damned!* she thought. She pondered who or what it might be that stepped on their porch next. There was never time to lie low or run too far. The only option they ever had was to stand and fight. Their lives and the lives of others depended on it.

Later in the day, the mail came, a letter from a foreign country arrived. The next chapter of their lives was being written. Jen thought, *Oh shit, here goes...* It was addressed in English, but there were Russian alphabetical letters on it as well. Jen knew how to read just about any language she came across and Russian was no exception. The letter came from the Russian Museum Consortium. It was a request to help the Russians find lost art and artifacts, much of which was plundered long ago.

She read the letter then threw it on the table in the kitchen. It said they were needed and to call to make preparations as soon as Jen and Morgan were able. Jen rolled her eyes. She wasn't sure they needed to be going to Europe, at least not without visiting Scotland and her new father figure. She thought about him and smiled. He was kind to the girls since meeting them a few years back. Her son now knew some of his family, which also made her happy. They talked to him via video chat a lot. Technology was great.

Morgan came in from the yard soon after the letter came. She entered the kitchen and saw it on the table. She looked down at it and didn't say a thing. She knew what it probably was. She felt a little bit frightened and thus Jen felt it, too. Jen didn't like sharing feeling with Morgan that much. There was a line to all things and sharing feelings crossed that line.

She gave Morgan a stern look and asked her what was going on. "Morgan, what is it this time? You're making me feel scared and I hate sharing without knowing why."

"I had a dream a few nights in a row about an ornate room where I was looking at my face in a mirror. I used to have that dream a lot when I was a girl. It went away, but then, the other night the dream came back. This time, there was this guy standing behind me, saying things in Russian to me. He was creepy. He had white skin and black hair. His beard hung to his waist. And he had this staff with a green orb that glowed on top of it. His eyes glowed green, too. He told me he was waiting for me and called me 'Catherine, my love,'" Morgan explained.

"Oh, okay. I thought it was something scary…" Jen said, trailing off. She started to feel her own fears then. She wondered about the new puzzle, but it felt like a few pieces were missing. Confusion was her next set of thoughts. It would be a while before they got all the pieces together. She walked away from Morgan, who stood there looking scared and slightly taken aback to it all. She wondered what the man meant by what he told her.

The day passed quickly. There was much research to be done on the new subjects at hand. It took them the rest of the afternoon to dig up things on the missing Russian art and Rasputin, this was the only clue they had as to who the man in Morgan's dreams might be. Morgan had no idea he was who was emulating until she saw pictures online of him with Alexandra Romanov of Russia. They had no clue he was the demon Aremis, strong and old, who wanted to control them and make them his. This thought never crossed their innocent minds.

The mysterious connection between Catherine and Rasputin didn't go unnoticed, however. She wondered why Rasputin from the 1900's would have anything to do with Catherine the Great of the 1700's. The only answer she had, thus far, was one word: *supernatural*.

"'The world is my oyster…' Just try not to get blood on it, k?" Jen said to Morgan randomly in the middle of researching. She looked up and smiled at her friend when said it. She loved occasionally quoting some of her favorite battle lines.

Morgan smiled back at Jen. "'While that thought is sardonic in nature and admirable as it might seem, you must accept the truth…this is not over.'" She brushed her long blonde hair behind her ears and looked at the screen of the laptop on her desk with a sigh that said, *Oh God, not again.* Quoting battle lines was silly fun at times of sheer boredom.

"'Because it never will be. We decide that every time we decide to live,'" Jen said. She smiled at Morgan with a mischievous smirk that said "We're crazy!" then returned to her research. Morgan returned the facial expression and said nothing. The battle lines they'd quoted were their own from over the years. This gave way to archaic hardening, wild expressions of knowing, their past was always with them.

It was a long day of links and printing documents they found over the Internet so they needed the banter. A file folder was made labeled "Russia." They printed the copies in Russian because they read the language and were tempted to think the Russians might tell the truth in their language because most English speakers couldn't read it. That theory worked in their favor because they found out things most Americans didn't know. They, however, weren't most Americans. They were ghost, witch, vampire, and demon defeating bitches no one wanted to mess with. Finding out the truth was like discovering gold in a copper mine. It was good.

Morgan also smiled when she opened her mind to the good memories of the last few years. Pandora, the vampire they befriended, left her knowing lots of spells and how to use them. The sadness of that time was, she left so her friends could live a normal life. As it turned out, that wasn't an option for Jen and Morgan. Morgan was glad to have Pandora's knowledge. The spells came in handy when Jen and Morgan had to battle a set of pissed off witches who thought Morgan killed their friends the previous year. The new witches didn't know the ghosts of Warren and Blake burned them or how good Morgan was at being a witch. Her fast education wasn't a deterrent of a lack of power by any means. She could do almost anything they could and they studied for many years. It didn't take the ghosts of Warren and Blake to help Morgan and Jen stand against them.

The next year, Jen and Morgan defeated a couple of demons and a few more witches. Every year since 2005, something came their way. Their new life was getting old, even though they knew their mission was to save the world from all evil beings. It was the job behind the job, hidden from the world, done in secret. There were absolutely no bonuses and no accolades when you killed creatures who wanted to murder you for standing in the way of their goal for domination. Jen and Morgan toughened themselves up doing the impossibly real things they did. Insanity carried them through a lot of rough parts when they needed it. It was same insanity that carried them through the first mission. It kept them alive while they were up against the ghost of an ancient, angry Viking warrior.

They raised a kid amidst the inner war always going on in their world, which, unfortunately, was set apart from the real world. The boy, belonging to Jen, was about four years old. He knew to hide when his mommy told him to and not to come out of his hiding place until she came for him. It was the only way to keep him safe from all the evil his mother and her friend dealt with. Their methods were over-protective, but logical because they loved Warren's baby boy. The two friends continued to live together for safety reasons. It wasn't out of love for each other as friends. They'd talked about selling the house and moving into separate places before the baby was born. It didn't happen, mostly to protect the boy.

Chapter Twenty-eight

Being trapped in the Underworld never detoured Aremis A.K.A. Grigori Rasputin from his goal, even if that meant causing bloodshed up above with his mere thoughts. He created evil dictators. There was so much blood on the ground in Russia at one time, it seeped through the dirt and straight into the pits of the Underworld. The demons feasted well for years. Revolutions took place and more blood was shed all over the world for the centuries. Territory was fought over above the beasts, more crimson goodness slipped through the cracks in the earth, sliding down into the primordial hell fires below.

Evil reigned in Russia for a long time due to the creatures buried below them. The people never understood they were controlled by otherworldly forces. The only ones who *did* know had already given their souls to evil in order to accomplish a dark goal. Some prayed for power and immortality, while the others had no idea demons were real; they prayed for evil reigns to end and the wars to be over.

There were silent times in Russia where no wars or bloodshed was present, in those lulls, the demons would make something happen. They hungered for chaos, famished and starving for the nectar of human lives. Aremis was one of the many millions of demons who craved vengeance and blood. The difference between him and the millions of others was that he somehow grew to be a favorite of Lucifer.

It was last known that he was looking for Catherine and he was about to happen upon her doppelganger to fill with her soul. He would have her forever. He helped her in her first life to win territories and gain rule over the serfdom of the land, which was wicked fun for him. He used his power to plant evil, hate-filled ideas in the hearts and minds of men for centuries. In this new generation, he mainly wanted her, all of her. He would have her soon. Not only did he thirst for the soul of his Catherine, but he wanted his other favorite queen by his side as well. Alexandra and Catherine had always given him what he needed to succeed in his warring 'life' and they would do so again. It was only a matter of time before he had them back and they did his bidding willingly.

It was time to conserve his energy, he would need all of it when they came to him. He already had the plan in motion. It was a simple plan, no more invading her dreams until she came to him. He wouldn't need to invade her dreams as much, he could take their minds because he would be closer to them. If Catherine didn't remember who she was, then he'd have no choice but to remind her. Alexandra, on the other hand, would be different, but her mind would be his, too. It would only be a matter of time before he had both of them bent to his will. He would put the spirits of his queens into the bodies of those girls.

It never took long to convince someone who wasn't too stable of their being insane. Those vessels were always one step away from the ledge. This was something he always felt about Catherine's vessel. Alexandra's vessel he saw in the memories of Catherine's. The two of them had no idea, they've been connected somehow their whole lives. It would come out in Russia though. It would be something they would have to learn to live with or not. He wanted his women back too badly to give the vessels any choice.

His game was played by his rules, the two women would play along whether they liked it or not. Aremis always did business this way, you either play or you pay. His demon eyes glowed green as he salivated over the plan to bring those women to their knees and make them his.

With greasy, grimy strands of hair falling in his face, he smiled a sharply wicked, knowing grin. His Catherine and his Alexandra were on their way back, he felt it. He wanted Catherine much more, but he loved them both and wanted them both by his side.

His Alexandra with her darker hair and blue eyes was not coming, but her ancestor was. He knew she was a distant relative of Alexandra, but she would do as a vessel. She even looked like her a lot except her eyes were brown. His Catherine was blonde with green eyes. Her vessel was almost a mirror image, a doppelganger.

Aremis' demon eyes glowed green and brightly. He saw his reflection in the mirror of the room. It was with discord that he looked at his true form; dark, deadening, sharp, and scary. Behind him, he saw gold gilding on the walls and white paint. He remembered the room he was standing in. He lived in a room not far from that one. It was after nightfall. He was standing there looking in the mirror, thinking about his queens, burning inside over the return of his women.

That would mean his return to power over Russia. The people would get what they deserved for trying to kill him twice, especially after he healed the son of Czar Nicholas trying to show good faith. That really pissed him off. Aremis must not have been convincing enough for the cousins, the rat bastards were actually smart enough to catch on. After that, he was condemned to the Underworld for a long while. He could only partly control things above him and he hated it. After a while, Aremis had his strength back and the people forgot about his deeds. It was time for him to come back and show them all. Bloodlust was also on his mind. The blood excited him beyond reason.

Aremis had pictures in his mind of the past, all those times he caused bloodshed. It made him smile; toothy, yellow, wide, and sharp. His passion had been one in the same all those years. He did it for the blood. Even being sent back into the Underworld was worth every drop he sent to his kin below. To many, he would have been known as a proverbial vampire when it came to the crimson liquid. His joints ached for it.

While looking in the mirror, he saw the Underworld and all the people down there counting on him to get them what they needed. Fires raged and ravaged people, screaming took place all around. Some called it hell, he called it home. He only answered to one person, and Lucifer was a demanding king of hell. The common goal was souls and bloodshed. Keeping the world in chaos wasn't easy. Aremis wasn't the only upper-level demon out there, but he was the one Lucifer trusted to get the job done.

Aremis thought about his people in the Underworld, imagining it was raining blood, slowly putting out the fires, soaking the rocks and caverns at the bottom of everything. It was only a daydream, but it was the best one he ever had. He imagined the whole earth would be on fire, all the humans were either dead or dying and the seas were red. Fire was falling from the sky, landing in the water with a bloody splash. He smiled at that, which was his deepest wish. Armageddon was such a lovely word to Aremis. He saw more things that pleased him, but he didn't have time to spend daydreaming about his favorite things. He had to get the stage ready for his queens to come back to him. It would take time, the human world was a complex place in present times.

Aremis in Rasputin form was once again thinking about the past and the future. He was also thinking about how pleased he was, knowing his plan was working. And how ready he was for the violence that would come from it.

Demons would be released upon the earth and there was nothing to be done to stop it. He was looking forward to seeing the humans trying to exterminate each other, there would be blood coating the streets of St. Petersburg.

The fountains would overflow with crimson liquid and people would run screaming in the streets only to be caught like rats and killed in front of a courtyard filled with others made to watch it. *There's nothing like a mass execution*, he thought and smiled his most wicked smile. He was consumed with how the blood would flow into the cracks in the streets and seep into the Underworld, unleashing more of his kind.

Aremis stood before a big window as the rain poured and thunder boomed overhead. Shadows cast themselves over the walls behind him as lightning flashed. The streets were soon wet with rain and he looked down at them, soon he would be seeing red rain falling, hitting the streets below. His desires would be made a reality.

He walked away from the window smiling, he felt a strong force was coming his way. Aremis didn't however, feel apprehensive about it. The thought of more of humans coming only made him smile more. He thought, *the more the merrier*. They could invite everyone they knew and it wouldn't be enough to stop him. He was only bidding his time until he had the vessels of his queens under his spell. Soon, so soon, he would reign on earth as his master did in the Underworld. Then Aremis' master would be able to come and join him in the new hell he would make in the mortal world.

The curtains billowed at the open window on the other side of the room. It was still raining and the white sheer curtains were wet, but blowing because the wind was howling, whirling the thunderstorm all over the land. It was the rainy season in Russia.

Chapter Twenty-nine

Jen and Morgan discussed the letter in much detail after they researched the possible angles of why it was sent to them.

"Do you wanna go? I mean, hey, it will pay well. And being responsible for finding some of the oldest paintings in history would be a nice bit to add to our resumes," Jen said.

"I know, but I don't know. My dreams make me feel like we shouldn't," Morgan said.

"I understand, but this could be an opportunity to learn more about the culture and everything," Jen explained.

"I get the feeling this is gonna be like Salem without the help of anyone. A possible disaster," Morgan said with dread. "I can't stand walking into those situations."

"Yeah, it drives me nuts too, but I think we need to help Russia. I mean, come on…just think of it. We really could help them recover some of their national treasures. How cool would that be?" Jen said. She was always the more persuasive one of the two, it usually caused trouble. She never brought up thoughts of supernatural elements, they always happened to pervade cases the women undertook. She just wanted to do the job.

"I know it would be very cool to help them, but I have a feeling we won't be leaving Russia the same as when we get there," Morgan said. The preternatural was what Morgan was concerned with. That's all she thought about, especially lately. The mood in the room changed to worry.

"God! Stop it! I know what you're saying. We have time to study up on ways to protect ourselves. We have a few days before we have to tell them if we're going or not. Just think it over. It could be a chance of a lifetime to help the Russians uncover and discover the missing and stolen artifacts. We took some kind of invisible unwritten oath to find what's hidden, remember?" Jen asked, trying to get her to relax and think about the job.

The wind kicked up outside and clouds were moving rapidly across the sky. Sioux Falls was experiencing a longer rainy season than the few previous years. Flower planting was out of the question that spring. Thoughts of planting hadn't entered Jen's mind, instead, her thoughts consisted of a new mission, one where they weren't consumed with saving the world.

She didn't know how much of her destiny was tied with Morgan's. She knew nothing of their relation to the Romanov family. She only knew the Romanov's had been executed by people who captured and held them because of overzealous rumors spread about them. She was going to discover a lot of things being covered up by demons and how long ago it started.

She knew centuries danced by with many wars; casualties of war, disease, famine, and hardships fed the demons all that time. She didn't know demons, of course, caused every event in history propagating evil. Humans were led to believe it was their true nature to be angry and violent. The violence was actually brought on by evil conspirators they couldn't see. The demons whispered in the ears of rulers, telling them things that made them angry or willing to fight. It never took a lot to make a raging monarch begin a war. The violent past of Eastern Europe was no secret. The constant battle over territory kept them angry and fighting for centuries. When the land lines were determined, the people decided they hated the harsh rulers and revolutions broke out. Demons ruled Earth and humans while God ruled the skies. In the present, there were still wars on the ground and violent acts all over the news. No one understood demons ruled the planet as long as they have. It was about time for a change. She would soon find out how much of their history was marred by the existence of demons and the true evil they could do.

While she was unable to do magic, Jen studied it anyway as a means of knowing that might come in handy in the future, for a precautionary measure.

A few days later, the two friends decided to go to Russia and help the museums find their cherished artifacts. It was supposed to be another job. It was a job that would take them away from home for three months so they had to get their papers in order and that took a little time and effort. Visas weren't easy to get unless everything was neatly squared away. They wrote a reply email to the museum that requested their help, telling them that they'd be there as soon as their papers were ready and arrangements were made for them.

***

Morgan awoke from another bad dream about a palace and a room with a mirror in it where she saw herself. She woke up next to Jen on a plane. It was dark inside the cabin of the aircraft, she was sweating. Jen looked at her through the darkened haze as if to ask, *Are you okay?* Morgan nodded. It was a lie. Jen felt otherwise, skittish and a bit scared. She knew it came from Morgan.

The two of them had a strong connection from all the time they'd spent together. It was only natural for Jen to respond to her moving and shivering sitting next to her asleep. Morgan had always dealt with the screaming of Jen in her dreams and Jen wanted to return the favor by being there for her in her time of need.

Jen softly whispered, telling Morgan she'd be okay. She also told her, they were about to touch down in Russia. Morgan wiped the sleep and tears from her eyes. She put her tray table up and buckled her belt. A stewardess came over the airwaves and told them to get ready for descent in both English and Russian.

After they landed, they got their bags and went outside. Morgan saw the sign with their names on it, held up by a driver. All three people piled in a tiny taxicab and drove away from the airport. It was cool in Russia compared to the U.S. in the spring and summer. Chilly winds blew all around them. Morgan got the chills just thinking about being on Russian soil. She was already scared. It was the place of her nightmares. She didn't care that they had a job to do. She wanted to go home from the moment she arrived. Normally, she wasn't the skittish one of the two. She'd always looked out for Jen when she got scared, but now it was her turn.

The taxi took them to the Neva River side of Pushkin into Saint Petersburg. It had beautiful scenery even with the cloudy skies making things appear darker. The streets were damp and the air was chilly, but the flowers were starting to come up and the trees were starting to turn green. The buildings didn't look cheerful by American standards. They appeared stark in the cloudy skies. Shadows were everywhere, watching their gloomy entrance into the city.

The stern glares of the people's faces weren't convincing of happiness either, they saw many on their way to the little apartment they'd be staying in while on Russian soil. The people were as gloomy as the weather. The taxi pulled up in front of a three-story apartment building, it looked like the cheeriest of all the buildings they drove passed. The driver said in Russian, "This is it. That will be fifty euros for the long ride." The two women understood him. They got out of the cab then grabbed their bags, paying the man his money.

Before Jen and Morgan got inside they had to find all their information on the building so they could use passcodes to enter. After that was done, they found their apartment on the third floor and went inside. It was large by Russian apartment standards and would accommodate them well for three months. The apartment had white walls and wood floors. It was nothing fancy, but still nice. It was set up for eight patrons, which meant two bedrooms, two sleeper sofas, and two full bathrooms. The place was light and airy. It was also bigger than they'd thought when they first reserved it online. It had all of its own bed linens and towels. The washer and dryer were in the kitchen with the fridge and stove. They had cable and high-speed Internet included, but they didn't plan on having time to watch TV.

Morgan planned in her head, she was there to work so she could get home faster. Her train of thought led to her body shivering. Her fear was coming to the surface again.

"Morgan, you're scared of something. What is it? I can feel it," Jen said.

"I don't wanna be here. I'm really scared that something is going to happen to us. Those dreams didn't *just* start. I had them as a child then they went away. If they came back there has to be a reason. I don't like being here. Something isn't right. You know every time one of us gets a bad feeling, something's going to happen. I have that feeling now," Morgan said.

"I know. We have a job to do. If we do it fast enough maybe we can get back home quicker," Jen said, filled with Morgan's foreboding feelings.

"I'm telling you, something fucked up is gonna happen. It's imperative to be fast," Morgan said, still shivering.

"I understand, but what can we do now? We just got here. It would be rude to not at least act like we're grateful to these people. We don't know how they might react. They might find American rudeness harsh and try to hurt us over it. We don't know them," Jen explained to Morgan. "You've got to calm down."

"Why is it our roles have reversed all of the sudden?" Morgan said.

"Because my nightmares went away and I'm sane. I've had more sleep than you in the last few days, I guess," Jen said. "We gotta pull ourselves together. We can't have them thinking we aren't capable of handling this task. We have to be professional."

"I know that and I know my emotions don't help, but I can't shake this. We just need to be careful," Morgan warned.

Having said their peace, Morgan and Jen went to unpack their things and put their books out where they could find them easily. It didn't take too long so they made a call to the office of the Russian Museum Consortium. Aremis answered, knowing it was the girls who were phoning in. He temporarily changed his form to be a museum worker so he could get the two of them to Russia. He would be "working" closely with them on the job. He was pleased to hear from them. He gave them an address and told them to report in two days, so they could adjust to the new surroundings.

After she hung up, she started shaking. She could feel it more than ever, coming to Russia was wrong. She didn't know what to do so she phoned Warren Sr. and talked to him. She explained why she thought they needed him and Sir MacAfee to come. He agreed something strange was on the rise and said they would make a flight out the next morning.

She felt better knowing she could bring in some heavy hitters who would come for no other reason than to put her at ease. Her bond with Warren Sr. and Sir MacAfee was almost as great as Jen's even though there was no relation between them. They bonded over the battle for the golden statue of King David I of Scotland a few years back. It was a tumultuous, mind shattering battle, but without each other it would have been certain death. Bonding over their experiences together made them family and family was all they had left.

Chapter Thirty

Jen looked out the window of the flat she shared with her best friend. Even Russian rain was dreary. She didn't like the rain, the gloominess overcast her heart. It was like a set of chains she longed to be free of. She sighed and went into the big living room, sitting on one of the sofas while Morgan paced the room, probably thinking about taking up smoking so she wouldn't have to keep pacing. The laptop was on and shining brightly. The Internet worked fine. Morgan pulled up a short history on the town of Saint Petersburg. Called Sankt Peterburg by the natives.

Jen stopped watching Morgan pace and started looking through the maps and pamphlets about the area they were in. She had a feeling she wouldn't need them, that trip was not for pleasure whatsoever. She decided to stop reading and try to sleep a little on the couch in the living area. It was going to be hard to sleep later, but she didn't care, plane rides were exhausting. She took her long dark hair out of its ponytail bindings and shook it out. It felt better to be loose. She laid on the sofa and covered up.

When she awoke about two hours later she couldn't locate Morgan. The door to the flat was open and no one was there. She jumped up and ran through the open door leaving it ajar. She ran, mindlessly freaked out and not thinking straight, all the way to the bottom of the stairs. When she got to the main door she swung it open with a loud crashing sound. The big door almost hit her square in the face, but she didn't care. She found Morgan standing in the rain on the sidewalk. She was dazed and looking at the sky as the rain hit her eyes and ran down her face. She didn't seem to mind being drenched to the bone. Jen could tell she wasn't completely present by looking at her.

"Morgan. Morgan? What are you doing out here? You're soaked. What the hell are you doing?" Jen said, exasperated. She was worried something happened to her best friend. Morgan stood in the rain like a zombie. "Morgan! Damn it! Answer me!"

"The rain is pretty don't you think? I think it's pretty…" Morgan just rattled off.

"Are you nuts? What's wrong with you?" Jen asked. She was starting to get scared.

"No. Are you? Crazy people scare me," Morgan said still looking up.

"Come with me, you're wet. You need to come back inside before you get sick," Jen said trying to get her friend off the street. It scared her that Morgan was acting like she cracked up.

"No, I wanna look at the rain, Mama. You can't make me go in. I'll tell Daddy on you. He lets me," Morgan said. She had the memories of a child and thought she was a child. Something happened to her while Jen was sleeping. It wasn't good.

Jen just went with it, her brow furrowed and she acted like a mother would have in that situation. "I said come in the house now. Your father isn't here right now to protect you. Get in there before I spank your fanny!"

"Okay! God, Mama! You don't have to be mean to me! Geez!" Morgan said. She stopped looking at the sky and went into the building. She stomped up the three flights of stairs like a child. When Morgan looked confused as to which door was hers, Jen stepped in front of her, leading her inside the third story apartment so she could lock the door for the night.

Morgan went in and sat on the floor with her legs curled underneath her. She made a pouty face, her blonde hair sticking to the sides of it, looking at Jen with sheer contempt. Jen told her to get up and go change her clothes before she caught a cold. At first, she didn't want to, but Jen stood up as if she would go over to her and spank her, this made her start moving. Soon, she came out of the room with clothes in her hands, looking at them like there was something wrong.

"Those are yours. You aren't a little kid, you're an adult," Jen said to Morgan.

"No, I'm not. I'm eight. Mama, I didn't know you were dumb. Gosh!" Morgan said, pouting.

"Morgan, you better get those clothes on! I'm not playing with you!" Jen was getting angry.

"Okay, okay. Mama, when did you get so mean? I don't remember you being this mean, like yesterday," Morgan said. Clearly she'd lost her mind. After she came out of her room, Jen wasn't angry anymore.

"I'm not your mama. I'm your friend, Jen. Something is wrong with you. You are grown up now," Jen told Morgan.

"What? No, I'm not! I'm eight! I'm not big. Where's my mama? Take me to my mama! I want her! Take me to her!" Morgan screamed because she was terrified.

"Shut up! Stop screaming. Your mom is dead. Don't you remember? She and your dad died in a plane crash when you were fifteen. Please, Morgan, come back to me, please remember who you are!" Jen was overwhelmed and didn't know what to do next.

"I don't remember you. Why? If you're my friend, then how come I don't know you?" she asked calmly as she looked at Jen with wonder.

"That's because something is obviously wrong with you. I have no idea what happened to you, but I took a nap then woke up and couldn't find you. I found you in the rain. Now you act like you don't know what's going on," Jen said.

"I remember the man from my dreams. He came here and talked to me in my head, he called me Catherine like he always does and then he went away. After that, I woke up outside in the rain," Morgan said, still thinking with her childish mind.

"We need to get you some help. Something's wrong with you. Really, you are grown now. You're not eight. You're thirty," Jen told Morgan. She was trying her best, to no avail, to get her back the way she was.

"No way, thirty is old. I'm never gonna be old," Morgan said.

"Oh, dear God, please help me. I need you so much right now," Jen said as she looked up at the ceiling of the apartment. She closed her eyes and prayed in silence for a few moments, crossing herself in a Catholic manner. She sighed then looked at Morgan, who sat on the ground looking up at her dumbfounded.

"What the fuck? Why am I sittin' on the floor? My butt's wet. What happened?" Morgan said with her eyes wide in fear of herself.

"Um, Morgan, how old *are* you?" Jen asked her.

"I'm thirty, dumbass! What's wrong with you?" Morgan scowled at her. Then she looked at her again, eyes widened with horror. "What did I do?"

"Something happened to you. Your mind wasn't right. You were eight years old," Jen explained to Morgan.

"What? What the fuck?" Morgan was in shock. *What have I done?*

"You thought I was your mom and I was being mean to you. You were gonna tell your dad on me," Jen said with tears in her eyes. She was scared and didn't know what to do. So, she did the only thing she knew she could do, which was to ask for God's help.

"I did that? Oh no. I think I know what happened. I went in my room and shut the door when I noticed you were asleep. All of the sudden, my brain let all the dreams loose I've ever had of that Rasputin guy. You know the one, back from when the Romanov's ruled Russia. Even the dreams I used to have as a kid, when I was eight years old. I think I lost my mind for however long that was," Morgan said, she was also crying.

Morgan got up off the floor, hugged Jen, and cried like hell. It opened the floodgate between them. Jen cried, too. They let the waterworks flow for what seemed like hours but, it was only ten minutes or so. Once they calmed down and pulled themselves together, they both decided they didn't need sleep.

The door was locked. Jen and Morgan had popcorn and Russian movies to watch. They decided to keep each other company all night. Neither of them was tired and both girls were too scared to sleep. It was a good thing they knew Russian or the movies wouldn't have made any sense. It was something to do while they waited for backup to get there in the morning, by then, they hoped the rain would let up.

In the corner of her room, shadows Morgan couldn't see were peeking in on her. She was unaware she was being watched. Surveillance for Aremis.

**

Aremis softly crept into Morgan's mind. With a whooshing of emotions, he opened the floodgate inside her head, crashing into her subconscious. He quickly filled her mind's eye with all the images he could think of at once. He coated her memories with crimson. The blood was the lynchpin, turning her mind to mush. She came back relatively fast the last time, but it would be harder and harder for her to return, until she was herself no more. She would be his Catherine forever. His plan was to break her, make her his possession. Slowly, he would make her revert to childhood then he would make her into someone else entirely. The first episode went well. He broke through the barrier of her mind like he did when she was a child. He controlled both Catherine and Alexandra in their day and would do so again with their descendants. He would make good wives out of them yet. The time hadn't come try his magic on the other one, but he would get to that. In due time, they would both be his, the descendants of the adulterous, murdering cads that bore the children etc., would be his.

He already had their honeymoon picked out; first they would dine on the flesh of the humans and drink of their blood, then they would vacation in a warm place where they would consummate the arrangement in the fiery pits of hell in front of the master himself. Willing or not, those women were his. The master said Aremis could have them both in every way possible.

His shadow demons were watching them. He knew how the other one made the first mind trip go away. Their God would only help them so far then they were his completely. He thought the whole concept of God was a misconception to give the humans something to have faith in, something they thought they could trust and they were wrong.

If there is such a thing, this God, humans can't trust him. He lets demons wreak havoc on the world. If God loves the humans so much, why doesn't he ever help them stop the violence? Those thoughts made Aremis laugh.

Many times people believed there was a ghost haunting Catherine's palace but, that wasn't true. It was Aremis laughing about recent insane thoughts. He was quite mental. One had to be in order to initiate plots that got kings executed, thus adding famous blood to his collection of souls killed because of the wars caused and his plans to soak the Underworld in red.

Aremis did think it would be interesting to clue the women in on their true heritage. They had no idea they were related to the Romanov family, through mistresses and Paul, the son of Catherine the great.

One of the women was related through the royal line because of a mistress that was kept secret or the child would have died. He never knew he wasn't a true Romanov. And Paul had his own mistress and had a child.

The whole family line, beginning with Czar Paul, were born half demon and half human because of Aremis disguising himself as Sergé, the true father of Czar Paul. None of the descendants of Aremis knew they had demon blood, therefore, they couldn't go against him because they didn't know they had the ability. It was the reason some of them could do magic, but they never knew demon's blood gave them their powers.

It would be fun to tell the two women he wanted about their true nature. Aremis smiled and looked upon the rainy night instead of the rainy day. It was dark in the palace. All the candles were out and people went home for the day. His ruse would only have to hold for a little while until he broke them.

Chapter Thirty-one

In the morning, the sun was shining through the third story window of the apartment building Jen and Morgan stayed in. The TV was on and they were cuddled up on the couch sound asleep when loud pounding on the door and ringing phones woke them suddenly. They both jumped to their feet and picked up their phones, running to the door. As they opened the door, the phones stopped ringing, Warren Sr. and Sir MacAfee stood in the opening.

"Hi," Jen said. She hugged them and showed them into the apartment. Morgan hugged them next and closed the door behind them.

"Scared me to death," Morgan muttered. They were both still asleep but had their eyes open.

"Yester'dee when ye called askin' us tae come 'ere, ye scared us tae death, lassie," Warren Sr. said to Morgan. "Ye dinna look sae scared righ' now."

"Da, we stayed up really late because we didn't want to fall asleep. Yesterday, when I took a nap, she flipped out. Her mind reverted to childhood. She thought she was eight again. She thought I was her mom and I was mean to her. She was remembering stuff from before I knew her and prior to her parents' deaths," Jen told him. "We were so scared, we tried to stay up as long as we could."

"Sir MacAfee, did ye remember tae bring a copy o' the document we found while researchin' what Morgan told us 'bout las' nigh'? We foun' somethin' ye might find verra interestin'," Warren Sr. told them.

"Yeah, I brough' tha copies. Jus' cause I'm old, dinna mean I'm thick," Sir MacAfee said as he dug the documents out of his suitcase.

"I kin it, MacAfee. Now, let's show 'em." Warren Sr. laid documents all over the kitchen table. "Here's tha most interestin' part. You lot are related tae the Romanov family. Both o' ye, cause o' mistresses at different times in tha timeline. An' one o' ye wouldna be 'ere if it weren't fer tha fact, tha last mistress o' Czar Nicholas knew not tae say anythin' tae anyone about tha wee son she had. She kept 'er laddie secret an' he had no idea he was related tae them. The other mistress' son, he kin it, what 'e was, but kept it secret fer fear o' death. The Romanov family became a hated royal family in Russia. The las' ones were executed b'gunfire an' buried in a mass grave. All but two o' tha children were buried wit 'em. Those wee nippers was buried in another grave, yards away." He was pointing and gesturing as he explained the family history to the girls.

Jen and Morgan sat listening to him with shock in their eyes. Neither one had any idea they were related to Romanov's, neither of them even knew they had *any* Russian blood.

"An' in addition tae this, we found out how yer related. Catherine the Great and Czar Peter couldna have a bairn. A man named Sergé was allowed to have an affair wit the queen an' they produced a wee son, later raised by the queen mother. Paul knew no one but Peter, the king, as his father an' hated his mum. He didn't know he was half demon. Sergé was just a cover. In all o' our research o'er the years inta tha strange goings on all o'er tha world, we discovered a lot o' bloodshed an' violence was caused by a lot o' demons," Sir MacAfee told them. "An' we believe tha' may be what's happening here, righ' now."

"We're half demons...well, that explains a lot..." Morgan said dazed by the truth.

"It does. It explains your abilities," Jen said.

"Yeah, but if that's the case, then how come you don't have powers of some kind?" Morgan asked Jen.

"Mayhap, she does, they jus' haven't been brought tae tha surface yet," Sir MacAfee said.

"Who the hell wants demon powers? Yuck. I don't want that shit brought to the surface," Jen said in disgust.

"Ye migh' find ye dinna have a choice. Just like everythin' else ye lassies been through. It might be somethin' ye ha'e tae temporarily embrace in order tae fight," Warren Sr. told her.

"We know you guys won't be around for forever and we truly need to learn how to do things without assistance, but do we have to learn the demon stuff now?" Jen whined.

"I slowly been educatin' ye both 'bout supernatural things since we met. I'll be teachin' ye everythin' I kin 'bout demons as well, and yes lassie, ye have tae learn it now. Ye may need it tae help ye. I'll no be leavin' ye defenseless against somethin' tha' be meanin' tae kill ye." Warren Sr. looked weary from the journey and the questions. His face had the lines of a well-seasoned teacher and spellcaster. He was a man of many secrets, but with Jen and Morgan, he could share some of them. It made him feel better to know he didn't have to hide a part of himself from them.

It was a long morning for the two older gentlemen so the women let the fellows take naps to sleep off their flight from Scotland. There was still so much for the researchers to filter through their curious minds. Jen and Morgan read all the documents littering the kitchen table and talked about what being related to the Romanov clan must have meant. They pieced together some of Morgan's dreams with the new information. Chills from the shock of their newfound ancestry ran through both of them. They had to acknowledge the fear of knowing they came from demons.

Since the past was all they had to learn from, Jen and Morgan tended to remember their lessons. At least, that's the excuse they used to hold on to the past, using those lessons to survive the new life they lived. History had a way of repeating itself and this new life was filled with violence. Images of people and tragic events constantly hung in their minds like war photos; black and white, grainy and real. The Vietnam War was no place to go or come back from, neither was the type of life Jen and Morgan lived. The only difference between that war and this one was the fact of living a secret life from the rest of the world. Everything seemed surreal and although nothing should have shocked or scared the girls, things often did.

Later in the day, after the gentlemen were sleeping, Jen stepped into the first bathroom in the back bedroom, part of the master suite. After she finished up and was washing her hands, she glanced up into the mirror. Everything was the same; from her light olive skin, her raven hair, those dark brown eyes, to the same scars on her face. The only thing that changed was the split second she glanced up and saw her eyes glow green. She wasn't sure of what she saw, so she looked again, seeing nothing out of the ordinary. It scared the hell out of her, but she decided to temporarily keep it to herself.

While Jen was in the bathroom, Morgan was alone for a few moments in the kitchen looking over the papers scattered on the dining table, sipping a cup of coffee as she read. Her mind was once again a sea of thoughts, emotions, and images colliding; trying to simultaneously fight their way into her head. Blood soaked the images. She had the mind of a child again. She rose from her chair looking for crayons. Morgan wanted to draw, but she only found pens and paper. She made a face, disappointed, then picked up the pens and paper, finding a place to sit on the floor to draw.

Jen came out of the bathroom looking around the big apartment until she found Morgan sitting on the living room floor, huddled over a pile of paper with a pen in her hand, rapidly applying it to the top page. Jen stood in the doorway, looking into the living room with confusion. It didn't take long for her mind to spark a memory. She knew Morgan reverted back to being eight years old again.

Jen silently walked over to Morgan and watched her draw something furiously fast. Morgan sketched something with Russian writing around the edges. The middle was a picture of Catherine the Great drawn by Morgan. Jen opened her mouth to respond to the drawing but couldn't. She was in awe of it. She never knew Morgan could draw at all let alone perfect sketches of people. It was odd and intriguing.

There was no time to waste, Jen had to wake Morgan from her trance before it was too late and she slipped into childhood forever. She looked at the ceiling and imagined the sky above. Closing her eyes, with her head held high, Jen prayed to God to save her friend once again from what was ailing her. At first, it wasn't working. She opened her eyes and Morgan sat there drawing like her life depended on it. Jen closed her eyes hard, so hard it hurt. She prayed to God loudly with as much concentrated force as she could muster. Morgan began to scream like someone grabbed her suddenly by the back of her hair and pulled, trying to rip it out of her scalp. Morgan rose from the floor and stood in Jen's face, shrill cries of pain escaping her, angry and hysterical. Jen was screaming prayers in earnest when the older gentlemen came walking into the living room having awoken from their naps because of the noise.

Shouted prayers could be heard bellowing throughout the room, carrying and echoing on the whole third floor of the apartment building. The Free Masons hurried back to their room, grabbing their weapons, rosary beads and their Catholic bibles. Morgan's screams of anger and pain reminded them of the many exorcisms they'd witnessed and helped with. Even though the gentlemen were getting older, they moved faster than they had in years.

Warren Sr. and Sir MacAfee laid their hands on Morgan and began reciting exorcism rites in Latin. "Exorcizo te, omnis spiritus immunde, in nomine Dei." They crossed themselves. "Patris omnipotentis, et in noimine Jesu." They crossed themselves again. "Christi Filii ejus, Domini et Judicis nostri, et in virtute Spiritus." They crossed themselves once again. "Sancti, ut descedas ab hoc plasmate Dei Morgan, quod Dominus noster ad templum sanctum suum vocare dignatus est, ut fiat templum Dei vivi, et Spiritus Sanctus habitet in eo. Per eumdem Christum Dominum nostrum, qui venturus est judicare vivos et mortuos, saeculum per ignem. Amen."

After the long Latin rites, the two men did the same things, they both spit into their hands and touched Morgan's ears and nostrils, each touching the right ear and then the left one. "Ephpheta, quod est, Adaperire. Be opened!" They both shouted. After that, they both took turns touching Morgan's nostrils and saying, "In odorem suavitatis. Tu effugare, diabole; appropinquabit enim judicium Dei. And to you, oh devil be gone! For the judgment of God is at hand."

While the two men performed the exorcism, Morgan writhed, shrieking as if she were being killed. She screamed so much all the neighbors were in the hallway shouting things in Russian like "Are you all okay in there?" No one said anything back to them. The group kept their minds focused on Morgan and the demon possession that made her act like a child. Soon after the rites and prayers were done, the interrogation began. Each of the kindly men asked Morgan questions starting with the simple stuff first. "What's yer name, lassie?"

"Morgan, duh!" she said.

"Okay, where'd ye live, lassie?"

"I live in Sioux Falls, South Dakota, but I'm currently staying in this apartment in Saint Petersburg, Russia. Why in the hell are you guys staring at me, acting like something bad just happened?"

"Something did. Just answer the questions and we'll tell you what happened after it's over," Jen said.

"How old are ye? Sorry, I kin it this sounds crazy to ye righ' now but, it won't when we explain it tae ye," Warren Sr. said to Morgan.

"I'm thirty years old. This is nuts," Morgan said, rolling her green eyes.

"Maybe so, but we just want to know it's the real you in there," Jen said.

"What year is it, lassie?"

"It's the twenty-first century, people. I have an iPhone to prove it. Guys, I'm fine. I promise. Whatever was going on must be over now. Seriously, I'm okay, we can stop now."

"Okay girly, ye did all right," Warren Sr. said hugging Morgan.

"Da, what happened to me? Why all this, the bibles and the rosaries?" Morgan asked him. Jen, Warren Sr., and Sir MacAfee took turns explaining what happened to her. Her eyes grew wide with shock and awe. After a little while of explaining, Morgan started to cry. Her fear had been realized, something evil had its grip on her soul and her mind. She was going crazy, being stamped out of her own mind, and replaced by her former self. Was her demon half trying to take over? Or was it an evil plot to destroy her cast upon her by some pissed off witch or demon?

Chapter Thirty-two

Aremis in Rasputin form spied on Jen and Morgan and the Free Masons from the shadows in the corner of the living room. He dared not reveal himself during the exorcism. It was not the proper time. He only wanted to watch the methods the group used to extract the demon he put in Catherine's vessel. He put it there to let them know he could find his way in.

The next thing on the agenda would be to start playing with the mind of Alexandra's vessel, make her think she's going crazy too and get her to believe she was seeing things, such as the glowing of her demon eyes. It was time to bring her true form forth then make her into a complete replica of Alexandra. Time was growing short and he was impatient. Immediately after the exorcism passed and the mess was cleaned up he'd start on her. The women would never set foot in the museums as free women, but as his queens, the rulers of Russia.

Thoughts of Totalitarianism excited Aremis. Together they would start with Russia then the rest of the world. The three of them would be a force to be reckoned with on Earth. He waited a long time for the world to be ripe with fraught situations and angry libations. It was time for the middle act of his little melodrama to set itself center stage. Lights! Camera! Action! It was Jen's turn to start feeling him. Morgan was already on the fast track to madness.

Aremis would break the wings off of those little butterflies and throw them on the floor for all to see and laugh at. He would turn them pale and broken into the shells of themselves, never letting them go, rotting, just like him. They would become hostages to their own minds, bent completely to his will. Russia would see his power and run screaming into the streets only to be shot down where she stood. Then the rest of the world would see what he was made of.

The sun was setting on the day, bitterly setting in shades of red, from the deepest crimson to lightest pink. Standing at the third story window, the gang was looking out at the sky as it turned from blood red to other shades as they painted the sky with oranges, yellows, and blues until black ink with star specks dotted the night. Light fog and city lights obscured some of the view, it looked like a typical quiet night in Saint Petersburg, Russia.

Shadows bounced off of the walls of the apartment. Sleep was calling the people who stood at the window watching the last sunset in the sky. They couldn't have known it was the last, but somehow Aremis felt they did know. Such feelings were rare in humans, but those four were exceptional. There were powers there he could sense, but couldn't put a finger on. He normally didn't have a hard time figuring out the weaknesses of his prey. Watching the two older men, he was baffled by what surprises they might have in store. Now wasn't the time to be intrigued by the enemy.

That night was the night Aremis would take his passionate queens into his arms and wave away all worry of the things to come. *That night* he would have time with his brides. *That night* the bloodshed would finally begin and nothing held him back. All other things were irrelevant. That night was the night of broken dreams and thirst. His wanton need to taste them, his sweet young women, grew by the hour. They didn't have a clue who or what he was, this didn't bother or deter him from his goal. That night while they were sleeping he would simultaneously invade both of their minds and not let go. He would have them before dawn. They would walk away from the modern world upon his command.

Too much time and too many years were spent plotting his plan and it was finally coming together. He waited, plotting his revenge on Russia since his 'death' in 1917. Almost a hundred years went into scheming, plotting, and planning to insure his desires were sated.

As Aremis waited patiently for the vessels to fall asleep, he watched them from the shadows. He waiting for the perfect time when all four souls were too tired and had no choice but to go to bed. His lovely ladies each went into a bathroom to change into their nightgowns, one wore gossamer lace and the other satin. *How lovely they are,* he thought to himself. Even though they both went through things that were comparable to hell, they remained delicate and fragile on the outside. Both of his women wore their hair long. One of them had the darkest auburn hair and the other blonde. When they pulled their hair out of the restraints from the day, it fell down over both sets of shoulders, hitting them both passed their breasts. Aremis sighed as he watched them. Soon he would be able to touch them and feel all they had to offer him, including their beautiful hair for him to caress.

After the ladies dressed for bed, they gathered in the living area, waiting for the older gentlemen. After the Free Masons returned, the group decided nothing could be done sitting up waiting for the final shoe to drop. The four souls decided to try getting as much sleep as they could. The atmosphere in the room changed, even Aremis felt the shift in feelings that radiated outward. Morgan's empathy made them all scared, he felt it, almost smelled the fear. She was afraid of flipping out again and becoming a child-like demon or worse. Aremis smiled from his shadowy hiding place. She wouldn't be able to undo his assault of her body. There was no reset button once they were fully in his grasp, which would happen soon. Aremis was a patient demon and they were worth the wait.

Time crawled by for Aremis, ticking by one slow second at a time, approaching the moments he waited for. He stood silent, looking out at the starry night from the castle home he lived in and loved most of his demon career in Russia. A gentle breeze blew in his face, caressing the broken, shattered, and fragmented pieces of his skull that made the flesh hang lower on his forehead. It was easy to disguise the disgusting features of his face with mental images of someone else, using it to invade the mind of his Catherine's vessel. If she saw his real face, it would have horrified her to complete madness.

Aremis breathed in a fake breath of air ushering passed his face. He stood there with overwhelming joy filling up the empty parts of him. He hadn't felt happy in almost a hundred years and was glad Lucifer granted him that gift while he, Aremis, fulfilled his mission to take over the world in his dear boss's name. He closed his eyes and saw nothing but red coursing over black, he smiled a misshapen toothy grin.

He opened his eyes and focused once more on the task of retrieving his women. Aremis looked upon the shadowy places again and saw them sitting in chairs discussing some plan that wouldn't work with their comrades. That also made him smile. They thought they could defeat him. It almost made real tears from laughter form in the corners of his eyes from the lunacy of their juvenile minds, thinking it would be so easy. He had no tears, but he still thought the gang was pretty funny.

It would only be a matter of hours before his ladies would be awakened and summoned. All he had to do was wait it out. Hours passed in the succession of a snail's pace, from the first twinkles of twilight to the nearing dawn. He twiddled his thumbs for a few hours to make the time pass. The sky was grayer outside than it should have been. Dark gray fog, with a few plumes of red making it appear dark purple, crept into the open windows and down the narrow streets, covering the land and sky. No noises came from the streets. No birds chirped from the eaves of the buildings. There was nothing but the haze. That was Aremis's cue.

***

Plucked from her bed by hellish nightmares, Morgan was breathless and shaking. Scared, she sat in a corner of the bedroom. *Who am I? What am I doing?* She looked down at herself, her mind was racing with thoughts. *What am I wearing? Some sort of under thing resembling a bedgown? Dressing gown? Something unfamiliar…* She looked around the room, nothing was familiar to her.

At that moment, Morgan, or the body of Morgan and the soul of someone else, heard a voice call to her from the shadows. *"Catherine, it's me Sergé. You must listen and do as I say. You are in a bedroom of an apartment building in St. Petersburg. You must go out of this bedroom and to the next bedroom. It is down the hall two doors from this door. You must go in there and get the other woman. She is named Alexandra. Bring her to me. You and she will be my brides. After you get her, leave the apartment and get a 'cab,' this is a carriage that moves without horses and has a motor. You will open the door and climb inside the motor carriage, telling the man to bring you to the Winter Palace Hermitage Museum, the Peterhof Palace."*

"Yes, we will come to you," Morgan/Catherine replied aloud in Russian. She rose from the floor to retrieve the other woman. *Whose name is Alexandra? And get a motor carriage. What is a motor carriage?*

Catherine bowed her head in respect of her lover and told him she would gather up Alexandra and meet him in the Palace of Peter the Great. Although not knowledgeable as to nightwear, she found something to drape over the undergarment she wore and quietly left her room in search of the other lady of the house.

***

Townsfolk stared out their windows at the two ladies in their nightgowns walking around the large city. The people wondered what they were up to, walking around town like that. Whenever one of the women would look up at a window with faces gawking at them, people quickly disappeared from view. The green glowing eyes resonating from Catherine and Alexandra petrified the locals. They'd never seen anything like the fog or those women before.

It took the two ladies a while to walk to the castle but, they both knew where they were going on foot. They'd been afraid to charter a motor carriage, which was too loud for them. Their lover would have to wait a bit longer to receive his brides. He salivated thinking of them in their nightgowns even though he knew he wouldn't see them in flowing silks and satins until later, after their first meeting.

Once the two female figures reached the gates of the Peterhof Palace Museum, Winter Palace Hermitage, in St. Petersburg, Russia, the doors swung open. Both women, glowing eyes, wild hair, and flowing gowns, entered the grounds. They remembered who they were on the way to the palace, each knew their lives. Each woman yearned to see their love. Entering the palace, looking around at their surroundings, the women smiled, remembering fondly lives past.

Catherine smiled knowingly at Alexandra. She took Alexandra's hand and they ran up the stairs, into one of the bedrooms. The two women stood raiding through the closet of one of Alexandra's old rooms. There, hung in the closet, were clothes of the time period Alexandra ruled beside her husband Nicholas. Catherine thought the clothes were funny looking, but they would have to do until they made it to her venue.

There were no tight constrictions like she was used to but, Catherine would manage. Those two women had been out in the world and saw with much fright, the clothes the other women were wearing. The new wardrobe was better than what they'd seen on the streets. It made them both wonder what year it was and how come there were so many, many buildings in the city.

The motor driven 'taxicabs' were a sure fire way to get a person killed in their minds. They were instructed to take one, but Catherine and Alexandra decided to walk the whole way. The noise and motion frightened them. Most of the fountains and ornate things around the palace they recognized, but the colors were different, much like something that was once new and turned old with time. This discovery also made the ladies wonder what year it was.

When the women were finally composed and dressed, they returned to the front steps of the Winter Palace. The huge stone steps were where they decided to sit and wait, staring out at the grayish-purple haze of the morning, looking out at the tail end of the Neva River. Voices in the heads of Catherine and Alexandra were faint whispers from the original owners of the bodies they took over to be mortal again. These light sounds were easy enough to silence while they killing time awaiting their love to come for them.

When the two queens felt his presence, they rose from their spots on the back steps of the palace and ran inside. The large hall that was held up by golden pillars shrank as they ran the length of it, skittering to a halt to reach the front gates and the entrance from the street. There they waited for him to arrive and take them to Catherine's Palace where they would hold up for a little bit.

***

While the ladies waited, Aremis was sending his shadow demon armies to differing parts of St. Petersburg to make ready for a battle with the humans over their domain. There were many shadows for the demons to hide in and wait for his commands. It was clear, the day would live in infamy in the history of the world. Some would grow to call it Armageddon, but there was no true name for what they would experience other than Hell. The city would pay for trying to do away with him all those years ago. Pity and mercy were not options on the day that would last forever. Blood would stain the streets and soak into the dirt below, thus pouring into the porous holes in the ceiling of the Underworld, feeding all the deadly, destructive souls living there. It would cause the true uprising to begin then the world would pay.

Aremis thought about his plan for world domination while he was transporting himself through the shadows to be with his lovelies. The time was nearing. He felt too happy to be given his reward for thousands of years of faithful service to the Devil. A sated smile crossed his lips as he appeared on the street outside the gates of the Winter Palace. His women rushed to the gates to meet him.

Chapter Thirty-three

Sometime in the night, the Free Masons fell asleep. When they awoke in the morning, they poked around the quiet apartment looking for the girls. The two young ladies, Jen and Morgan, were missing and the front door was wide open. Immediate red flags began to sound silent alarms in their heads. They began walking around the apartment calling the names of the ladies. They got no response, so the men began looking for evidence as to where the two women may have gone. No luck there either. The men hurriedly got dressed so they could out and search for the women. As the Free Masons, filled with fear, were about to walk out of the open apartment door blue swirling lights came rushing into the middle of the room. Warren Sr. knew it was his son. He grabbed MacAfee by the shoulder, silently asking him to wait.

The bright blue lights swirled around Warren Sr. and Sir MacAfee. Warren Sr. grinned from ear to ear, he missed his son. A tear came to his eye. It had been three years since he had seen the lights carrying his boy to him the first time, but he would never forget it. Blake and Warren always came for a reason. Jen and Morgan told him when they saw the boys it was because they needed help.

"Da, you guys won't find the girls in time. They will only get hurt if you try. They have to fight this fight alone without your help. They're possessed with the souls of old queens and under the control of a demon. An ancient and powerful one," Warren said.

"This demon has caused half of the world's wars and transgressions. He has a hold on them only they can break. They're still inside their bodies. All they have to do is fight like hell to end the possession. They can do it too! We came to warn you not to try to get involved. The ones that possess them right now don't know you and will kill you. Not only are they queens, but they're the meaner versions of them," Blake explained to the Free Masons.

"So we're supposed tae sit here an' let those precious lovely lassies do it by themselves?"

"Yes, Da. There is nothing you can do for them. I'm sorry. They must do it on their own. You forget Morgan's a powerful witch. Once she's freed from the possession, it'll be easy to free Jen. And the talisman, that'll help them too. She'll be able to access it once she's about to escape from the place she was shoved into in her mind," Warren said.

"Jus' lookin' at ye, ye make me miss ye more. Ye havena called me Da since ye was but a wee laddie on the moor," Warren Sr. said to his son with a tear running down the lines in his face. He wiped away the tear and seriousness took the place of sadness.

"So, we just sit here and wait! I canna stand waitin'!" Sir MacAfee said. "Those girls're family! I dinna like it one bit!"

"MacAfee, old bean, cool it! Boys, how dae we deal wit this?" Warren Sr. asked them.

"You have many powers of your own, Da. You need to use them to scry for the girls and open a channel so you can see them in your minds. There may be a way to communicate through the channel to tell them you're waiting for them. You have to tell them, they need to fight as hard as they can to regain their bodies from the queens," Warren said to his father.

"Bro, it's time to go," Blake said. He looked up at the ceiling as if he heard something.

"Already?" questioned Warren Sr.

"Yes, we only have a little while to come help," Warren said to the men.

"Okay, we'll do as ye say. I'm so sorry, boyo, we canna help them. That's why we came here. To help." Warren Sr. gulped down his pain.

"I know you did. I thank you for being with my family when I can't be. I love you, Da," Warren said as the blue lights returned all around him and his friend.

The lights grew brighter as the two figures vanished inside it. The blue glowing light grew brighter still, until the ghosts were gone. The lights faded away, but the pain of missing his son would never leave. Warren Sr. knew he'd never get to have him back, not really.

Warren Sr. and Sir MacAfee set to work. They cleared the table and made ready to scry the girls and open the channel between them. Papers were pushed to the floor and piled in the corner of the kitchen. The table was then covered with a full sized map of Russia. The crystals were found and spelled upon. It took a while to get the response they were looking for. They tried many times using different spells. Finally, an idea struck them, scry for ancients.

Finding the bodies was easier than creating an open channel between the four souls. That took energy and patience, both of which was waning. It took a while to break through the barriers the demon had in place in the minds of the women. It was not going to be easy, but breaking through could be done. It was midday before the gentlemen could finally break the barriers separating the mindsets of the two girls from the queens who possessed them. In gentle whispers, the Free Masons called out to the souls of Jen and Morgan.

The older men knew they were heard by Jen and Morgan. Once they felt connected to the girls, they told them to fight, to shout, to scream, to never give up. Letting them know they could get loose of the possession. It would be hard, but they could do it. The last thing the two men told the girls before they discontinued the spell was how much they loved them and believed in them.

As the Free Masons whispered those last words, the earth began to shake outside the apartment and threw the men out of the trance they used to break through the walls and into the minds of the women. The apartment shook hard and splinters fell from the ceiling. Knick-knacks fell off of shelves crashing to the floor. The men knew they shouldn't go near the window, but they crawled over there anyway. Peeking over the edge of the window, they saw a huge crack in the street and red plumes of smoke rising from it. Through the steam, black shadows formed into demons. A large army was assembling outside, waiting for them to run. A big question running through the minds of the Free Masons was: Why were they there? An even bigger question was: Where would they run to if they had decided to run? While pondering these things, the demons saw them. The shadow demons smiled, bloodlust on their minds.

The Free Masons crawled away from the window. With the miscellaneous items scattered all over, it took them a while to find their crystals and spell books. Those were the most valuable things they owned. The Free Masons tried to fortify the apartment with enchantments and protection spells to keep the demons at bay as long as possible. The guys felt they knew why the shadow army was watching them. Their job was to babysit the Free Masons while Aremis was busy, to make sure the old goats didn't interfere with his plans. His queens and world domination. Otherwise, all other life could fry. With demons outside their door, the Free Masons hung tight, there would definitely be nothing they could do for anyone if they were dead.

Chapter Thirty-four

Between the nighttime hours and dawn, two tiny whispering voices became roaring shouts echoing in the heads of two queens. Savage migraine headaches, with blinding white lights crossing their vision, prevented them from preforming their marriage duties with their lover. Aremis wasn't happy. His eagerness began to disintegrate. The women told him about the loud voices in their heads. He could only quail the voices into silence for a little while. After that, the queens had to fight it back on their own and they were failing. Both women were miserable. They begged to cut out their eyes and end the excruciating pain. Thinking was out of the question and modern over-the-counter medicine was foreign to them. The only thing carrying the two women through the situation was knowing it wouldn't be long until the voices subsided forever and the bodies they inhabited would fully belong to them.

In the meantime, Aremis taught them about many things they missed out in the centuries they'd been dead. He rapidly educated the women, telling and showing them modern conveniences such as phones, computers, and cars. He also told them of the history of Russia up to the modern era. Hearing about her own death, Alexandra Romanov wanted retribution. This made Aremis happy.

He looked like Rasputin to Alexandra and Serge to Catherine, but he was something entirely different. When he looked upon the faces of his brides, he saw their anger and displacement. He had them following the path he wanted them on. For his plan, he needed them angry; he could use pissed off monarchs, ready to fight.

The next part of the plan was to take the queens to the palace of Catherine. There was enough blood seeping into the cracks of the Winter Palace. Time was nearly upon them to take the other palaces by force. In the days following, there would be blood everywhere. It would be as he pictured it in his head, visions of red seeping into the Underworld.

***

Red coursed over black once again, the visage of time's past would concrete the new way of life inside death. All throughout the great kingdom, life would drastically change. If the citizens got angry, that would only add fuel to the fires of the Underworld, thus making the Lucifer extremely happy. It was eminent, the world was seeing its last days of freedom, its last days to stand up and fight against whatever awful force was breaking the world apart bit by bit.

The streets in St. Petersburg were quiet and lined with demon soldiers. Cracks from the earthquake were all over town. The soldiers were lined up and ready for the fight to begin and the battle to be won shortly after. The scene was reminiscent of dictators of the past making ready for the chances of an uprising against them.

No one spoke a word. No one had to. Everyone knew something was amiss with their world. There were no great moments of awe. People remembered the horror stories of the past and felt them deep inside themselves. It was no time for emotions. It was time to watch and wait, then decide what could be done. The governing forces in St. Petersburg stood affront to the silence filling its city streets. They had no idea what was causing the weather and no clue to be scared, for some reason, they were anyway. It hadn't occurred to the citizens of St. Petersburg to give over to thoughts of a demon takeover in their town.

***

The gray-purple haze was bogging down more and more, coming to earth and meeting the ground. The trees were droopy and the branches were limp, leaning toward the earth, and their leaves were sadly withered. They stood rooted to the ground, inanimate.

Soldiers made of shadow with green glowing eyes stood on the street making their presence known to the citizens of St. Petersburg. As silent as they were, they were also ominous in appearance. Looking as if they would strike at any given time, awaiting their orders from the commander.

Warren Sr. slicked his curly, black, graying hair back while in the bathroom of Jen and Morgan's third story apartment. It was a place that held shadows well in the corners from the lack of natural light, that day it held many shadows. He looked in the mirror above the sink and thought, *How are we gonna help 'em? M' son said we couldna help 'em, but there has tae be a way. There jus' has tae.* He looked sallow and wrought from worry about the young women he'd grown to love after they fought side by side in the town those girls called home. He washed his face and wiped it off with the towel on the hanging rack beside the sink. He put the towel in the hamper and opened the bathroom door. Sir MacAfee was sitting at the kitchen table reading the spell book with his glasses on so he could see the pages better. Warren Sr. looked at MacAfee with interest as to what he was reading.

The older man was reading the spell on opening channels again more thoroughly. He thought he found a part they neglected. The part they neglected would help them to be able to stay inside the heads of the girls longer so they could talk them into ousting the spirits inhabiting their bodies.

It would take more energy to stay longer in someone else's mind, but it had to be done. The men had to get to the spirits of the girls and get them to understand what they needed to do. They needed to be loud, EXTREMELY LOUD. They had to drive the queens out of their bodies in a hurry before they no longer had control and their spirits died out. It took a while to get through, but the girls understood their newest mission. It was now up to them to enact it. The men both sat back after having drained all their energy on the spell to unlock the mental door, giving them the foothold they needed to get into the girls' minds to tell them what needed to be done. It was up to Jen and Morgan.

Now they waited.

***

Piercing resonance inside one's head, including the echo, might be as strong on the outside as inner shrills cracking the cranium, blinding a person's vision.

Alexandra, with glowing green eyes, was trying her best to scratch at the voice inside and get her head to open so it poured out. Her eyes glowed brighter as tears formed and flowed from the corners, down the sides of her face. The pain was too much to bear. She glanced at Catherine who wasn't screaming yet. Alexandra kept blinking her eyes as she was shrieking and a striking realization came to her. She thought to herself, *Am I the only one in this body?* It turned out, she wasn't. Jen was screaming from the inside, trying to get out and back where she belonged. Her soul was starting to vanish from its rightful place, but she wouldn't be evicted so easily. She was taxing her soul, but she would fight with every fiber left to remain alive. Alexandra could feel it, she was in a tug of war with the person whose body she unknowingly stole.

Jen shouted loudly at Alexandra. She had no idea of what else to do but yell at her. She had no idea she had her own powers and could have stopped the possession of her body at any given time. She was consumed with thoughts of her four-year-old son Warren III, this made her bellow until she was almost hoarse. She got a stroke of brilliance and was quiet for a bit. She was deep in her mind, buried and far away from her body snatcher. She let Alexandra think she was having a reprieve. It was far from over. What the queen heard next was maddening laughter, the serial killer kind. After the laughter, Alexandra only heard silence inside her head. She thought it was over. She had no idea she would soon be in for a violent end.

***

Aremis knew something was starting to go wrong with his wonderful plans. He heard his queens scream and squeal in pain from the other room as he continued to plan his life and their rule of the world. He had to be at least a room away from them so he could maintain proper thought. All the noise was distracting him from his plans. Something Aremis didn't know, Jen and Morgan were trying like hell to take their bodies back by force. He assumed his women were having trouble adjusting to their new bodies and their new lives. He thought, eventually, they would come to terms with it.

There was a twenty-person dining table in Aremis's war room. It was a dark mahogany wood, with detailed webbing and delicate carvings in the wood. There were only ten chairs sitting around the table and a huge set of maps on top. Red marker was scrawled across Russia. The other maps were of other countries in Europe he wanted to conquer after he had complete control of Russia. A map still rolled up in the corner of the table, the North American continent, was lying there untouched. The United States needed their ass handed to them for a long time and he was going to be one to do it, silver platter and all.

***

Catherine had agony written on her face, but she wore it well. She was beautiful despite the torturous bellowing in her head. She was silent save for telling Alexandra to quit screaming. This noise only made the situation worse for both of them. She, Catherine, had no idea she was wearing a powerful talisman around her neck. She had no clue of its value, she thought it was just a pretty piece of jewelry. It looked like a big red ruby on a gold chain. She thought it might be someone's treasure, therefore, it was her treasure. She was fighting off the owner of the talisman in what she perceived as *her* mind. Occasionally, the screams grew faint enough for her to hear her own thoughts. In those rare instances, she thought about what it was like to rule Russia in her time and what it would be like to rule Russia in modern times. She would smile to herself thinking those thoughts. That was the only time her sullen expression changed.

Morgan devised a plan to regain her bodily domain. She'd tell the truth about herself. People thought they knew her, they had no idea who she was. As a child, her parents dying was the best thing that happened to her. She loudly told Catherine the Great what her past life was like. In desperation, if it meant destroying the spirit living in her body, she would recall the memories of being her daddy's whore. Memory for memory, she shouted at the walls knowing the queen heard it, possibly saw it too. She told her about the abuse and the prostitution. The drugs and the parties her parents took her to and left her at. The nights she'd run all the way home after someone she was made to sleep with would pass out.

She told Catherine how happy she was the day she got taken into custody and found out it was because her parents died in a horrible fiery plane crash. She'd spent a few years getting arrested and being bailed out by the people who took care of her and had no friends most of her life. Hatred was her only friend until she met Jen.

All the disgusting information flooded Catherine, images upon images, smells, feelings of fear, and the lust the radiated from the men Morgan was thrust into the arms of. The queen's head hurt so much she threw up while lying on the cold marble floor of the palace. After the first stage of her plan took place, Morgan chanted spells as loud as her voice would let her. The magic incantations rang in the ears of the queen, causing her to shiver. Aremis ran into the room to see why the screaming continued, just stared at her in wonderment. He couldn't hear what she was hearing. He thought she was going crazy on the floor shivering and mumbling.

Occasionally, when she blinked, the green glow disappeared from her eyes for a split second. In that small time frame, she felt gone from the world again. When she blinked again, she returned to being.

She'd been gone from the world for three hundred years before Aremis brought her back. She didn't understand what he was up to or why he wanted revenge on Russia. Catherine hadn't been awake long enough to understand and she didn't care. She prayed for death. Being mortal hurt like hell. Catherine spoke inside her head, *"Just kill me, I can't stand this! Please, God, just kill me! Whoever keeps yelling at me, just kill me!"*

Morgan followed orders from the queen that one time. She shouted every bit of magic she could think of, every spell and counter-spell she knew that might help. She even evoked curses, hexes, and protection spells in the few minutes since the queen begged her to end it. The green glow blinked away longer and longer with the passing of time. Morgan called on the power of the talisman while her body was shivering on the floor, turned toward the window instead of the Aremis and Jen.

Just then, a red glow caught the attention of Aremis and Alexandra, they both turned toward the light. It was Catherine on the floor facing the window. She turned onto her back. Her body started to hover about an inch off the ground, long blonde hair hung off her shoulders touching marble. Her eyes were flickering from green to normal. The necklace she had on was the source of the red light. It got brighter and brighter until it was so bright she started crying out in pain again. The talisman was ripping Catherine out of Morgan's body a piece at a time. The true battle had begun.

Chapter Thirty-five

The Free Masons sat on their hands, worried to the point of adding lines to their faces and further graying their hair. There was nothing to be done except wait to see how things panned out for the young women they loved like daughters. It was heartbreaking.

The two older men paid no attention to smoke floating in from the window. They were consumed with conversation about everything they'd seen and heard that day. As Free Masons, it was their job to record it for the sake of the job. The records of all events natural and supernatural they had anything to do with went into a book. It was the only thing they could do without harming the situation or making it worse, although they couldn't stand knowing the girls had to go it alone that time.

Purplish-gray hazy came into the window of the living room, flowing like a plume of purple smoke. It was only the smoke of shadow demons checking the men out and watching them to make sure they were not plotting a way to get out and run after the queens.

The air was still and the light was dim in the apartment. It was hot being three stories up. The haze finally did produce a misty red rain that looked like blood spattering the streets below. The change in events didn't put Warren Sr. any more at ease than the silence did. Sir MacAfee tapped his feet on the floor, anxious. Warren Sr. gazed at his friend with sadness, then sternly scowled at him, silent telling him to stop fidgeting. He looked at the window and without saying a word Sir MacAfee straightened up.

As if their feet were planted in concrete, the gentlemen stayed in the apartment for the sake of the girls and the town. The demon armies stood still as long as the men didn't leave. Outside they were standing tall, motionless, and silent.

The Free Masons thought it was better to keep the demons where they were as long as possible.

Rain that looked like the crimson red drops of death landed on the windowpane. The droplets ran together forming a bigger drop of bloody water. They stared at it as it stood on the wood of the window sill. The ground shook once more but, only enough to make the droplet run off the edge of the window and fall three stories below to the cobblestone sidewalk. After it hit, it split and ran in all directions in the cracks.

***

In the Underworld, the heat was blazing, Lucifer had a temper to match. It was taking far too long to gain control of the Russian people, something must have gone wrong. He hadn't heard anything from topside in so long, he was about to go up and check on Aremis. His favorite war demon usually didn't let him down. He couldn't go up and finish the job either because he had to stay out of sight for now. Too many of the Christians and Witches could undo him. It wasn't easy to die, but being dislodged from vessels sure did suck. The humans thought they could kill him. They were wrong, but thought they had more power than the fallen angel. Soon, he would go up and show them. He would make them all burn. For now, Lucifer sat on his throne of fiery stone thinking about the blood flowing through the cracks in the ground and he wondered why it wasn't. Up top, there must have been something going on.

***

Finally, the screams coming from the body of Morgan subsided, she blinked in the red light coming from the talisman. Her body softly hit the floor and she rubbed her eyes. They were her eyes, pale Irish green like always.

Aremis growled at her. She looked at him and saw his true decayed form and nearly shrieked in terror but stopped. She straightened her back then turned from him with a scowl on her face, looking toward the body of her friend.

Morgan turned her attention toward Alexandra, whose eyes were glowing green demon's eyes. The queen was staring at Morgan in horror. Morgan rubbed the back of her head with her hand and got up off the floor, looking at the 1900's dress she wore. The getup made her laugh, which made her concentration return. She focused her eyes on Alexandra. She knew she had to get Jen back and expel the queen, but she wasn't quite sure how.

She started walking toward Alexandra, away from the window and the puke from earlier. Alexandra started backing up, screaming, "No! No! No! Witch, stay away from me!" Morgan wasn't hampered by being yelled at in Russian, she was having her way.

She was almost across the room when Jen started laughing from deep inside her body again.

The green glow of Alexandra's eyes shot out like headlights on a car. It was painful for her. She knelt to the ground, closing her eyes, wondering what was happening to her. When she opened her eyes the beams were still there, light green lights, glowing. Her long raven hair shielded her face, but the light showed through the hair that fell over her shoulders like a mask.

Morgan stopped where she was when she saw the light pouring out of Alexandra's eye sockets. She was watching and waiting for Jen to surface. All the while, the demon Aremis was pissed off. He tried to touch Morgan because he wanted to end her life for messing up the plan. When he reached her to give her death's grip, the talisman shocked him and threw him into the wall with a crash, caving in the marble panel. Morgan didn't feel a thing. She started coaxing Jen out of her brain and back into her body.

"Jen, I know you can hear me. Keep doing what you're doing. I think it's working."

"Mo, I know it is. I finally remembered I have powers, too!" Jen said through the flash beams coming from her eyes. She was still crouched on the ground, but it was quieter as she fought her battle with the queen. Jen fought hard and finally got her to renegotiate the body. She battled with Alexandra in her brain, scraping and clawing the walls. In the end, Jen fell to the ground, silent as if she fainted.

"Wake up, Jen! Wake up!" Morgan slapped her repeatedly, screaming for her to wake up. The only light in the room was red and the outer gloom was slowly passing. Neither of the ladies paid any mind to it. Morgan kept slapping Jen. Finally rousing, she shielded her face with her hand.

"Okay, you can stop that shit, it hurts," Jen said. Having used all her strength, she was weak but alive.

"We gotta get the hell outta here, girl. This ain't no place to be. I knocked out the demon that had us captured, but he ain't dead. I never fully killed a demon before. I don't know if I can," Morgan said, still scared and stressed out.

"The Free Masons, maybe they know. We have to get to the apartment," Jen said.

The ladies ran out of the palace and down the street, skirts billowing. The sun was starting to peek through a few grayish purple clouds in the sky and the red rain was steaming up and drying. Demon soldiers were fading into the shadows. Vapors were evaporating in the spots parts of the army had been previously.

It wasn't over yet, Aremis wasn't done. Morgan knew it and felt a shiver run down her spine as she ran. Her fear consisted not of the same fear she used to have as a child, but now she feared her magic wasn't going to be good enough to defeat him. She was deep in thought on the long trek back to the apartment. She and Jen ran the whole way from one side of the island to the other. By the time they returned, the ground was stained red, but dry in many places and red puddles lurked in other spots. The ground in some places where the cobblestone streets fell apart took the women by surprise. There was no time to waste on the mystery of what happened.

The apartment was quiet when they ran inside. Jen and Morgan both started shouting for Mr. O' Connell and Sir MacAfee. Finally, the men came out of hiding realizing the girls were back and themselves.

"Girls! You're back! Ye got away!" Mr. O'Connell was overjoyed. He'd spent the day worried and helpless to their plight. Seeing them again made his heart beat a little more level. "How'd ye do it? Did ye hear us tellin' ye what tae do?"

"Yes, we did. How did you know to go inside our heads where we were?" Jen smiled asking him.

"The lads showed up again. Warren and Blake tole us. Was amazin', jus' like las' time. All them lights…" Sir MacAfee said, trailing off as he looked into the other room, remembering.

"It's awesome they came to you. It took more than simply driving them crazy to get them to give up. We had to make them sick as hell then they begged to die. It took hours of screaming at the top of my lungs using magic to get Catherine to let go. Finally, I was able to use the talisman because I was back in my body, which kicked her out fully," Morgan explained.

"I finally came across the notion that I'm half demon. I kept screaming, getting so loud she felt like she had to claw her way out then she started begging to be let out. I amplified those feelings in both souls. I just kept letting it get bigger and bigger, then boom, no more queen," Jen said, laughing.

"We knocked the demon out, but he won't be that way for long. How do you kill one? I have no idea. Pandora never told me how to fight one, let alone kill one," Morgan asked the Free Masons, who stood grinning ear to ear at the sight of them.

"It migh' take a demon tae fight a demon, not a witch. Ye say ye 'ave powers, Jen? Demonic powers? Tha' could come in handy. Let's read up on it a bit, shall we?" Sir MacAfee suggested.

"Right," the group chimed in together.

The four of them picked through the books and papers strewn all over the apartment after the quake. All things demonic were taken to the kitchen table. As small as it was, it was the common area for the group to gather and pass the information back and forth between them.

***

Morgan didn't know what they'd find reading through all the material on demons, but they had to pinpoint something. They couldn't let Armageddon happen like Aremis planned. He planned on death, war, and revenge. She remembered seeing his war table on the way out of the palace. It looked serious. She saw his battle plans and all the strategy he put into it. The memories of seeing it made her shiver. She thought about Jen, her little underestimated best friend. She had powers now, knowing that made Morgan smile. She used to wonder if Jen would ever get any powers of any kind or would she be moral support and the brains her whole life. *Well, that was cool.*

"Morgan, you okay?" Jen asked her, concerned with the wide grin that suddenly spread across Morgan's face.

"Oh, yes. I was just thinking how cool it was that you have powers now. And now it's *your* turn to save the world," she said proudly.

"I'm not happy about this, you know! Fuck! I didn't ask for this, just like you didn't ask to be a witch!" Jen exclaimed.

"I know. I think it's cool." Morgan was once again smiling at Jen. Morgan's empathy made them all feel her pride. She beamed silently, but the rest of the group felt her feelings.

It felt like the reading was taking forever. There was a lot written about demons.

It was only about an hour for the hazy skies to return. The shadows darkened and the demon army returned to their posts. Aremis was awake and he was angry. Far off, a bellowing wail cut through the silence. Rage radiated from that cry all the way to the other side of the island. Shivers coursed down the backs of all four people sitting with the window open in the third story of the apartment building.

"Now, that's jus' annoyin'. Close tha winda would ye, lassie?" Warren Sr. said to Morgan when she was getting up to go to the window.

"Sure thing, Da." Morgan closed the window and returned to the others at the table. "What are we going to do to destroy that sick asshole?"

"Well, first things first. We've got tae see what Jen can do wit those powers so we know wha' we're workin' wit. Ye kin?" Logical as always, Sir MacAfee suggested the best starting point they had.

"Okay, where do I start? What do I do?" Jen asked.

"Well, if I were you, I would try a 'Charmed' move and see if you have any powers that come from your hands," Morgan suggested.

Jen smiled. She lifted her hands, palms facing outward, then tried to blast something. No eruptions of lightning or balls of light came. Fire streamed from her hands, hitting the sofa, causing a small fire. She closed her hands and the fire vanished.

"Cool!" Jen smiled and her eyes lit up.

The fire on the couch still burned so the men dug under the sink for the fire extinguisher and put it out.

"Okay, besides fire, what else are demons supposed to be able to do?" Morgan was curious.

"Says here, they've tha power tae get inside yer head an' control ye. Jen, ye should try it," Sir MacAfee said.

Jen stood in front of the group, staring hard into their eyes, trying to concentrate on them, trying to control them. It took a few minutes, but finally, her eyes glowed green and she had them in her power. She told them to hug each other and they did, warmly. Then she told them to stop and they stood there as if nothing happened. The group stood straight as arrows, dazed. All she had to do to turn off the power was mentally tell it to stop and her eyes no longer glowed.

Jen was excited. She informed the group that she controlled them, making them hug and then making them stop at her command. They were confused because they couldn't remember it.

"So now what?" she asked. Jen was antsy to use her new powers and end the war before it started.

"We dinna kin what's gonna happen if we go up against the demon, Jen. Ye jus got yer powers. Ye aren't even sure they'll work, are ye? I'm noot, but hell, I'm noot sure o' anythin'. I thought for sure we'd seen it all, but me assumption was sae wrong. If ye die,

I'll never be forgivin' m'self fer allowin' ye tae go out there untrained," Warren Sr. said, his heart heavy, his Scottish thick, he was filled with fear.

"But Da, we have no choice, you know that. There's no other option here. We have to kill him before he starts a monumental war that could end us all," Jen said.

"Aye, we kin it. In short, we send you lot, then hope and pray, ye've enough power between ye tae do 'im in. Damn that plan sooks!" Sir MacAfee said, surprising them with a lack of refinement, which wasn't his nature. His Scots was thicker and less coherent when he was angry.

"MacAfee, if there was anythin' else tae do, we'd be doin' it. We canna go because he'd use us as a weakness against 'em. Remember what m'laddie said, we canna help 'em this time. It's a fookin' shame, aye."

"Okay, okay. We got it. So, we're gonna use all the power we got. We're going to try our damnedest to kill the bastard. I did bring a few spell books. Maybe I can cook him as revenge for the dreams that asshole gave me all my life!" Morgan exclaimed. She was seething and wanted payback. She grabbed her book of shadows off the coffee table and started flipping the pages. She wanted revenge, that was true, but she also wanted to stop Armageddon, too. She knew it wouldn't be easy.

"We can try. I'm not sure we *can* kill him. We've gotten lesser demons, but he's Aremis, the right-hand man of Lucifer. I looked it up on the net, he's powerful as hell and no one defeats him unless he gives in as part of a plan," Jen said. "It's going to take every skill we possess to try it."

Shocked by the news, the four people sat in chairs at the dining table in the kitchen, silent.

Chapter Thirty-six

Aremis shook his head. He was confused. How the hell did those bitches do that to me? He thought. Where did they get the strength? Baffled, he sat still shaking off being thrown into a wall. He pondered witch powers. He had to kill those women before they tried to foil the plan. His master said Russia was ripe for the picking again. *So how do the two women factor in, now the possession is over? It's simple, they don't. They will have to die.* If Aremis was lucky, they would be the first of many.

The thought struck him, his plan was convoluted. He wanted to make them his brides, but it hadn't worked as he planned. The idea saddened him a bit. Their beauty would be lost. He would make examples out of them for all of St. Petersburg to see. The time was upon him to prepare for death and destruction.

The shadow demon army was still standing by and the gray-purple haze returned to the day, which meant his powers were back because he was awake again. He knew where the women were. Shortly after high noon, he would have his revenge for their part in fucking up his plan. The summer would not end in a total loss, by autumn Armageddon would be in full swing.

Only one part of the plan was screwed up, the other part would take place as intended. Before Armageddon got underway, the town would get a big show. It was turning out better than he thought it would. Aremis would have the demon armies herd the people to the back of the Peterhof Palace where the huge fountain was standing. That was where he would kill them as an example to show the crowd who was in charge. Blood would soak the streets, even if it started out being the blood of two beautiful women, it wouldn't matter if they were the first to bleed to death, as long as the blood soaked the ground and raised the demons. Hard and cold, their soulless bodies would burn on the pier. The flames would take them fast and sorrowfully.

He sat pondering, smiling at death. That was his true favorite thing to think of. What's love but another means to an end? He decided early on, if it didn't work out, he would be done with them early enough not to screw up the rest of the plan. He ran his bony fingers through his almost non-existent hairline. He thought of what death brought to the table and how hungry he was. As he waged war with happiness and sorrow, he thought about how important he would make those two bitches' deaths. They'd be his first martyrs in the battles to come.

In the center of town, demons made of shadow were preparing for destruction. Somewhere else in the town of St. Petersburg the demon army was watching and waiting, reporting back to their master of the happenings inside the apartment. There were shadows, hiding, watching all over the apartment. Talk was big. It excited the demons because they knew their master would love to know what the two former queens were up to. To the demon's knowledge, the women weren't aware they were being watched, which would be to the master's advantage. He would know and be ready for them.

***

The quick-witted survivalists knew they were being spied on. They didn't know how exactly, but they figured it out due to when they were possessed, Aremis knew how to get inside their heads and what forms of torture to use. In order to know those things, he had to be watching them. The girls used their phones to communicate a plan to the men and to tell them the real things they had to say, otherwise, the shouted conversations taking place around the apartment were for show only.

They couldn't eradicate every shadow in the apartment, but they had the place lit up like the brightest summer day back home. Lamps sat in corners, things were covered and doors were closed with blankets covering the bottoms. Jen faked her powers, Morgan read spells she had no intention of using, the Free Masons practiced their Catholic exorcisms. What they did had to appear real, so reports were authentic. In text messages, the real plan was forming. Real spells were discussed and a plan of action for Jen and her powers. The stage was set.

The current battle would be the hardest one to date. Both women were warriors, but not as seasoned as the Free Masons were. The men would hold open books, tell them the opposite of what the pages said, giving them time to read a caption and move on. One of the women would silently read what was pointed at, text a response, then keep moving through the plan. That tactic was for the spies. What was really happening, they were reading up on Aremis and his powers, looking for weaknesses. It could be done.

There were a few things that weakened him, but they were there nonetheless. The group studied hard in the time remaining. Rage was his biggest weakness. They had to use their heads or he'd kill them straight out, no fooling around.

As time drew shorter, the sun glowed blood red through the haze, burning its way into the folds of vapor. The room was bathed in red light as it streamed harshly through the third story window. That was the sign they waited for. It was time to go to him. Soldiers waited outside to take them to the fountain in the garden of the Peterhof Palace. What was once a happy meeting place would have tragic memories attached to it from then on, in their minds.

People were scared, it was evident as Jen, Morgan, Warren Sr., and Sir MacAfee passed them in the halls and on the sidewalks, looking up at them through the haze and blood red sun. They wore their fear on their faces.

The march to Peterhof was endlessly slow. Soldiers in the rear of them pushing them onward toward their demise didn't sit well. In the history of long walks off short piers, this ten minutes seemed like an eternity. Boots clicked on stone for miles. Listening to the sound made the group feel like they were marching to their deaths, followed by the Reich.

The citizens of St. Petersburg came from all corners of the common with soldiers behind them, herding them into the middle of it. Gray cobblestone was covered with the bodies of hundreds maybe thousands of people crowded close to the fountain, but far enough away to have a substantial amount of moving room. At the center, closest to the old fountain, stood a man, or at least, he looked like a man. The scariest looking man on Earth at the moment. He had wild green glowing eyes and a staff that held a green glowing orb. He had an evil, steely grin made of layers of razor sharp teeth.

Jen, Morgan, Warren Sr., and MacAfee were thrust toward Aremis, who stood at the front of the fountain at Peterhof as if he owned the place. Smug self-assurance exuded from him. He glanced down at the low fountain, thinking it would do as a place to catch the blood he planned to spill.

Tall and proud, Jen and Morgan stood, heads held high, as they faced Aremis, grinning with madness. Jen had her hands behind her back looking straight at his demon eyes as her wicked smile curved higher on her face. She looked like she had a secret she couldn't wait to tell. She wore rage in her eyes and never broke eye contact with the demon. Her friends smiled too, but not as hauntingly. She was small, Aremis probably thought he could squish her, but she had news for him.

Aremis wanted to wipe the smiles from their faces so he started with the older men. He raised a hand and they both fell to their knees in pain. The girls stooped to the ground to help Warren Sr. and Sir MacAfee.

"Your sentiments are looked upon with no favor. You will die, you insufferable bitches," Aremis said.

Jen and Morgan stood tall again. Anger made Jen begin to shake. She raised her hands to Aremis and he saw the hellfire come from her hands. It shocked him seeing it come from her. She almost hit him, but he moved just in time.

"You son of a bitch!" she shouted. "Stop it! Stop hurting them!" Jen screamed at him.

"Why would I do that? You hurt me. Why should I care about two old humans?" he said.

As Morgan stood in the windless courtyard, her talisman began to glow. She squinted her green eyes, facing Aremis as she raised her hands, blasting him with a great jolt of her witch's powers. He fell to the ground, laughing at her. Morgan's anger grew into rage. She pointed her hands at the demon, blasting him with every bit of power she had left. He hit his head on the ground, concaving the space, his glowing green eyes facing the hazy gray-purple skies. He withstood the blast. When it was over, he rose to his feet gingerly then smiled wickedly, pointing his scepter at her. She stood her ground, ready to hurt him.

Jen stepped in front of Morgan as her eyes flashed glowing green. She could see what he'd previously hid from them; his true appearance would normally drive a person insane by merely glancing upon it. She momentarily gasped at the sickening sight of him. Then she looked upon his façade with the reverence of pity for a second. She quickly recovered her thoughts and they returned to murder. The intense madness took over again. The color of her eyes changed from glowing green to bright red lights peeking from under her eyelids. Rage-filled tears slowly streaked down her dirty cheeks as she stared at her enemy, seething.

"Kick his ass!" Morgan shouted from behind Jen.

Jen nodded.

Aremis was shocked by what he saw in the face of his opponent. When she took control of his body he didn't know how to stop her. The bony, cloaked figure rose in the air above the crowd watching the spectacle. Aremis dropped his scepter on the sidewalk by the fountain and the bulbous globe attached to it shattered, filling the air with a misty green fog momentarily.

Aremis felt the bones of his skull cracking. His hollow, green, glowing eyes were fading as his head began slowly rip in two. What flesh was left on his face split, black oozing blood ran onto his neck while he screamed. The gray matter of his brain covered in ink was seen by the crowd.

Screams of horror were heard behind Morgan who turned to see the faces many people momentarily. Some of them passed out and were on the ground. She looked at Jen again. She felt the immense rage coming from inside Jen's tiny body. Morgan cocked her head to the side as she watched her friend murder their demon enemy slowly.

After she got to his mouth, his head was flopping on both of his shoulders so she ripped it off with her mind, black blood spraying out. Some of it hit her face, but she stood perfectly still. Next, she started tearing his arms completely out of the sockets. The sound it made resembled tearing scrap cloth for bandages. Then came the cracking, crunching bones as the appendages separated, falling on the gray cobblestone sidewalk in front of her. His legs made the same sounds as they fell. Black ink-like blood pooled around the pile of body parts below the floating torso. When Aremis's chest cavity began to splinter as it split in half, she covered her eyes but continued to break him in two. Blood as black as the darkest night washed over the remaining pieces of the demon onto the cobblestones below. Jen slowly rolled her head on her shoulders, cracking a few vertebrae, looking at the dead demon's body as she stood solidly in her footing, rage poured off of her.

Outside of killing Aremis, Jen had no concept of other things going on. Morgan came up behind her and put a hand on her shoulder. She turned, almost willing to tear her best friend apart until she realized it was Morgan, trying to get her to stop.

The horde of shadow demon soldiers was gone and the sun was shining in a blue sky. There were people standing around them in awe. The two Free Masons were picking themselves up off the ground. There was black blood everywhere along with a sizzling, shrinking pile of demon body parts.

Warren Sr. came up to Jen and Morgan, looked at Morgan and said, "Remind me not tae piss off that lassie. Wow!"

"I didn't know I could do that!" Jen said, surprised by what she did.

"Well, I think somebody best say tha forgettin' spell. People're staring at us…" Sir MacAfee surmised.

Morgan went with Sir MacAfee toward the crowd, they both chanted the forgetting spell to the whole group standing around. It took a few minutes to get them to go back home with the belief nothing happened. Morgan also magically mopped up the remains of Aremis, the dead demon. The group left no traces of being at the Peterhof palace, that day or any other.

The only bad thing about erasing other people's minds was they got to forget—the group had to remember everything. Back in Sioux Falls, when they went around saying the spell to make the neighbors forget, they knew they had to deal with the truth. The same would be true of Russia.

After the spell was finished the crowd dispersed and the group walked back to the apartment. It was a sunny day, but the gloom they felt loomed over them like heavy rain clouds. Deep down, they knew it wasn't over.

***

Amidst the sunny blue sky, there were no signs of what happened minutes before. Down in the Underworld, Lucifer was seething. Aremis was dead and the plan for Armageddon was gone with him. No chaos that day or at least not according to any plan. If there was going to be bloodshed, the big boss was going to have to go off-script and get his hands dirty.

"We need a new plan," Lucifer said out loud for all the minions in the room to hear. "I was supposed to get Russia today, but it didn't happen. Somehow, those stupid bitches won the battle. Any ideas?"

All the minions stood around and thought. One finally said, "Why don't you go up there and take it? You're way more powerful than Aremis was."

"I could do that, but what real fun is that? I can take anything anytime I want, but the games are so much fun. The humans are fun to toy with." Satan smiled.

"If you want to begin Armageddon, then just take it, Master. You're so powerful, more powerful than a couple of human females. It would be easy for Armageddon to start. You know the angels would come to protect the humans. After that, you kill the angels, you win."

"Hmmm, you bring up a few good points. I've wanted to kill some of my brothers for a long time. They're such pains in my ass," Lucifer said.

It was time to take matters into his hands and crush whoever stepped up to him. What fun to be back on the battlefield. As far as anyone would know, he was coming to take revenge on the female humans that killed Aremis, which he did want revenge for. The only thing that boggled his mind was how they were able to kill an ancient demon with only half-demon powers.

He had time to figure it out. It was only slightly after noon in Russia. He would attack at night, using the darkness as cover. Also, the four humans would get comfortable, thinking the battle was won since they killed Aremis. *Wow, are they wrong!*

Lucifer had six hours to wait and plot to exterminate the humans to enact Armageddon. He saw in his mind; lands barren of richness, trees gray and dead, water running blood red, and skies filled with smoke from many death pyres that would come to be. People's heads would be impaled on long sticks coming out of the ground stained with the blood of thousands. Lucifer sighed at his dream of the perfect world.

Six hours seemed like a long wait to get the future of planet Earth started.

Chapter Thirty-seven

The walk seemed long, never ending, in fact. By the time Jen, Morgan, and the Free Masons made it to the door of the apartment building, they were exhausted. Too much precious energy was used up, sleep was all they thought about except the fact, they knew it wasn't over. There was something too easy and sadistic about what Jen did.

In all their years as Free Masons, Warren Sr. and Sir MacAfee never saw anything like what Jen had done. They'd seen demons fight before, but none of them had the powers she had. None of them were able to rip someone apart on a whim with their mind, it was reminiscent of tearing tissue paper and letting it float to the ground into a puddle of mud.

Not knowing exactly what was going to happen next, the group decided sleep was the only option in order to be awake and focused in case something else came their way before they could get the hell out of dodge. Hours later, after trying like hell to get their minds to shut down, the gang decided sleep was not an option, so caffeine had to be.

The sun was setting and the animals near the Neva River were too quiet, like the night before, when Aremis mentally led the ladies to him. The silence was a prelude to the still darkness soon to cover the island. No lights and cheery club music filled the air to invite anyone in. The whole city would be shrouded in darkness, hauntingly awaiting the next assault on them. No one knew for sure what was coming. The air was thick with vibrations, something evil was on its way. There was no set battlefield like last time, the whole of the city was it. Jen, Morgan, and the guys had no idea what exactly was coming for them. To presume too much would cost them dearly.

Flickering lights in the apartment meant something was near. Since the place was lit up like Christmas in July, there was no viable way for whatever was coming to force its way through the shadows. It would have to come to them face to face. The lights flickered again and momentarily went out. When the lights were restored a messenger demon was standing in the middle of the room about to get blasted. He held up his hands as if to say 'Stop!' to Jen.

"Hold on now! I was sent to deliver a message and nothing more. My master, Lucifer, told me to tell you to meet him on the pier by the Neva as the first star appeared in the night sky. It will be red," the messenger demon said to them. "He said he would prefer that the old men stayed home, but he knows they won't, so bring them if you must. So, you have witnesses to your deaths." The lights flickered once more and the messenger was gone.

"Oh shit! Lucifer wants us. Now, what the hell are we supposed to do?" Morgan said.

"Pool our powers, that's what we do! An' read like mad, lassies. We've no time tae fool aroun' 'ere," Warren Sr. said rapidly.

"But how the hell do you kill a fallen angel? A very *old* fallen angel," Jen asked.

"That's why we need tae work fast. Pull up anythin' ye can find on Google an' other spots. We'll be lookin' in tha books," Sir MacAfee said.

The team spent the next couple of hours researching how to kill Satan, demonized creature that he was. After two hours of finding no information to use to kill him, no spell, no power, no ritual that would do it, everyone decided they would prepare mentally because there was no way out of a death match with the oldest and most powerful of the fallen.

"The first star's out, it's time tae go now." Sir MacAfee was watching the skies for the sign.

Before they could walk out the door, the room turned white with light and no one could see, temporarily shielding their eyes. An angel stood in front of the door.

"You cannot win this fight. You must not go," Michael said to them.

"We have to go. If not, he might endanger all of St. Petersburg and the world. We can't allow that," Jen said.

"You can fight him, just you. The others can't, he'll kill them. It has to be you. If they come, they die," Michael said.

"How am I supposed to fight him alone? I'm only half-demon and really far back in my family!" Jen asked.

"You have some power in you, if used properly, it can get rid of him. You are also part angel. I don't have time to explain it to you now, but you have the power in you. Lucifer was one of us long ago and has his own angel powers that none of his minions knows he has. He may not even know he has them still himself. You, being a descendant of his, makes you have both as well," Michael said. "Dark and light in the spectrum. If you call upon both sides of yourself, you can defeat him."

"Well, how do I use those powers? I just found out a day ago that I had powers, period," Jen said.

"It will come to you, like the demon powers came when you ripped Aremis apart. Just believe in yourself and it will come," Michael explained. After he was finished the blinding white light filled the room again and he was gone.

All four people backed away from the door. They turned in toward the apartment.

"Um, Jen, I think tryin' this on yer own's foolish," Warren Sr. said.

"My fucking ass! She's not going alone. I will *not* allow it!" Morgan cried.

"We might not have a choice, Morgan. Just like the fellas didn't have a choice yesterday, but to let us go and hope for the best," Jen told her.

"Morgan, if ye think I be wantin' 'er tae go off an' get killed all by 'erself, ye've lost it. I dinna want the mother o' my wee grandson goin' off tae kill demons alone," Warren Sr. said.

"Everybody, I think we better hurry the hell up and decide. Look…"

The only star shining turned blood red, the sign they waited for. It was time to go, Lucifer was getting tired of waiting.

"Okay, she goes, but we won't be far behind. And no, I don't give a damn if he knows we're there," Morgan said.

Everyone grabbed their jackets and walked out the door. It was a chilly night in St. Petersburg that evening. The pier wasn't too far from the apartment building. It was situated on the Neva River but was closer than Peterhof palace. The group scoped out hiding places once they got close enough to the water. After their hiding places were found, Jen walked the rest of the way to the dock at the pier. All the boats were strapped and tied down. The water was choppy and black in the night. The sky was now filled with red stars, blood specks over black fabric. It was the darkest night Russia had ever seen.

The short walk lasted only a minute or two, but it felt like an eternity to Jen, who was nervous and a bit flustered. Her stomach was tied up in knots and her emotions were wary. She made sure to tie her long dark auburn hair up so she could see in the blackness of the night. As she neared the pier, a hooded figure with a white face came into focus. His black eyes and blond hair were the first things she noticed upon approach. As she drew closer to him, he removed the hood of his cloak and his long white-blond hair came folding out of it.

His smile was something out of a magazine, it hypnotized the senses and left masses of people in awe of him. Although he'd fallen, he was still beautiful. His eyes were black pools of shining ink. His white skin held a bit of rosiness that only fair skinned humans could convey. If he'd been human, Jen would have assumed he was Russian.

"So, you came all by yourself, little child. Why are you alone?" Lucifer said to Jen.

"I may be a young to *you,* but I'm no child. Children don't defeat ghosts, vampires, witches, and demons," Jen said matter-of-factly.

"I suppose not. What a resumé you have, young one," he said.

"You didn't summon me to talk about that. What do you want?" Jen asked.

"Revenge, dear girl. You killed my right-hand man. I don't take too kindly to having my demons ripped apart by some teeny, tiny five-foot-nothing brat like you," Lucifer said, seething.

"It was his stupid plan that got him killed. I don't kill people unless they fuck with me or mine first. Blame it on the one it should be blamed on, then let it go, man," Jen explained to him.

"I can't do that. I hold grudges, you see. Your pitiful friends hiding behind walls and around corners can come out now, so they can watch you die," Lucifer said as the rest of the gang came out of hiding. They stood far enough away so no one got hit with what Jen planned to assault Lucifer with.

Jen closed her eyes and whispered something to herself. She whispered so low Lucifer might not have understood what she said had she not spoken of God. She opened her eyes and smiled mischievously at him. The whites of her eyes glowed brightest white making her brown eyes look like black circles surrounded in lightbulb white light. She took a step back. Opening her hands facing the palms at him, she began. Jen's eyes turned red where the black rings were, causing them to turn a shade of pink.

Lucifer expected angel powers or demon powers, but not both. His black eyes were huge circular pots of ink. He was seeing something entirely new. He didn't believe he had the ability since he'd fallen. He used his demon powers so much he forgot his angel powers altogether. He watched the colors in her eyes merge, becoming pink. He saw her outstretched palm facing him and stood, not knowing what to expect from this human he knew he had no power over. A strange tingling sensation crawled all over his body and his skin was burning from the inside out. Then it was bleeding and bubbling as if he were surrounded by fire and melting off the bone. The pain started to surge through him in engulfing waves. Lucifer raised his hand and tried to extinguish the internal fire Jen started inside his body. Her eyes glowed brighter pink and her mind held up against his assault. She blasted him mentally and the fire on the outside began to grow taller than the bloody and bubbly body of Lucifer, one-time angel of the Lord. His screams were deafening. Jen held strong and true, staying her course.

The rest of the gang stood by watching the show with awe and amazement. No one knew what a mad bitch with a lot of powers looked like until then. They wouldn't soon forget it.

It didn't take long for the screaming to die down in volume. Jen thought the fight was beginning to end so she let up. It wasn't over. Lucifer started to regenerate and laughed at her as he was reforming.

"Is that all you got? That tickled," he said, laughing louder, taunting her.

"No," Jen said. After that one word, solid, flat, and whispered, she continued using her powers on him, heating him up from the inside out until he was a puddle of goo on the dock. He reformed after she stopped again.

"Woman, you're going to have to do better than that to get rid of me." Lucifer smiled.

"I'm not done yet, you son of a bitch," she whispered as her pink eyes glowed brighter than they had earlier, venomous resolution lighting the way. She blasted him again and again. Finally, she blasted him with everything she had. He heated up and imploded. Body parts flew all over the dock then evaporated as if made from black vapor. The dock was left clean and Lucifer was gone.

Morgan, Warren Sr., and Sir MacAfee came running up to Jen as she was about to fall onto the dock. Morgan grabbed her when she saw her going down. The light went out of Jen's eyes. All the lights and sounds of the city returned, making the island night noisy around them. The sky returned to normal as four people hover low on the wooden planks of the dock beside the Neva River. Jen was gently laid on the well-worn boards. The three friends who leaned in close to check her vitals noticed she was barely breathing. One of them went off to find a cab while the other two sat by and watched Jen. To them, the nightmare never ended, their friend wasn't waking up. The older men were having a hard time trying to maneuver her into the cab.

Finally, after a good amount of time, the group was back into the apartment settling in for some sleep and watching over Jen. She was out for the count after all the energy she used up. Everyone was also packing their bags, getting ready to leave Russia as soon as possible. Just as Morgan was getting ready to make up the couch on the other side of the living room, bright white light engulfed the apartment. Michael, the archangel, returned. He stood, looking warily at the group.

"She has done well. She didn't kill Lucifer, but she did send him back to the Underworld. He can't come up here or be summoned for some time. He must recover from what she inflicted on him. And yes, she will recover from her wounds," Michael said.

"How the hell did Jen even do all that? She fried him from the inside out," Morgan whispered.

"She combined her two different powers, like I told her she could. She used the powers that both God and Satan instilled in her. She did exactly what she was supposed to do. She used her powers and put Lucifer down in the pit where he's supposed to be," Michael explained.

"So now what? What happens to her?" Morgan asked.

"She will sleep it off. After that, she's going to remember everything and will still have powers. Make sure she only uses them to fight the good fight. She needs to be looked after and you need to make sure she doesn't use her powers to create evil. It will turn her into a demon," Michael told Morgan.

"Okay, I can do that," Morgan said.

The bright white light came again then Michael was gone. The Free Masons and Morgan sat on the other couch facing Jen, staring at her while she slept, agape and in awe. She never knew her best friend had it in her. Someone who, without rage, could become so undeniably dangerous. *That five-foot-six-inch tall petite person is scary beyond all thought or measure*, Morgan thought. The sentiment was truly hard to fathom.

Chapter Thirty-eight

A few days later, Jen woke up feeling a lot better. She was up and around as if the events with Aremis and Lucifer never happened. Her memories confirmed the truth. Her head reeled with questions.

When it came time to leave, the gang agreed, parting was bittersweet, but wouldn't last forever. They agreed to meet again soon on home territory to see the littlest O'Connell. They all missed him, but his grandpa and MacAfee decided they'd go home first before taking another plane ride to visit their little bud. Jen and Morgan needed the time to heal physically and mentally before they got to see the gallant men of the Secret Order of the Paranormal-Free Mason Chapter again soon. Although there was great love in their hearts for one another as a family growing closer, it was hard. The mind had to ponder things on its own. That was something both Free Masons told them time and again in the few years they'd known Jen and Morgan. To take time for themselves, no matter how difficult things seemed to be.

Jen and Morgan arrived about twenty hours later, back across the pond in the U.S.A. Touching down in Sioux Falls, South Dakota where things were a sight for sore eyes, even though they were tired. It was happiness. They found terra firma. As the touchdown happened, a part of Morgan's empathy went into hyper drive. Something was going on at home, she felt it. Eeriness filled her as she walked off the plane in a haze. She was staring off into space at baggage claim.

Jen snapped her fingers in Morgan's face to get her attention.

Is it time, so soon after returning, to start looking for something else no one knows exists? Or do we wait until it surfaces on its own? Morgan thought.

"Morgan whatever you're thinking…no way," Jen said.

"I have a feeling we were stepping in it again. Something's going on here too. I don't know what, but something is," Morgan said, worry spreading across her face.

"The second we get off the plane? Really? Do we have to do this shit *all* the time?" Jen was annoyed.

"Princess, you know this *is* what we do now. No going back, not at all," Morgan said dryly.

"I know, but five minutes would be nice occasionally. By the way, don't call me princess," Jen said as pink lightning flashed across her eyes. She laughed out loud. When Jen laughed so did Morgan. No one standing near them understood why they were laughing, but some of the people smiled anyway. Laughter was laughter.

On the way home, Jen and Morgan looked at their town as if they saw parts of it for the first time. There were shadows and lights they could have both sworn weren't there before the Russia trip. As they passed the falls, there were lights glowing from behind it they never noticed before. Many colored balls of light could be seen in the twilight. Neither Jen nor Morgan paid complete attention, they thought the lights must have been new to the tourist attraction. After the Suburban passed the falls, Morgan started to cringe behind the wheel. She had to pull over. Her middle was wracked with pain and she suddenly felt like her head was going to explode. Jen sat there confused asking Morgan what was wrong and what to do. Finally, Jen got out of the passenger side of the truck and walked to the driver's side. Morgan gingerly slid over into the passenger side. Jen drove away from the side of the road. She made it all the way home without an incident, but she was scared for the pain-stricken friend sitting beside her. The queerest thing happened when they made it home, Morgan was no longer in pain, like it never happened. She was fine when they went inside their house in the dead of night. It felt like weeks since they last laid eyes on it. Cautiously, they entered, peering around corners as they checked all the rooms for any signs of strangeness.

The ladies looked in all the corners and closets to see if anything or anyone was hiding in the house. It appeared that the house was vacant, save for them. The two of them were so tired they decided to go to bed. Soon, both women had pajamas on and teeth brushed. They quickly said good night and exited to their bedrooms.

***

While Jen and Morgan slept like babies, a drow with silver hair and skin as black as soot, peered in through the window, craned its neck and laid its elven ear to the glass, listening while standing silently on the back deck. A knife scraped against the hard surface, shrilly carving a line down one of the windows. The drow would return with a small force in tow to talk to the witch and the demon. If they didn't have what he wanted, he'd kill them, simple as that. With yellow eyes, the drow peered into the house more intently before leaving. *They must know where it is. They're the only ones who know about it besides us, the few that still remain.*

The drow was named Draven. His partner for life, Edina, the High Priestess of the drow commanded him. Her silver hair and red eyes, beauty unsurpassed, made her too hard to defy. She sent him on this mission. She said the two mortal women had the object she was looking for. So, he sought them out. His job was to retrieve the object then go back to his world and live in darkness with his Edina. The job seemed simple enough and the night was young. He sat down on one of the chairs on the back deck soundlessly with his curved blade in hand. He looked up at the stars remembering them vaguely from his younger years having only seen them a few times in his long life. Draven was a hundred and fifty years old. In drow years, he was young by far. His childhood was brief and dark, spent in the caverns of his home under the ground. His city was dark and he liked it that way.

Sitting outside in the human world, he observed the sky with the vision of mole people. When it finally adjusted, he could almost see gas trails coming from the stars as they passed. Humans couldn't see it without telescopes but, his eyes were almost like night vision goggles without being burrowed hundreds of feet underground. His fluid form stood suddenly, not making a sound. He swiftly walking away from the home of two human women he would visit again after he gathered his henchmen.

PART FIVE
Angels, Demons, and the Devil

Chapter Thirty-nine

Draven's footfalls echoed in the silence of the dark night. The sound bounced off the walls of the otherwise quiet home. Boots were a bad choice of footwear, he surmised. Wooden floors resounded every click of his heels. He removed the boots, carrying them in one hand and a curved silver bladed dagger in the other.

On the second story of the house, he heard shuffling sounds. *Damn Edina*, he thought. *I woke them!* He hid in the hall with the three other drow he brought with him. The others heard his thoughts, every drow had a mental connection they could talk to each other with, like having a private telephone line in their heads. These were the strongest of the drow army, so he recruited them for the current mission. He didn't know what powers the witch and the demon possessed and didn't want to take a chance.

The hall light flicked on and could be seen down the stairs, the drow sank back into the wall as if the light were going to melt their flesh off of the bone. No one downstairs breathed for fear of being caught too soon. The elven men heard female voices mumbling and getting a little louder as two shadows were at the top of the staircase. Out of nowhere, an eerie light was seen at the top of the stairs closest to one shadow. The hallway was shadowy and light pink.

What's that? thought one of the other drow who was beside Draven, looking up at the light from their place in the shadows. *What would cast a pink glow? A scepter?*

No. From what I've heard from demons in another part of the Underworld, it's the one called Jen. Draven thought to him. *She has demon powers.*

And that means what exactly? He thought back to Draven, not convinced it meant anything.

It means she might have the power to vaporize us, idiot! The mental conversation came to an abrupt halt as the shadows and the pink light grew closer to them. The drow stiffened; four blackened forms with silver hair, prepared to confront the humans in order to get the object back their queen, High Priestess Edina, sent them to retrieve.

Mumbles were being heard by the drow once again.

"Would you shut up and listen a minute?" Morgan mumbled low to Jen at the top of the stairs.

Both women were pajama-clad and glassy-eyed, only having woken a few moments before when they heard a loud noise in their silent house. No human knew they were home yet. So the thought of whatever was in the house being a person was out of the question. Morgan thought it might be a demon coming to exact revenge for sending Lucifer back to Hell in a handbasket.

It was no demon seeking revenge. All the lights in the living room area of the house came on suddenly scaring the drow stiff, making them remain still. Jen and Morgan were still at the top of the stairs, descending them when the lights were magically turned on courtesy of Morgan, the witch. Draven didn't know how to respond to this, he stood still and waited for Jen and Morgan to come to him.

"Who and what the hell *are* you?" Jen asked Draven as she rounded the corner of the living room with her eyes lit up, ready to strike.

Draven stood staring at the wonder of her eyes for a moment before he spoke slow and broken English. English was not his first language. He normally only spoke an old form of Elvish. He said, "I come…to talk…with you…you have…object…I want back. You give…you live."

"What object? What the hell are you talking about? And you *better* talk or we'll kill you without letting you explain why you broke into our house," Morgan said, furious, looking at the strange intruders.

"We want object. Edina says…you have," Draven said in broken English.

"I think Edina's sadly mistaken. She's your queen, I presume. She sent you here to die, my friend. If we did have said object, we wouldn't give it to you," Jen told them in a deep whisper.

Draven looked at Jen with a deep fear. He hadn't known Edina would send him to his death intentionally. Jen stared, glaring at Draven, his yellow eyes gazed into hers. He saw them, glowing brightly then lightning crossed them. Before he died, Draven saw his whole existence flash before him.

Draven grew up in the dark. His world consisted of cavernous wilderness below the underbelly of the earth. Dim candlelight was the only source of light in the homes and buildings carved out of the sides of underground mountainous regions. The brightest thing most drow ever saw was the lake of magma that rested at the base of the highest underground volcanic mountain there was in existence, Mt. Hellfire.

No flowers grew at the bottom of Mt. Hellfire, it was too dark and the top of the Underworld wasn't porous enough to let in any light at all. There was one huge factory that worked with metal and fabrications alongside the lake of fire that came from Mt. Hellfire. The queen of the realm, Edina, had a good number of her subjects working in the factory as slave labor. She made them use the magma as a blacksmith tool in huge quantities. The forced laborers made Edina all sorts of contraptions out of the metal they made and refined for her.

Aside from the factory by the lake of fire, the land was barren and hard. All the rocks were jagged and walking out there was useless. Draven tried to explore the landscape by the river many times but failed at every attempt to get past a huge crater in the expansive darkness. However, that was before he grew up and fell in love with hell. Edina was hell.

Edina was everything a male drow could want and more. She tested and used every conquest she ever had. Draven was no exception to the rule. She played with him as if he were a child. And she used him to get what she wanted. Her beautiful face could do a lot to him as well. Her sparkling red eyes glittered her way into his heart whether he liked it or not. And her flowing golden locks wrapped around him in their bed.

There were nights when Draven would brush his golden blond and silver hair aside and rise from their bed only to walk to the window and gaze out over the drow made dimly lit sky of their otherworldly home. He often wondered what the overland was like and hoped beyond hope that he would one day see the surface of the earth. He wondered what he would see and would that world be anything like his own. He knew deep inside himself that there was more to the world than where he and his people were living. He felt it like he felt his own hands run through his golden and silvery hair.

Edina had it in mind that Draven would see the overland, but not for a good reason. She never had good reasons for doing anything. She said she wanted something that some of the people up there had. She was sending him to his death and he had no idea. He just wanted to see what it looked like topside. She had already been up there and used her resources to do things and make deals with humans. All Edina had to do was use her power of persuasion on them and she got what she wanted, it was easy.

Draven's desperation to see that world was widely known. She knew how to instruct him about that world and how to get him to go up there like there was a mission. There was no mission, she was tired of hearing him go on about it and she was tired of him period. It was time to get a new companion.

When Edina told Draven about the 'mission' she wanted him to go on for her his yellow eyes sparkled. She saw the glimmer. Her plan was going to go off simple and easy. She easily made up an object, lying, saying it was stolen by two humans with powers. She told him the humans were female, one was a witch and the other was part demon. It took her a few days, but she 'educated' him about Jen and Morgan, two random humans she'd heard about through the Underworld grapevine. Her friend 'Lucy' talked about *them all the time with a vulgar disgust. He hated them so there must have been something to it.*

Edina showed Draven pictures of them she'd gotten and given descriptions of them to him. By the end of a few days, he knew a lot about people he'd never met. Lucy's knowledge served as a base for Edina's. Neither of them knew the true lion's den he was about to enter, although Edina had her suspicions.

Jen's eyes glowed bright pink. She lifted the palm of her hand to them and mentally imploded each creature one by one. Each drow, Draven first, let out a bloodcurdling scream of pain before he exploded. All the antimatter of the bodies went up in smoke and vanished before their eyes.

Both Jen and Morgan would have sworn they heard a woman laughing out loud. It was an evil, ominous sound. As soon as they heard it, the wind carried it away.

"What the hell *were* those things?" Jen said.

"Some other mythical creature I'm sure we'll run across tomorrow. We better see how they got in so we can fix the point of entry and go back to bed. This is bullshit. We can't even sleep anymore. Damn things have no idea how much sleep we've lost in the last few months after being possessed pawns." Morgan was mad and rambling.

Both of the women walked around the house and saw one of the dining room windows was broken and glass was all over the floor. Morgan went into the kitchen and got the tape measure. The whole way in there and back she was cussing under her breath. When she returned, she measured the broken window. Then she and Jen went to the garage and found some scrap wood big enough to cover the hole. They brought the wood back into the dining area and secured it in place over the window with screws. In the morning, Morgan would call someone to fix the window.

After the temporary repair work, the women made sure the house was locked up and the alarm was on. Jen swept up the glass in the dining area. While she did this, Jen noticed something she hadn't seen before. On the floor was a golden ring with a gold and black crest on it. She grabbed a tissue and picked up the ring to get a better look. After the golden statue of King David I, she knew not to pick up mythical objects or touch them with her skin in case there was something wrong with them. The ring got put away for another time when it would be better to investigate. After it was secure in the wall safe and the mess was cleaned up downstairs, the phone started ringing. The caller ID flashed, Mr. O'Connell was calling. At that late hour, it must have been important.

***

Scottish and Irish Myths of the Banshee

[Scotland]*In the ancient times of Ireland and the surrounding provinces, Scotland included, there were many myths about the banshee, one that started with the ancient kings of the realm. Families with someone about to die would see the banshee around the day of death. The person that saw her was the one going to die.*

Once a soul was plagued with seeing a banshee there was no turning back, death would come to them shortly after, be it hours or days. Fear has in the past sent some folks off on a reckless spree of evil and others it's pushed toward God. No one knew why these omens appeared for the Celtic world. It was never explained and would always remain an urban legend.

Ban Sith, the banshee, more traditionally in Irish culture, were there for the sake of warning; or taking the traveler to their destination. Wailing that could hurt the ears and blind a soul was something done when a person was in danger of being taken against their will and taken into the 'Otherworld' by force. Some people didn't want to be taken at all.

There was a banshee looking in upon Mr. O'Connell of the clan O'Connell in Carlisle—border town of England and Scotland. His castle home was the heritage home of his forefathers and the place where the banshee always came when it was time to take one of them to death's doorstep. Knowing the banshee was nearing him, Mr. O'Connell called his old friend Sir MacAfee to his side and they talked over a plan to leave, not knowing that she would follow them to the land of America.

In all the lore about banshees, it doesn't tell anyone how to get rid of one. Drastic and nonsensical thinking also made it impossible to lift one. No one knew if one could be lifted. At the castle, the library had been sifted through and the Free Masons had already made calls to everyone they knew who might have known something. No one knew a thing about ridding oneself of a banshee. Although they did mention that her wail could render someone sightless and mindless should someone make one made enough to wail to her full potential.

On the ancient land of Ireland, it was also speculated that Druid magic was hidden. There was a forestland little known in history as Druidia, where the Druids lived and practiced their craft in secret. One thing Mr. O'Connell knew, banshees were a mythical product of Druid rituals and magic as an omen of death for any Celtic king. Being an ancestor of kings, he was no exception to the rule.

Chapter Forty

Spring was turning to summer in the United States, winds were dying down in some places and picking up in others, and the temperatures were rising, the rain was abating in most areas. It was greener and a little warmer. The ground was drying out and the mud was returning to dust. Spirits ran high in that part of the world in summer, especially for Jen and Morgan, the two ex-research assistants turned supernatural fighters. Years passed since their first battle with an entity and they freely agreed to get rid of another spectral nuisance.

Mr. O'Connell worried about the entire thing. *Am I cursed? Am I dying? Am I supposed to die?* He didn't want to die and leave his family behind. He wasn't ready to go. These thoughts toyed with him all the way to the U.S. and the girls. If they weren't able to figure out a way to defeat the ban sith, would he have to die anyway? So many thoughts consumed him, he was unable to sleep the whole flight.

When the Free Masons landed at the Sioux Falls, South Dakota Airport in the U.S., a few days later, Jen and Morgan came to collect them and take them home. No one said much on the ride. Everyone felt the fear. Everyone knew this could be their last chance to see each other alive. Fear was not all the family reunion was about. It was also about the fight. Some men wanted to die a natural death, not one at the hands of something that shouldn't exist. Mr. O'Connell was one of those men. Warren Sr. and his family were together to fight any way they could.

Banshees can be unseen when they follow someone to wherever it is they think they can hide. Calla followed close behind the red Suburban as Morgan drove all the way to the middle of the quiet street in the neighborhood she and Jen lived in. Morgan was well aware of the mystical tail they had but couldn't see.

Once the gang was back at Jen and Morgan's house, everyone split into conversations about what happened since they last saw each other. Jen told the men they were still fighting unknown creatures like the ones earlier in the week. They'd discovered what they were by searching them out from the brief memories both of them had had on the morning Jen used her powers to implode the creatures. They were discovered to be drow, elven creatures from underground with evil intents. Morgan sat back and listened as Jen told the tale of the drow from what they discovered about them after the fact. Morgan's concern turned to why the gentlemen came to Sioux Falls, they were having a banshee problem. One part of the problem, Warren Sr. was the only adult who could see Calla. She was always in the room with them.

"Lassies, I assume ye got a plan?" Warren said with consternation in his voice.

"Yeah, Da. We got a plan of sorts, I just hope it works. We don't want to lose you to a banshee or otherwise. All the layover time gave us time to research and think," Jen said.

"I kin it ye would, ye always do," he said rapidly, looking in the direction of where the banshee sat perched giving him a look of painful sorrow. He glared at her.

"She's here, isn't she? With us, right now?" Morgan asked.

"Yeah, she been wit me fer days now. MacAfee's tha only one what helped me stay sane since seein' 'er tha firs' time at home. I think he's good at spreadin' his empathy or he cast a spell on me or somethin'. It helped whatever he did."

Sir MacAfee winked at them; older, frail, and looking tired, the gentleman still had a few tricks up his sleeve. His powers were well-defined and seasoned. He didn't have to talk to cast a spell. He had the power to mentally cast them, whereas Morgan had to say the words aloud to get her spells to work right. MacAfee was doing correspondence training with her from Scotland and she was doing better. The knowledge she gained was being written in her own book of shadows when she learned something new and had it down.

Sitting in the living room of the house, the girls and the Free Masons watched as Little Warren ran past them all and stopped dead in his tracks. He looked at Jen. "Mommy, what is that?" He pointed at Calla. "It's looking at me! I'm scared!" he cried.

"Baby, come here to mommy. Let me try to explain. It's a ghost. You see it because you're special and Grandda can see it, too. Don't worry, it won't hurt you. It's not here for you," Jen said trying to reassure her son.

"Little guy, I know it's not like when you see your daddy's ghost. When you see daddy and Blake it's different and there is pretty light because they're like

Angels. This one has no light probably, but she isn't here to scare you. She's here for other reasons," Morgan said, also trying to help him understand.

"Mommy, Mo, why is it here then?" He wanted the full explanation and the girls didn't think a six-year-old child, no matter how smart he was, would understand his grandfather's life was at stake.

"Well, this migh' be hard tae understand, wee laddie, but Grandda's tha one she's here tae see. Dinna fash yersel'. It's gonna be fine," MacAfee said, empathy radiated through him and into the whole of the room. Jen and Morgan felt it coursing through them. Calmness spread into the whole house like a warm blanket covering them. He looked at Little Warren, blue eyes shining and black curls glistening in the sun. He was innocent and the four adults wanted him to stay that way as long as possible. He stood there smiling and then MacAfee took something small out of his pocket. It was a small round metal disk. The picture carved into the metal surface was St. Christopher, the saint of protection. "This here was yer da's when he was yer age. I found it in tha house in Scotland an' asked Grandda if I could bring it tae ye. It'll help ward off things tha' may have ill will toward ye."

Little Warren put the metal around his neck and hugged MacAfee, after that he when over to where his grandfather sat and hugged him too. He looked down at the metal, looked up again and saw his mom and her best friend watching him. He smiled at them both then bounded up the stairs in a noisy jog.

After Little Warren left the room, the four adults huddled up and started talking about their plan of action. Calla could hear them, not truly understanding what she heard. It confused her as she was an ancient being, she wasn't evolved enough to understand their plan to use another primitive Celtic power to undo her thus erasing her from the family. In whispered words, the group formulated that the Druid magic, runes, and other ancient methods were going to be employed in order to end the banshee's hold on Warren Sr. It was their only chance and it might not work, but they were willing to try anything. *What else do we have to lose?* Warren Sr. wasn't ready to die yet. Time was growing short again; Calla was there to take Warren Sr. out of the mortal world soon. She was his ride to the other side.

The sun was setting on the day, darkness was calling out, ready to be heard, to tell a tale of woes unimagined by the normal human. The stars were dancing to the sad nighttime tune along with a waxing and waning moon. The shadows were following suit in the room, growing. Lights were being turned on in every room, placed to illuminate every corner. The tempo of the meeting was heightening, almost exciting.

With two empath witches in the room, the gang could feel the adrenaline and shear passionate thought of saving someone from death. Voices grew and fell shallow and soft, then grew again like the rising and falling ocean tide. The discussion went on for hours and the plan was in a code language so Calla had no idea what they were saying.

"Ye really need tae calm down. Me and Jen's gettin' a fooking headache from all yer empathy shit. Both o' ye," Warren Sr. finally said after hours of dealing with their high, excited spirits. He rubbed his temples and looked exhausted for the first time in the whole time the girls had known him. He looked older than in his early fifties momentarily.

"Yeah, guys, just because we all know how to speak in Old Norse doesn't mean it has to be so lively. You guys are too excited about this. It shouldn't *excite* you knowing we have to kick something else's ass," Jen said, going to the little bathroom in the hall downstairs and grabbing the Excedrin Migraine out of the cabinet, popping two in her mouth, rinsing them down with water.

"Girl, why you getting all bent about this? We figured it out. Finally, we got one figured out before it gets bad, we gotta use all our wits on the spur of the moment, without real time to come up with anything. And I think this plan'll work," Morgan said.

"Mo, I hope it does. That would be great, but if not, I'll do my best to keep our Da with us, you know that," Jen said looking at her would-have-been father-in-law who blushed then smiled at his girls faintly.

MacAfee said in Old Norse, "Ladies, we aren't here to let him die. We came to save him. Rest now. We need to be in top form as tomorrow is most likely going to be a bitch. We need to be able to properly prepare to rid the O'Connell family of its ghost." That was the only word Calla understood of the whole passage and she shrieked loud enough for the whole house to hear. It was horrible and ear piercing. No one but Mr. O'Connell could see where she was, but they all knew her location from the wailing.

"Fucking BITCH! Shut up!" Morgan shouted hands over her ears. Warren III awoke screaming and crying, frightened at the sounds downstairs. The group of four raced up the stairs to his room. Upon entrance, the boy screamed louder thinking the ghost was after him too. Jen was the first one through the door, pushing all the others out of her way to get to her baby first. She held him as he cried, so scared.

"Baby, what's wrong? Did that shouting just now, wake you?" Jen inquired of her young son as she hugged his crying form.

"It wasn't Daddy. It was the mean ghost who's after Grandda. I heard her screaming!" he exclaimed as he cried in his mother's arms.

"Shh. It's okay. We're going to get rid of her maybe as soon as tomorrow," Jen said. There was sorrow in Jen's expression. The two empaths standing in the doorway felt her feeling and both frowned, looking at each other. "Da, come tell him, please. Let him know you're going to be okay."

"Laddie, your mum's right, I'm gonna be fine. Nobody's gonna get yer old grandda, especially no ghost o' an old hag like her. We got us a plan, boyo. No worries from ye now," Warren Sr. said to his grandson, hoping he was being reassuring to the young boy. "Sleep now, an' in the mornin' me and MacAfee'll teach ye somethin' fun, okay? We'll teach ye some stuff yer da learned when he was a wee laddie like you." Warren Sr. smiled thinking about some of the things he taught his son when he got to see him after his mother took him to live in America.

After Warren III went back to sleep all the adults left the room, three of them whispering protection spells on the room as they went down the stairs and back to their battle plans. Worried thoughts swirled in Warren Sr.'s mind of how the banshee was going to die, it seemed almost impossible, almost. They had minimal experience with spirits. The ancient stories and ancient forms of magic would have to be enough.

Chapter Forty-one

Stars hung in the sky, bright and stunning, white dots marking the night. Silent and in deathly rapture toward the morning hours. As the stars still danced with the moon, the sky was the darkest shade of blue.

Calla was tall and beautiful with her fire red hair and emerald green eyes. She was the epitome of a Scottish queen. She'd been luring her charges for thousands of years, she didn't understand why this time was different. Downstairs in the living room, Calla was still lurking in the corner, watching everyone. She stayed silent the rest of the night. She listened to the conversation even though she didn't understand it.

***

The group was getting a bit restless and enamored toward sleep. Druid magic and rituals were the plot to stop the banshee. It was all they had, all that was clear. Everyone was getting fuzzy in the late hour. Sleep was taking over, the night was calling them all, pulling them in, lulling them into thinking it would be possible to catch a few hours of sleep.

Morgan fell asleep in her comfy chair, blonde hair tied back in a messy ponytail, holding her grimoire. It slowly started falling out of her hands. MacAfee went over and took it gently from her. He put it on the small end table next to the chair. The talisman turned around Morgan's neck, the red stone glinted from the light in the room. Calla saw the talisman and kept her distance. Jen got a light blanket out of the hall closet and put over Morgan so she could sleep soundly.

Mr. O'Connell sat on the couch with his eyes heavy, in his thoughts. He felt bad about bringing the banshee to the family, but he knew he had no choice because he knew no one else who might help. They'd grown close over the last few years. There was no other alternative, either bring her to them or die. Dying wasn't something he was ready for. He'd missed so much of his son's life and had the chance to know his grandson and his mother. He wasn't ready to give that up. He loved them. Being of the Order, he knew the plan wasn't a sure thing, but he had great hope it would work. He wanted it to. He was so tired, he dozed off thinking.

Jen and MacAfee were the only ones still awake. It was time for them both to find a place to lay their heads. Jen decided she was going to sleep in her room so she could be close to her little one. Sir MacAfee went upstairs and slept in Morgan's room so he could be there faster if anything happened. The power was divided evenly. No one wanted to take them all on sleepless and angry.

The night hung there still and solid, quiet and yet there was Calla in the far corner of the living room waiting to take her charge from the world. She figured out it might not be as easy as the others she'd taken, but she was still there to serve her purpose.

***

Morning came sooner than anyone would have liked. Warren III woke up and roused the others, he wanted his breakfast. His little face showed no signs of fears from the night before. Although he wasn't the picture of happiness, he still wasn't talking to his mommy or the others of his fear. He had no knowledge his father visited him in the night while everyone was sleeping to make sure he was okay. That was something Warren and Blake did every night without the true knowledge of the others. Jen and Morgan had their suspicions, but couldn't prove it, nor did they worry about it because they were the only good Angel-typed beings they'd ever known. It made Jen smile on several occasions thinking the men might be looking in on them still.

As breakfast was slowly being laid out on the table, the five human inhabitants of the house sat quietly. Warren III was bouncing in his seat, black curls bouncing and blue eyes dancing. His grandda smiled with recollection of his own son at that age. A small amount of noticeable mist cast its way over his eyes, but he blinked it away, still smiling at the boy.

Morgan felt his emotion and so did everyone in the room. Everyone looked at her, she shyly smiled and the mood in the room lightened Being an empath wasn't something she wanted, but Morgan used it to balance out her witch's anger. Her empath powers came to her in overdrive after the Russian trip. It took a bit to learn to control them better, but with MacAfee there to help her, it was easier to sort out. She still had moments where no one was safe from her emotions. This left her feeling a bit despondent, but she dealt with that aspect too. Pandora never told her she would become an empath as well as a witch. Maybe she didn't know. After the empath episode, everyone ate silently. It was too early to start arguing over who needed to knock it off with the powers before nine am.

Research needed to be done and MacAfee was done early, so he was at the helm first. He found out Druids did have magical powers and they used them to stop others from harming them or their lands. No true documentation of actual events was left from the time of the ancient Celtic Druids, but enough about their time and their legacy survived to find out what was needed through his connections in the Free Masons. Some scholars noted in things MacAfee read, the Druids performed their rituals of blood sacrifice in white robes with a golden bladed knife. He wondered if they would have to scare up those outfits to do the magic necessary to lift the banshee from his friend. They most likely wouldn't because there was no sacrifice involved in ghost removal, at least not to his knowledge. Soon after reading all the white robe stuff, the others entered the room MacAfee sat in with a laptop and notebook, writing hurriedly. He said nothing but kept scribbling.

Jen got Warren III situated, playing in the corner farthest from the ghost. Morgan got her book and laptop out went to research alchemy. Mr. O'Connell gave Calla the death stare. A bit later, Morgan took Warren III to his grandma's house.

The four grown-ups came together and made a circle in the center of the room. There was a round Persian rug on the hardwood floor where they stood. Jen bent down, peeled it up, and tossed it aside. The four of them knelt in a circle where the rug once was.

In the center of the wooden area, there was already a sign of protection. Morgan waved her hand over it and it temporarily disappeared. Putting her long blonde hair behind her ears, she stared down at the empty surface of the floor.

"Now what?" Morgan wondered.

"We wait just a minute. I think there be somethin' comin'. I can feel it," MacAfee said.

"So we just sit here exposed? Are you fuckin' crazy?!" Morgan exclaimed.

"Shh…can't you hear it?" Jen asked.

No one heard the faint noise, but Jen. They saw demons materialize in droves in front of them. Jen blinked hard, pink lightning was cast over her eyes. Her dark brown pupils turned glowing pink, she put her hand in the air facing the demons that came to kill them. She looked straight at MacAfee with a slight look of disgust, then turned back to the demons, her long raven hair flipping fast as she turned.

"Why did you come?" Jen looked back at her room full of targets.

"Just kill 'em, Jen. Don't worry about why they're here!" Morgan snapped.

Jen *did* just kill them. Demons exploded as fast as they materialized. Black smoke temporarily left a trail from the death of the demons when she was done eviscerating them all. After the demons were gone, something had changed no one noticed until then. Calla was visible to them all now. Everyone looked around the room then back to the circle. MacAfee nodded, looking down at the center of the circle.

It would be easier to kill her if they could see her and MacAfee knew it so he had Morgan take up the seal that protected the entire house. He couldn't tell them because they would have argued with him, Calla didn't need to know.

The next thing to be done, four candles and four crystals were laid out around the circle on the floor. The four adults sat around the circle making ready to summon the Druid ability to curse her and rid the world of her existence. Jen and Morgan both tied their long hair up so it would be easier to complete the mission. Sitting in the circle, Jen closed her dark brown eyes and opened them to reveal pink lightning streaking across her eyes, the hue changed to bright pink once again. Morgan closed her green eyes and concentrated on her talisman, which began its low glowing red, pulsating and growing like a strobe light until the room was bathed in it. Both men sat calmly focusing on the task at hand. After everyone was ready, the four of them took the others' hands, calmly they sat in the circle, power overflowing, radiating outward to fill the room.

Calla got scared standing in her corner so she screamed the loudest, roughest scream she had. It was believed the banshee's wail could kill a person were they exposed to it for long. It was maddening, the four adults held their hands over their ears and continued with the ritual. Soon the curse was showing signs of working and she was fading into nothing, as was her banshee's wail. The four people held on as things spun around the room and the house shook on the foundations. The wind blew things around the room fierce and fast, trying to break the hold each of the humans had on one another, but they held strong.

Calla faded into ethereal existence. The wind stopped blowing and objects fell to the ground, smashing glass on the hardwood floor as it fell. Jen put her head down so as not to get by falling debris. The ritual lasted mere minutes, to the group it seemed to last for forever. They all unclasped hands then looked around at each other and the state of the living room, slowly surveying the damages.

"Oh, holy Lord, look-it. We did all that!" exclaimed Sir MacAfee. "I canna see 'er though. Can ye, old son?" He looked at Mr. O'Connell.

"No, I canna see 'er anywhere, boyo. I think we got 'er." He sighed with relief. He looked at his girls, hoping the drained looks on their faces meant it was over. "An' ye, lassies? How're ye farin'?"

"Da, I'm okay. I'm just tired. It takes a lot out of me to use that much energy and concentrate that hard." Jen said.

"I'm okay too, but worn out." Morgan was so tired, in fact, she wasn't thinking about restoring the demon protection spell to the house like she should have been. She forgot about it. All she wanted was to take a nap before cleaning up the mess and retrieving the little guy from his grandma's house. The talisman received a small stress crack she didn't notice too.

"Okay, I say, we nap 'fore gettin' the lad. If I'm tired, ye must be beat." Everyone agreed with Mr. O'Connell and slept for a solid two hours that evening, waking up to find the rest of the place in shambles. Someone had been in the house while they were sleeping but was gone when they awoke.

Chapter Forty-two

Lucifer sat upon his throne of human bones, eyes red with the blood of innocents. His hair was white-blond and his body was as bony as the skeletal remains of the dead he so proudly called his own. His cloak was tattered and worn in places, black as the night and waxen as the skin beneath it. His bare feet were charred on the soles with long yellowed toenails. He hadn't fully healed from being made a fool of weeks ago in Russia. No one in Hell was stupid enough to mistake him for a weakling, even in his degenerated state. Anyone who did saw exactly what their king was made of.

The non-picturesque forms of all who opposed Lucifer were hanging before him on the Wall of the Discarded. He saw the wall as art, his expressionistic view on creative ways to kill. It was one of the many artistic things surrounding him in his palace in Hell. He had many others. The Wall of the Discarded happened to be in his main office, but he liked to mix it up.

Earlier in the evening, he sent a few minions to check out the house belonging to Jen, the last human he did battle with. She happened to live in Sioux Falls, South Dakota, U.S.A. A place he also had a strong foothold. He knew she was strong, but he wasn't sure the extent of her powers. She's the first person of his line he ever knew to have dual abilities. He only knew about having either the power to do good or evil one at a time, never together. He was curious as to how she'd do in a real battle with him. It might even be fun.

Lucifer's thoughts raced, roaming to places in the inner sanctum of his mind; he was thinking of ancient times, before humans had true knowledge of him and his workings, when 'witches' were the cause of things people couldn't deal with. They weren't smart enough to deal with the fact the demons were sent into the world, causing damage and possessing whoever they could get their hands on, in order to cause chaos.

Tall grass blew in the wind off the northern coastline of England. The hillside was scattered with tiny villages, thatch-roofed houses and candlelit windows in the night. The laughter of children was heard as they ate their meager dinners and were regaled with tales of silly things their fathers' made up to see them smile. It was a quiet night by the ocean.

Lucifer saw in his mind's eye, the night turning bad for the people in a village by the sea. His demons came in the dead of night, giving the animals diseases, making plans for the villagers to burn each other out of their homes, believing there was witchcraft afoot. The village burned to the ground and all the people save for one died. That one person was responsible for spreading the widely rampant plague, sweeping like wildfire over the land. In those medieval times, people thought witches were responsible for everything unknown to them. But no, his demons infected and infested them with diseases no one knew how to cure.

There were raids and pillaging done by kings who were unwittingly possessed by the Devil's minions. Also, there were wars and death, plenty of blood to soak into the ceiling and walls of his underground home and feed his people for decades.

As Lucifer awakened as if from a waking dream, he smiled fully showing his jagged and always bloody teeth. He was a madman in the highest degree, he wanted vengeance for being humiliated by a damn human who isn't completely human! *That damned Aremis had to mate with humans! Idiot! No wonder he died a bloody death. If they find the grail, my plans are finished!*

The Devil sat in his chair strumming his fingernails on the base of the arms where his hands rested. He was pissed off and the underlings knew it, they stayed away from him so he wouldn't kill them because he was angry. He had thoughts of taking Jen's 'precious' son from her and either turning him evil or killing him. The thought made his little, wicked heart smile.

He sat in his chair remembering things all day. It was sweet to relive those times he had his way with the humans and almost won his piece of ground every time. It also made his anger grow knowing there were goody-two-shoes humans out there who thought he was something to be trifled with. His plan, this time, was a good one and would hurt people. Then if it proved successful, he would use the boy and his powers to finally get what he wanted, Hell on earth. Children could be trained and the damn adults always tried to stand in the way. Possessions gone wrong were proof of that. He wouldn't have to seek possession of the child. He would be a teacher after he exacted vengeance on his mother and her friends and they were dead.

***

After waking up two hours later, upon closer inspection of the house, Jen and Morgan surveyed the damages during the banshee attack and the house shook itself loose of its foundation. The place was worthless on the open housing market, it was wrecked. When they first went to sleep it was only the living room, a couple pictures off the walls in other rooms, but after they woke up, the whole place was destroyed. How they slept through it was beyond them, but they had. There was stuff thrown about everywhere, broken dishes and furniture, pillow stuffing and paper was all over the house, someone had fun.

"What the hell happened to the house?" Morgan said loudly so the others could hear from different rooms.

"I have no idea, but it wasn't this trashed when we fell asleep!" Jen shouted from her room through her open door.

"Did ye remember tae restore the demon protection spell, lassie?" MacAfee yawned as he stepped out of the Library.

"I don't remember ye doin' tha' before we went tae sleep," Warren Sr. said.

"Shit! I didn't! Damn it!" Morgan chastised herself. "I'd better go restore it so no more happens without our knowledge." She quickly walked down the stairs and out of view of the others, long blonde hair whipping in the breeze she made as she hurried. Chants could be heard in her womanly voice from the center of the other room.

"Well, guess we clean this up 'fore we get the lad, eh?" Warren Sr. suggested.

"Aye," MacAfee agreed. He nodded to Jen, who nodded back. Jen used her mind to push things together while MacAfee used his warlock abilities to rid the house of the debris, making fast work of the top floor of the house. It took them only a few minutes to clean all the broken things up and put things right in all the rooms. The trash bin filled quickly. After Morgan finished her spell she used her powers to help with the cleanup too. Top to bottom, the house was cleaned in half an hour. The group got in the suburban and went to get the youngest O'Connell from his grandma's house.

On the way to get the little one, the girls could have sworn they kept seeing weird things. As they passed people in traffic, both women thought they saw the occasional set of green glowing demon eyes temporarily flash before their vision. An uneasy feeling settled over the group and the ride across town into the inner city of Sioux Falls became quiet. Jen's mom lived not too far from their old place of employment. It got easier for Jen not to want to go to the museum and kick their old bosses' ass every time they drove by with the passing of time. She thought she probably still would if given the chance, but Morgan wasn't stupid enough to pull over anywhere near the place.

It took a little bit to get Warren III from his grandma's house because the Free Masons had to explain what was going on. Over the years, since the bout with the vampire, the girls started telling Jen's mom what was happening so she would always be aware and keep her head down. Hiding was the best thing they knew for her to do. Morgan safeguarded Jen's mom and her home with the best protection spells she learned them from MacAfee. He'd been a great international teacher in her magical learning, the Internet helped with her research into the craft also.

After telling Jen's mom what happened and getting the little one, the group left the inner city portion of Sioux Falls and went back to their subdivision. After dinner and some conversation about what would or should happen since the banshee was gone, there was a strange cold feeling that swept the house. Morgan was the first to say she had nothing to do with it, but she felt it strongly. It swept through her like the winter wind, chilling her to the bone. Something was coming, but they didn't know what. Morgan was no psychic.

Moments later, the walls were bathed in bright blue familiar light. Two spots in the middle of the living room glowed bright and the swirling lights made it impossible to see so they all closed their eyes a minute until the blue light began to fade away. All that was left were the human forms of Warren and Blake. Jen and Morgan looked at each other and smiled broadly.

"Son, somethin' wrong?" Warren's father wanted to know, scratching his head with wonder.

"Unfortunately, yes, Da. When you all cursed and rid this world of the banshee, you opened a whole can of worms on this house. Not to mention, the demons who came in here pillaging while you were sleeping." He looked at Jen. "Baby, you can give up the lacy panties I like. It's okay, really." He giggled and winked at her, making her turn ten shades of red. Warren turned back to his father. "Da, this house is sour and the spirit world is in turmoil. You need to get these three out of here. Take them home with you, you have plenty of room and we can all watch them there." He sighed and looked at his son.

"One more thing…the devil wants a piece of your ass, guys. Jen really pissed him off when she used her powers on him. She's strong and he doesn't understand it. Something else, you need to find the Holy Grail. It seems like bullshit, but it's not. The grail is the only thing to help you get rid of him for good," he said. "About this house, too much fighting, too many rotten things have fought their way to this land. This piece of ground wasn't meant for that. You've spiritually desecrated it somehow. The negativity levels are wrong. You can't stay." He was looking at Morgan, staring at her, taking her in, from the top of her blonde head to the tip of her toes. He still loved her. He always begged to go on the information missions with Warren and be visible so he could see her and she'd *know* he did.

"So what are you guys saying? We have to kill our house? How do we do that?" Morgan was the first to say it.

"Warren, you better tell them," Blake said with a serious demeanor.

"You have to burn it to the ground, blow it up. I'm sorry, but that's the only way. Get what's valuable to you out first, but it needs to be cleansed. Fire is the only way," Warren told them sorrowfully. "We know you two love this house, but we love you and want you to live. Eventually, this place will kill you. All the fighting you do, the objects, the magic, and ancient energy that passes through here...it's not safe anymore."

"Damn. Well, there goes our retirement. I'm kidding, guys. It's just a house. We can eventually get a new one," Morgan said. "And the Holy Grail! Fuck! Just how do you suppose we find that?"

"No worrying about that now, babe. You'll find a way," Blake said.

"Okay, it's settled then. You take the girls to Scotland with you, Da. Do you agree?" Warren asked.

"Aye, an' I kin it ye only come tae us where we can see ye if it's important. Since yer here, it must be."

"Right. I hate to do this, but we have to go. They give us limited time to be seen here. We love you and take care of yourselves!" Warren looked at his son who stood silently throughout the whole ordeal, staring at him. "Hey you, kiddo, it's me, your dad." He smiled brightly at his son. If he could have cried, tears would have streamed down his face while looking at his beautiful son.

"Hey, Daddy. Mommy talks about you all the time," he said, looking at the spirit of his father, smiling. "She said you see me sometimes even when I don't see you."

"Mommy is right. I do see you all the time, I watch you always. I love you very much."

"Sorry, dude, it's time to go. I hear them calling us back." Blake didn't want to go either, but he knew they wouldn't get to continue to visit if they disobeyed. He gave Morgan one more loving look. "We love you all and we'll be watching, as always."

Blue swirling lights came back, swirling fast and bright. As fast as the room lit up, it faded away, the room was back to normal.

"So that's it then, we kill this place and move on?" Jen sighed. "So how are we gonna do it?"

"I don't know yet. Give me some time to think about it," Morgan said, not happy having to leave a place she loved. To her, there were good memories within those walls. More good than bad.

The Free Masons were busy talking to Warren III about his father and his friend, explaining what was going on in a way he'd understand. They explained why he saw his dad and what it meant. He knew his father had been around before, but he'd been too young to remember it. He was also learning what the colors of the lights meant that invaded the house sometimes. Red meant Morgan was using magic. Pink was Mommy. Green usually meant demons, or to him, bad people trying to kill his Mommy and Aunt Morgan. Blue was his daddy.

Jen and Morgan began discussing the plan to burn and or blow up their house then find the Holy Grail. The search could begin from anywhere, moving to Scotland wouldn't be a problem. Material possessions weren't the issue. Trusting what to ship and what to carry with them was the issue. Their basement was a makeshift vault for objects that looked harmless while left untouched, in fact, those artifacts were some of the deadliest in existence. Jen thought and came up with a plan. They would put the objects that needed to go in the catacombs in a coffin and claim it was their dead relative and they were taking them to Scotland to be buried. It worked with captured vampires, so why wouldn't it work with dangerous objects? The books would have to go the same way. Their prized possessions or most dangerous smaller things were going with them on the plane into the coach compartment of the aircraft itself. Morgan never let her book of shadows out of her sight for a minute. Jen's source of power and knowledge was inside her head so it didn't need to be hidden.

"So, it's decided then," Morgan said.

"I guess it is. These are our last days here," Jen sighed. She didn't want to leave but knew there was no other choice to be made. The house would burn or explode and a necessary new life would begin. "It's going to be all right. It's just a house."

Morgan put an arm around Jen's shoulder hugging her. "Yeah, but it was our place with our stuff and all that. I know. This isn't the end. You know, we gotta live to fight another day. That damn Devil's gonna try something massive. Intuition tells me, we need to find this grail, then kick his ass once and for all. All the worldly evil has got to stop. I know it's a balance thing, but lately, if you watch the world news, it's not balanced. There's pure evil going on all over the world right now."

"Yeah, I know." Jen was sad. She knew Morgan was right, but that didn't change her feelings. Morgan picked up on her emotions and a tear rolled down her face as she stood hugging her best friend in the middle of the living room.

Nightfall fell upon the two-story yellow house with the blue shutters and the pretty rose bush in the front yard. Sleep took them. They dreamed silently through the night. The land was cursed, sour to the core. The girls' home would be gone soon. They knew their sentimental attachment was petty but they were trying not to feel hurt by letting go.

Chapter Forty-three

A few days passed, filled with going through items and old research files, getting the dangerous artifacts packed away and ready to ship to Scotland. Bags were packed and flight arrangements were made. Jen and Morgan were busy going through the house, getting rid of old pieces of their lives. Memories, things they'd tucked away in draws and closets, came out of their hiding places in both their hearts and were placed in front of them. Warren Sr. and MacAfee were helping pack away objects and books, and occupying the little one with anecdotes about his dad. They also taught him magic tricks and card games, things fathers and grandfathers did while sharing time with children they loved. The heavy lifting was done by coffin movers, they didn't ask questions they just put the boxes on the truck, took a card with an address to ship the crates to and were gone.

The day everyone left for Scotland, their plan for the soured ground came into full view. They'd make it look like random arson. Someone suggested explosions.

Standing outside, in the dark, under a beautiful blanket of stars, Jen and Morgan each had an old wine bottle in their throwing hands about to light up the cloth wick. Zippos in both their other hands, the girls looked at each other with that same insane expression they got when things got nuts and they had to do something badass yet wicked. Jen winked at Morgan, the talisman around her neck twinkled in the night under the stars.

Launch of the first round of Molotov cocktails was a success. One hit the living room window in the front of the house breaking the glass, lighting up the drapes, and igniting the wall beside it; paint began to peel and fire grew up it. The next one hit one of the upstairs windows, breaking the bottle and exploding into the library. Fire immediately spread through the old books they weren't taking with them. Rapidly growing shades of orange light could be seen from across the street, the yellow siding and blue shudders started to melt.

The smallest Warren was strapped into his seat in the back of the Suburban with the window down so he could see. His grandfather stood by the door telling him it would be okay.

Sir MacAfee was ready to hand the girls more Molotov cocktails when they needed them. Everyone wore gloves, not to get fingerprints on everything, leaving DNA. Jen and Morgan wore black pants, leather jackets, and boots with their hair tied up. There was no way to get DNA on anything. Jen wondered why the hell she even owned that particular pair of pants, but they were obviously purchased for a reason her mind hadn't thought about at the time. Morgan looked at Jen and smiled again, she knew what Jen was thinking because she saw her look down at her feet with a bit of angst.

"Okay, Chica. Let's finish this." Morgan looked in Jen's eyes and saw the starting of temporary tears. "We gotta…it's all right. We got us, remember that. Did you remember to turn the gas on?"

"Yep, okay." Jen sighed back her tears and lit the rag at the end of her second makeshift bomb and threw it with her good arm. It shattered the other front window and fire caught on the curtains. Morgan threw the next bomb hitting the roses. All the blooms flamed up individually, it was utterly beautiful and strangely terrifying at the same time. Jen got her next shot from MacAfee, lit it and launched it, hitting the second story bay window, shattering glass again. Jen looked into her mind for a moment. *She was in the kitchen standing in front of the stove where she'd just blown out the pilot light. She wasn't going fast and had one thing left to do before leaving the house. The rest of the gang had text her phone telling her to get on with it. It made her sad and she remembered her sorrow when she turned up the pilot light on the hot water heater then ran up the basement stairs, out of the kitchen, then out the back door of the house.*

Standing in front of the red Suburban, Jen looked at the place as the curtains lit up. She and Morgan got inside the 'truck' and made sure the windows were rolled up, with the others bent over in the seats just in case. It was only seconds after the girls got in the SUV when the entire house, on fire and raging with smoke, exploded. Glass and ash burst outward while wood splintered and crashed into the street. Sheetrock dust and debris flew in all directions, some of which hit the Suburban parked across from the house. Little Warren looked at the damage and screamed, the noise scared him. His grandfather tried his best to calm him.

After the debris stopped flying, Jen, Morgan, and the gang peered out the windows of the Suburban in awe, they were looking at nothing, a fiery void, devoid of all they remembered. Water, fire, and ash remained in place of their beloved home. Fire rose high in the sky and black smoke billowed up. After the explosion, a few matchsticks on fire, some exposed plumbing and a visceral amount of smoke as black as shadows remained on top of a concrete crawl space foundation.

Sirens could be heard amidst the roaring of the fire. Warren Sr. drove away quickly from the scene of the crime. Their destination was the airport. They had a flight to catch.

***

Lucifer sat on his throne, cursing the existence of some useless mortals. He wasn't happy they somehow found out about the Grail, the one thing that could undo him completely. He talked to his Scottish minions and had a plan set up to distract the women from their goal. If it didn't work, whoever didn't do their jobs would die, then the mortals would die too. In his head, he heard them talking about what they did to their house as they sat at the airport whispering to each other. Jen, his enemy entirely, was crying and her 'daddy' was consoling her. It made Lucifer want to throw up. Of all the human emotions, sadness made him the sickest. He felt bile rise and descend in his throat.

The King of Hell cleared his throat and smoothed down his long white-blond hair. As he rose from his throne, hell shook and his minions retreated into the background. His formidable form crossed to the gated portion of hell. Looking at his lake of fire soothed him. Seeing the faces of the forlorn trapped there for eternity gave him inner peace. He looked around his gated world at his blood-covered, muddy, cracked, and fire laden roads. He loved his world, but there was a half-blood human and her companions who were threatening its existence.

The time to wait around was drawing to a close and the plan was laid out before him. He knew what he had to do. If it went wrong, the balance between good and evil would be thrown off. There would be a new king of hell if he were gone, but not until everyone noticed, which could take a while. Until then, the minions would be left to themselves.

In the meantime, Lucifer walked and thought, his tattered cloak smoking from walking on the burning grounds of his kingdom. All good things were coming to an end, he could feel it. He ran a bony hand through his hair, thick, and long. He looked at his world imagining its non-existence. It worried him. Those women had power they shouldn't have. And power he couldn't take from them or use against them. An angel's power is strong, being combined with a part of his own made Jen too strong to kill in the normal manner. And the blonde had some sort of talisman that helped direct her powers as a witch. It was an old talisman. He would have to pull out the big guns.

He wasn't too worried about the Free Masons. They were old men in the mortal standing. They knew magic, but it was nothing compared to the two women, they had untapped power they probably had no idea how to use.

The tension in hell was mounting, blood sinking into the Underworld, seeping into the porous earth. The humans were helping with the chaos because of their own stupid, weak minded thoughts. It was easy to control a person who wasn't strong enough to keep his minions out. Their stupidity was to his advantage. Armageddon should have taken place months ago, but since it didn't, Lucifer had to calm the minions and make his stand at a later date. There would be no need to possess the women, he would go toe to toe and kill those bitches were they stand. However, only after he got the Grail from them and destroyed it. That was where the hidden minions would come in. In Scotland, the demons were already watching and waiting, ready to start enacting Lucifer's plan to distract the women from seeking the Holy Grail. If they did find it, the minions would make sure the women gave it to him.

As a safeguard in his efforts, Lucifer also had a nanny demon put in place who would take hold of the child, if necessary, to get the objective accomplished. One thing about the Scottish demons versus the American ones, they passed all the demon hunter tests. No one could see their green glowing eyes and the traps didn't work. Demons could go to church if they wanted and salt had no effect. It would be harder to kill something they didn't know for sure was there.

As he stood on the edge of the stream that fed the lake of fire, Lucifer surmounted the idea: all was not lost, not yet. For the moment, the plan would take a slow stance and the demons he picked would edge their way in, earning the trust of the clan O'Connell.

He envisioned the death of his enemy at his own hands and smiled widely, sharp teeth sticking out against his cracked lips breaking the thin skin. He sucked in the blood, black as crude oil. He licked his lips and they healed. Lucifer's eyes glowed green then red as he looked at his lake of fire one last time for the evening. Tomorrow was a different day, one he felt was filled with the promise.

Chapter Forty-four

At the airport, Morgan, Jen, and the rest of the group sat in chairs pulled close together so no one could hear what they were saying to one another. There was a whole conversation in hushed whispers going on as everyone stared at them. No one in the subdivision could find Jen and Morgan, but they had a cell number so the police called them and told them their house burned to the ground. The two women learned how to lie well over their time fighting the supernatural, it was time to pull out their best acting skills.

As Jen spoke she held her sleeping son on her lap. He had no true idea what was happening and was too tired to care so he slept, his curly hair itching his mother's arms. His t-shirt was rumpling up his back from the movement as he slept. His long eyelashes fluttered. Jen looked down at him and smoothed his hair lightly to keep it from itching her arms so much.

"Okay, so that was the cops. I think we did good Jen, acting like it was a surprise to us the house was on fire," Morgan said.

Jen nodded. "Mmm hmm."

"I told them we were out of town and had been for a day."

"And they bought it because we go out of town all the time?" Jen asked.

"Yes, I think they did. So we should be in the clear. As for our next steps, I think we should be careful. I don't know about you all, but I thought I saw demon eyes watching us as we got the boy earlier."

"Oh god! I thought that was just me!" Jen exclaimed quietly.

"Apparently not, lassie," MacAfee piped in. MacAfee was old and getting tired. He was beginning to drift off as he sat in his chair.

"MacAfee, old son, jus' go tae sleep. It's okay. Me and the lassies'll watch out for ye til it's time tae get on tha plane." Warren Sr. patted MacAfee's hand.

Sir MacAfee smiled wearily at his friend, closed his eyes, then folding his arms and hands onto his chest he leaned back in his chair. Airport chairs weren't comfortable, but that's what they had. A long time ago, MacAfee learned to go with the flow of the situation. Being an Elder Wizard with the special sect of the Free Masons was no easy or comfortable task. As he slept, MacAfee heard the voices of his companions. He rarely fell into REM sleep any place other than his own bed. He must have been exhausted when the demons tore through the house in Sioux Falls, he didn't hear a thing that day.

As MacAfee slept, Warren Sr. told Jen and Morgan about his home, the place closely bordered Scotland and happened to be in England, after centuries. It was his ancestral home, his whole family generation after generation lived there. It was a great stone building, a castle, in fact. It was still intact after the wars and fighting. Many years later, it was succeeded back to England.

Warren Sr. thought the family might have rebuilt the castle after all the turmoil to preserve the family heritage. It also held a lot of family heirlooms. Some were dangerous and some were there to state someone's history at the time. An example was the golden statue of King David I, it was cursed a long time ago and had its trappings. Only the O'Connell's could handle the artifact without getting the plague and dying. A set of Irish witches wanted it a few years ago to unleash hell on earth. It had other dangerous powers aside from the curse, which was why it was hidden away from people in a tomb, in the catacombs beneath the castle. Raising a demon army was out of the question. The castle was a great treasure trove of historical artifacts and memorabilia, most of which, wasn't cursed and was on display around the house. As he was explaining his home to the girls, Warren Sr.'s eyes lit up, he loved the place and all it beheld. He actually missed being there. He saw it all in his mind. The exterior, the field it sat in, the flowers that bloomed in the summer, the water he saw out his bedroom window all year around. He even saw the dock he needed to have repaired first thing when they returned to the castle. He thought he might take them out on the Loch in his boat.

Warren Sr. was happy to be taking his family home with him, he wouldn't have to miss them anymore. No matter why they were going to be there. No matter what they faced in the future. Nothing mattered at the moment except happiness. Those moments were rare for him after his son died. He might have had the small group under surveillance since the lad was born, without their knowledge until they met him, but he knew he could trust his girls now. Not to mention, the fact, he'd grown to love them.

It was a long journey to Cumbria County, England. First, the plane landed in Heathrow then the group hired a cab to take them all the way to the county, where they were met at a boarding station by one of Mr. O'Connell's drivers. After they got their things and piled into the back of a large black sedan, the older gentlemen sighed with relief. On the flight, there had been a lot of card games, coloring pages, and books read to Little Warren to occupy his time until he fell asleep. In the cab and car, he was wide-eyed, staring at everything with wonder. The second Warren Sr. stepped out onto the landing of his home, he breathed a sigh of relief. He was back in his native surroundings again.

Jen and Morgan knew they would have to try to appear normal to the outside world now. Whether they could pull off a ruse of that magnitude was yet to be seen. They didn't need jobs, the inheritances still paid the bills. And dating felt like a strange thing to do, still mourning and in love with dead men, it didn't seem feasible. Having jobs would give them a chance to search for the Holy Grail and feel out the people in the area.

A few months passed, Jen and Morgan were acclimating, but the little guy was having nightmares about Sioux Falls and all he witnessed. He still heard the banshee wailing in his head and saw images of the old house set on fire and blazing. There were no solid leads about where to search for the Grail, but the jobs were going okay. Warren Sr. had a few connections and he used them to get the girls part time work somewhere people would keep an eye on them in case of danger.

Scotland and the surrounding countries being Celtic, people had a natural sense of the old ways; superstition was alive and well and belief in the paranormal was real. Jen and Morgan didn't act as if they acknowledged any of it, but they were listening all the time. They were learning from the people in their new land without making them aware of it. As time passed on, a lot of growth in adverse culture took place. They also thought it was pretty cool living in a castle. As the summer drew to an uneventful close at Carlisle Castle, the fall rang in upon them, bringing a lot more rain than they were used to and a sense of foreboding.

Chapter Forty-five

One day, while still searching through books in the library at Carlisle Castle, Jen stumbled across something written in Scottish Gaelic about the Grail in the back of an old book, almost too old to open. She slowly thumbed through the handwritten script bound with the oldest string bindings and trimmed in crumbling visages of glue and binding tape. The book looked homemade and the ink faded on the cracked yellow pages. The last page of Scottish Gaelic script was the most important of all. It told of the last place the Grail would be in the early part of the twentieth century. The oddly bound antique book turned out to be the journal of the last keeper of the Grail. It was a record of where the object had been for centuries.

"Hey Morgan, I think I have something. It says here in this old journal the Grail was scheduled to be moved in the early twentieth century. It's a record of everywhere it's been throughout its existence! That means we only have to track it from the 1900's until now!" Jen exclaimed.

"That's exciting right there! So, we need to look for other journals. Maybe Da can get a hold of some others dated later." Morgan smiled. "Freakin' finally!"

"I know, right!" Jen did the happy dance, showing jubilance. The trail was finally about to come to a head in a good way.

"Okay, so we go talk to Da after a quick check in on the little guy. I'm curious as to whether or not he's getting along with his nanny."

"Yeah, me too. He started acting a bit strange after she came to live here." Jen screwed up her face and looked up the hall at the staircase. "Let's go quietly check in on him."

Jen and Morgan crept up the narrow servant's stairs, beside the door to the catacombs, and up into the second-floor hallway. As they moved along the hall, they heard faint words coming from Little Warren's room. It sounded like he was being scolded by the nanny, who was also a teacher of sorts. Upon entering the room, quietly and quickly, the girls came upon Little Warren and his nanny Mirabelle. She was teaching him. He knew his ABC's and how to count, all his shapes, and his colors. Mirabelle was teaching him how to write sentences she found in books. After that, she would teach him sentences in different languages. He was learning to read and write in many different languages. He was exhausted at the end of his days with her.

Warren III caught sight of his mommy and Morgan and his eyes lit up. He didn't move from his chair he just smiled at them briefly. Mirabelle turned around looking at Jen and Morgan. She seemed slightly perturbed but smiled anyway. Her slim rigid figure in her long skirt and black ladies' boots stood taller than both of the other women. Her bright red hair was tied up in a tight bun at the top of her head. Her glasses were perched on the end of her nose as if she'd been leaning over Warren III as he tried his best to please her with his sentences. She tapped her foot, which meant it was time to go so they could get back to work.

Jen and Morgan turned to leave and saw a small pleading look on the little guy's face temporarily, it faded as Mirabelle turned back to him. The girls quietly left the room, closing the door silently and walking down the hall a bit before either of them said a word.

"Did you see the look on his face, Morgan?" Jen asked. She looked her best friend square in the eye. She was worried and pissed off.

"Yeah. I'm not real happy right now either. We need to watch that girl," Morgan surmised. "She might have been having a rough time with him. You know how he is when he doesn't want to do something."

"I know. He's stubborn, just like his father."

Jen and Morgan went down the hall further, walking back down the narrow staircase back into the kitchen then into the first-floor hall leading to the library. Their stacks of notes were where they'd left them, all the books were on library tables in the exact places they'd been taken. The girls looked at each other and stacked their notes into one pile, placing the books back on the shelves. It took a few minutes and a bit of climbing to get everything put back in its place. After it was done, the girls grabbed their notebooks and piles of papers, leaving the library as they found it. All the notes and research led Jen and Morgan to speculate they were slowly zeroing in on their goal. The next thing to do was ask Warren Sr. if he could find anything out via the Free Masons. He had international connections in high ranking offices, someone might know something.

Hours passed and everyone was preparing for dinner in the great dining hall, like so many other nights since the girls came to live at Carlisle castle. As Jen walked into the wood-paneled hallway she saw the same old paintings lining it. The pictures were of long-dead relatives of the clan O'Connell. The upper floor of the castle was now carpeted in the Modern era, walking down the hall was silent. She heard no sounds except faint voices as she walked past the door to Mirabelle's room. The door was ajar so she peeked in and saw Mirabelle alone but talking to someone. She speaking in hushed whispers about almost getting caught today when Jen and Morgan came in the room with Little Warren. Someone, the person Mirabelle was talking to, stopped talking and Mirabelle looked at the door. She saw a flickering shadow of someone standing there. Before Mirabelle could get to the door, Jen ran as fast as she could to a room across the hall and closed the door. She stayed there for several minutes to make sure no one would catch her eavesdropping. She sighed in relief and went on her merry way to the dining hall. She found herself on the wooden floors in front of the rug under the table, looking at everyone, feeling guilty. It was good the maids and other servants were not allowed to eat in the main dining hall. She looked around and relaxed a bit.

Everyone looked at Jen like they wanted to say something to her about why she was the last to arrive, but they didn't. She was looking around the room, taking in the slight cream-colored walls with all the paintings of Warren O'Connell's clan members hanging on them. As her eyes moved over the walls, she felt the others' eyes on *her*.

"Dear lassie, what is it? Ye got somethin' on yer head jus' now, we can all tell," MacAfee finally piped up.

"Yeah, what the hell did you do? You look guilty, girl!" Morgan said.

"Morgan, I did do something, but not what you think. We can't talk about it here and now," Jen said as she looked at her son.

"After dinner an' tha lad's in bed, we'll have a meetin' in tha drawin' room then," Mr. O'Connell said. He looked worried.

"Okay, Da, sounds good." Jen relaxed and thought about food, she was starving.

Dinner hour passed with no discrepancies, the normal dinner chatter and laughter. A glass or two of wine with the meal always made both girls giggly, it took some getting used to when it wasn't the norm to drink with your supper. It helped them relax, when bedtime came, it helped hush the nightmares either of them might have thought about having, each awoke in the morning rested. That night the girls regaled them with tales of work, telling their three listeners of the funny things about working in the house of Canterbury. They described the way the tourists stared at them as if they shouldn't be there either, wondering what they had going on, being American now working in England. The tourists wanted their backstory, but neither Jen nor Morgan said a thing about their past.

Later in the evening, Warren III was put to bed and Mirabelle went to her room for the night. The adults met in the drawing room. The room was filled with dark oak paneling lined with the heads of stuffed game arranged beside and over fireplace walls, scotch glasses and full decanters sat on tables near some of the plush sitting chairs. Shelves on either end of the room were filled to the brim with books spanning hundreds of years in age. Some were bound after the parchment was discovered in the vaults below the ground floor, somewhere in the catacombs of the castle.

Sitting on the couch near a set of chairs closest to the fire, Jen was almost ready to spill. Mr. O'Connell lit a cigar and looked at Jen, thoughtful before he spoke. To him, the conversation seemed like it would be an important one so he thought of the proper start to his line of questioning.

"So Lassie, do tell us why yer were lookin' guilty enterin' the dining room earlier this evenin'. We dinna kin what ye got up tae."

"Da, I accidentally eavesdropped on Mirabelle. I heard voices and followed them. Her door was cracked so I stood there listening. She was talking to someone, but I couldn't see anything. After I stood there a minute, she saw me, so I ran and hid."

"Ah! No wonder you looked guilty as hell!" Morgan laughed. "Nosy!"

"Dude, shut up! Remember what you said earlier in the day about that crazy woman looking after my son?" Jen was getting slightly irritated.

"Calm down, girl. I'm just messing with ya. Yeah, oh god, it was creepy. We were about to leave after checking in on the midget and he gave us this look like, 'please help me' but it vanished as soon as Mirabelle turned back to him and we left the room. She was seriously pissed we came in there, like we interrupted something of utmost importance to her. I was pissed off when I left the room and so was Jen," Morgan explained.

"Well tha' puts 'er on tha watch list then," Warren Sr. said.

"Also, we found out something else today. We know where they moved the Holy Grail in the turn of the Twentieth Century," Jen said quickly.

"She found it in an old journal that must have belonged to one of the keepers. It was hidden in your library," Morgan explained to the Free Masons.

"Well, there's a reason for it. Tha clan O'Connell had a keeper in tha line in recent centuries. It's no me, but me father or one o' his bunch was said tae 'ave been tha one who took it to its restin' place. Wherever tha' may be."

"Your family just keeps getting cooler and cooler all the time!" Morgan exclaimed, smiling widely.

"Well, that brings me to my next question then, Da. Do you know anyone who might know how to locate it?" Jen asked, ignoring Morgan's last comment.

"Yeah, an' I been workin' on it while ye been researchin' on yer own in the library. I havena got any news back yet, which means they're still searchin'. Soon as they get it done, they'll be lettin' me know. Keep it hushed up, cause now ye mention it, I dinna trust tha' nanny, but we need tae act like noothin's wrong an' we're no watchin' 'er." With that, Mr. O'Connell bid everyone good night and got up to exit the room. As he crossed the floor of the drawing room, Mirabelle ran up the stairs as fast as her human form would take her. She heard everything the group was thinking and planning. She would tell her master about the new information as soon as everyone else in the house was asleep. Excitement coursed through her.

***

No one noticed Mirabelle eavesdropping. Everyone disbanded and went to bed. It was getting late and the group was tired. Mirabelle was in her room smirking. She knew what was happening in the castle and what the humans *thought* was going on. They were so wrong about what her master had in store for them. At two in the morning, the sky was pitch black, not many stars were visible in the Northern Hemisphere. Carlisle was dark. The only lights on in the castle were some in the hallway leading the way to the privy. The only noises to be heard were the faint far-off sounds of old men snoring.

Mirabelle lit a candle, saying a summoning ritual, calling out to her master. "Bagabi laca bachabe, Lamc cahi achabade, Karrelyas, Lamac lamec Bachalyas, Cabahagy sabalyas, Baryolas, Lagoz atha cabyolas, Samahac et famyolas, Harrahya," she whispered.

Lucifer appeared before her in his black cloak. Mirabelle smiled at him. She told him the information she gathered about the humans from earlier. Her master seemed pleased at first then he looked at her with hateful reproach.

"Mir, my girl, in a way you've done well. In another, you've screwed up. You were not supposed to accost the boy so soon. I wanted to wait until winter so the women wouldn't be able to leave so fast. You know England and Scotland and all the surrounding lands are hard to get away from in winter."

"Sire, I'm sorry. Do I fail you?" She bowed before him, eyes on the ground.

"No, you haven't failed me. I know the next move to find their precious Grail. It's time to put the other part of the plan into action. Tell Aiden and Errol to get ready for their part of the plan. They need to start as soon as possible, tomorrow, in fact."

"I will do that immediately, Sire. And thank you." Mirabelle bowed once again before the King of Hell.

"For what?" Lucifer asked her.

"For not killing me," she said.

Lucifer leaned in close to Mirabelle and whispered, "My dear, servant of the dark, you will die, but only when I say you will and *only* then." He was close enough to her he could have used his magic to make blood pour from her eyes if he wanted to, but he resisted. He backed up a little, took her hand and kissed the top before he bid her farewell for the evening then vanished.

Mirabelle sighed in relief, she might live long enough to complete her mission, which so far had little mishap. After the conversation with the only soul to incite fear in her, she was exhausted. She took the pins from her long hair and let it flow down her back, she usually wore it up every day and only took it down at night. Her long, thin red hair fell down her back in rings from being up so long. She shook it out further and tried to get comfortable. Her white nightgown was long and not frilly. She needed to be warm. Living in England and the surrounding countries her entire life, human and demon, she remembered the temperatures in accordance. It was coming into the fall, which meant colder nights and bigger blankets.

Right before Mirabelle slid into her bed she made one phone call and simply said to a male voice on the receiving end, to start with their part tomorrow. She hung up her cell phone and put it on the nightstand beside the bed. She got up from the bed, flipped back the warm covers, then slid inside thinking and smiling. *Tomorrow*, she thought.

As the few stars sparkled against the blackness of the night and moon shone over the castle to be waxing and waning, sleep took the whole place as its prisoner. The main gate was closed and locked and the magic protection spells were in place. Everything was quiet and everyone at Carlisle was dreaming while Lucifer was busy torturing souls in the bowels of hell.

Chapter Forty-six

As the dawning of the sun came upon Cumbria County, people started to rise within the walls of Carlisle Castle. The maids and servants rose early to prepare for the day. Mirabelle rose with them. Her only preparation was to be up and dressed, ready to receive her charge, to teach him whatever stupid thing came into her head that seemed semi-logical to teach a young boy, in case her snoopy employers came into the room.

Slowly the residents of the castle awakened one by one, all five people were once again in the dining hall waiting for their breakfast so they could go about their day. Dressed in sweaters and black pants, both women were ready for their jobs, the men always wore suits. It was something they'd grown accustomed to, having spent many years with the guise of businessmen, never mind they couldn't sell anything to save their souls. The little one always wore his jeans and sweaters, his black curly mop detangled every morning.

***

It was an uneventful morning in the House of Canterbury. The rain made Jen and Morgan's jobs far from interesting. There were no tours of the house to give, no history to talk about to visitors, no sign-ins for guests. It was the start of the off-season until Christmas. Both women were busy putting things away from the summer season in the entrance hall of the huge house when someone snuck up on Morgan and scared her, she squealed and almost took a tumble off a ladder.

"Who are you?" Morgan said, angry at being scared, her heart still racing in her chest.

"M'name's Errol, miss. I be lookin' for who migh' be runnin' the place today. I've some things tae discuss wit 'em," Errol said in a perfect Scottish accent. "Wouldna be you, would it, lassie?" He looked her in the eyes, his bright blue ones staring into her soul, making her shiver.

"Umm, yes, that would be me," she said, being to flush all over her pale skin. Her cheeks went rosy. "How can I help you, Errol, you said your name was?"

"Well, lassie, firs' off, you can tell me yer name. And second, it's off-season here, so tha place can be rented out for gatherin's an stoof now. M' friends and m'self would like tae rent 'er out for tha weekend comin' up." Errol smiled at her with his perfect toothy grin, it reminded her of someone she loved, his appearance even reminded her of him in some small ways.

"My name's Morgan. Yes, I'll have to check the datebook for you on those days, but this week is when the house can start being rented out. After we get all of the seasonal items put away." Morgan tried to act casual, it wasn't working.

"Well, go on, check tha' then fer me an I'll stay righ' here an wait for ye." He knew he was flustering her and he enjoyed it. Lucifer gave him the easy job. He winked at her.

Morgan climbed down off the ladder gracefully. As soon as her feet hit the floor she walked over to the desk closest to the main door of the entrance hall. She flipped the big book used for scheduling tours and rentals. As she looked down at the pages, she glanced up occasionally, smiled and quickly looked away again. When she did, she would put her blonde hair behind her ears so she could see the pages better. Finally, she looked up and spoke to Errol.

"Yes, I think that'll be fine. So you want to schedule this coming weekend. The whole weekend?"

"Aye, lassie, I do. Put it in the names of Errol and Aiden MacQuinn. My cousin an' m'self," he said smiling brightly at her, trying his best to lure her in with his charms.

"Ah, how nice," Morgan said glancing up from writing them into the time slot. "That will be two hundred pounds sterling for the weekend."

Errol ran his fingers through his blond hair quickly then grabbed his wallet out of his back pocket and paid Morgan the fee. He tried to act as if this was his first time flirting with a girl, but it wasn't. His line of work was seducing women for his master's use. Right now he was working Morgan with his smile.

"Um, hey, would ye be interested in comin' this weekend as well? You're welcome tae join us, ye know. Somethin' 'bout ye tells me ye need some foon," he told Morgan trying his best not to get too forward right away.

"Maybe. It's been a while for me," she said sheepishly.

"Okay then, I'll see ye there. If ye have a friend, bring 'er. There'll be a lot o' people fer ye tae meet and talk tae…American girl."

"You caught that, did you?" Morgan giggled.

"Darlin', ye canna miss it." Errol was smiling with the light dancing in his eyes.

"Okay, I'll see what I can do."

"See ye on tha' weekend then. Bye fer now." Errol smiled one last time his biggest smile then turned and left the House of Canterbury.

As he walked away, Morgan thought about Errol and how much he reminded her of Blake. Her favorite things to remember about Blake were his smile slightly dimpling his cheeks, his eyes dancing in the light, his attitude and confidence that never came out sounding arrogant. He was her light. She remembered the moonlight seemed to dance in Blake's eyes on those starry nights when he would hold her while they sat on the porch in Sioux Falls enjoying the night sky. The new person who walked into Morgan's world reminded her of what she missed and everything she would never have. For a few moments, she went into the closet where the coats were kept and got down on her knees, she put her hands over her face and cried.

***

Later in the day, when Jen and Morgan were on their way home, Jen told Morgan a similar story to the one she experienced, weeping and all. They hugged each other in the car as the driver drove them back to the castle. It was a rainy day in England as they reached the border city where they lived. Both girls wanted to reach the castle's land where it felt safe and loved. They wanted to hug all the guys. Upon reaching the road to Carlisle Castle, Morgan felt chills and worry run down her spine. Pink lightning flashed across Jen's almost black eyes, she felt the foreboding too.

"Something's happening in the castle," Morgan was the first to blurt it out.

"Yeah, I feel it too, not just from you. Something's wrong."

"Driver, speed up!" Morgan shouted at him.

Carlisle Castle was just out of view until the driver sped up. It looked normal, but that meant nothing to Jen and Morgan. Normal was always anything but. Before the car could get to a complete stop at the entry gate the girls were out of the car and running to the entrance. With the code punched into the alarm at record speed, two bodies ran, brunette and blonde hair flying in their homemade wind. Skittering to a halt in the entry hall, Morgan and Jen ran into each other, nearly falling down. Both women screamed the names of Warren Sr. and MacAfee loud and repeatedly.

"Shhh! Stop screamin', lassies." Warren Sr. hurriedly came walking down the stairs into the entry hall. "Ye felt somethin' didn't ye?"

"YES! What is it?" Morgan said, she was still worked up. She looked at him in earnest. Her empathy was on overdrive, ready to spill out at any moment. Keeping the energy of that power at bay was making her insides boil.

"Would ye both calm down? It's not gonna help anyone."

Lightning flashed in Jen's eyes. "Tell me now. What's wrong with my son?" It flashed again threatening to take hold.

"Yer too in tune with the lad, seriously. He fell, tha nanny sais he was walkin' down the stairs an' fell down the last few, landin' on his side. He's okay, except tha coma," Warren Sr. said with sadness. His eyes were red rimmed from crying.

"Where's MacAfee?" Jen asked quickly. She started shaking and tears were running down her face. Her long hair was a wet mess, she smooshed it down and out of her way.

"He's wit' the boy o' course. Tryin' tae heal him. So far, he's no had success, but he's still tryin'."

The girls and Warren Sr. almost ran up to Little Warren's room, where they saw him, pale and sweaty, in his little bed looking as if he were asleep. Someone put his pajamas on him and there was a cool towel on his forehead. Mirabelle was sitting beside his bed in a chair. Beside her was a table with the water basin on it for dipping the towel on the little boy's head. Mirabelle was reading a book to Little Warren. She looked up and frowned, looking over at the boy. She was good at faking concern.

Little Warren was lying down in his bed hearing his mother cry over him and he felt her hand clutch his, but he could do nothing. His mind was trapped. He was trapped. At first, there was confusion as to how it happened but then he remembered, for months Mirabelle's ideas were washing over him, into his head. She was trying to turn him into a bad boy. He didn't want to be that. He defied her and she pushed him. He saw her eyes as he fell. For a split second, they glowed green. His mommy told him green eyes meant demons. That scared him and after he saw that, all he remembered was his mind waking up, but his body wouldn't. Terror struck his mind and he shouted loudly inside his head trying his hardest to wake up. At first there was nothing, his voice echoed back against his mental walls, but he kept working at it. He kept shouting, focusing all his inner energy on breaking the barrier that grabbed hold of him and trapped his mind. He continued to fight hard against whatever force was holding him inside himself while the world thought he was in a coma, stuck away from them. He kept hearing his mother's sobs and shouted louder.

On the outside of Little Warren's mind, where the other people were, everyone saw Little Warren's eyelids flutter. Jen was speechless while watching her son. She wondered what was happening to make his eyes shift, in mid-thought she saw his eyes fly open glowing bright green. The five adults gapped in awe. His body rose up out of the bed and hovered in front of his mother. Jen said nothing, she watched as her son's eyes turned to pure white light too bright to look at. The whole room was bathed in it. Little Warren hovered in front of Jen for a bit longer, then the light vanished from his eyes and he almost dropped out of the air. If Jen hadn't caught him, he would have hit the ground. His coma was over, he was alive in all senses of the word, hugging his mommy tightly around the neck.

Mirabelle shrunk away from the crowd. After she reached the door, she ran to her room when she saw the white light coming from her charge. *No one mentioned the brat has his own powers.* It scared her.

Chapter Forty-seven

Lucifer bit his lip hard enough to draw black blood from it. He was angry. How the hell did that kid get angel powers? he thought. The one woman had both, but how did the kid get the good ones? He strummed his fingers on the arm of his throne, pondering what should have been obvious. His father gave the kid those powers. Now there was a third possibly formidable force against him. Mirabelle didn't push the kid hard enough to kill him like Lucifer really wanted. She was going to have to work harder and if not, she would pay for screwing up. First, he would torture that bitch then he would burn her bones slowly. She would already be a pile of black goo by now if it weren't for him anyway. So why not just end her the way she would have gone years ago?

Lucifer hoped the other two minions had better luck. It would be slow, but suffering at the hands of people who deliberately looked like lost loves was sinful, his kind of plan. Using pain and one's true desires against them was wicked, he loved being bad. The loss of their greatest loves was something holding them back, something to use against them. He sat deep in thought about how to destroy his enemy when Errol and Aiden both walked into his chamber. Lucifer looked up at them. He sighed and waited for them to tell him anything useful. Each told him the story of how the women accepted their invitation to the party over the weekend at the House of Canterbury. Each told similar tales of flirtation and slow, but growing anticipation they'd felt for the women when asked come. Lucifer smiled, part of the plan was going as he pictured it would.

When the two male demons exited the room Lucifer looked at the tall ceilings in his inner chamber, blood dripped down on the floor slowly gathering in puddles here and there. Out his window, he saw the fiery pit and knew it deserved at least two more souls to join the ones he'd already collected over the centuries. When he got their souls, he wouldn't drop them into the lack of fire first thing, he wanted to play with them first. He wanted to ruin those pretty faces, strip their outer shell so he could then destroy the inner one. He wanted to eviscerate them a little at a time so Jen would know how it feels to be blown up. Only she wouldn't be able to put the pieces back together like he could.

Molten waters spanned out before him and he looked at the faces once again as they rode the orange tides. He stood at the edge of the lake and stream feeding the fiery waters, he felt soothed staring at it. He knelt beside it and picked up a piece of old stone. As he held it in his hand, he thought about all the evil he could do with Jen and Morgan and others like them out of his way. He could eliminate five in one meeting at Carlisle castle. He kept thinking and decided to throw the rock, skipping it across the small river, hitting dead people in the head. He laughed hard for a minute as the people groaned when they glided passed him. His aspirations lifted momentarily, he returned to his chambers in high spirits. As for the rest, it would either work itself out or it wouldn't, but when the time came, people would die, that was worth smiling about.

After the small Zen session at the lake of fire, the King of Hell rested. If he still had a beating heart, it would have been calm and collected as he closed his eyes.

***

Days passed and the residents at Carlisle Castle lived on. Things went back to the routine they'd formed, meshing with the three new members of the household. The weekend was nearing and the invitation was looming in the heads of both Jen and Morgan, as they hadn't quite decided to go or not.

Warren Sr. and MacAfee were having a hard time convincing the girls to go and enjoy themselves. After what happened to Little Warren, fun was the last thing on either of their minds. Even if he acted as if nothing had ever happened, Jen and the rest of the gang knew it did.

***

At the House of Canterbury, everyone was making ready for the festivities over the weekend and Jen and Morgan kept thinking about both of the men that asked them to come. At one moment, Jen questioned it and the next she was wondering why someone would ask her on a date of sorts. By the look of things, Morgan was questioning it also. One thing they both thought: What would Warren and Blake think about it?

"You know, I think they might want us to do this. We're still mortal. We still have needs and wants in this life, remember those?" Morgan, the current voice of reason surmised.

"Yes, I know, but it feels weird possibly moving on," Jen said.

"Yeah, it does, but I think they want us to. Ya know? Like, we'll see them again, but not until later on, whenever that is. We can't stop here with our hearts. That isn't right. We'll always love them and that love will never fade away. Neither will our *want* to be loved by someone who can touch us and we can always see. I know they still love us too, but they can't hold us, talk to us when they want to, or kiss us like they used to." Morgan sighed. She began her task of preparing the room.

"You're right. I wish you weren't, but hell if you aren't." Jen walked into the next room and started putting toiletries out on the counter and towels in the basket.

"Ya know, I think we should go. I think it would be good for us," Morgan said loudly from the other room. "We need to have some fun. It's been too long."

"Maybe." Jen was busying herself, but she smiled a little.

On the way home, both women started talking about how it might be fun to go to the party they were invited to. They even started feeling excited, an emotion Jen and Morgan almost forgot existed. The emotion spread throughout the vehicle, even the driver smiled, he never did that. After dinner, the conversation went to their weekend party plans. Mr. O'Connell was glad the women decided to go. He was ready to push them out the door on Friday night if they said no. Six years without so much as a date or phone call from another man was too much. His girls mourned still, he knew that. He also knew it was time to try something different.

There were no stars that night, rain clouds hung over the full moon in the ink pool sky. The castle grounds were silent and the lights were dimmed. Warren Sr. was standing at the window in his bedroom looking out into the night, thinking about what he was recently told about the Holy Grail and where to find it. He thought about it with trepidation. Could he send his girls out there alone? He knew they could take care of themselves while he and MacAfee made sure nothing happened to the boy. Did he want to risk it? He pondered those thoughts for a long time until he decided he needed to go to sleep and think about it in the morning. He'd tell the girls what he found out after the weekend was over and they'd had a bit of fun. His last quandary of the night was how his grandson got powers of his own and how the little lad was to use them. Mr. O'Connell of the clan O'Connell, a descendant of the kings of Scotland, closed his eyes, resting his weary mind for the night. When he drifted off, he saw images of the Sudan and the Rainforests of Africa. Then his mind flashed to soggy streets of Seattle, Washington in the rainy season. Images of places flooded his mind for what seemed like hours, but it was only about thirty seconds. The final image was of a lot of deaths. He was surrounded by his little family including MacAfee. In the final image, he saw fire all around the five of them. They were standing on a hilltop in the middle of a molten lake of fire. The only thing he heard was the laughter of someone he couldn't see, but he knew he'd heard the voice before. Fiery orange eyes glowed at him in his mind, then glowing momentarily green. He could see a pair of eyes floating in midair leering at him. Then he heard an annoying noise and awoke in a cold sweat. His alarm clock was screaming out its *Meep! Meep! Meep!* sounds at him.

He ran his sweaty hand through his graying black hair. It didn't feel like the new day would be a good one. He saw the gray rainy sky through his window, the gloom wasn't helping his mood. Something new was the red damp spot on his pillow. He didn't notice it until he got out of bed. He walked into his bathroom and looked in the mirror. There was a red line drying up across the top of his forehead. He took a washcloth and washed away the drying blood to reveal a thick scratch all the way across. There was no way to hide it. Warren Sr. shrugged and brushed his teeth then went into his closet to find a suit for the day. It was a somber day so a somber gray was his choice. He picked his tie and turned around to turn off the light. As he walked out of his oversized closet with his suit on and his tie around his neck, he turned to face the full-length mirror in his room. He saw the long scratch in the mirror. *How do ye explain what ye dinna understand?* Soon he was ready for the day, making his way toward the dining hall, not thrilled at the idea of trying to explain. When the maids caught site of Warren Sr., they gasped. He looked at them and went on his way into the dining hall where the others were awaiting him. When they saw his face, the others came rushing toward him. They were clamoring to know what happened to him. He told them the truth as he understood it. The lot of them stood in awe.

"What do you mean, you were dreaming and it turned scary? You woke up looking like this? What the fuck, Da!" Morgan said.

"Aye lass, that's exactly what I mean tae say tae ye," Warren Sr. said slurring his Scottish, he was tired.

"Sit here, Da. We want to look you over. MacAfee, please," Jen rationally said.

Mr. O'Connell sat in the chair on the end of the dining table as always and MacAfee got up and stood beside him, looking at the large thick scratch, not speaking. He was in his mind. After a few moments, MacAfee spoke low, stolid, blunt, and to the point.

"Gather 'round, lassies and lad. I've only ever seen it once in all m' years o' workin' for tha magical sect o' tha Free Masons. I know the laddie might be a bit wee tae hear it, but it could be helpful later on. This was done cause tha Devil invaded yer mind, old son." The Scottish accent appearing to come out thicker the more upset MacAfee became. "Tha last part o' tha dream, he was puttin' them images in yer head, ye kin it. He means tae mess wit ye while the lassies're out lookin' fer the grail. He might be tryin' tae possess ye somehow. He's tryin' tae crack ye like tha one demon did wit them ladies there in Russia."

"You're kidding! Not this shit again!" Morgan exclaimed.

"Yep, looks like it, lass," MacAfee said, confirming it.

"Damn Devil! I can't wait to fuck him up!" Jen was pissed off. "Fucking wonderful!"

"We kin it, he'd try somethin', didn't we?" Warren Sr. asked. "Using me tae get tae ye, that's not abnormal, girl."

"I know, but damn it! Why not just come after me directly? I was the one that blew his ass up, remember? Not you!" Jen shouted, pink lightning streaked across her brown eyes.

"Where's the fun in that? Knowing you could blow him up again takes the fun out it, don't you think?" Morgan said, trying to use her logic.

"Hey, it's Friday, dinna let it spoil yer good time. You girls go tae tha party tonight and have foon, stop worryin' about this. MacAfee'll be here."

After the conversation, Warren Sr. hushed the group and the maids came in to serve them breakfast. Jen was sitting in her chair fuming, but she still ate. Her movements were quicker when she was mad as hell, she clicked her fork against her plate too hard a few times. Morgan kicked her under the table and she scowled at her, giving her a look that told her to calm down and drop it.

As the girls were leaving for work, Warren Sr. and Sir MacAfee hugged them both, telling them not to worry. Sir MacAfee put protection spells on the castle after the girls left and set to healing his friend. It didn't take long to get the scratch to look like a scar. MacAfee was a great healer.

Chapter Forty-eight

The rain didn't let up until the afternoon at the House of Canterbury. The day was passing slowly. At about three o'clock, when Errol and Aiden walked into the entrance hall of the house. They each took a look around and smiled when they spotted the girls at the reception desk doing the paperwork for the week. Jen and Morgan didn't see them come in. The two Scotsmen snuck up behind the desk and 'scared' the women who turned around flabbergasted. Jen almost killed them as her powers instinctively came to the front of her being, before her glowing eyes appeared she saw them and calmed herself.

"I guarantee you, scaring me is not something you want to do, guys," Jen said.

"She's not kidding. You just about got the pointy end of that ball point pen in her hand there," Morgan covered. "She's a psycho, that one," she said, trying to play it off, laughing.

The guys laughed and asked if they were going to join them later in the evening. Jen and Morgan said they decided to come to their party, thanking them for the invite. Errol asked if everything was ready on the top floor of the house, it was assured, everything was made up according to their specs. When all their questions were answered, the men walked away, saying they had to go get ready for the party. When they did, Morgan rounded on Jen.

"Dumbass…" she said, scowling.

"Yeah, whatever," Jen said, rolling her eyes at Morgan. "So, I'm a dumbass psycho, fine by me."

"I'm beginning to think working with the public isn't such a good fit for us anymore."

"Tell me about it…" Jen said as she continued to go about her tasks.

Later in the evening, people started to arrive at the House of Canterbury. The event was by no means a prestigious one, but the guests were dressed.in nice suits and casual dresses. The girls ended up bringing the right attire and avoided a trip back home. Jen wore her hair long, dark, and straight down her back, flowing over the top of her black dress, which hugged her hips and fell to her knees in a nice elegant pleating. Morgan wore a red knee-length dress to go with the talisman hanging around her neck. She finished her look off with low black heels and little makeup. Simple but classy, just the way each woman liked things.

***

The evening started out well, the girls had a few drinks, mingling with the small crowd, introducing themselves. Everyone else was from one of the countries that made up Great Britain except Jen and Morgan. Strangely, it felt good to be in a room with so many different people, vastly different than Americans. At a certain point in the night, Errol and Aiden asked the girls to join them in the center of the room. The men happily introduced Jen and Morgan to the entire crowd. Wine glasses were raised as cheers were said. The girls drank enough alcohol to make them flushed in the face and warm.

In a few quick motions, the crowd zeroed in on Jen and Morgan. The group surrounded them, flashing their green eyes, moving in closer. Several rows of sharp teeth came their way. Both women were not scared. They stood still as people converged on them. Jen closed her eyes. When she opened them, her eyes glowed bright pink. She held Morgan's hand, lifting it toward the crowd. Not a word was spoken aloud, but demons exploded, vaporized in seconds all around them.

Errol and Aiden, eyes glowing and teeth showing, backed away from the crowd. The two men were in awe at what they saw. It made them run for the exit. Glasses full of wine hit the floor, shattering. Demons took that as their cue to scatter and ran like they were set on fire. The doors became stuffed with demons trying to get away from the two women standing in the center of the room, killing them one by one. A few moments later, the two women stood alone in a large room in the Canterbury House. Jen blinked a few times, as her eyes returned to normal she let go of Morgan's hand.

"Well, no one told us Europe was full of demons, but now we know the bastards are everywhere." Morgan sighed.

"Let's go home, I'm tired." Jen was not feeling well having used up a bunch of her energy.

***

MYSTIK LEGENDS

A cab was called after midnight to take Jen and Morgan back to Carlisle Castle where their beds awaited them as did the passcodes and security spells. Jen was nearly asleep when the cab pulled up outside their home and Morgan paid the fare. When Jen and Morgan walked into the entrance hall of the castle their shoes were so loud it woke the others. People came running down the stairs.

"Dude, you guys need to back up and get her a chair," Morgan said. Someone materialized with one. Morgan loosened her grip on Jen's arm, sitting her down. She looked everyone squarely in the eyes and said, "There's a reason we don't go out and have fun like normal people. Tonight proved the point."

"Damned room full of fuckin' demons..." Jen trailed off.

"What'd tha lassie say?" Warren Sr. couldn't hear her.

"She said 'Damned room full of fucking demons.' And yeah, she's right. They got us drinking something that was probably drugged and tried to kill us. The whole place was swarming with 'em! We were clusterfucked almost."

"Clusterfucked..." Jen repeated, giggling through her exhaustion.

"She got us through it though. That's why she's so tired and delirious. There were too many of them. She didn't get them all, but she got a lot of them. And man, that surge of power she had going on, was the good stuff. She had me by the hand when she was killing 'em and whoa! It was amazing how she held on that long."

"Clusterfucked…funny word…" Jen was still laughing.

"She needs to go to bed. I think we can finish filling you in when we all get up tomorrow. I think we need to quit those jobs. The Grail needs to be a priority now. Lucifer's not stopping. I know it was him who sent a whole room full of demons after us. It had to have been him."

"Yer righ'. We need tae get her tae bed. Lassie needs 'er rest. Come on, Jen, let's get ye tae bed," Warren Sr. said to the still laughing Jen, grabbing her by her arm, hoisting her onto her feet. Warren Sr. directed her up the stairs and down the hallway to her bedroom and opened the door. As he hugged her goodnight, he told her to sleep well. She calmed down, hugging him brought her back to herself as her eyes were closing. She told him good night, shutting the door behind her.

Morgan went into her room, next to Jen's, took off her clothes then put on her pajamas. She was tired too. She was tired of fighting and living that nightmare of a life. She was tired of everything in general, but she knew, if nothing else, they had one mission left. They *had* to get the devil to finally stand down or they would never have peace.

***

Meanwhile, in the kingdom of Hell, there was a conference going on in Lucifer's main chamber hall. His plot to destroy Jen and Morgan was falling down around his knees. Using Errol and Aiden as distractions didn't work, instead, the women killed more of his demons. After hearing the story Errol and Aiden told him, he sat infuriated by those two mortal females. This proved Jen and Morgan wouldn't be so easy to get rid of. Sitting at the table with blank looks on their faces, both men knew what was most likely coming next for them. Their boss knew if the plan kept getting fucked up, there would be no Armageddon then no true freedom from Hell and no chaos or calamity. Seeing his burning orange eyes up close made both men nervous. He was a lot scarier in person than when he was summoned.

Lucifer put both bony hands on the table made of stone. The two demons saw white bony fingers barely covered in skin and long graying to black fingernails. He stared coldly at them, waiting to see which one would and start spewing excuses as to why the job didn't get done. Neither man said anything.

"Okay. Which one of you dumbasses wants to tell me how and why you messed up?"

"We almost had 'em! I swear! Then tha dark haided one's eyes lit up an' demons started vaporizin' in thin air," Errol managed to choke out.

"Apparently, you didn't almost have them, you idiot, or they'd be dead by now!"

Errol started choking on his own spit, coughing up masses of black demon blood. He kept coughing until he finally choked on a large clog of his own blood, hit his head on the stone table hard, and became motionless, devoid of life.

Lucifer looked at Aiden. "Do you have anything to add to this tale or should I just rip you to pieces?"

"Please, sire. Dinna kill me, I beg o' ye. We was convergin' on 'em when demons started dyin'. I promise, it's no our fault. Ye ne'er told us they was that powerful, sire," Aiden said, pleading for his life.

"Oh, well…see ya later, in the river." Lucifer raised his hand to Aiden. He rose to his feet and started screaming. Aiden's head was being pulled apart from inside the middle of his skull. His face was being ripped in two. Black blood washed down the front of him in sheets of liquid. His blood-curdling wail only lasted a few more seconds then his mouth tore apart. Once Aiden's head was split down the middle, Lucifer decided he had enough and lowered his hand. The body fell to the floor with the head flopping around on both shoulders. Lucifer looked at the dead demons and shrugged, leaving their mess at the conference table then exiting the room. *Mirabelle had better be doing a good job or she and those two fuck ups will be dead,* Lucifer thought.

Chapter Forty-nine

The morning sun shone through the castle windows early in the morning in the middle of summer. There was nowhere to go or anything needing doing that day, but the whole household rose at their regular time on Saturday. Breakfast was eaten with little talking, everyone got dressed as if there was something going on.

Jen still looked tired and felt it. Her long hair needed a wash to get all the demon vapors out of it but she didn't care, it felt like she'd drank a whole bottle of wine the night before although she knew better.

Morgan looked at Jen in the hallway on the way to the library, she was worried her strength wasn't coming back as well as it used to. A good night's sleep was usually all it took to restore her energy. Jen felt her worried vibes and just shrugged, walking away from her down the hall to check in on her son.

Once she got to Little Warren's room she made it a point to knock on his door, then she entered his room. Mirabelle was in there with a blackboard with a lot of words and foreign language writing on it.

When Little Warren saw her, he ran to her. "Mommy! Are you okay, Mommy? You look sick."

"Yeah baby, I'm fine, just tired still. How're your lessons coming?"

"They're okay. I can say 'nice to meet you' in five languages. And Mirabelle is teaching me to write what she said are 'salutations' too," Little Warren told her.

"Well done, baby. I was just coming in to check up on you. Then I think I was going to take a walk around the castle. If you get done soon, maybe Mirabelle will bring you out to see me outside."

"Mirabelle, can we?" Little Warren asked.

"We'll see, there is still a lot left in this lesson." Mirabelle was trying to flake out. She didn't want to spend time with anyone who was capable of killing her so easily. "Come sit so we can get back to work."

Little Warren looked up at his mother and frowned. He hugged her then released her. "Okay."

"Bye, baby. Learn lots, okay? Love you!"

"Okay, Mommy. I love you too!" The little one was disparaged, but couldn't say so in front of his nanny, he was scared of her and knew what she was, but he couldn't tell a soul. He remembered what happened before the coma, she pushed him down the stairs after he saw her eyes momentarily glow green. He thought he'd remember seeing her like that for the rest of his life. He would remember the fear too. His grandda told him he wouldn't always be so small.

Jen exited her son's room, leaving quietly. Everything there looked and felt normal. There were no hidden scowls, no look of fear on her son's face. Perhaps she and Morgan imagined it. As she was moving down the hall, Jen looked at the pictures on both sides of the walls, kings and queens of old, the collection was vast. She was impressed with how well the paintings were cared for. Her da must have taken special care when one of them needed fixed or restored to its original state. She wished she knew more about the people her son's bloodline. Her head was in the clouds thinking about ancestry and she almost fell down the front stairs, but she grabbed the banister just in time.

In the library, Morgan was reading up on the destination of the Holy Grail. Da gave her the destination location in the morning after breakfast so she would be able to study up on her surroundings before they got there and were in the thick of it. There wouldn't be time for her to figure it out once they arrived because there were going to be a lot of obstacles to tackle, she had a feeling.

Books were laid out on the floor of the library in order of possible acquisition position. Morgan was laying out a battle strategy in her head for when she and Jen got close enough to the Grail. It wasn't going to be easy to gain access, there would be demons to fight.

Warren Sr. was in the drawing room, pinning sewing pins to a map, trying to help the ladies find the safest route to the location of the Grail. MacAfee was in his Merlin tower practicing spells to arm Morgan with, in the event she should need them.

Jen was out running in the courtyard, end-to-end and corner-to-corner, making laps around it. As she ran, her thoughts began to race also. She knew she needed to be training or doing something to prepare for the impending journey like everyone else, but all she could do was run. She needed to mentally prepare for what they were up against, she was thinking about Warren and how she missed him. She thought about how life changed the day he died and never went back to what she'd known prior to his vicious murder. Their life was one terror after another, it never ended. If not for loving her son, a driving force in their lives, would the women have had what it took to stay alive in this new nightmarish hell? *I just don't know.* She shrugged off her morbid thoughts and kept running.

At the end of the day, after plans were set up and hashed out, everyone gathered after dinner in the drawing room yet again. Maps were draped on tables while strategies were discussed. Everyone agreed, Jen and Morgan would go in alone because it would be easier to hide only two people. If the whole entourage was with them, it might end badly. Also, someone had to watch Little Warren and his nanny. Everyone was unsure of Mirabelle, even though she didn't show any signs of being anything or *anyone* other than what she said she was, especially after the coma.

***

Jen and Morgan made travel arrangements to the last known location of the Holy Grail. According to the last word from inside the secret organization of the Free Masons, they'd be journeying to Qumran off the shores of the Dead Sea. There were caves that held pieces of the *Dead Sea Scrolls* until the late 1940's and 1950's, about a ten-year span, researchers finally having thought they recovered the remains of the scrolls, stopped looking for them in the eleven caves. Jen and Morgan were to go there and search out the Holy Grail. If they couldn't come across it, Lucifer would surely kill them because their powers wouldn't be enough, no matter how strong they were.

Upon their arrival, to their knowledge, Jen and Morgan were about to be in another cave. The first one since their time in Missouri years ago. When they arrived in Qumran, it was dark and the caves were darker. The man who took them to the cave entrances gave them a lantern and a few cautionary words about the caverns in the Middle Eastern part of the world. He told them they were holy and things happened inside no one could explain. The reason it took about ten years to get all the pieces of the Dead Sea Scrolls out was because incidents keep happening, like spirits telling them to leave the caves alone. Jen and Morgan didn't discredit the man, but they didn't completely buy the myths either. They'd been in caves with ghosts who wanted to kill them. A big difference between then and now, the girls learned how to defend themselves against spirits. They weren't stuck, they weren't victims.

Jen and Morgan took the lantern into the ground floor of the largest of the caves. The light spread over a vast array of cavernous décor; stalagmites and stalactites, some stood floor to ceiling, creating pillars. Drips were heard in the background and there were bats on the ceiling so Jen and Morgan had to keep quiet. When either of them spoke, it was nothing above a whisper.

After exploring for a few minutes, the girls circled back toward the entrance where there were flattened spots in the earth that made good places for sleeping. As Jen laid down for the night she looked around and shivered. She didn't want to be in a cave, they were not a place she would frequent again without memories chasing her. She wanted to be done with the mission quickly, she wanted to get the hell out of there as soon as possible. Morgan felt the same way, it radiated outward into Jen.

In the morning, Jen and Morgan awoke early from their mutual nightmare. Lucifer had a fun time last night. He put the two women in the same nightmare dream world. Somehow, the dreams were invaded by another, stronger force. God came into the hellish nightmare and saved the women, waking them at dawn. Normally, God would let a person work it out on their own or be a sight unseen, but that time he made Lucifer run for the mental hills. In the dream, God told Jen and Morgan the true location of the Holy Grail. When Jen and Morgan awoke, they left the caves, going to the Israel Museum instead.

Hidden in plain sight, the Holy Grail sat amongst a bunch of clay jars in a crate at the Israel Museum in a storage room collecting more dust. It was the most ornate, but it looked like a clay jar nonetheless. It had inlaid bits of gold, horribly tarnished after its centuries in existence, and it was heavily guarded by demons.

Jen and Morgan knew it was probably guarded, they were too close to the goal. There was always something standing in their way, now was no exception. Knowing the Grail was heavily guarded, the girls needed to get in and find it with a minimal mortal body count.

Standing at the back doors of the museum, Jen and Morgan thought for what seemed a long time. Then Jen said, "Fuck it, just open the door. I'm sure they won't suspect that."

"Okay." Morgan closed her eyes tight and her talisman glowed, the back alleyway was bathed in red light. The door swung open and the two women ran inside a dark room. "Um, good plan. We can't see shit!" Morgan whispered in case the room was filled with the enemy.

"Do you hear that?" Jen said, hearing a popping and fizzing sound.

"No. I don't hear a thing."

"It's a popping and fizzing sound. This room is filling fast," Jen whispered.

"You know I can't hear demon shit."

"Well, prepare yourself," Jen said to Morgan in one final whisper before the lights came on.

Jen and Morgan were staring at a room full of demons intent on killing them. Jen and Morgan stood tall, back-to-back, surrounded by evil. Morgan said a spell under her breath and for a few seconds, it seemed like there was a barrier around them. It wasn't strong enough to withstand all the fireball blasts and evaporated. Jen's eyes glowed pink. Demons moved in on them. The frontlines started screaming and vaporizing. Morgan burned all the ones in her line of sight. The girls made fast work of the room full of demons. Demon dust was flying in the air, it smelled like burned things in a house fire. Jen and Morgan remembered that smell. They both heard the maddening cry of an angry king of Hell. The girls paused for a minute then Morgan said they needed to hurry, they ran around looking for crates marked in Hebrew reading *Dead Sea Scrolls.* Finding the boxes they needed, Morgan opened them with her mind using a powerful spell. Looking through the crate packing, Jen heard another loud popping and fizzing noise.

"Now tell me you heard that," she said in her normal volume.

"Heard what? Again, I can't hear demons arrive."

"Well, hon, I think we're about to be invaded by–"

"Invaded? Ladies, you just fucked up, big time," Lucifer said, seething.

Both women turned around and saw him, cloak hanging on his white bony frame, fingers poking out, and feet bare. He stood on the concrete floor ready to make the earth shake if necessary. His feet were apart and his lips were ready to utter the world's oldest curses.

"Transport! Damn it! Transport!" Jen screamed at Morgan.

"Where do you think you're going?" As he uttered those words, he saw dust swirling around then nothing in front of him. He laughed out loud. "Silly bitches, think they can out run me! Now that *is* funny!"

Chapter Fifty

About ten seconds after Jen and Morgan arrived back in Cumbria County, Carlisle Castle became a flurry of activity, voices rose and fell, and bodies were moving in a rapid pace. A plan was being formed without much previous thought as to how it would play out. Lucifer was coming for them.

"You're fucking serious aren't you? We can't use her as bait! You're crazy as hell!" Morgan shouted.

"What other option do ye see here?" Warren Sr. said to Morgan.

"The bastard already wants a piece of her ass!" she reminded Mr. O'Connell.

"I know. I say we bait him, bring him tae us faster so we can get on wit it already," Mr. O'Connell said. "No sayin' I want tae mind ye. I don't."

"No fuckin' way, man!" Morgan shouted as if Jen wasn't in the room.

"Um, we could always use the Grail," Jen piped in.

"What? We don't have it. I didn't see it," Morgan said.

"Uh, yeah. Right before Lucifer came, I snatched it and hid it on my person," Jen explained, smiling. Everyone gaped at her in surprise when she produced the clay cup with golden metal surrounding it from under her thick, long sweater. "Yeah…yeah…"

"You're amazing. You know that don't you?"

"Yeah, *we* are amazing. Did she tell you guys how we killed a room full of demons to get it?" Jen asked.

"And I mean *we* because she did her thing, too. We were up against a fuckin' wall of 'em!"

"We *literally* don't have time for this. Has anyone seen the little guy lately?" Morgan wanted to know.

"Las' time I saw the bairn, he was wit' Mirabelle," MacAfee said. "I doubt gettin' him down here's gonna do anythin' but distract ye."

"I want to see my son. It's been days since I've seen him," Jen said as she marched out of the drawing room door and into the hall leading to the staircase. She was still holding onto the Holy Grail as she jogged up two flights of stairs, lightly ran down the hall, and into Little Warren's room without knocking. Her baby was just about to go to sleep. Mirabelle was standing above him uttering curses in a language Jen knew to be Ancient Satanic. She didn't hear Jen come in.

"Bitch, I will *kill* you if you don't step away from the boy! *NOW*!" she shouted at Mirabelle.

Mirabelle stood up, looked at Jen with her green glowing eyes. "Took you long enough. Humans are so stupid." She faced Jen completely for a moment then turned back to the boy and picked him up, getting ready to carry him off into the Underworld. "Ah-ah, I wouldn't if I were you. You might blow up this brat of yours."

Jen's eyes were glowing red, not pink that time. Little Warren's eyes were closed. When he opened them, no one could see because of the white light emitting from them. Mirabelle dropped him onto the plush carpet. Little Warren looked straight up at Mirabelle and said, "I don't want you anymore, you're *MEAN!*" After he told her off, she started boiling from the inside out. Her skin started melting, her eyes were like sauce pouring out from the sockets. She screamed out in pain as black blood poured out of her mouth and onto the floor. Her bones were showing through the spots where her skin was falling onto the rug in chunks. Finally, she hit the floor and bubbled into nonexistence. Little Warren returned to normal and ran to his mommy who caught him in her arms and carried him to the drawing room where the others were waiting.

"We heard screamin'. What happened? Where's Mirabelle?" MacAfee asked.

"That fucking bitch died. She tried to steal my kid!" Jen replied. She was mad as hell and it was written all over her face.

"So ye killed 'er? Ye canna jus' kill people," Warren Sr. said.

"She wasn't people, she was a demon. I didn't kill her, *he* did. Remember how his eyes lit up when he came out of the coma a while back? He has powers, too!"

"Oh boy…this could get interesting fast!" Morgan exclaimed.

Jen looked at her son when she put him down on the couch. His curly black hair bounced as she placed him there. His blue eyes were full of tears. He never killed anyone before, he was only six years old. He was innocent.

"I have an idea. What if it's him and not me who's supposed to control the Holy Grail? He's innocent and pure, I'm not. I have the Devil's blood in me more than he does. I mean—"

"Ye migh' be on tae somethin'. We better act fast. When Lucifer gets 'ere, it's gonna be a madhouse round 'ere," Warren Sr. said. With that, everyone gathered up things that were needed and moved out into the main entry hall of Carlisle Castle. Jen heard loud popping and fizzing and warned the rest of the group Lucifer was coming. Holy water was poured into the Grail and Little Warren held onto it, standing in a corner of the room waiting for the signal to drink it.

***

Similar to fiery waves crashing on rocks made of brimstone, Lucifer appeared in the entry hall in Carlisle Castle; sudden, smoky, molten ebbs lapping at a human shoreline. He was laughing and angry. His appearance didn't scare anyone, everyone stood watching him cross the intricate wood floors. In the four corners, the adults faced him. He walked to the center of the room with his long white-blond hair floating over his shoulders, his cloak billowing behind him, his bony stark white feet showing. He was almost begging the group to *bring it on!*

Jen stood in front of her son as he held the Grail in his hands awaiting the signal. She spoke first, "Here I am. I'm the one you want. Leave them out of this!"

"Not on your life, sister. They protect you, so they die, too," Lucifer spat.

Jen walked out of her corner, eyes glowing pink, lightning crossing her vision, ready to fight. Lucifer couldn't breathe, she mentally closed off his airways. He was choking, his hands went to his throat, he was coughing and trying not to retch as Jen walked up to him in the center of the room.

Lucifer started laughing. "Is that all you got?"

"No," she said, feeling déjà vu. She concentrated hard and began to imagine imploding a monster, just like the last time she fought him. She could see the flush in his cheeks, he was starting to feel his organs cook, then it stopped. His color turned back to normal bone white. Last time, he wasn't ready for her, this time, he came prepared.

Lucifer reached out and grabbed her by her tiny head. He had a handful of her raven hair, clawing into her scalp, blood ran down both sides of her face. Her glowing eyes faltered a minute and returned their brilliant shade of pink. She let out a yelp, he was hurting her, trying to expose her brains, pain ripped through her, starting at the top of her head. His grip grew tighter on her, his hand became a vice, clamped onto her skull. The blood continued to cascade down the sides of her face. The horrific pain nearly made her start pleading for her life when she caught a glimpse of her son drinking from the Grail in an attempt to save her. As Little Warren dropped the cup on the ground, the sound of metal hitting stone echoed. Everyone turned in his direction, watching the little boy.

Little Warren's body hovered several feet off of the ground and his eyes lit up the walls with the most brilliant white light ever seen in the mortal world without causing blindness. As his small body hung in the air, everyone watched the light as he made his way to the middle of the room and hovered there.

Morgan, MacAfee, and Warren Sr. ran to the center of the room. Little Warren hovered in front of Lucifer, who gaped in awe at the boy. He couldn't believe a child was able to possess the powers of God. The sizable magnitude of the situation held the king of

Hell speechless. His grip loosened on Jen's head and she struggled to get away from him. He felt her movements, snapping back to reality, he returned his gaze to her. Lucifer tightened his grip once more, hurting her again, causing her to cry out in pain as the blood began to mat her hair, sticking tendrils to the sides of her face.

As Morgan closed in on the circle of people, the talisman burst into shards of colored glass on the floor. She looked down at red shattered pieces on the ground in shock and frowned. She thought she'd lost a big part of her magic. As she pivoted her head back up, she saw what was going on next with the boy.

"LET HER GO!" bellowed the boy with the voice of a man, scaring Lucifer who let go of Jen.

"Who the hell are you?" Lucifer asked.

"I THINK YOU KNOW WHO I AM! I AM THE ALPHA AND THE OMEGA! THE BEGINNING AND THE END!" bellowed God.

"My father, you show up. Long time, no see, Daddy," Lucifer said sarcastically, laughing, mocking God.

"GO HOME!"

"Well, Daddy I can't do that. Where's the fun?" Lucifer grinned at the child's body.

"GO HOME!" God shouted once more.

The child who was inhabited by the soul of God pointed toward the large ornate antique wooden double doors as they flew open and the wracked horrid body of Lucifer flew out backward. The doors closed behind him, creaking on their hinges. Once outside the doors, Lucifer found himself back in the depths of Hell. He tried to resurface and couldn't. God placed him on lockdown in the Underworld. His father banished him! He was pissed off, but there was no revenge to be had because God was *God*. Even though he could eviscerate anything or anyone at any given time, there was no competing with the almighty. Although he was merciful, Lucifer knew in the past he wasn't always. He slammed his fists against the wall of his chambers and screamed in rage, so hard and loud it shook the Underworld.

***

After Lucifer returned to Hell, the gang stood there looking at the spirit of God still embodied in the child. His eyes lit the way to the other side; as bright as Heaven, angelic was the bodily host of God as innocent as the day he was born.

"Your son is good. Take care of him, he's special. One day, he will help you fight this battle of good versus evil. You'll always fight this battle because you're one of the only ones who stands in the way of evil fulfilling their dream of killing all I've created," God said to Jen.

After the Lord said his final words, he left the child's body as it hovered a few seconds longer in the air. Jen prepared to catch him like last time. Little Warren looked like he was passed out. The crowd stood around Jen with Little Warren in her arms. She was crying, she looked like hell and didn't care. Her son saved her life, so did God, thus proving his existence. God saved everyone in the room from a fate worse than death, being taken to Hell and tortured for an eternity. Little Warren was taken straight to bed, he needed rest.

Jen still had dried blood caked down the sides of her face and Morgan's talisman was gone. It was hours after Little Warren was taken to his bed before anyone noticed it.

***

Morgan went into the hall, green eyes shining through the mist of tears forming. She remembered what happened to her talisman. She grabbed her cell phone out of the key dish downstairs. She moved her blonde hair out of the way and dialed Pandora, waiting for it to ring.

"Hello? Morgan, are you all right?" Pandora asked from the other end of the phone.

"Yes, I guess I'm okay. The talisman is dead though," Morgan said, explaining what happened.

"Oh goodness! Well, here's a little secret I didn't tell you about the talisman. It wasn't real."

"What? It had to be real. How come it glowed when I used magic?" Morgan questioned her friend.

"Because I made it that way. With the little bit of magic I'm still able to do, I cast a spell on it. I had to find a way to get you to have faith in yourself, didn't I? You're a wonderful witch, you never needed help, but you did need confidence in yourself."

"No way, there's no way," Morgan replied.

"Uh, yes way. You always had the power inside you. It radiates out of you and into the fabric of this world," Pandora said, smiling on the other end of the phone line.

Morgan and Pandora spoke for a while longer. Morgan explaining everything that happened since she left until their fight with Lucifer earlier in the evening. Pandora agreed with her about the little guy being something special. By the end of the call, Pandora agreed to come visit the family at Carlisle Castle soon. Morgan ended the call on a happy note, clicking the end button on her phone. She walked back into the room with Little Warren and the rest of the adults who watched as he slept, sweaty black curls clinging to his damp forehead.

Jen looked at Morgan and sighed, she knew what was going on and felt bad about the talisman being gone. Morgan smirked and looked at the boy with concern. He would be sleeping a while, they knew it. When the energy was used to defeat evil, there was always a period used for the recovery. In the years to come, Little Warren would have those periods of sleep often. The others knew how important his life was going to be now, too.

Later in the evening, sleep fell over every soul in the castle, silence sprang forth crawling on like a slow eternity until the light began seeping through the windows, pouring over them with earnest. The shadows disappeared. The fight from the night before began to feel like a dream rather than a memory, but they wouldn't soon forget the devil was in the details.

Chapter Fifty-one

Light broke through the ancient stained glass windows, entering the terrarium, hitting the blooming pink and red roses, turning them shades of purple. As the sunlight splashed off the white walls making the room brighter, more placid to the interior of the room, sparks of brilliant light lit the tiles of the floor, the white glow gave off the deceiving appearance of heat.

A slim figure walked through the terrarium, casting mild shadows in the abundant light. He ran his left hand through his curly black locks, looking out at the winter landscape, smiling at the frost crystals twinkling on the grass outside. His ocean blue eyes sparkled gazing out upon the centuries' old stone courtyard benches, faded to black crumbling relics of many generations of kings.

Splinters of light hit Warren's eyes, blinking, he thought back to his childhood momentarily. He thought of how his mother and his Aunt Morgan used to hug him while teaching him life's lessons and fighting the forces of evil. He smiled. His loving heart never tarnished all those years, his innocence remained intact. He was careful to keep his heart as pure as possible, helping him keep the angel powers he possessed. With all the fighting, it was hard to dial back the rage inside. He innocently didn't understand why people would want to harm him when he'd done nothing to them. His mother explained to him once, sometimes there was no reason for evil people to act out. He had to protect himself and others.

Warren glanced around the room noticing the roses and the light as it grazed the tops of the flower petals changing the casting of colors. The scent of them was sweet and methodical. He once again remembered why there were such things in the world. They were put there to remind everyone God was good and created all things, big and small to be enjoyed and rejoiced over.

In the years Warren spent training, he learned a lot about the source of his powers. He learned about angels and demons, the ultimate fight of good versus evil, and why he must remain vigilant. Threads of his knowledge posing more and more questions of curiosity over the years, he learned acceptance of the good and bad.

Warren sucked in his breath, smelling the roses then exhaling, still thinking about times when he didn't have faith in himself to do the job. His heart used break thinking about fighting demons and witches who were always trying to kill him. Warren being alive and as powerful as he was made him a danger to the Underworld. He didn't consider himself special, he was a humble young man. His mother and the rest of his family taught him to be not only a respectable person, they taught him to be good, to love others, be generous and kind without fail, the most important thing they taught him was to be a man who cared. His heart broke with every demon he killed, yet he still did his job with love in his heart.

In his years of training, there was always one more death threat and one more idiot demon who tried to start Armageddon. So far, the tally of dead demons was adding up nicely. Warren stood mentally noting that observation. He saw swirling colors at the back of the room, reflecting off the stained glass windows. He turned his head. Shades of familiar blue light gleamed as they lit the room, showering it in overcast. Warren's father appeared with a gentle smile on his face, looking proudly at his grown son.

"Da, you came."

"Yes. I wouldn't miss this day for anything in the world," Warren II said.

"And you're right on time too, as always." Warren smiled slyly at his dad's ghostly figure.

"Okay then, let's show them sonsabitches how this works!"

Warren and his father left the terrarium and entered the entrance hall of the castle where a grouping of the ugliest demons they'd ever seen, stood tall, waiting for them to attack. Slowly, Warren walked with confidence into the middle of the old intricate room. Wood floors inlaid with different designs explained to him by his grandfather, laid out a path of innocents saved and evil souls lost.

Jen and Morgan stood in the hallway watching Jen's grown son as he did his work. Demons screamed as they exploded one by one without Warren touching them. Jen smiled proudly as her boy, now a man, made light work of ten or more demons in another attempt to claim and turn his soul to the darkness.

Warren smiled at his dad, who looked his brilliant son in the eyes. "Happy birthday, son!"

PART SIX
Legacy

Chapter Fifty-two

Dear Journal,

In complete transcending thoughts, I thought about weeping, the joys within, and hearts broken about a million times over. I'm not sure where or when I inherited empathy, but sometimes I could feel the pain. My heart, however, didn't break all over the floor, my heart was something of a lover's mystery to me.

I harkened dark, I loomed in shadow and in secret, my mysteriousness saved for someone who might understand I was a sliver of hope, a beacon in the cold, dark night. I had yet to find the one who understood my desires and could fulfill them while the celestial presence engulfs me. I walk alone in my journey, much like the two who came before me have done, unable to see passed the need to rid the world of evil forces. It came so easily, willing to destroy me.

Now, I sit in the dimly lit ancestral castle thinking about the future, as I'm the heir of kings and the only one who can stop the evil that searches me out, I am filled with a heavy sense of longing. I want a normal life which I know I will never have. It's not what destiny has chosen to lay at my feet. Do I hate my mother for this life? No. I couldn't love her more. She and her best friend raised me to the best of their ability, always teaching me something new and valuable in the process. I love them both.

In truth, I don't know why I have such a heavy heart. I wish I knew what some normal guys felt, but they get to feel it because of me. I was told, I'm the one who keeps Armageddon at bay with every creature killed by my hands and my mind. I've done away with demons, witches, ghosts...you name it.

So why the heavy heart and the deep reflection? I felt, throughout my history, certain pieces of myself may definitely be lost to the world, not something I want to happen. My heart carries the burden of never having love and keeping it. When I was a child, I was taught, most people don't see what I've seen and they wouldn't believe supernatural beings exist. For me, this meant keeping a lid on what I can do, therefore never getting close or trying to gain another's confidences.

I want love, even if for only a short time. I want to feel the love my mother still has in her heart for my father. She still wears tears on her sleeve for him, I've seen her when she thinks I'm not looking. Thoughts of the day my father died course through her memory as if it were yesterday. She sees his ghost sometimes as she's awakening from a night of restless sleep, those days my mother smiles all day and looks at me fondly. I look a lot like my father. I wonder if she's remembering any particular day or random thoughts of him, she never says. I don't envy my mother or her friend, those two women have been through hell in my lifetime. I wish they'd find peace somehow.

My grandda and old MacAfee have always tried to protect me, now it's my turn to protect them. As they grow frail with age, I'm still a young man, thank goodness. I don't know what I'd do without those two old guys to teach me as well.

It turns out I'm also the first and last of my kind. I researched it myself, there has never been another human given my powers AND I'm the last of a line of kings. My ancestors on my da's side didn't have supernatural powers when they ruled at Carlisle castle, formerly a part of Scotland. I won't tell you about the Jacobites and the English always fighting, or the takeover that would break your heart. I'm sure you already know about the bloody past, so I won't go into that. As I said, no one has my powers, not even my mother. Her power stems from the use of an angel and demon mixture. My power is pure white, without dilution. I know this because I'm probably the only human who's truly seen God. He's as real as you and me. He told me he was bestowing some of his power to me in the use of fighting evil. His angels visit all the time to check in on us, making sure we're all doing well.

No matter what mom thinks, I know how she thinks, she isn't evil even though she's used her powers to kill. My mom has saved the world more times than I can count. It doesn't matter she used to only know about her evil powers, God gave her some of the whiteness too to balance her out, making them neutral inside her and giving her the ability to rid the world of evil. Since I was six years old and learning about my powers, I have seen my mother and my aunt bust more ass than I can count! I think they were scared before because they thought I might be a distraction or someone might harm me. When I came into my powers every fight was a lesson for me. I knew what to do as soon as my mother's eyes streaked with pink lightning. How well I knew them intrigued me. Something I always saw in their faces certain times of the year made me sad for them. Back to the deep topic at hand, full circle, in fact.

Love isn't an easy subject for me, I've hidden my heart for so long. It's not that I've never been in love or was terrified of it. I love a vampire, someone I know I can never have. Not because I didn't want her. I'm a realist. I know she's centuries old and I'll die one day, hopefully as an old man. She looks like she's my age, but she's not. I also know she went through hell to save my little family. She's known me since I was a child and yet, I still love her. So, with this feeling I have, I wrestle with myself all the time. How do I go on knowing I love her and we can't be together? I have no choice. I have to do my job with only half a heart and all of my brains. That's how I was taught, by two lovely women who do it every day. Sometimes sadness creeps over me, invading my thoughts with darkness, then I remember what I was taught and fight to feel the light inside me grow, extinguishing the dark shadows hiding in the corners of my soul. Then I pray for solace in the dim lit mornings when I'm alone and have a chance to speak directly to my maker.

I was raised with the knowledge of both good and evil as I've said but, I am a true believer. I've made believers out of the others the night I really came into my powers for certain, which was the night I was possessed by the spirit of God. He temporarily used my body as a vessel to rid my mother of Lucifer, the first of the fallen angels and the king of Hell. While alone, I often think back to that memory and smile because God helped me save my family. I don't have much of one, but what I do have I want to keep until it's time for them to go to God.

I don't understand everything there is to know about love or God or the light, but I'm learning. Being of a brilliant mind is good, I suppose, but in the case of love, I wish I were normal.

Warren James O'Connell III

Chapter Fifty-three

Morning light drifted in through the high castle window, shearing off the tops of the blooming plants, casting them almost yellow. Moss grew up the side of the castle, protruding into the cracks of the bricks and mortar holding the place together. Many of the windows were small casement windows trimmed in white paint peeling a little with age and wintertime having fallen hard in the region for a few years in a row. Ivy started to climb one side of the ancient castle, inching its way to the windows and sky above them. The sun was bright and warm, not like the sweltering U.S. summers. A summer spent at Carlisle Castle was unlike one spent in America. The whole U.K. was at least ten degrees cooler at all times with more rain and less sunshine. When the orb of light decided to grace their lands with its presence, the lush green of the well-kept gardens and surrounding lawns was beautiful. The plants were maintained to look as though they were never touched but always alive with color, splashing the lawns with reds, pinks, oranges, yellows, and purples. The trees in the gardens had moss on one side of them, turning their brown trunks a shade of green, making them look almost as old as the castle with which the gardens were maintained for.

A sullen figure loomed in the window of one of the tall towers overlooking the gardens and lawns in the back of the castle. Silently, the figure moved from window to window as he journeyed down the staircase leading to the expansive area below him. He wanted to go sit in the sun and bask in its rays while he could because there was always something to be done, whether it was training or something else of the menial variety. He could never claim he lived a dull existence, but he wanted to appreciate the small things in his life as well. To sit in the sun alone with his thoughts was something he always cherished.

He was built much like his father; medium height and slender build, muscular and fit, curly black hair and ocean blue eyes. Warren III had a bit of freckling here and there his father didn't have, but only on a few places on his body. There weren't too many years left until he'd be as old as his father was when he died. Warren didn't worry about it like his mother. She hoped he'd make it passed the day and not be killed by one of the numerous things he fought. He thought her feelings on the matter were odd and overprotective, but she kept an eye on him nonetheless. Being watched was nerve wracking even if she did do it out of love.

As Warren made his way outside, he saw the sun peeking in over the bushes into the courtyard before he reached the gardens and his own special thinking spot. He remembered his summers at the castle. He had vivid childhood memories of playing and laughing with his family. A huge smile graced the face of the man who was once an innocent little boy. He remembered every bit of love and attention they gave him.

Warren closed his eyes as the sun beat down on him, it felt good on his skin. He was silent, hearing the chirping of birds and the wind slowly whooshing around him. His mind was clear and his senses were heightened. He heard the rustling of the grass as he stood in the middle of the gardens. He opened his eyes and instead of them being bright, brilliant blue like the ocean, they were white and glowing with the heavenly light coursing through him like an electric current, charged and ready to go. He saw something in the distance that displeased him.

A horde of demons was coming quickly to try to kill him yet again. Nothing was sacred to demons, they could give a shit less about what the mortal beings liked. Several yards away from the gardens, demons vaporized and swirling black vapors wisped away on the wind. Others came and went, vanishing the closer they were to the lush green lawns of the castle until none of the horde was left. Warren smiled and blinked his eyes, breathing a sigh of contented relief. The demons didn't come close to touching his family's land.

Stuck in his thoughts, Warren walked into the castle, standing in the main entryway looking at the wooden tiled floors that showed his reflection, smiling. Memories of the day he found out he had powers like his mother came rushing in. Thinking of all the times his loving family surrounded him and aided him every step of the way, carving him into the soul he'd become, made his heart feel light. As he stood staring at the tiles a pair of old sneakers came into view. He recognized them immediately. He looked into his mother's brown eyes.

"Hey, Mum. What are you up to? Wearing the old sneaks?" He laughed.

"Hey, boyo. Why are you grinning? What did you do?" Jen asked.

"Fought some demons in the back yard, no big deal. Still, what's up with your shoes?" Warren was still giggling.

"Ah, just memories. These are my ass kickin' shoes," Jen declared, smiling at her son.

"And whose ass you been kickin'? Or are you gonna kick?"

"Yours if you don't wipe your feet! Look at you! All that mess you made, boyo!" Jen was laughing as the light pink warning lightning flashed in her eyes at him for fun.

"Hey whoa! Mum, chill out, okay? I'll take care of it." He laughed out loud as he looked at the mud trail his shoes made on the floor where he stopped walking. He held his hands in the air as if he were at gunpoint when he saw the lightning in her eyes.

"Okay, son. You take care of it. I was actually going outside. It's a nice sunny day." She winked at him, smirking.

"Mam?" he asked.

"Yes, my boy?"

"I love you, Mam!" Warren declared.

"I love you too. Are you okay?" Jen looked him over, not seeing signs of harm.

"Yeah, I'm fine, just wanted to tell you that." He turned to her before walking away, hugging her, then leaving her standing there pondering what he might have been thinking.

Warren walked into the main dining hall of the castle where the maids gathered and asked where the mop and buckets were kept so he could clean up his mess before his mother came back into the castle. He wanted to surprise her by doing the clean-up himself instead of having the maids do it, which would have been easier. He came from her, she might have had a little money, but didn't have the maids do everything for her. She didn't feel right about it.

***

"You're the best research team I've ever known," Warren said, running his fingers through his curly hair.

"We're the *only* research team you've ever known," Morgan said, chuckling, light dancing in her eyes. When she laughed, she was beautiful. Her long blonde hair sweeping over her shoulders and her green eyes glittering in the light of the day.

"Son, why are you trying to butter us up? Do you need help with something?" Jen looked up at her son and smiled widely at him, shaking her head and giggling.

"Yes, my beautiful mum, I do. I have something, I found it the other day. I want to know what it is and what it means." He picked up a box with symbols on it. Before he could hand it to them, both ladies gasped. Jen and Morgan knew exactly what it was.

"Where did you find that?" Jen asked her son.

"When I opened the front door to leave the other day, it was sitting on the ground in front of it. So, I quickly brought it in. I had a feeling there was something special about it. Why would someone leave something like this at our house?" he asked.

"Pandora's in trouble again," Jen said.

"Was there a note?" Morgan asked, worry spreading over her.

"No, no note, just the box," Warren said looking concerned too. Pandora never dropped something off without saying hello to them.

"All right, we need to start a search for her. Morgan, call her. I know you probably won't get a response, but try anyway."

Morgan nodded, took her cell phone and left the room to try it out. Jen had been right, there was no getting in touch with Pandora that way, which in the past it never failed. She always picked up the phone when Morgan called. Morgan walked back into the room and shook her head looking sad.

"Okay, time to take this into cyberspace. Oh, this is bad. Son, I wish you'd alerted us sooner. What you're looking at is old, ancient Egyptian, as a matter of fact. If I remember the history correctly, it was made for Pandora for her eighteenth birthday around the time she was turned. She learned to use it after she found her way back home and acted as if nothing happened to her, but everyone knew something was wrong. Almost all her magic was gone. She was good at it too. She'd been learning since childhood. She taught Morgan, but she couldn't show her a lot of things. She still had the power to control the box when we met her years ago," Jen explained to Warren.

"And it showing up here means she's in trouble somehow. We have to find her." A tear formed in the corner of Morgan's eye as she thought about her teacher and friend.

***

Green glowing eyes radiated off the walls and onto the ceiling. Shadows clung to the walls lit by candles and a small amount of moonlight allowed to poke through the boarded up windows. Shattered bones lay scattered over the floor of the room. The walls were dirty with the blood of many deaths. Spiders made their homes in every corner of the old house, spinning their webs as they ebbed in darkness down the sides of the decrepit manor house, decay replacing ancient finery.

In the dark, creatures with unspeakable intentions finished feasting on the flesh of the last humans to pass by the long forgotten house hidden by the scraggly woods near the water's edge. The floor crunched with dead leaves from many seasons of autumns past. The creaking floorboards in some of the rooms told stories of how old the place was. Once upon a time, two hundred years ago, the house would have been seen as beautiful, owned by a slave master.

Demons walked the halls of the house, clawing the spongy plaster as they slunk down the small corridors. The green glowing of their eyes flanked the solitude in mysterious ugly waves of strobe light. As the small group walked the house they searched for hidden spaces, cubbyholes, and rooms behind the walls. The box was nowhere to be found. She wasn't talking and they couldn't find it. The master would be displeased.

***

Morgan took the box in her hands, flipping it around on all sides, investigating it. She turned it over, sitting it in her lap. She saw a yellowed piece of parchment paper affixed to the bottom of it. Gently, she placed a fingernail underneath the edges, popping the paper off the box.

"See. What'd I tell ya?" Morgan glance around at Jen and Warren.

"Never leave any stone unturned, son," Jen said.

"Well, how did I know she'd hide it?" Warren questioned them.

"You didn't, but we suspected. She's not stupid. She knows what she's doing. She knew we'd eventually find it," Morgan said.

"I never thought she was." Warren scowled and looked at his feet.

"Okay, open it. I want to see if she left us some clues to find her." Jen was feeling anxious.

"All right." Morgan popped the wax crest sealing the letter together in the middle, unfolding the piece of thick paper. "I wonder why she went old school, that's weird."

"Maybe, because she had no choice?"

"Maybe. Okay, here goes–

Dear gang,

I've sent you the chaos box as you can plainly see because I'm in danger yet again. This time, demons found me. I don't have long to write this. I'm in an abandoned plantation house in Louisiana. Come find me fast. I'm afraid they mean to kill me. They were after the secret, as per usual, about the box. I've said nothing. It's been awful, please help me. You're my only hope of keeping it safe.

Love,
Pandora

"–And that's all, folks," Morgan said, folding the letter.

"Looks like we have another mission after all and this time it's a rescue mission," Jen said.

"No, you don't. I got this. Remember, you retired and I'm the one who does the fighting these days." Warren was beginning to be deeply worried.

"Yeah, but she's *our* friend, we have to go after her," Morgan said, almost begging to join him.

"No, I've got it. Seriously. I can handle it. Me and a room full of demons, no big deal," Warren stated, crossing the room.

"Son, are you sure?" Jen asked. Worry crept over her.

"Yes, Mom, I got it." Warren filled with anger, turning away from Jen and Morgan, tears began to sparkle in his eyes. "I mean it." He walked out of the room, stiff and serious.

"Oh, he's gonna do something stupid. I can feel it, he's pissed," Morgan said.

"Damn it. Well, he doesn't know we know, so he's trying to hide it, but he sucks at it."

"Well, we're going to have to tell him sometime. Might as well be sooner versus later," Morgan said.

"I agree. He's only ever loved her and he deserves to know we wouldn't be mad at him for it," Jen said, sighing.

***

The stars shined, reflecting off on the water, glittering in the night. Wisping willow branches hung low over the edges of deep, dark, cavernous places on the bayou. The silence gave way to sounds of the night, things ebbing in the distance, growing steadily louder into a locust and cicada symphony. Crickets chirped in the misty fog as Warren walked onto the scene. He ran his hand through his black curly hair thinking about how to save her, his own heart's desire. Warren thought about the last time Pandora spoke to him about anything personal.

"We can't!" Pandora exclaimed.

"Why not?" Warren didn't want to believe her. He wanted a valid reason they couldn't be together.

"Because, I'm a vampire and you're not!"

"You keep saying it like it matters. So you're a vampire!" Warren's heart always broke when he fought with her, which they did every time they got closer. He couldn't help how he felt.

"It should. I could kill you so easily and not even mean to!" Pandora turned away. She could feel her resolve beginning to mentally tear her in two.

"You wouldn't though."

"How do you know? How do I know?" she questioned.

"All I know is, I love you. I've always *loved you," he said, looking her straight in the eyes.*

"You don't know what love is. You're so young!" she shouted.

"Yes, I do. And for some reason, it's always been you!" Warren stared at her.

"Oh my God! You're so infuriating! You don't know what you say!" Pandora turned away.

"Pandora, just look at me. Look at me, please. You know what I say is true." He lightly grasped her arm, trying to turn her.

"It's impossible, Warren. Just impossible. It can't happen." She stood still, crossing her arms over her chest.

"But why? If you love me too, why can't it?" He didn't understand.

"Because…"

"Because why?"

"It goes against everything, that's why," she whispered.

"Who cares? I don't care!" He was furious.

"You should. It's just not right. I'm sorry." Pandora was gone as quickly as she arrived and hadn't spoken a word to Warren for months.

In his memories, he'd cried, heartbroken. Now, he stood in the bayou, looking around at the night with conviction. He was there to get her back, no matter how much she thought things were impossible for them.

Chapter Fifty-four

Dear Diary,

I've been a vampire for so long…do I still have my humanity? Can I be what he needs me to be? Why can't I see past this being wrong? And how can I love someone who, to me, is just a boy? It's impossible, but true. I'm in love with a child, yet he's not a child. He's a man.

I've never loved anyone like I love him, yet, I'm not supposed to. Everything inside me says it's wrong, except my heart, it aches to be near him. Why? I've never had this trouble before. Maybe because even though he has the innocence of a child, he has the bravado of a strong, sensitive, caring young man? It's true, I've known him since he was a child. I watched him grow up. I've seen him develop his powers. They're strong. This spirit he uses to exhibit his powers, I didn't think He was real, it turns out His light is immeasurable within Warren. I didn't believe it until I saw it for myself.

He doesn't know, but he's had my heart for a while. It's been a struggle hiding it. I've fought with him because I know it's wrong. I can't let him love me, but I know he does anyway. I've spent a lot of time away his family (my family) because of it. His heart is strong, I'm afraid it consumes him. I'm scared my own feelings will engulf me. Once the fire is allowed to ignite, it could take us both down.

If there was a way I could be with him without it hurting him, I would seek it out. I don't see how. I've spent many pain-filled nights wishing for a solution. I've lived in sorrow for the past few years thinking about it. I know he's tried to go on, as have I, to no avail. Everything always leads back to him.

I've often wondered about my mortal soul. If I hadn't learned to shut it off so much then maybe that would be the key to happiness with him. I've contemplated ways to turn it back on, if it was possible. I have no idea if it would work, or if I'd be spinning my wheels. It hurts knowing how much I've hurt him already. This inner battle with my heart and my head is gruesome. I want to be able to love him freely without holding it in. I'm pretty much lying to him and myself every time I tell him I can't. I feel his heart breaking as much as mine does every time I deny it out loud. The more I deny it, the more I tell him I can't, the more I wish I were able to look in his amazing blue eyes and tell him the truth. I hate lying to him.

He knows what I am and he doesn't care if I could kill him instantly. It doesn't scare him. If it did, things would be much easier. I wouldn't have to continually break his heart. I wish he'd find a nice mortal girl, but I understand what he's thinking, the humans wouldn't get it. He's so special, loving, and innocent. He deserves more than me, so much more. Yet, I can't deny it anymore. I love a mortal who's good and fights the evils of this world by the grace of God. Everything inside me telling me to fight my feelings will hopefully subside one day.

Pandora

***

The stench of death and decay surrounded Pandora. Her senses heightened, it made being in the basement of the old plantation house almost unbearable. Her golden eyes saw the minute cracks in the walls, the tiny termites crawling in and out them, the buzzing of bees outside in the evening. She heard the cadence of crickets and cicadas calling to the others across the bayou waters and swamplands. She couldn't see where her attackers took her, but she knew her whereabouts, she knew she was somewhere in the southern have of the United States, having been there before. She remembered the immense heat, the night sounds, and eeriness of the landscape after nightfall. The bayou was beautifully spooky. It was the only place she'd ever smelled so much raw death and emotion in the air.

Pandora didn't sweat much being dead already, but if she had she would have been soaked in it because the basement was like a furnace even in the night. Her pure silver restraints kept her from moving too much or getting free of the old house. The demons that captured her put vampire proof restraint on her. She was strong, but the silver burned her wrists, keeping her subdued.

When she heard the floor begin to shake above, she cocked her head to the side listening to the movement. Gentle footfalls could be heard then clawing on the walls, swishing of leavings, and bodies thrown into walls shaking the floors so hard silt from the old boards floated downward. The sudden screaming gave way to more thuds and crashes. She saw bright light coming from cracks in the floor boards. She shut her eyes as more mists of dust rained down upon her. She prayed he'd come to save her and he was there now. When the screaming stopped, she opened her eyes, still hearing the sound of someone walking above her. The bright white light was gone. Pandora heard the inside basement door creak as it flew off its hinges, busting into the side of the upper wall. She saw a beam of light flowing from the darkened doorway.

"Pandora! You down here?" Warren shouted.

"Yes," she said weakly.

"I'm comin' to get ya, love," Warren said in his British accent.

"Please hurry."

"Be there once I navigate the bloody stairs o' this rat-hole." Warren used his flashlight stepping on the boards that still remained intact. Pandora heard the loud creaking as he made his way slowly down to the dirt floor basement. The dark night was casting no moonlight in the small windows of the damp, dirt filled hell she'd been trapped in.

"I knew you'd come," Pandora whispered when she knew he was near her.

"I will always come for you. Always," Warren replied.

"I know."

"Let's see about getting you out of here." Warren set his flashlight down after he saw her and the type of chains trapping her. Sterling silver was pliable and soft, but deadly to vampires. He took the chains in his hands, bending them until they gave enough to break. Her wrists were bound by big silver bracelets, he had to scrunch her hands through them. It hurt her so he tried to do it fast. After she was freed, he picked up his flashlight as she held onto his bicep and he led her back to the stairs.

"I know another way out. There's an outside entrance. They didn't use those stairs to get me in here," Pandora said.

"How'd they get you in here?"

"Over that way somewhere. I think there's a cellar door to the outside." The closer she got to the outer wall the more she was assaulted by the smell of honeysuckle, her ears came alive with the sounds of night creatures. "Yes, this is the way out."

"Okay," Warren said as he led the way, shining his light on the wall in front of him. As he got closer, he could see the two chained cellar doors. The chains were rusted steel, entwined together, and locked with a huge older style padlock.

"Shine the light directly on the chains. I can try to pull them apart. They look like iron or steel so they won't hurt me to touch them."

"All right." Warren watched Pandora as she rounded him and went to the doors.

She pulled hard on the rusted metal, breaking links, releasing it from its place on the door, then the thick metal clanked to the ground. She almost smashed the doors when she opened them, revealing the dark of night.

"If you'd follow me, I'd like to go now." Pandora faced Warren. The two people climbed through the large opening into the night. As soon as Pandora was in the open air she breathed in a huge breath. The dank, dead air filled her lungs for too long. "And where exactly are we?"

"A very old plantation house in Louisiana," Warren told her.

"I wasn't completely positive, but figured it was something of that nature."

"Yep. I was hoping you'd help me navigate away from it. I can't see that well in this darkness. The bayou without a moon is a black ink death march, you ask me," Warren said.

"I can help you, don't worry. And if I haven't said it, thank you." Pandora smiled even though he couldn't see her.

"It's all right. Let's get you out of here. I want to take you home to see Aunt Morgan and Mom." He held onto Pandora, listening to the sounds of the bayou.

"Oh, I would love that." She sighed, glad she wasn't stuck in the dank basement anymore.

As Pandora led Warren away from the ramshackle house in the middle of brambles and overgrown grass. She hedged the garden statues, black and crumbling with age. Warren followed using his flashlight once they got away from the overgrown mess of neglected plants. He walked slowly, thinking about nothing particular. In his silence, he heard the midnight cadence of the bugs. He saw lightning bugs flittering around lighting up the scenery a little bit at a time. It had been years since he'd seen and heard any of the sights and sounds of the United States. When he delved into his memories, the last one he could remember contained fire and explosions. He shivered.

Pandora heard the quickening of Warren's heartbeat, she slowed down, letting him catch up to her. When he reached her, Pandora grabbed his hand, her wrists healed a little after the silver chains and restraints were removed.

"Do you think you can lead us away from here?" he asked.

"Yes, I know I can. It smells old and dirty near the house, but the further we get away from it, I smell water and animals," she said.

"How long has it been since you've fed?" Warren wondered.

"Umm…the day before I came here and I have no idea how long I've been here."

"You need to eat." Warren could see in her darkened eyes she was ravenous.

"Does it scare you?" Pandora looked down at the ground, seeing every individual blade of grass.

"No. I just want you to heal," Warren said, staring at her, observing her wounds in the moonlight.

"Good." She lightly smiled. "You're right. Nourishment equals healing a lot faster."

"When we get far enough away from the house you need to hunt. I'll stay back and wait," he said.

"Yeah." Pandora sighed as she walked hand in hand with Warren.

Chapter Fifty-five

"Yep, I'm safe. You ladies worry too much. I'm fine. I think I'm almost there. I see a faint green glowing not far from here. I have to go. Stop worrying and tell Mom, I'm okay. Love you too, Aunt Morgan." Warren clicked the off button on his phone and put it in his pocket. While he walked over the hill, he saw the glow of green lights come into clearer view. The reflection was cast by demons, off what remained of tall windows. Not much remained intact after years of decay rotted the abandoned plantation house hidden in the woods near the edge of the river in the Louisiana bayou.

As Warren reached the steps to the front entrance, he noticed most of the porch was gone so he crept to the back of the house. He hunkered down beside one of the large broken window holes, listening. He heard clawing, scraping of walls and skittering of leaves on the floor. He knew he'd have to move fast to get in the house. His mind was prepared. He was angry because of who he came to save. He'd always protect his love, always.

He looked in through the huge hole in the pane where a large sheet of glass used to be. He couldn't see any of the glowing eyes roaming around so he took a chance. Warren strolled slowly into the house. He didn't make a lot of noise, but he did hear the floorboards begin to crack a little under his weight. He focused on his task: getting in and saving Pandora. Soon, the room was bathed in a brilliant white glowing *light radiating from Warren. He lit up the entire house. Demons came running into the room and were blasted against the walls. Some died instantly and some thudded to the floor. The ones left alive got the mental onslaught of a pissed off God-boy. Warren blew some of them up from the inside out. As they baked and boiled, screams of intense pain were heard momentarily until their human forms gave out and exploded.*

The light bathed the decayed and placid walls of a once grand home of rich evil people. The woodwork was of artisan proportions from the 1800's. It split like rotted knotty pine when a demon hit the side of the wood because termites had eaten it to bits. The former gossamer lace curtains fell like a ghost's shroud upon the demon, wrapping it in thin white fabric that tore like ancient bandaging on a rotted corpse in the grave. Two glowing spectral green orbs were seen through the old curtain before Warren walked up to the demon, tearing the fabric from its face so it saw the person who would end its existence. As it exploded, Warren's mind raced. A familiar voice inside his mind told him the feelings of rage were wrong. God told him to rid the world of demons, but to do it without rage, do it with the love in his heart he held inside for all lives, not just one. A tear found its way to Warren's cheek as he blasted more of the demons who captured Pandora.

When he was finished, Warren took a knee and prayed. He asked his Lord for forgiveness in his momentary rage. He prayed for the souls he killed and for the Lord to forgive them as well. As he stood, Warren rubbed his eyes, wiping away the tears. His flashlight was turned on and as he walked the house looking for Pandora, he smelled dead demon vapor amongst the rot and decay. He noticed how badly the musty old house was falling to ruin as he passed through its corridors. Warren finally found the basement door leading to the dirt floor basement. He ripped the door off the hinges with his mind. Soon after it crashed into the wall behind him, he was carefully made his way into the underbelly of what was once a beautifully crafted home.

***

Warren sank into his recent memories as he waited for Pandora to return to him in the dark. He rested against a tree staring off into space. Then he thought only about her. He knew they were doomed, it wasn't destiny for him to love her, but he did anyway. He knew a part of her felt the same way. He wished she'd stop fighting herself and let it be. He knew the reasons how he felt supposed to be right and he didn't care. Sure, vampires were predators. Sure, they lived off of blood. What did it matter? He knew he wanted her, only *she* mattered when it came to his heart. He knew it was a childish notion with precarious, convoluted appeal, but he also knew she was the only woman he'd ever known besides his mother and his aunt who he didn't have to hide from or lie to. Even God told him it wouldn't work, but he lived with the pain of his feelings far too long.

"One thing you're going to have to do. Please, stop staring off into space like a daydreaming child," Pandora said as she walked up to Warren. He was lost in his thoughts.

"Oh, sorry about that. I was just waiting for you. You look like you feel better," he said, seeing the golden rimmed color return to her eyes.

"Yes, I feel better now. I found a few small animals."

"You ready to go?"

"Yeah. I have one question, though. Who wanted the box this time enough to try and kill me again?" Pandora asked.

"I don't know. I'm sure there was something behind the horde of demons kidnapping you," Warren replied.

"Makes me wonder if it wasn't a plot orchestrated by the devil himself. He's been after your mom for years now."

"And the fact he never gets past me…"

"You left her and Morgan to come save me, so we better get going. They might be in need of some assistance pretty soon," Pandora said.

"Why don't you call them? I'm still looking for our ride up the bayou. There should be a little boat around here somewhere." Warren pulled out his cell phone, handing it to Pandora, who checked and saw there were no bars.

"No signal. We'll have to wait until we get closer to people, I think."

"Yeah and I wonder how many missed calls I'll have." Warren laughed.

"Okay, chuckles, let's find the boat."

"Yes, indeed." Warren walked along the river's edge, watching for the tiny boat with only room on board for a few people yet large enough not to get carried away by the current. Finally, a few miles from where they began the journey away from the house, the boat was waiting, tied to an old dock.

"Is that the boat you came here on?" Pandora asked.

"Yep, it's tiny, but it did the job. There should be a captain on board someplace. Yo, Cap'n! Can ya hear me?"

"Ahoy, there! See ya found your lady friend. Good. Now we go sailing up river the way we came!" The captain noticed what most people who first meet Pandora notice; she was a beauty, exotic but pale at the same time. Her movement was fluid and she had the strangest set of gold-rimmed eyes anyone had ever seen. "So your friend there, she always so quiet?"

"Yeah. She's pretty shy," Warren lied to the captain.

"No problem. I think we should be up the river in about a half hour. That do ya, young friend?"

"Yes, that's great. We have to get home as soon as we can. We have folks waiting on us back there," Warren said.

"Where's home, sonny?" the captain asked, curious of the accent.

"The United Kingdom."

"Wow! You're a long ways from there, I tell ya!"

"Oh, yeah. We're taking the red-eye out as soon as we get to the airport. Our family is very worried. Aren't they, hon?" Warren knew she would have spat needles at him if she could for calling her that, but he didn't care.

"Yes." Pandora said nothing else the rest of the boat ride but glared occasionally in Warren's direction.

"Somethin' wrong with her?" asked the captain.

"Nah, she'll be fine. She just wants to go home."

"Well, that's all right then." The captain kept his hands on the wheel as the little boat chugged against the current.

The water sloshed around the outside of the boat as the captain drove it down the river, maneuvering it, avoiding sand banks in the middle and low hung tree branches until he pulled over at a dock on the side of an embankment. When he anchored the boat, he helped Pandora onto the rickety old dock. Then Warren climbed up behind her. The captain followed and went to the building sitting on the side of the dock that looked like an old shed or shanty. He came out producing a receipt for the money Warren paid to take him up the river. Warren asked where they could catch a cab, the captain told him they'd have to walk up the road and there'd be a house about a quarter-mile, they could get help finding a ride there. Warren thanked the captain then took off walking for the house with Pandora in tow. When they got there, there was a light on upstairs and one in the back. Warren decided to go ahead and knock on the door.

An older couple lived in the house. An elderly man came to the door with a shotgun in his hand, when he found out it was out of town strangers asking about a ride to the nearest airport, he put the gun down. He told them to step inside and wait. A few minutes later he came out of the back of the house dressed and ready to drive his little car into town. Pandora and Warren followed the man outside and to the car. After the ride was over, Warren tried to pay the man for his troubles, but he wouldn't take the money. Southern Hospitality, he called it. Warren smiled and waved as the older man drove away leaving them at the gates of the little airport in the small town.

"Strange. What the hell is Southern Hospitality?" Warren asked Pandora.

"Well, they have pride, you see. They just help to help, it's their way," she explained.

"Ahh, I see. That's new." Warren smiled.

"Not really. It's an old custom, even though this is the first time you've witnessed it. It's been a long time since you were on U.S. soil. You were about six the last time you set foot on this piece of dirt and you definitely didn't live down here," Pandora explained.

"You've known my family that long? Damn…"

"You were a baby when I met the girls," Pandora said, looking into Warren's eyes.

"Wow."

"Now you know why I find some of our conversations so weird," she said.

"No, you mean arguments," he said, glancing at the ground, kicking a pebble.

"However you want to categorize them, it makes no difference."

"I know."

"The plane tickets?" Pandora asked, watching Warren as he stared intently at small stones.

"Right. We need to get you outta here before the sun starts coming up." He sighed.

"Agreed. I don't think my burning, smoking skin would be good for other people to see."

Warren walked into the airport with Pandora behind him. He purchased two tickets leading them to a bigger airport and a direct flight out of the United States straight to Heathrow. From there, they could get a car to take them back to Carlisle Castle, situated on the border of Scotland and England where his mother and Aunt Morgan were anxiously awaiting their return.

***

Almost a full day later, Pandora and Warren got off the plane on U.K. soil. It was gloomy with darkening gray skies. The air was damp and the ground soggy, Warren felt at home. Heathrow was a huge place, but he explained to his mother where they would be getting off the plane before he boarded the first small aircraft in the U.S. When he led Pandora outside to wait for their ride, a misty light rain began to fall around them. Pandora looked up at the sky then shut her eyes. She enjoyed it. Several minutes later, a car pulled up that Warren recognized. He opened the back passenger side door and let Pandora get in first then he slid in beside her. He was shivering from the rain, but he didn't care, his thoughts turned to the mission ending and being near his home.

In the dark, he couldn't see the moon or the stars with the clouds covering them. He did something he rarely did in front of Pandora or his mom, he bowed his head and talked in his mind with the Lord about everything that transpired over the last forty-eight hours. He previously asked the Lord to watch over his mother and his aunt while he was gone on the rescue mission, now he asked if they had any trouble. The response he got caused him to slightly panic, he asked the driver if he could speed up. The little roads leading to the castle were muddy and well worn, the driver sped up only a little for fear of getting stuck in the muck.

When Warren and Pandora finally reached the castle, it didn't appear different. It was the same as it always was on the outside. The only difference was the pink light flashing in the windows. The pink lightning couldn't be seen from the gate or the gatehouse out front. The car stopped at the large front doors leading to the grand entrance of the structure. Warren told Pandora they needed to hurry as he quickly got out of the car, running for the doors. Warren flung one of the doors open to the sight of his mother being flung against a wall and Morgan kneeling beside her shooting invisible daggers from her eyes at Lucifer himself. Warren's eyes lit up bright white the instant he caught sight of the devil.

"Oh good, you're back. This is getting really boring. Your mom's no fun to play with anymore." Lucifer smiled at Warren.

"DO NOT touch her again!" Warren shouted at him.

"Aw, why not? Killing her would be a little bit of fun."

"Because, this time, I will evoke the *full* power of your father."

"None of you are any fun anymore," Lucifer said as he raised a hand in Jen's direction, sweeping her bruised and bloody body against the wall again.

Warren stood in the middle of the floor facing Lucifer as Pandora ran to aid the girls. Warren raised a hand into the air, wind began to blow around him and he hovered off the ground a few feet. His glowing eyes pulsated until white light bathed the entire room. The booming voice of God told Lucifer to go or finally feel his wrath. Lucifer laughed loudly. Through the vessel of Warren's body, God raised his other hand in the direction of he was standing, soon the devil was screaming in pain. He knelt on the tile floor. Soon, the black shroud that covered him was a pile on the tiles with nothing inside it.

Warren's glowing eyes subsided and he was lowered from the air. As soon as his feet hit the floor, the wind died away. He turned in the direction of the women and ran to them. Pandora and Morgan stood and wrapped one of Jen's arms around themselves, standing on either side, holding her upright. She was knocked out from the heavy blows Lucifer threw at her, but she was alive.

Later that night, after Jen was put to bed and sleeping soundly, Morgan went to her room, leaving Warren and Pandora to themselves. Warren walked Pandora down the stairs to the catacombs of the castle. There was a safe area set up down there for her. The family made her a sun free bedroom in the safest place they could think of. Instead of telling her good night and leaving, Warren followed her into the room. She lit the candles and sat on the edge of her bed. He stood above her looking down at her face.

"All right, damn it. I give, you win." Pandora sighed.

"Win what?" Warren looked at Pandora, seeing a look of love on her face for the first time.

"Me." She smiled at him.

###

Mystik Legends Easter Eggs:

*[Chapter 9, smaller Catholic exorcism rite, in Latin] *"Ave Maria, gratia plena: In nominee Patris et Filii et Spiritus Sancti. Profectus indedaemon. Vade et amplius noceat nemini. Profectus inde daemon. Vade et ampliusnoceat nemini!"* They both said it together and repeated it together, crossing themselves as they did. They both looked up and listened.

*[Chapter 31, toward the bottom, Catholic exorcism rite, in Latin.] "Exorcizo te, omnis spiritus immunde, in nomine Dei," they crossed themselves, "Patris omnipotentis, et in noimine Jesu," they crossed themselves again, "Christi Filii ejus, Domini et Judicis nostri, et in virtute Spiritus," they crossed themselves once again, "Sancti, ut descedas ab hoc plasmate Dei Morgan, quod Dominus noster ad templum sanctum suum vocare dignatus est, ut fiat templum Dei vivi, et Spiritus Sanctus habitet in eo. Per eumdem Christum Dominum nostrum, qui venturus est judicare vivos et mortuos, saeculum per ignem. Amen."

After the long Latin rites, the two men did the same things, they both spit into their hands and touched Morgan's ears and nostrils, each touching the right ear and then the left one. "Ephpheta, quod est, Adaperire. Be opened!" They both shouted. After that they both took turns touching Morgan's nostrils and saying, "In odorem suavitatis. Tu effugare, diabole; appropinquabit enim judicium Dei. And to you, Oh, devil be gone! For the judgment of God is at hand." (Explanation: This is the real deal. I wanted to be as accurate as possible where it counted. Don't try this at home. Demons aren't real, they don't inhabit people, and this is a fiction book.)

*[Chapter 45, Devil summoning spell, said over a cup of blood] Mirabelle lit a candle, saying a summoning ritual, calling out to her master, "Bagabi laca bachabe, Lamc cahi achabade, Karrelyas, Lamac lamec Bachalyas, Cabahagy sabalyas, Baryolas, Lagoz atha cabyolas, Samahac et famyolas, Harrahya," she whispered. (Explanation: This is another "Don't try this at home" egg in the story. It's real, but summoning or even trying it is something we see in movies, TV, books, and games.)

Terms:

An <u>athame</u> is an important ritual tool, with many uses, but was not to be used for actual physical cutting.

<u>Dru·id</u> /ˈdroo͞id/ noun- (1) A priest, magician, or soothsayer in the ancient Celtic religion. (2) A member of a present-day group claiming to represent or be derived from this religion.

<u>Drow</u> -noun- A fictional race of dark elves in various fantasy settings, such as Dungeons & Dragons.

<u>Scrying</u> comes from the Old English word descry meaning "to make out dimly" or "to reveal." Adding the prefix/suffix 'be' (often 'gye' in Germanic languages), gives us the modern word 'describe'. (Simple explanation: This method can be used to find something or someone. It usually involves a map and crystal or a map and the person's blood you are looking for (in fiction.)

Tal·is·man / ˈtaləsmən/ ˈtalizmən/ noun- An object, typically an inscribed ring or stone, that is thought to have magic powers and to bring good luck.

Teleportation involves making an object or person vanish from one location and reappear at another.

Wic·ca /wikə/ noun- The religious cult of modern witchcraft, especially an initiatory tradition founded in England in the mid-twentieth century and claiming its origins in pre-Christian pagan religions. (Wicca/Wiccan)

About the Author

Jennifer Oneal Gunn is the author of *Mystik Legends*, *Devil's in the Details (and the Reboot)*, *The Revenging the Evil Series (The Story of Jake and Holly books)*, *The Heart of a Woman*, and *Squishy Face and the Moon*. She resides in Missouri with her daughter, who loves drawing and cats.

Like me, follow me, and rate this book. If you like it, please review it!